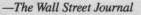

**Also by Homer Hickam**

*Torpedo Junction*

*Rocket Boys (a.k.a. October Sky)*

*Back to the Moon*

*The Coalwood Way*

*Sky of Stone*

*We Are Not Afraid*

# THE KEEPER'S SON

## HOMER HICKAM

St. Martin's Paperbacks

THE KEEPER'S SON

Copyright © 2003 by Homer Hickam.
Excerpt from *The Ambassador's Son* copyright © 2004 by Homer Hickam.

Map © 2003, Mark Stein Studios

All rights reserved. No part of this book may be used or reproduced in any manner whatsoever without written permission except in the case of brief quotations embodied in critical articles or reviews. For information address St. Martin's Press, 175 Fifth Avenue, New York, NY 10010.

Library of Congress Catalog Card Number: 2003054964

ISBN: 0-312-99949-6
EAN: 80312-99949-0

Printed in the United States of America

St. Martin's Press hardcover edition / October 2003
St. Martin's Paperbacks edition / September 2004

St. Martin's Paperbacks are published by St. Martin's Press, 175 Fifth Avenue, New York, NY 10010.

10 9 8 7 6 5 4 3 2 1

To John Gaskill and Rany Jennette,
sons of the keepers, guardians of the light

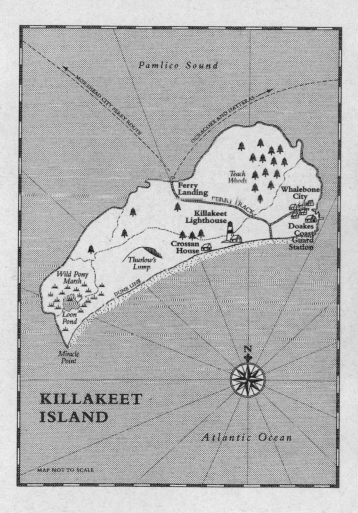

Pamlico Sound

MOREHEAD CITY FERRY ROUTE

OCRACOKE AND HATTERAS

Teach
Woods

Ferry
Landing

FERRY TRACK

Whalebone
City

Killakeet
Lighthouse

Doakes
Coast
Guard
Station

Crossan
House

Thurlow's
Lump

Wild Pony
Marsh

DUNE LINE

Loon Pond

Miracle
Point

N

# KILLAKEET
# ISLAND

Atlantic Ocean

MAP NOT TO SCALE

"Guess now who holds thee?"—
"Death," I said. But there
The silver answer rang—
"Not Death, but Love."

—Elizabeth Barrett Browning,
*Sonnets from the Portuguese*

# PROLOGUE

The old wicker rocker creaked as Josh pushed back and forth in it, back and forth, back and forth, his bare feet slapping against the boards of the pizer with each rock. His chin rested on his chest and his hands restlessly worked up and down the arms of the chair. Every minute seemed to last an hour and it was only nine in the morning. According to the chart his father had told him to follow, sunset would occur fifteen minutes after six and then "civil twilight" twenty-five minutes later. That meant there were nearly ten, unending hours that had to pass until he could do what he most wanted to do, what he had always wanted to do. Josh was not a boy who cared much for waiting, especially not today. It was going to be one of the most important days in his life, but first darkness had to come. Today, September 12, 1924, Josh would light the lamp in the Killakeet Lighthouse and he would do it all by himself.

Before Josh lay an apron of brown sand and the vast, great Atlantic Ocean, but he did not look at the blue-gray sea as either vast or great. It was simply his front yard and had been for all of the fourteen years of his life. The tall spire of the Killakeet Lighthouse cast its shadow across the sand toward the Keeper's House where Josh impatiently rocked on the pizer, as a porch was called on the island. As the day wore on and the sun sank lower, Josh knew the shadow of the tower would gradually move until it pointed at the ocean.

Then, just before the shadow dissolved into the encroaching darkness, he would follow the schedule his father kept every day of every week of every month of every year. He would climb the 266 steps of the black iron staircase that spiraled inside the tower, carrying with him a three-gallon can of kerosene. Along the way, he would pass the brass plaque his grandfather, the second keeper of the Killakeet light, had placed at the third landing. It was inscribed with the words from the old hymn "Let the Lower Lights Be Burning":

> *Brightly beams our Father's mercy*
> *From His lighthouse evermore;*
> *But to us He gives the keeping*
> *Of the lights along the shore.*

Near the top, the stairs spiraled into the watch room where Josh would pour the kerosene into a holding tank, then pump air into it until there was enough pressure to feed the mantle in the lantern room above. Next, he would crank a clockwork mechanism and raise a sixty-pound weight on a wire rope. As the weight descended, it would turn the giant lens.

A dozen more steps would take him to the lantern room where the Fresnel lens sat like a huge glass beehive. He would pull back the curtains that protected the lens, then light an alcohol-spirit lamp to vaporize the kerosene coming up from the watch room. After the vaporized kerosene soaked the silk and zirconium mantle, he would light it with a long candle. If he had done everything just right, the kerosene would ignite and the mantle would begin to burn, to *incandesce* as the chemical reaction was called. Next, Josh would activate the clockwork mechanism, and the great glass structure would begin to slowly turn on chariot wheels along a circular track. There were eight prism panels, each with a glass bull's-eye that was designed to transform the illumination from the mantle into an intense cylinder of light. As the lens turned, its bright shafts turned with it, like the projecting spokes of a fiery wheel.

At sea, the light would appear as a brilliant beam for

precisely two and three-quarters seconds with an equal period of darkness, each flash a warning of the deadly shoals offshore. To the north sat the lighthouses of Ocracoke, Hatteras, Bodie Island, and Currituck Beach. To the south was the lighthouse at Cape Lookout. Up and down the sandy islands off North Carolina, the Lighthouse Service had set up these great towers with their flashing spokes of light to warn the freighters, tankers, warships, fishing boats, banana boats, and every other kind of vessel that they were passing through what had been called for centuries the Graveyard of the Atlantic. Below the waves were the skeletons of hundreds of ships put there by sudden storms bashing them against hidden shoals. But the ships would be safe as long as they heeded the flashing towers, and as long as the keepers on those shores kept the light.

Josh glanced at the shadow of the lighthouse. It had barely moved since he'd last looked at it. It was as if the sun had gotten stuck in the sky. Frustrated, he took in a deep breath, let out a long sigh, and rocked some more. Josh's father, Keeper Jack Thurlow, had gone up to Bodie Island to see the keeper there and inspect a new rotation clockwork design. Keeper Jack had worried for days about leaving Josh alone, not only with the responsibility of lighting the lamp but also having to tend to Jacob, his baby brother just turned two. Josh knew his father wanted to go and finally convinced him to make the journey. Josh was, after all, fourteen years old and had proved himself a responsible son. He had done so much since his mother had died, not only working around the lighthouse, but also raising Jacob.

Josh rocked a little harder, as if he could force the sun to move along. Jacob was playing in the sand in the shadow of the lighthouse. Josh had made certain his brother was well covered with a sun suit and hat. He was a happy baby and knew how to entertain himself, sometimes to Josh's consternation. He'd caught Jacob in the sun-drenched room his mother had called her "art palace" that very morning, playing with a spilled box of beach glass. The room had been left virtually untouched since Josh's mother had died during Jacob's birth. Josh knew why. One time when Doc Folsom had come by for a game of hearts, the Keeper had taken a little too much whiskey with his cards. Tears streaming down his whiskered cheeks, he'd confessed the "palace" was the one place in the house where he could still sense his wife's presence.

Josh felt the same about the room. After he'd carried Jacob outside, he had returned and sat down in his mother's chair and touched the implements of her art, the small pliers she'd used to bend the silver and gold wire, the glass beads and beach glass and shells she had strung with the wire to make bracelets, anklets, broaches, necklaces, and pins. Then he'd taken a deep breath. He could almost smell her, a wonderful mixture of soap and the vanilla extract she liked to dab behind her ears. He'd scooped up the beach glass Jacob had spilled and traced his fingers through the smooth, translucent chips, loving the way they sounded like tiny, tinkling bells. Josh had accompanied his mother on many expeditions up and down the length of Killakeet in search of beach glass, which were pieces of broken bottles ground smooth by the workings of the surf and the sand. The rarest of all the beach glass was that off the *Alexander Hamilton,* a bark-rigged screw steamer that had fetched up on Bar Shoals and been battered to pieces. Among its cargo had been a few boxes of a rare California Syrah wine called Rose of Sharon. Over the years since, the red glass of the Rose of Sharon bottles had been turned into ruby-colored gems that occasionally washed ashore. It had been those pieces that Jacob had spilled. "No, Jacob," Josh had told him sternly, and even slapped the boy's tiny fists, making him drop the tightly held scarlet glass. Josh was no tyrant as a brother, but he knew Jacob needed discipline. The boy had cried a little, but when Josh went outside to look after him, he seemed to have forgotten all about it and was happily playing in the sand.

As he rocked, Josh occasionally glanced at the ocean and the seabirds flying past. He saw a trio of pelicans, a lone gull, a squadron of mergansers, and a sea hawk. His mother had run a bird hospital right there on the pizer of the

Keeper's House, not easy with more than a dozen cats on the premises. His mother had so loved her cats. Many of them were still around, good mousers all, and gentle creatures. They liked to sleep on his mother's grave, which was soft with grass and warm in the sun.

Josh missed his mother. He missed her with all his heart, missed everything about her, her gentle ways, her sparkling laugh over something he or his father had said, her joy of life on Killakeet Island, her dedication to taking care of its creatures. He would go visit her just before he went up on the tower to light the lamp. The Lighthouse Service had graciously allowed the Thurlows to have a family cemetery behind the Keeper's House. Josh wanted to tell his mother about getting to keep the light, and he also needed to tell her how Jacob was doing, and how much of her he could see in Jacob's face. He wanted to say he missed walking the beach with her, looking for beach glass. There was always so much he wanted to say, so much he could never possibly say it all. He always tried very hard not to cry when he talked to her, although he rarely succeeded. His father said there was no reason to cry, that she was gone because God needed her more than they did. Josh hoped God was happy but it seemed sad that the Almighty Creator of the Universe might be so needy as to take a mother away from her children.

Something small drifting along on the blue water caught Josh's eye and he stood to see it better. It wasn't a dolphin since it didn't appear and reappear. He thought it might be flotsam from the wreck of the *Bertha Gaskill,* a brigantine that had gone down in a storm just off Hatteras the past winter. Ever since, her planks had been floating in, and even a big section of her wheelhouse had come ashore near the Crossan House, the summer cottage of a rich Yankee family that sat about a mile south of the lighthouse.

Josh wanted to see what the thing was on the water. The best way to do that was to climb the tower and have a look with his father's binoculars. He didn't want to leave Jacob alone so he picked him up and carried him on his hip and started up the spiral staircase. Jacob burbled happily and clutched Josh's shirt with his tiny hands. He was a cute little boy with a mop of sun-whitened hair and big, blue eyes and strong, inquisitive hands. Josh had to remember to always empty Jacob's pockets before he took him in the house. He never knew what he would find in there, sand, sea oats, even the occasional cricket or beetle. Once, he'd even found a flattened penny with Josh's name stamped on it. Josh had forgotten who'd given him that penny or that he'd even lost it, but crawling around in the sand, Jacob had found it.

Josh tediously climbed the steps, one after the other, until he reached the lantern room. He picked up the binoculars off a hook on the wall and shifted Jacob with one arm onto his hip, then went out on the high parapet that encircled the lantern room. The wind struck him there as it always did. Wind ran like a constant river across Killakeet but it was always especially strong atop the lighthouse. Jacob giggled and squirmed and Josh worked to control him. "Stop wiggling, Jacob," Josh scolded. "Hang on to me and don't let go! It's a long way down!"

Jacob settled into his arm, chewing on his collar, giving Josh a moment to look at the dot on the ocean. He was astonished to discover it was a little boat, with its mast neatly stowed on its deck. Josh had never seen anything quite like it. It had a blunt bow and a square stern and a tiny cockpit. It looked very fast.

Josh wanted the little boat. The people of Killakeet had made their living for years fishing and what they called "wrecking," the taking of what the sea had stolen from one to give to another. Josh could already imagine how proud he'd be to show the little boat he'd "wrecked" to his father and how jealous the other boys would be when he sailed circles around them with it. He managed to play a neat little scenario across his mind, how the people up in Whalebone City would say what a clever boy Josh Thurlow was to go out and catch that smart little boat.

"Look, Jacob," he said. "See the boat?"

Jacob proved himself a true Killakeeter. He looked and squealed, "Bo!"

"Yes, bo! Our bo! You want it, too, don't you?"

"Bo! Bo!" Jacob giggled.

Josh took another look, noted the direction of drift, and went back down the staircase, arguing with himself all the way. What he wanted to do more than anything was to hop in his father's workboat and give chase. The workboat was a boat better sailed with two men but he'd taken it out alone before. He could easily do it. Why, he said to himself, he could be out and back in just a few minutes.

But what to do with Jacob?

The solution, when Josh forced it into his little scenario, was simple. He would take Jacob with him. Jacob had been on the workboat many times. He was a Killakeet baby, after all, and naturally loved the ocean. The more Josh thought about it, the more perfect his plan seemed. He would get a tarpaulin in case of rain, put Jacob in the workboat, and they'd both go out and catch the little boat.

It was a glorious day, the skies blue with just a cotton-puff cloud or two, the winds fair and light. Tonight, it was going to be a full moon, which meant a high tide and the water would be deeper over the shoals. It was going to be an easy sail. Josh expertly steered the workboat through the breakers and they were off on the chase. Jacob squealed with delight as they bounced through the waves, but once past the breakers, Josh realized it was going to be more difficult to find the little boat than he'd thought. He stood up and still couldn't see it. It was too low in the water and his own sail blocked his view. All he could do was head off in the direction he'd last seen it drifting. He tacked back and forth to cover more area. As he did, Killakeet slid past him. Before long, he'd passed Miracle Point, seven miles south of the lighthouse, and was out on open water.

*There it was!* Josh saw the little boat for just a moment as a wave tossed it up. It was farther out than he expected and he realized a little piece of the Gulf Stream must have grabbed it and drawn it east and then north. Josh tacked toward it, beating up against the wind until he was in the Stream, too. He felt the insistent river of warm tropical water grasp the workboat. Josh knew he'd have to work hard to get out of it after he caught the little boat. He looked at the sun and realized it was already well past noon. From willing the time to pass faster, now he wanted it to slow down. The lighthouse was just a tiny sliver of alabaster on the western horizon. *I'd better catch her quick,* he said to himself, even as he knew he should give up the chase, take Jacob home, and be ready at twilight to light the lamp.

But Josh didn't give up. He kept chasing until at last he tacked up to the boat and got a hand on it. To his delight, he discovered it was just as pretty and special as he thought and it looked brand-new, too. Its hull was painted a bright, cheerful red. He inspected the stiff new painter attached to its bow. Someone had not tied it off very well and the sea, being the sea, had grabbed it for itself. But now it belonged to Josh, and Jacob, too.

Josh took the little boat in tow, tying its painter to the stern of the workboat. He checked the sun. "We got to get back and light the lamp, Jacob," he said to his brother. Josh was worried now. What would happen if he didn't get back in time to light the lamp before darkness? Not only would his father hear about it and never trust him again, true disaster might occur. The ships at sea depended on the light. They could pile up on Bar Shoals without it. Josh had to hurry but it was difficult to get across the Stream, which was determinedly pushing him north. He would have to point the bow of the workboat directly southwest, he decided, and let the wind blow him across. With the Stream pushing him northeast, it would average out and he'd go mostly westerly. But that meant the hull of the workboat would be against the full power of the Stream. It would be hard to steer but he was confident he could do it. He *had* to do it.

The wind picked up, the way it will off the banks as September afternoons wear on. There was a chop on the sea that hadn't been there a minute ago, too. Josh got up to adjust the sail. Jacob kept getting in his way. He tripped over him and Jacob started to cry. "I'm sorry, Jacob," he told the baby.

Then, when he turned his back, he heard a splash and to

his horror, he saw that Jacob had fallen in. The workboat was moving along with the wind behind it. The Stream was insistently carrying Jacob away. Jacob's face was in the water. Josh had no choice. He dived in and swam as hard as he could. The Stream carried him and within a few strokes he had Jacob, who sputtered and started crying again. "Please, Jacob," Josh begged. "Don't cry. It's going to be OK."

But Josh wasn't so certain. Now he had to catch the workboat. He should have reefed the sail before he dived in. All the canvas was shaken out and the workboat was, if not a fast sailer, a steady one.

With one arm holding Jacob, Josh swam after the two boats. He had always been a powerful swimmer, and even against the Stream, he managed to catch the stern of the little red boat just before she passed. Desperately, he grabbed her with one hand and with the other lifted and dropped Jacob into the cockpit. Then Josh went hand over hand to the workboat and climbed aboard. He was exhausted from the swim and shaking from the terror of almost losing his brother.

The wind had shifted and was blowing even harder. Josh had to get to shore. He looked over his shoulder. Jacob was sitting in the little boat and had stopped crying. In fact, he was smiling at his brother. Josh got the tarpaulin and tossed it into the little boat's cockpit. "Stay under the tarp, Jacob," he said. "We're going home, don't you worry. We're going home right now!"

As he ran for shore, fighting the tiller, Josh looked over his shoulder every few minutes to check on Jacob, not that he needed to. He kept hearing him laugh as the little boat bounced across the waves. He was such a happy child and even the shock of being tossed in the ocean had not changed him.

The wind began to blow blister-hard now and it started to rain. Josh was having to use every ounce of his strength just to keep his heading, but still he kept checking the towed boat. Jacob had crawled under the tarp. Josh looked over his shoulder and saw Jacob's bare feet sticking out from under it. That was when the wind piled into him, a terrific gust, and knocked the workboat nearly over. Josh was tossed out into the warm fast current.

He came up swimming. The workboat had righted herself but her sail was a flapping mess. That was good, Josh realized. Otherwise the wind would have surely blown her past him. He climbed aboard and looked to make sure Jacob was all right, and that was when the greatest horror he'd ever felt coursed through his body. The little red boat was gone. The new painter was tied off on the workboat but the other end had come undone. Josh hadn't checked the knot. A landsman had probably tied the thing, some sort of granny knot that had come loose with all the bouncing around. The near knockdown had finished untying it and sent Jacob off on his own across the waves.

"I'll find you, Jacob!" Josh screamed desperately into the wind, then set the sail and clutched the tiller and began to turn the workboat around against the mighty Stream.

# PART ONE

GUESS NOW WHO HOLDS THEE?

# I

Dosie Crossan returned to Killakeet Island to the creak of saddle leather and the jingle of tack, leading a big brown mare down the ramp of the Wednesday ferry from Morehead City. When she had left the island a dozen years before, she had been a rich man's daughter, bright and cheerful and filled with boundless dreams. By November of 1941, Dosie had lived through the Great Depression, discovered what it meant to be hungry, put herself through college by selling encyclopedias door-to-door, and been fired as an assistant editor of a New York publishing house for taking a lunch break that lasted three days. She had also loved too often and been loved back too seldom and was as wary of most men as she was capable of skewering them with a few well-chosen words. In short, Dosie Crossan had left a girl of hope and returned a woman of experience.

Young and pretty women who appear world-weary are attractive to a certain class of men, which is to say nearly all of them. In her riding outfit of a white blouse tucked into jodhpurs, which were in turn tucked into knee-length brown leather boots, she was a "right goodsome package," as the ferry master had it to his skinny, long-legged mate, who had replied, "Yeah, and she knows it, too."

But Dosie didn't know it, which was much of the reason why love had not only eluded her all her adult life, but come very near to destroying her. It was why she habitually wore a wary, yet yearning expression on her otherwise pretty face. Men had often chased her and professed endless love to her, but she thought surely their attentions were mostly a sham and couldn't understand why they had done it. She saw herself, in terms of beauty, as needing more work than was possible. She was, to her thinking, neither tall nor short, her figure routine, and her face, though blessed with unblemished skin, uninspiring. Her brunette hair, which she considered her best feature, was silky, but only because she brushed it religiously, and it lapped down to rest lightly on her shoulders. Often, when she held her head in a certain way, a lock of her hair drifted across her cheek and it gave her, though she had no concept of it, a look of such vulnerability that men felt driven to protect her even as they longed to ravage her. Dosie had a clever mind, interrogative and incisive by nature, careful by design, but it was incapable of seeing herself as others did. That was a blank spot. She took no notice, for instance, of the ferry master, who had difficulty taking his eyes from her during the three-hour journey.

The ferry master was not a particularly imaginative man, but something about the woman who'd come aboard his ferry that morning had struck his heart like an ocean storm. Perhaps it had been the manner in which she had stood so proudly on the deck of the ferry and held her mare's reins and watched each seabird and leaping fish and spit of sand as if she were required to memorize each of them. How happy their sight seemed to make her! As he kept watching her, sideways, glimpses for a moment, then away to come back again, each time longer, the master's heart grew warmer until it was as near afire as a man approaching fifty could bear. And now, after landing, he watched her inspect her surroundings, her summer-sky-blue eyes, which had known sadness—a man can always tell—now aglow with something akin to joy, though all there was to see was a line of plank shacks and nets drying on wooden racks and a few workboats bobbing at rude piers. "I've never been so glad to be anywhere in my life," she said to her mare, startling the mate, who thought at first she was talking to him.

The big mare—Dosie had told the ferry master coming aboard that the horse's full name was Genie's Magic but she called her simply Genie—pawed at the sand as if not quite knowing what to make of the place. The master suspected she was a horse more used to being in green, grassy meadows, and not up to her fetlocks in brown, dry sand. If so, and if she was going to be kept on Killakeet, things were very much about to change for the mare and the young woman, too. Killakeet was sand and more sand piled onto sand, alleviated only by the sea and Pamlico Sound.

The ferry master sighed forlornly and went inside his cabin while barefoot boys dressed in bib overalls ran up from the shacks and then stood openmouthed at the sight of the big horse under full English tack. Genie tossed her head when one of the boys crept over and touched her saddle, then stamped sideways with a low rumble in her throat.

"Be careful!" Dosie snapped, and the boy ran away, stopped, and spat in the sand in embarrassment. The other boys stood scuffing the sand with their toes and wiping their noses with the backs of their hands. Dosie's heart sank at the sight. They were so threadbare and hangdog that she thought of the pictures in *Life* magazine of ragamuffin Polish children made orphans by the German army. *I must make it up to them,* she thought.

"I'll give a nickel for each of my trunks if you boys will help move them," she called. Then she nodded back to the ferry where sat four steamer trunks and the mate gazing at them and scratching up under his cap. It had taken two husky dockworkers to get each heavy piece aboard, and the mate was strapped to figure out how he was going to manage to get them down into the sand by himself. He doubted a tip, too.

The boy who had touched Genie's saddle stepped out in front of the other boys and said, "I'll give a penny a trunk to the *one* boy who helps me. Who's it going to be? You, Huey? Well, come on."

To the relief of the mate, the two boys ran up the ramp and attacked the first steamer trunk, half carrying it, half dragging it into the sand, then they ran back for the next one. Back and forth they went until all four trunks were at the bottom of the ramp.

Dosie called the boy over. "What's your name?" she asked as she gave him his twenty cents from her pocket.

"Herman Guthrie, ma'am," he said. "My maw's Mrs. Abby Guthrie, who heads up the Fish Market ladies. My brother's Fisheye, engine man on the *Maudie Jane,* that is to say the patrol boat out of Doakes. Paw's dead, drownded a year ago, but before that he was a fisherman, mostly mullet and menhaden when they run."

"Well, Herman," Dosie replied, made a little breathless by the historical family recitation, "I'm sorry to hear about your father. I'm Miss Theodosia Crossan, but friends call me Dosie."

"Oh, I know very well who you are, ma'am," Herman said. "It's known all over Whalebone City that you was coming, by the men who came acrost and got your house ready."

"And is it ready?" Dosie asked, amused.

"Oh, yes, ma'am. Quite ready, I'm sartain."

"Herman, I need those trunks taken to my house. If I pay you an adequate fee, can you manage it?"

Herman looked dubious. "That's a far piece, all the way acrost the island and down the beach past the lighthouse."

"Shall we say two dollars a trunk?"

The boy's eyes nearly popped. "Yes, ma'am. I reckon I can manage!"

An elderly man and a woman had wandered up from the shacks. The man, dressed in coveralls and a faded cotton shirt, and the woman in a cotton housedress with a flower pattern and a gray sweater over it, had spent the time alternately pondering the horse and Dosie's negotiations with Herman. "Hello," Dosie said to them, after Herman ran off to gather his troops.

"Right fine weather for a trip across the sound," the man responded. The way he pronounced it, it came out sounding like *roite foine*.

"I was glad it was calm," Dosie said, after taking a moment to interpret the Killakeet brogue. "I was afraid Genie would get seasick."

"What kind of horse is she?"

"She's a quarter horse," Dosie answered.

"Well, young lady, if I *[Oi]* had a quarter, I'd *[Oi'd]* give it to you for her, that's for sartain. So you are here to open up the Crossan House?" When Dosie nodded, he said, "You see, Etta, I told you the Depression was over. Why else would the Crossans come back?"

A hopeful smile formed on the woman's otherwise pinched face. "You don't know me, Miss Dosie, but I'm Etta Padgett. I used to come by to pick up your laundry."

"Why, I do recall you, Mrs. Padgett," Dosie said, pleased that she really did remember after she mentally subtracted a dozen years and a few cares from the woman's face. "How are you?"

"Tolerable. And this is the mister. His name's Pump."

Dosie shook his hand. "I'm so glad to meet you."

"Well, little lady, same here. All I mostly ever saw of the Crossans was their clothes hanging on the line. Good to meet one in person."

"Is your whole family coming?" Mrs. Padgett asked eagerly. "I can still do the laundry with the best of them."

"Not yet. I'll be alone, at least for the next several months." Dosie hesitated, then added, "I'm on something of a spiritual journey, you see."

The couple shared a look, then Mr. Padgett said, "Killakeet Island's not a bad place for the spiritual. Queenie O'Neal used to hold sea-nances regular at the Hammerhead Hotel until one night the ghost of Blackbeard hisself showed up and turned their table over. You shoulda seen those ladies scatter, ran out into Walk to the Base a-squalling."

"She ain't talking about ghosts, old man," Mrs. Padgett growled out of the side of her mouth, then smiled sweetly at Dosie. "You know where I live, honey? Just two tracks back from Doc Folsom's infirmary on the Atlantic side. The house with the gate curved along the top. You come see me or send word if you need anything."

"Yes, ma'am, I will," Dosie said. Then, seeing that Herman had successfully completed his subcontracting and that an entire army of barefoot boys were lifting her trunks across the island, she stepped into the stirrup and swung her leg over Genie's back, settling familiarly into the saddle. She clicked her tongue and said, "Walk on," and Genie did, following the boys and the trunks. They reminded her of ants carrying bread crumbs.

Before long, Herman fell in beside her, deciding his troops had no need of close supervision. In fact, they were racing one another to see who could get across the island with the trunks the fastest. He began to point out the sights. "This would be Teach Woods, ma'am," he said as the track led them through a vine-filled forest of live oak, red cedar, and juniper trees.

"Yes, I know," Dosie said. "It was named after Edward Teach, who was Blackbeard the Pirate. Have you looked much for his gold?"

Herman was astonished that Dosie knew about Blackbeard's gold.

Dosie laughed. "It's the same with every crop of kids here. When I used to come here for the summer, my brothers and I looked for it, too."

"You didn't find it, did you?" Herman asked suspiciously.

"No, and I remember how disappointed I was. Now I realize just looking was treasure enough."

"That don't make no sense," Herman said.

"At your age, it wouldn't. But give it a few years and it might."

Before long they had passed through the woods and reached a line of sand hills, six to eight feet high, that barred the approach to the beach. The track turned north behind the dunes to Whalebone City. Dosie could see its cluster of wooden houses and the moderately tall steeple of its church, and down the track that was called Walk to the Base, she could see the old Surfmen's House, a two-storied, white-washed structure with a lookout tower in its center, the glass panes sparkling in the sun. It had once housed the legendary surfmen who'd gone out in storms to rescue the crews of battered ships. Now, it was the headquarters of Doakes Coast Guard Station.

"I live up that way, ma'am," Herman said, pointing. "We got a nice house just back of Walk to the Base one street over toward Pamlico. Granpaw built it with planks wrecked from a sugar boat named *Carole English* fetched up on Bar Shoals around ninety-seven or so. The church there was built by wrecking the *Frances Clayton,* a goodsome schooner. I guess, come to think on it, there ain't a house in town what ain't been built from wrecking."

Dosie looked over the village, recalling the fun she'd once had as a girl exploring it. *I'll come visit,* she promised herself, *but not until I'm ready.* Then, she nudged Genie toward a notch in the dunes through which the boys and her trunks had disappeared. The roar of the ocean assaulted her as she and Genie passed through. Genie pulled her ears back and stamped her hooves and would have shied, but Dosie told her to stop acting silly and walk on. Shivering nervously, Genie obediently crossed the high-tide mark and entered the windswept strand of brown sand and pounding surf that seemed to go on forever.

And then there it was, a mile or so south, the great Killakeet Lighthouse, a dazzling white tower with a single black bar painted halfway up. "I had forgotten how beautiful it was," Dosie said, and then she breathed in the warm, salt-laden air, which felt like a tonic. The temperature had risen with every step toward the Atlantic side of the island. Killakeet was on nearly the same latitude as Bermuda and kissed by the same tropical water brought up by the Gulf Stream.

The boys carting the trunks scarcely glanced at the lighthouse, nor did Herman choose to mention it until Dosie kept going on about it. "I've been to the top of it," he said. "It's right high. And you can see the Stream out there, all a deep, thick blue."

"I never went up on it," Dosie confessed, "although I always wanted to."

"Keeper Jack would take you, I'll bet."

"Keeper Jack. There's a name I haven't heard for years," Dosie said wistfully. "I wondered if he was still the keeper."

"Oh, yes, ma'am. I guess he'll always be the keeper, lest he dies."

Dosie recalled that she'd hung back whenever her brothers had gone to the top, mainly because she had hoped that Josh, Keeper Jack's son, would offer to take her. But Josh, six years older, had never paid the slightest bit of attention to her even though she took every opportunity to stand near him, often sighing, and had once even given him a present of a flattened copper penny with his name stamped on it, made by a machine on the boardwalk at Atlantic City. He'd said, "Thanks," and put it in his pocket and never mentioned it again. When she'd left the island, her heart had been a bit broken by Josh's inattention. Now, she could understand why he had ignored her. When they'd last been together that summer of 1929, she'd just been an ungainly thirteen-year old, probably smelling of milk, which her mother made her drink more or less constantly for her bones. Josh had been a college man, home to visit, and sophisticated beyond measure. He had even smoked a pipe.

As they drew nearer the lighthouse, there was no sign of anyone on the parapet, nor was there anyone evident around the Keeper's House. It was a neat and cozy-looking white house with a chimney at each end. Several rockers sat on its porch, and clay fern pots hanging from chains swayed in the wind. "Keeper Jack's most likely in Whalebone City," Herman said. "Today's his poker day."

"I suppose Josh is at sea," Dosie said while nudging Genie away from the keeper's lawn, the only green grass they'd observed on the island. "I heard he joined the Coast Guard."

"I reckon so," Herman said. "He usually takes the *Maudie Jane* out every day, not counting weekends. Fisheye says he ain't never seen a man quite so happy to get out on the water as Ensign Thurlow."

"You mean Josh lives here on the island?"

Herman squinted up at her as if uncertain he'd heard her right. "Why, yes, ma'am. He's been here for a couple of months now, come in from duty in Alaska. He commands Doakes Station and captains the patrol boat."

"Well, I'm surprised," Dosie said, and she was. "Does he live at the lighthouse?"

"Oh, no, ma'am. He stays at the hotel so he can be near his boat." Then, as if quoting someone, Herman said, "There ain't nothing more important to a Killakeet man than his boat."

While Dosie considered the news of Josh Thurlow, they kept going south, the Crossan House gradually creeping into view. It was precisely as she remembered it, perfectly suited for its location, driftwood gray, a cedar-shake roof, a porch that wrapped nearly all the way around with plenty of rocking chairs, and dormer windows on the second story. It was a sturdy, unpretentious house, with a charm given it by the wind and sea that had battered and weathered it now for over thirty years. She recalled that her father liked to call it the "unpainted aristocrat," though officially it was called the Crossan House.

When they reached the gate, Dosie held back. She sent the boys to carry the trunks to her room, which she described as the one at the top of the stairs, and to the right, having the best sea view. They seemed to know right where to go. Every one of them had been inside, Herman explained, and more than once. The house had never been locked in all the years it had been unoccupied, and every so often, a boy just had to poke through it, just to see if anything had changed. Of course, no one on Killakeet would ever think of stealing anything out of it.

Before she went inside, Dosie asked Herman if he was interested in being hired on a more permanent basis. "You want me to fetch and carry?" Herman asked.

"A bit more," she said. "You will come after school each day—an hour afterwards, let's say—which will be around one in the afternoon, correct? You will first go to check on Genie in her stable behind the house, make certain her stall is mucked out, and she has proper feed and water, and so on. I would also like her brushed each day, and if I haven't ridden her, you will take her for a walk. I will teach you how to do all that. Fetch and carry as you say to the grocery store, of course, when I need it, and odd jobs about the house. Could you do all that?"

"Surely, ma'am."

"There's something else you must know, Herman, if you're going to work for me. Sometimes, I may get very quiet. I probably won't talk to you and my eyes will be red from crying. Pretty soon, though, I'll get better. Just do your work and don't be frightened. Do you understand?" When Herman nodded his head, Dosie continued, "On Saturdays, I will want you here during the morning only, and on Sundays not at all. Fifty cents a weekday day, a dollar on Saturday. What do you think?"

Herman thought fifty cents a day and a dollar on Saturday was about as much money as any boy on Killakeet Island would ever make. But he allowed a little caution. "Why will you get quiet, missus?"

"I'll be thinking about over there." Dosie waved vaguely westward across the island. "And how it makes me sad."

"North Carolina? I ain't never been acrost to it but my paw used to go to buy whatnots, and he never came back too sad as I recall."

"Well, not North Carolina," Dosie explained. "Just over there and beyond. I've come here to rid my thoughts of it, to cleanse my soul, you might say, to find a purpose in life if there is one."

Herman didn't know what to say to any of that, so he didn't say anything, smart boy that he was. Dosie climbed down off Genie. "What's your decision?"

"I'm your boy," Herman answered without a moment's hesitation.

"Then I am your boss and you are my employee. I will pay your wages on time and you will work like the devil." She offered her hand. "We'll shake, like Americans."

They shook, the bargain was sealed, and Miss Dosie Crossan began her spiritual journey on Killakeet Island with Herman Guthrie along to fetch and carry.

# 2

Within a few hours of darkness, nearly all the lanterns in the little houses of Whalebone City were extinguished and its people abed, resting up for another day of work on and along the sea. Outside, the cry of the wind and the drumming of the Atlantic and the hiss of the sand provided the island's nightly symphony, a performance that too often kept Josh Thurlow awake, entirely because he could calculate with precision what the blended melody of wind and sea and sand meant.

For most visitors to the Outer Banks, it was the unpredictability of the elements that gave the place much of its charm. But to Josh and the lifelong residents of the islands, the elements, though often swirling and violent, were not confusing in the nonce. They were all a part of an overall and understandable arrangement that could be used to deduce that which was, and that which was to come. Windspray against the skin, the ocean a certain color, clouds gathering on a particular arc of the horizon, or the distinctive snap of a sail or a flag, each told its own story. They were predictors of storm or calm, and whether the wind would soon change and its direction, and its near velocity, and the coming height of the waves and strength of the surge. The ability to forecast based on the elements was a requirement to catch fish, and Killakeeters existed only to catch fish, with a nod to culling clams and oysters, and, of course, the keeping of the light.

Usually, when sleep wouldn't come, Josh would get up from his bed and draw on the silk robe he'd been given in Ketchikan by a fancy girl who'd favored him, and stand at his open window and breathe in the island air, and look over the stars if there were any, and watch the flashing lamp of his father's lighthouse. He would allow himself then to think again how it was impossible that nothing of Jacob or the little boat Josh had put him in had ever been found. Even after those seventeen years, it ground at Josh's soul. If he stood long enough, fatigue would usually set in and he would fall back into his bed. If that didn't work, there was always a bottle of Mount Gay rum to help him through the night. Josh had spent a little time on Barbados, an island as warm and lush as the rum it produced. When he took a glass of Mount Gay, he could almost transport himself back to a time of tropical breezes and friendly women. It was a comfort.

One night, Josh dreamed that Jacob was outside the hotel. He distinctly heard his brother's baby voice call out, *"Bo! Bo!"* Unnerved, he pulled on his robe and went down the steps and outside, taking note that he was sharing the porch with three gulls and a pelican, all former patients of the bird hospital kept intermittently by Queenie O'Neal, the Hammerhead's proprietress. For some reason, their presence irritated him. "You boys get on out of here," he rumbled in his best captain's voice.

The gulls, all males, blinked at Josh, then went back to sleep. One of them had been brought to Queenie with a fishing line wrapped around its wing. Another had managed to get a hook snagged in its beak. Queenie had snipped the hook off and used petroleum jelly to fill the hole, and it had healed nicely. The third gull had lost a leg, somehow, probably to a bull shark, which tended to be aggressive in the fall. Queenie had dipped the stump in extract of goldenrod to kill the infection. The pelican was an ancient creature, a well-known island character everybody called Purdy. Purdy had simply checked himself into Queenie's hospital, never to leave. He waddled a few steps at Josh's reproof, then tucked his head under his starboard wing. It was well-known that

Purdy had once been married to a pretty little thing, but he had outlived her and no longer seemed much interested in making eggs with any one of the young, rowdy females down on the dunes. Josh shook his head at the old bird. "You know a good thing when you find one, don't you, Purdy?" Purdy made no response, which was a response in and of itself.

The houses of Whalebone City were all dark and silent. Walk to the Base, which led to Doakes Coast Guard Station, was empty, not even a dog to raise its leg. Still bothered by the dream, Josh breathed in the air, made tangy by the salt spray that hung everywhere, and chided himself for wanting to look for his brother up and down the sandy streets. A creaking sign, nudged by the light wind, interrupted his concentration. It was Doc's sign, announcing his infirmary. It reminded Josh that it was Doc who had brought him back to Killakeet, back with a letter and a lie.

*Dr. Jonathan Barksdale Folsom,* Josh thought grumpily, *the most beloved man on Killakeet Island and an incurable busybody.* Doc had sent a letter to Josh just this past April and it had turned his life upside down. Josh was eight years then with the Bering Sea Patrol under the tutelage of the famous Captain Falcon, a well-known Coast Guard brawler who picked fights with fur-seal poachers. The letter was waiting for Josh when Falcon's cutter, *Comanche,* tucked into Unalaska for fuel and ammunition. It was a letter that nearly tore Josh's heart apart, a carefully crafted message that Josh took as word that his father was dying and that if Josh wanted any time with Keeper Jack at all, he'd best come back home and *tout de suite,* as Doc had put it. Captain Falcon believed that the men who served under him had no family beyond the *Comanche* so he was reluctant to let Josh go. At last, he had been persuaded after Josh saved his life—it was at least the third time and so finally made an impression—and wrote the letters necessary to have Josh reassigned to Doakes Station. Once back on Killakeet, however, Josh discovered his father had indeed been dying, but only as all humans on the planet are from the moment they are born. After Josh had gone to his father and managed a restrained interrogation as to his health, he determined that Keeper Jack was, in fact, sound as a Yankee dollar and perhaps sounder, considering the Depression that had persisted for nearly twelve years. "You lied to me," Josh had complained to Doc Folsom shortly afterward, finding the man contentedly rocking outside the planked-wood shack that passed as his infirmary along Walk to the Base.

Doc was a fastidious little man who wore old-fashioned shirts with cellophane collars, and bright red suspenders to lift his gabardine trousers. His shoes were polished wingtips, and his hat a brown derby, always worn at a cocky angle. With his Adolphe Menjou mustache, he was quite the debonair gentleman. At Josh's righteous charge, Doc had reared back in the rocker and grinned beneath his mustache and tucked his hands beneath his suspenders and allowed as how "a lie ain't one until it happens, my boy."

"What does that mean?" Josh had demanded.

"I wrote that your father would likely be dead within two years," Doc answered, without so much as a hint of either embarrassment or guilt, "and the two years ain't up. In fact, there is, according to my calendar, something like a year and six months to go."

And so it was Josh had returned in September 1941 to Killakeet Island, a place that reminded him more or less constantly of the awful thing he'd done, that of losing his brother, and the reason he'd left in the first place. After a while, he'd forgiven Doc for the lie that wasn't yet a lie, and suspended his speculation that his father had been a party to it, and accepted that here he was and would be until that time the Coast Guard decided it had a purpose for him elsewhere.

So Josh stood in the sand that night in late November and listened to Killakeet's symphony and thought of Jacob, his only comfort a terrible one, that the baby had perhaps drowned and drowning was an easy death. When Josh had asked, Doc had maintained its ease. "After the first breath of water," he said, "the lungs don't hunger anymore. You just go to sleep." Josh could only hope it was so, even while he doubted in his heart that it was, or that Jacob had drowned, in any case. A moth boat, for that was the kind of racing boat Josh had put Jacob in, was an eminently buoyant and seaworthy craft. It should have been able to ride out the storm, and Jacob should have been found sitting in it, perhaps wet and unhappy, but still *found* the very next day.

But he wasn't, nor was there ever so much as a trace found of him or the moth boat. And that is what frustrated Josh. *Impossible,* he said once more that night in the sand outside the Hammerhead Hotel, though not aloud.

Queenie O'Neal was a light sleeper. She heard Josh's footsteps on the complaining stairs, and the front door creak open and close. She knew it was Josh since no other lodgers were in her hotel. When she heard him fussing at the birds, Queenie feared he might be drunk on that Barbados rum he favored. If so, he would need her help. He was, after all, even at thirty-one years old, a motherless child. Queenie gathered her pink nightgown around her and went down the stairs and peeked through the window in the door and saw Josh standing barefoot in the sand in his silk robe, which was billowing around him in the light sea breezes. Queenie watched for a moment longer, then put on the embroidered shawl she kept in the parlor closet and went outside. It was the habit of Killakeeters to first cover the state of the weather to one another before launching into the purpose of any conversation. "A warm breeze off the Stream," she said, and he replied, "It'll bring in a small blow," and then Queenie got to cases.

"What's the matter, Josh?" she demanded. "Why are you standing out in the sand? Are you sick?"

"I'm just getting a breath of air, Mrs. O'Neal," he said.

Queenie stood with her toes curled against the cold boards and watched Josh breathe his air and it started her to wonder about a few things. It was well-known that Josh had experienced some hard times on the Bering Sea. He'd been engaged in some battles, according to what had filtered back, and he'd gotten involved with an Eskimo woman so the tale went, who'd died. All those things plus losing his little brother might make a man prone to sickness, the kind that was in his head, Queenie thought, and she might should ferret it out. "Maybe you need a sleep tonic," she suggested tactfully. "Doc left me some the last time I had trouble sleeping, that time I stobbed my toe."

"No, thank you, ma'am," Josh replied, and went back to his breathing with an occasional glance at the stars.

Queenie inspected Josh, as only a woman can. The boy had, of course, grown into a fine-looking man. What Thurlow man wasn't handsome, after all? Moreover, the Thurlows tended to come tall, which Josh was, and wide-shouldered, which he also was, and with good, square-jawed manly faces tanned from the sun and properly weathered by the wind, which applied to Josh as well, not counting the deep scar he had on his chin, which, rumor had it, was the result of a confrontation with a polar bear. Josh was, in fact, pretty much the spitting image of his father, subtracting forty years, of course, and imagining away the Keeper's gray beard. It was difficult to see much of his mother in him, however. Trudelle Thurlow had been a Killakeet Thompson, a clan of wreckers who tended to marry across to the coast. The Keeper had married her late in life, she a widow at twenty, her first husband drowned down by Miracle Point when a storm raised up and swamped his flat-bottom skiff. Trudelle had been olive-skinned with a high, intelligent forehead and sharp cheekbones and full lips, all of which added up to more than a little Cherokee, or so the speculation had gone. It was Jacob who had gotten his mother's face. Now that Queenie reflected on it, perhaps Josh had also received something of his mother's nose, though he'd gotten it broken brawling up there in the Bering Sea so it was hard to tell.

All of his physical characteristics Queenie absorbed in an instant, being a woman, as well as determining that that there was something surely churning inside Josh Thurlow. "You heard about Dosie Crossan coming back?" Queenie asked, knowing very well the answer, but hoping to discover more by his reply.

"At least a dozen people told me all about her and her

horse," Josh said, with an edge of impatience as if he were anxious to get back to his thoughts. "Have you seen her?" he added, and Queenie could tell by his tone that he was only being polite, not interested.

"No. Etta Padgett did, though. Said she's turned into a right fair-looking young woman, though she was wearing pants like a man. She hired Herman Guthrie as her fetch-and-carry boy."

Josh said, "I recall her, I think. Pretty little girl all dressed up in ruffles and such. Her brothers were hell-raisers. We got along famously. I nearly drowned one of them that time I built an undersea diving helmet out of a bucket and a bicycle pump."

"She always had a crush on you, you know," Queenie said.

Josh was startled. "Why no, I didn't."

"Boys don't usually," Queenie said, having gained all the information she required. "Good night, Josh." She glanced over her shoulder before opening the door and saw that he had already turned away, once again breathing and looking at the stars.

When Queenie returned to her bedroom, her mister, whose Christian name was Fred but went by the name of Buckets, asked her what was the matter. He had to ask her since she stood beside their bed and kept sighing and clearing her throat and nudging the edge of the mattress with her knee and leaning over and blowing on his eyelids until he was awake. "Josh Thurlow," she said, and her tone was doleful.

"What about him? Did he forget to pay the rent?"

"No. He's downstairs in the sand, blaming himself for losing little Jacob and who knows what else."

Buckets rubbed his eyes and yawned. He searched his wife's face. "Did he tell you that?"

Queenie regretted that she didn't have a woman to talk to, but a husband sometimes has to suffice at two o'clock in the morning. "No, he didn't tell me that. He didn't have to. Why else would he be standing outside looking up at the stars?"

Buckets gave it some thought and came up with an answer he considered might be helpful. "Coast Guard officers have to look at the stars a lot. They help them figure out where they are."

Queenie, however, was not impressed by her husband's explanation. "Josh was born on Killakeet Island. I guess he pretty much knows where he is."

Buckets yawned and thought it was all very sad but he didn't see how Josh Thurlow's problems were any of his business. "Are you coming back to bed?"

Queenie climbed back under the covers and lay on her back and listened to the wind hissing and the grumble of the endless surf. She heard the front door open and close, then Josh's slow footsteps on the stairs. "Poor man," she said. "What he needs is a wife."

Buckets's eyes flew open. "What good would a wife do him?" he demanded.

"Well, for one thing, she'd think up things for him to do."

"Wives are good for that, for sartain," Buckets readily acknowledged.

"Josh needs a wife and I guess it's up to me to find him one," Queenie said with conviction.

Buckets was pretty much awake now. His arm slid over. "Stop it, Mr. O'Neal."

"I need a wife, too."

Queenie resisted for a moment, then scooted in close. "Well, I guess we might find you one."

Buckets smiled. There was nothing like seeing a lonely, tortured man to put a woman in the mood for romance.

# 3

The *U-560* was a miserable, stinking, and nasty submarine. It was miserable because it was damp and cold, its crew never dry and never warm unless they could think of an excuse to be in the engine room when the big engines were running, which was miserable in its own manner because of the deafening noise. The boat was stinking and nasty because it smelled of diesel fuel and wet leather and hot batteries and dead cockroaches and moldy clothes and men who'd gone too long without a bath. At any time, a portion of the thirty-two-man crew were sick in their guts from the rotten food. As a result, the only water closet that worked was in constant use with nothing save filthy rags to wipe themselves off. For those who couldn't wait, open cans were liberally used, adding to the odorous squalor.

Despite the misery and the stink, the *U-560* was a brave and proud submarine. Its commander, *Kapitänleutnant* Otto von Krebs, was famous throughout the fleet for having *Fingerspitzengefühl*—the sure touch. Krebs was a master at sinking ships, which was, of course, the only reason the *U-560* existed. Its crew were mostly experienced men. For two years, they had toiled and sweated under Krebs's command, dedicated to finding and destroying every enemy ship they could find.

The second-in-command of the *U-560* was *Leutnant* Max Hodel. Max Hodel, or "*Leutnant* Max," as the boys called

him, did not have the sure touch, nor did he want it. He
wanted only to get the hatch open and smell fresh air, and
especially feel the sun on his skin. The lack of sunlight had
made Max's skin thin and wrinkled, like the skim on sour
milk. *Hurry up,* Max willed the Chief, who was handling the
buoyancy controls after Krebs's order to surface. *Hurry up
before I suffocate, damn you!*

As always, Captain Krebs seemed unfazed by the misery
and the stink around him. He eagerly peered through the
eyepiece of the attack periscope, waiting for its lens to break
the surface. "When we're up," he said, "you boys get the
hatch open in a hurry. I think the Chief just farted!"

Although everyone else in the tower laughed, Max didn't.
Instead, he studied Krebs for, he supposed, about the mil-
lionth time since he'd served with him. For the son of an
aristocratic Junker, there was little about him that was immediately impressive. During patrols, he usually kept his
brownish red beard untrimmed and Max often had to remind
him to get his hair cut. Except for his white cap, he wore
nothing to indicate his rank. He tended toward the unkempt
with his bulky gray sweaters and baggy leather pants and
sloppy sea boots. Nothing in his posture indicated he was a
leader. The expression on his face was kindly and inquisitive,
like one might expect from a slightly silly headmaster, and
his eyes drooped like an old dachshund's. He rarely raised
his voice, and he was quick to laugh. He was also quite the
egalitarian, insisting that the "von" in his name be dropped
when being addressed. "In a U-boat, Max," he had explained,
"it's quite enough to be an officer. As it is, we are looked
upon by our boys with some awe. No reason to raise the
stakes even higher, eh?" He'd winked when he'd said that.

Though he was not an impressive man physically, Krebs
exuded an intense, unrepressed excitement that was conta-
gious when he was on the hunt. He was like a small boy at
a shooting gallery, trying to show off to the crowd. Soon,
everybody was cheering him on. There was something else
undeniable about Krebs. He had an innate ability to survive
and to get his U-boat through all the hell His Majesty's Royal
Navy kept throwing their way.

Max and the crew were nearly spent. Even the *U-560* seemed exhausted with dozens of patched bullet holes and dents and a wooden deck splintered from an attack that Max couldn't even remember. Inside the pressure hull, valves dripped, hatches squawked against their corroded hinges, and the bilges were slopping over with vomit and urine and feces. The symbol of the *U-560,* a jaunty, grinning white shark painted on both sides of the conning tower, was pocked with orange corrosion. For Krebs and Max and the old hands on board, the war had started as an adventure. During those first few months, they'd ripped the Royal Navy and the English merchant fleet to shreds. They'd called 1939 and 1940 their "happy time" with millions of tons of enemy shipping sent to the bottom. But during 1941, the war had turned into a running battle. A lot of U-boats sent out from their bases in Germany and France were not coming back, or if they did, they were showing up battered and beaten by the British and Canadian naval forces.

In mid-November 1941, after a fruitless two months on patrol, the *U-560* had been ordered to a station off Norway to ambush a convoy from England to Russia. For ten days, all they'd done was stare at an empty sea while their food and water went sour. It was an odd sea, filled with icy mists that froze over the conning tower. Every morning, the lookouts had to carefully chip the ice off the compass, the engine room telegraph, and the torpedo aimer. Nothing mechanical worked without complaint. When the attack periscope was run up and down, it squawked from the ice dust that had crept into its sleeve. The Chief kept layering on the grease to keep it free, but even the grease had turned into a cold, thick gelatin.

Finally, at long last, freighters were spotted heading northeast along a well-traveled route. Krebs had followed them until he had the boat in a good position, then dived and launched four torpedoes, two each at separate freighters. The men of the *U-560* had heard the welcome thunder of four solid hits. Now, as was his habit, Krebs was going up to inspect firsthand the destruction.

Max prepared himself for instant action. It was his job to scramble up behind Krebs onto the tower bridge to see that the lookouts were all properly positioned and in their harnesses. He'd also make sure the twenty-millimeter-antiaircraft-gun crew were ready to ward off enemy aircraft.

Krebs was still peering through the periscope. "Where are you, English? No Royal Navy today? *Sehr gut!*"

Max felt the *U-560* level out. "Go on, Winkler," he said to a lookout. "Open the hatch."

Seaman Winkler was a bearded veteran. Max remembered Winkler as he'd first seen him only two years before. He'd been a pink-faced youth then. They'd all been pink-faced youths now that he thought about it. My God, those years of war had changed them all so much!

Winkler pushed the hatch cover over, then dodged a gush of cold seawater before turning his face up to catch the first welcome rush of fresh air. Krebs, turning his cap back around brim first, waded through the icy water. He drew on his leather jacket and waited while Pretch, the radioman, tied a towel around his neck and handed him his binoculars. "All right, boys, let's go," he said softly, and clambered up the ladder rungs.

Max went up the ladder behind Krebs and stuck his head out just in time to see the last of the water run off the tower. He took a deep breath of the cleanest air he'd ever inhaled. Krebs had gone directly to the forward lip of the tower fairing, where he was leaning on his elbows, calmly taking in the scene. The manual issued by the *Befehlshaber der Unterseeboote* (Commander in Chief, U-boats, that is to say, Admiral Doenitz) directed U-boat skippers to keep their boats submerged when attacking during daylight hours, but Krebs believed he could never see enough through either of the two periscopes, the attack periscope to look over the sea or the air periscope to check for aircraft. After assuring the lookouts and gun crew were properly stationed, Max went over to stand beside his commander. Not wishing to disturb him, Max said nothing. He knew that Krebs was taking his time, gathering in all that lay before him. Max did the same.

To the north, a freighter burned beneath a boiling plume of gray smoke. Men were jumping off it into the sea, an exercise in futility. They'd all freeze to death within minutes. The *U-560* had hit the freighter with one of Krebs's patented long-distance shots, at least a mile away. Nearer to the *U-560*, the other freighter they'd torpedoed had also stopped, its power plant, rudder, or propeller probably damaged. Crewmen could be seen milling around on its deck. Farther to the west, there were two more columns of smoke, evidence of other U-boats on the attack, vectored in by BdU after Krebs had sent out the alert describing the convoy to U-boat headquarters.

Max counted the ships. He could see eight freighters, though there were probably more in the gathering haze, which was part fog, part smoke. Two smaller freighters appeared to be reversing course, a foolish move since that would take them back past the crosshairs of the wolf pack. Six freighters were still pushing doggedly northeast. The whooping alarms of the British escorts echoed across the water. They were apparently on the scent of one of the U-boats. Max heard the rumble of depth charges and even felt them through the deck plates. *My God,* he thought, *how I hate the sound of depth charges! Even if I live another hundred years, I shall go to my grave with that sound ringing in my ears!*

Krebs heard and felt the explosions, too, but his reaction was different. He took on an expression of contentment. "That's very good, English," he said. "Keep your distance. I don't want to tangle with you today. I just want to have a few of your flock."

"Aircraft!" a lookout cried. Max opened his mouth to scream for everybody to get off the tower, but before he could, the lookout said, with obvious relief, "They're ours!"

Krebs studied the airplanes through his binoculars. "*Dreifinger,*" he said using the nickname of the stout German bombers. "About time you got here, assholes!" A few of the lookouts laughed, though most stayed silent, anxiously looking at the airplanes officially known as Ju-88s. They knew the score when it came to aircraft and U-boats. U-boats almost always lost. Everyone was hoping the Royal Air Force boys would stay home this day.

Krebs was in one of his talkative moods. "Thank God for the Russians," he said. "So inept in convoy. It must drive the English crazy." He studied the horizon, the smoke, the continuous alarms of the escorting destroyers. After weeks of frustration, he was having a good time. "I like the English," he said. "I wonder if they like us, too."

It was so ludicrous a question Max started not to say anything, but he was too tired to resist. "They love us. Why do you think their aircraft pound our cities every day?"

Krebs looked perplexed, then said quietly, "You are right to be sarcastic with me, Max. War is too terrible to enjoy but, my God, sometimes I can't help myself."

Darkness was beginning to encroach on an already gray and thoroughly miserable ocean. The sun had turned the western horizon into a streak of pale orange, but the east was dark and gloomy. Before the war, there would have been the comforting twinkle of Norwegian lighthouses and buoys, but now, as was the situation all over Europe, there were only murky shadows, all the lights extinguished.

Krebs decided to act quickly. The operational manual said the safest and best tactic for a U-boat at dusk was to submerge, follow the target, wait until night, then come back to the surface and attack. The logic was simple. If a U-boat was on the surface, it couldn't be discovered by the British underwater echoing equipment called ASDIC. It was also nearly impossible for an aircraft to see a narrow, gray hull on black water at night.

But Krebs was never one for the book. *Take advantage of the situation!* That's what he told all the novice U-boat captains who came to him for advice. The situation he saw was a convoy hopelessly disrupted, its escorts off chasing other U-boats, and the Ju-88s adding to the confusion. He could see jittery red flashes on the horizon, probably antiaircraft artillery from the British destroyers. The sheepdogs had their hands full and it was the hour of the wolf.

Krebs flipped the lid on the speaking tube and barked down to the engine room, "Give me full turns, Hans!"

Max asked, "What's the plan, sir?"

"I'm attacking."

"In daylight on the surface?"

Krebs ignored Max's question. The *U-560* was in a rare position, and he couldn't resist it.

"*Alarrrrrrrrrrrrrrrm!*" It was one of the lookouts, a man named Heinser, who screamed out the alert at the top of his lungs.

"What's wrong with you, Heinser?" Krebs despaired. "How can we sink ships with you yelling like a woman?"

Heinser was on his first patrol and had nearly reached the limit of his endurance. He had his arm stretched out with a trembling finger pointed toward the sky. "But it's an enemy aircraft, *Kaleu!*" he squeaked.

Krebs shook his head. "See to it, Max," he said, and went back to scouting the two Russian freighters.

Max raised his binoculars to look where Heinser was pointing. "Heinser is right to give the alarm, sir. It's a Liberator and it may have seen us. We'd better get below."

Krebs was in no mood to do anything but sink ships. "Not yet, Max. You boys, get that machine gun popping! I'll not be chased off by a bunch of high-flying, tea-sipping Englishmen!"

Max whispered furiously into his captain's ear. "*Kaleu,* if those tea-sippers turn around and make a low-level run on us, we won't have a chance."

Krebs ignored Max and puffed into the engine room voice tube. "Hans, I said more turns. Give me everything you've got. Understand? I want those engines *hot!*"

"*Jawohl, Herr Kaleu,*" came the muffled reply from the chief motorman. He sounded unhappy, but that wasn't unusual when demands were put on his engines.

The machine gun opened up, its empty shells spraying like metallic rain on the tower. Krebs put the *U-560* through several sharp turns, carving a snake trail of foam on the darkening sea. The gun crew kept banging away until the bomber disappeared into the gathering purple murk to the east. "Run away, you bastard!" one of the gunners yelled, and shook his fist into the air.

"You better hope he doesn't come back," Max muttered.

Krebs watched Max out of the corner of his eye. The man was starting to worry him. Usually neat to the extreme, Max had stopped shaving midway through the patrol and was letting his beard grow. It was coming out thin and wispy, giving him the appearance of a little schoolboy trying to act the man. He decided that when the patrol ended, he would let Max take an extended shore leave. Now that he thought of it, he might even take a bit of time off for himself.

"*Kaleu!*" It was Pretch, the radioman, his head pushed up through the tower hatch. "Signal from BdU. One of the *Dreifinger* got shot down. They want us to pick up the crew at these coordinates."

Krebs took the slip of paper and glanced at it. "These numbers don't make any sense. This would put us down around South America."

"Let me see," Max said, reaching for the paper.

Krebs crumpled the paper and tossed it over his shoulder where the wind caught it and blew it into the sea. "Radio them back," he ordered Pretch. "Ask them to resend the message. I want you to write it down exactly as it's sent. Be sure to ask them to repeat it as many times as you need to make certain you haven't missed anything. I must have precise coordinates."

Pretch hesitated, then a light of understanding came into his eyes and he disappeared below.

"*Kaleu,*" Max said, "those pilots won't last long in this water."

"If I go off on a wild-goose chase, Max," Krebs said quietly so the lookouts wouldn't hear, "I'll never get back in this position. On the other hand, if I sink those freighters, it might help our soldiers fighting it out in Russia. Think about that before you give me a sob story."

"We've been given orders to rescue our pilots. We should do it, or at least try."

Krebs took the time to explain. In a way, Max was a commander in training and it was part of Krebs's job to properly instruct him. "These are orders from officers with dry arses back in France who don't know the situation like we do. The *Dreifinger* pilots are probably either in a raft or drowned already. If they're in a raft, they can wait it out until I sink some ships. If they're drowned, they're drowned. Besides, the odds against recovering them are so high as to be ridiculous. What am I supposed to do? Wave a white flag at the English destroyers, ask them to let me go about a mission of mercy?"

Max heard Krebs out, then turned away, satisfied that the captain's explanation was logical, though cold-blooded. "You men," he barked at the gun crew, who were still congratulating themselves for chasing away the Liberator. "Stop fucking off and keep your eyes peeled!"

Krebs puffed once more into the speaking tube. "Hans! Dammitohell! More turns, man! The Russkies are getting away. If you can't bang your whores, I'll come down and do it for you!"

A muffled reply came back, something to do with his engines not being whores but pretty little girls. Krebs laughed. He was having a good time. "Chief, tell the torpedomen in the forward and stern rooms to choose the best eels they've got. Then tell both crews to stand by."

The Chief acknowledged from the tower control room just below the main hatch. His job was to keep the boat trimmed and maneuvered according to orders, and the various stations prepared for the captain's orders. He was, therefore, a man of great experience and knowledge who was spared only the weight of making the decisions that ultimately determined the fate of the boat. That was Krebs's job, with *Leutnant* Max backing him up.

Krebs rubbed his hands together in happy anticipation of the attack and also in an attempt to get some circulation in them. Max, ever watchful, handed him some fur-lined gloves and Krebs pulled them on, slapped them together, then cupped them to his face. His beard was filled with ice crystals but he wasn't cold. He stepped up to the torpedo aimer and sighted in on the fleeing freighter and then the stalled Russian ship. He called down the coordinate numbers. "Chief, are my torpedoes ready?"

"Ready on both ends, *Kaleu!*"

"On my mark. Forward and aft! Wait for my command. We'll launch from the stern first, then give it to them from the forward tube. Understood?"

At the Chief's response that he understood very well, Krebs again sighted into the torpedo aimer and called down more numbers. They had passed the damaged freighter, the men on the tower hooting and waving at the Russians. Most of the Russians had simply watched, their faces sullen and grim, but two huge women on deck had taken off their coats and exposed their massive, hanging breasts. They used their hands to lift them, pointing them at the U-boat.

The lookouts whistled at them. One of them called out, "O sweet milk cows, you would like us to rescue you, wouldn't you?"

"Shut up, you!" Max snapped. "They are trying to survive. You would, too, if death was staring you in the face."

"Look, they're shooting them!"

A man with a pistol in the crowd of Russians had shot one of the women. She had fallen, blood spouting from her head. The other woman was running, but the man, dressed in a brown army coat, fired into her back and she collapsed. Krebs looked over his shoulder and gave a calm, professional appraisal. "The Communist Party commissar on board, no doubt. Have a look, fellows. That's the kind of men we're fighting, cowards and murderers who shoot their own women." Out of the corner of his eye, he noted Max shaking his head.

"The Liberator!" Winkler yelled.

"Coming in low at six o'clock, *Herr Kaleu!*" Max called with precision.

Krebs knew he had no choice in the matter. He yelled through the hatch. "Take us down, Chief! Everybody below!"

The lookouts and gun crew dived for the hatch as the *U-560* started under. Nearly all the crew inside were racing forward into the bow torpedo room to make it heavier so the U-boat would plunge faster. It was a race with death.

Krebs was the last man off the tower. He jumped through the hatch and landed hard on the control-room floor. There was a loud pop and it felt as if somebody had hammered a huge nail into his left knee. He pitched over, grabbed his knee, his eyes screwed shut against the terrible pain. Startled crewmen looked his way but no one reached out to help. They might touch him for luck when he wasn't looking, but to touch him openly without his permission was something they were afraid to do. Krebs forced himself not to scream. It would terrify the men. Inwardly he railed at himself. *Stupid!* He'd hurt that same knee during a skiing holiday. He knew it was weak. A crewman pulled the hatch closed and clamped it shut.

Max crawled over beside Krebs, who'd found a spot by the periscope. "*Kaleu,* are you all right?"

"No, damn it," Krebs answered through gritted teeth. Then he said, "Max, you know I think we may have just bought it."

Max looked at his captain in disbelief. He'd never heard such pessimism out of Krebs's mouth. Then he heard the rattle of the sea closing over the U-boat and a moment of peaceful silence followed by the distinct sound of two splashes, like big stones tossed in a pond. In an instant, Max knew Krebs's assessment was hideously correct. If he could hear the Liberator's depth charges when they hit the water, it meant the *U-560* was too shallow. The deadly canisters were probably drifting down alongside the U-boat at that very moment, waiting only to go a little deeper before detonating with crushing force. Below was at least a mile of freezing black water, ready to take them for all eternity. He heard the Chief, as tough a man as ever existed, who'd probably not seen the inside of a church for decades, begin to say aloud a hurriedly fashioned prayer: "Sweet Jesus, sweet Jesus, save us . . ."

Max lowered his head, took a breath, closed his eyes, and thought of his wife, Giesela, and the baby, now barely a year old. That was when Krebs seemed to wake up. "Chief?" he called across the tiny control room.

The Chief raised his head. "Sir?"

"Surface! Blow all tanks!"

The Chief hesitated for a fraction of a second, then leaped for the control valves. The *U-560* hissed and shuddered, but since it was already shallow, it only took a few seconds to respond to the rush of air into the buoyancy tanks. The submarine popped back to the surface while the depth charges kept dropping. When they went off, the crew yelled and cursed as their submarine rolled and pitched, but its pressure hull did not crack. The men of the *U-560* were still alive. What Krebs had come up with had been absolutely brilliant. Max confessed to himself that he would never have thought of it.

Krebs calmly ordered the Chief what to do next. "Dive deep. Then hard to port. Those bastards are surely coming around for another try, but they always seem to bank to port, the side on which the pilot sits. We'll be off their track. It'll take them a bit to find our shadow."

The *U-560*, miserable and stinking and battered and corroded though it might be, responded smartly and fell beneath the waves while the crew whispered prayers of thanksgiving not to God but to their captain. For his part, Krebs clutched his sore knee, which had already swollen to the size of a melon. Max looked at Krebs, astonished at what he had done. By his quick thinking, the man had saved all their lives. But then Max thought again. If Krebs had listened to him in the first place, they wouldn't have been caught so unawares by the Liberator.

Minutes passed. The eyes of the U-boat crew stared upward at gray steel, imagining the increasing layer of protective water between them and the air. Lips moved in silent prayer, this time to God since Krebs wasn't doing anything. The Chief eyed Krebs. "Tell us what it is like to be raised in a castle, Captain." He nodded at the wide-eyed boys in the tower. "They'd like to hear it."

Krebs laughed. "The difficult part, Chief, is trying to remember which pretty fräulein is the upstairs maid and which is the downstairs."

"You bedded them both, just to fix them in your mind, didn't you, sir?"

"Well, of course. I knew someday I was going to be a U-boat man and would have to be a good lover. It is a requirement!"

The boys snickered. Their minds were, for the moment, off their predicament. Elbows were stuck into adjoining ribs over some private joke or memory. The Chief had cannily gotten them to thinking of fräuleins or perhaps mademoiselles. Krebs had, of course, known exactly what was up.

Then there were two splashes above. A man called out, "Here they come again!"

"*Scheisse!*" Max groaned.

Krebs laughed through the pain of his knee. "Really, Max. Such language!" He lowered his voice to a whisper so only Max could hear. "You know, there is nothing left to do except what has already been done. We'll either make it or we won't. Relax. Not a bad way to die, is it? Doing our duty for the fatherland and Uncle Karl?"

Max closed his eyes and held his breath. *Come on, you bastards,* he thought to himself. He was suddenly angry at the English, so angry he wanted them all to die. *Why did they keep fighting?* He hated them all, the dirty, stinking bastards! *Come on. Come on, you English. Kill us if you can!*

# 4

J osh rose well before sunup, dressed in his khakis, which
Queenie washed and ironed once a week whether they
needed it or not, and went down to the dining room to be
served his usual big breakfast of clabber biscuits, boiled
drum, and a half dozen fried eggs. "I see the wind's picked
up a tad," Queenie said, dishing the eggs directly onto Josh's
plate from a big black frying pan. "Did you get to sleep last
night at all?"

He answered with a lie. "I slept like a log. How about
you?"

"The same," she fibbed similarly.

Josh ate heartily. His mood was always better in the morning, and the anticipation of soon being on the sea was a good
part of elevating his disposition, not to mention Queenie's
good cooking. He emerged after breakfast in the brown
leather jacket he wore to sea, feeling contentedly full, and
finding the three gulls and old Purdy still dozing. This time,
their presence didn't irritate him. "Well, howdy, boys," he
said. "Still working on your nap, are you?" Not a bird moved
a feather, which pretty much answered his question.

Since Whalebone City was a fishing village, nearly everyone in town was already awake, even though the pale November sun was just barely thinking about pushing up from
the Atlantic. Josh spotted Doc Folsom outside his infirmary.
He was wearing his derby hat at its usual rakish angle, and

his fingers were tucked into his bright red suspenders. Doc spat in the sand and said, "Hello, Josh, my boy. Another glorious day along the Outer Banks, is it not? 'So here hath been dawning, another blue day: Think, wilt thou let it slip useless away?' That would be Mr. Carlyle, Thomas Carlyle, sir."

"A pretty poem, Doc, that's for sartain," Josh said, his contentment draining away. Although he'd forgiven Doc for his letter, he'd not forgotten it.

Doc was in an expansive mood, which was the usual case. "Why the poem's not pretty at all, Josh! It's deep, and I'm surprised you don't recognize how deep it is, you being a college man and all."

Few on Killakeet would ever challenge Doc his opinions, and Josh was no exception. Doc knew books, poetry, music, and would probably recognize an artist's brushstrokes just by looking at them. Josh was college-educated, but as an engineer, matriculating at the Virginia Polytechnic Institute on a Coast Guard stipend. After he'd graduated, he'd taken his commission in the service and gone off to Alaska. Josh figured he knew something about engineering and he knew the sea and the stars and boats, but he wasn't a learned man like Doc. Doc was even a bit of an anthropologist, keeping detailed records on every child born on the island since his arrival, which had been just after the Great War. He was going to write it all up in a scientific journal, he said, one of these days, when he got around to it. He measured the babies when they were born and kept track of their growth. "Killakeet is my Galápagos," he liked to say, "but instead of Darwin's finches, I have Folsom's babies."

Josh didn't want to get into a conversation with Doc so he headed on down Walk to the Base, seeing up ahead Hook Mallory sitting in a rocker watching his daughter Willow sweep the pizer of his general store. Willow was a pretty girl, everybody said that, only she wasn't quite right, which everybody said, too. Willow had started out normal enough. She'd even been Jacob's playmate for much of those first two years of his life. They'd been born only a week apart, and both had seemed so bright, playing together out in the sand and building castles and such. But, not too long after Jacob was lost, Willow had taken an odd turn, inwardlike. At first, people thought she was never going to talk again, and when she finally did, she never had much to say except things that made people suspect she was something of a hoo-doo, what Killakeeters called someone who could tell your fortune and place curses and such. Doc, as always, had another opinion. "The only thing hoo-doo about Willow is that she pays attention where most of us don't," he'd told Josh.

Hook and Josh nodded to one another and Hook said, "I think we're due a change in the temperature, one way or t'other."

"Most likely," Josh said, "and the wind will turn before the day's out."

Willow stopped her sweeping at the sound of Josh's voice. She had eyes that were a strange though beautiful color, like purple sage. Doc said he'd never heard of anyone having eyes that grand a color. He also said if Willow ever got married, it was going to be interesting to record if the trait was carried over to her kids. Willow was all of nineteen, just a few years shy of being an old maid by Killakeet standards. It wasn't likely she'd find a husband, being a hoo-doo and all, and fishermen being the most superstitious of fellows. Her hair was also red, unusual among Killakeet women. Hook said he must have had an Irishman on a limb of the old family tree.

Abruptly Willow said, " 'The waves have a story to tell me, as I lie on the lonely beach. Chanting aloft in the pine-tops, the wind has a lesson to teach.' "

Josh looked at Hook, who shrugged at Willow's pronouncement. Doc came up and lifted a book from the corner of Hook's pizer. "What's this?" he asked.

"It's a book of Robert Service poems I brought back from Alaska," Josh said. "I gave it to Willow. Her mama told me she liked poems."

Doc opened the book, ran his fingers down the page of contents, then turned to another page. He said, " 'But the stars throng out in their glory, and they sing of the God in man.' ' "

Willow didn't look at Doc but she allowed a distant smile, replying, " 'They sing of the Mighty Master, of the loom his fingers span.' " Then, losing her smile, she went back to her sweeping.

"Impressive," Doc said. "I believe she's memorized every word."

Hook looked doubtful. "Likely she just read that very part, that's all."

"What do you think, Josh?" Doc asked.

"I think I couldn't have remembered that even if I'd just read it," Josh said.

Doc studied Willow. "Yes," he answered to a question unspoken. "Yes, indeed."

The only church on Killakeet sat at the end of Walk to the Base, a sign tacked to its front proclaiming it the Church of the Mariner. Josh found Preacher sitting on the front pew, reading his Bible. Preacher, which was the name he went by as well as his vocation, had a drooping shoulder smashed to pieces in a West Virginia coal mine by a slab of slate rock. The rock had struck him like a sledgehammer, producing a day of hideous pain that had transformed coal miner Jeremy Fowler into Preacher of Killakeet Island. It had been God's will, Preacher said, considering the slate rock was a booby trap only God could have set.

"How do, Josh," Preacher said in a voice some maintained was like fingernails on a chalkboard. "Need a proverb for the day?" Being an outsider, he nearly always forgot to first comment on the weather.

"No thanks, Preacher. I just want my minute."

"The Lord's always got a minute," Preacher replied, and went back to his Bible.

Josh stood in the church between the pews and bowed his head. He wasn't particularly religious, but like all men who work on the sea, he had a sense of the enormous power of the Creator of vast waters. Josh made his prayers for Jacob, and for his mother, and his father, and for Naanni, the Inuit maiden he'd married in Alaska according to her tribal ways and who'd died in his arms. That was a story he kept to himself, even from his father. On the island, only Eureka Phimble knew it, and that was because the bosun had also served on the Bering Sea with Josh aboard the old *Comanche*.

After Josh was done with his prayers, he put a quarter in the collection plate and started on, but Preacher stopped him. "Josh, I've been thinking," he said. "This church was built from the planks of the schooner *Frances Clayton*. It is a goodsome building, tight against the wind, hardly leaks when it rains, nearly warm in the winter and almost cool in the summer, and a great enhancement to our community. But it is the result of tragedy. So how can it be good?"

Josh scratched up under his officer's cap. "Awful early in the morning to be considering that kind of thing, Preacher. I don't know. Ain't it in your book there?"

"I keep looking but I can't find it, if it is."

Josh had always found it best to keep his thoughts unencumbered of religious philosophy. He decided to believe in the Almighty, and be impressed by His works, but it made him uncomfortable to wonder how the Lord thought about things. "Well, I guess good can come from bad," he replied, lamely. "I mean here's the example with the church, if you want to look at it that way. Is that the topic of your sermon this Sunday?"

Preacher shrugged. "It don't seem to matter what I say. The men sleep through it, the kids all squirm, and the women think about what they're cooking for Sunday dinner. I can see it on their faces."

"Well, it's not that they don't appreciate you trying," Josh offered, glad to change the subject. "Killakeet went many a year without a real preacher. You were needed. I guess it's just that you're a landsman, you know. Maybe you ought to go out and fish some and then talk about that. The men will always stay awake when they hear talk of fish."

Preacher's eyes lit up. "Maybe I shall! Why, I could join

someone on their workboat. Who do you think I should ask?"

Josh appraised the thin, clumsy preacher and knew there was no fisherman who'd want him. Likely, he'd get seasick and otherwise get in the way. "Try Pump Padgett," he said finally. "Pump's boy's off lodging in Morehead City to go to school. He could use a hand. But don't tell him I sent you. Make it like it's your own idea. It'll go down better that way."

Preacher grabbed Josh's hand. "Thank you, Josh. You're a friend of me and the Lord."

"Well, we try, Preacher," Josh said, and escaped.

Fishermen walking toward their workboats saw Josh as he went on down to Doakes and waved, as did the clammers and oystermen with their buckets and rakes. His boys, the crew of the patrol boat they called the *Maudie Jane,* also came along, mixed in with their parents and wives.

Just before he entered the station, which was marked by a low fence anyone could step over and a gate always left open, Josh looked down the beach toward the lighthouse and caught sight of his father riding on the big gelding named Thunder. It was Keeper Jack's ritual to come into Whalebone City after the lamp was doused in the mornings. The Keeper was wearing his blue serge winter jacket, brass buttons agleam, and his cap with the Lighthouse Service crest. Though he was seventy-one years old, he still carried himself like a young man, and a proud one at that. For all Josh knew, back at the Keeper's House was one of those young women his father occasionally sent for from Morehead City. It was the stuff of merry gossip amongst Killakeet ladies how Keeper Jack would get out his big old phonograph and his records of classical music and play them for his "girlfriends." They apparently liked it. Occasionally, he had to come in and stay at the Hammerhead until one of the girls gave up her dream of being the Killakeet Keeper's wife and went home.

Josh waited until his father reined in Thunder, which wasn't hard since the horse rarely went much faster than a

slow man could walk. There'd been a time when Thunder
had lived up to his name, but these days he was content to
plod. "Good morning, Son," Keeper Jack said with two fingers to the brim of his cap. "Pretty night, wasn't it? All soft,
though I expect the wind to pick up."

"A little blow a-coming, I'm thinking," Josh answered.

The Keeper nodded, then patted Thunder's neck. "Come
see me when you get a chance, Josh. I'd like to sit a spell,
talk to you about this and that." When Josh said he'd do it,
Keeper Jack clucked his tongue and Thunder clip-clopped
on.

At the military dock, Josh found Ready O'Neal, the gunner's mate as well as the son of Queenie and Buckets, sitting
on a piling reading a Morehead City newspaper that was
about a week old. "What's the paper say about the weather,
Ready?" Josh asked.

"Haven't spotted anything, sir, but there's a Studebaker
for sale. I like them cars. Bosun Phimble gave me this paper
to look at the picture."

"You ever drive a car?"

Ready looked up, then shook his head. "You know I ain't,
sir. Ain't no roads on Killakeet."

Bosun Eureka Phimble strolled up to the dock at that moment. Phimble was the son of one of the famous Negro Pea
Island surfmen from up Hatteras way, not that anybody on
Killakeet gave much of a damn what color he was. What
people cared about on Killakeet was whether you could handle a boat or could fish worth a hoot or had a good eye for
wrecking. Eureka Phimble was pretty much the best there
was at all of them.

Josh took note of the poke sack Phimble was carrying and
hoped it was filled with cookies. His big breakfast was already dwindling in his gut, and Phimble's wife, Talkie, was
a great baker. She was also the island's schoolma'am, teaching grades one through six in the island church, eight to
twelve o'clock each day. The older kids, those few who went
on with school, mostly went across to Morehead City and
lodged there.

Phimble offered up the poke and Josh stuck in his hand and discovered it was indeed filled with cookies, peanut butter ones at that. The bosun pointed at the headline on the front of the newspaper, which said, "Battle in the North Atlantic." "You know, sir," he said in a conversational tone, "we're going to get into that war sooner before later."

Josh reached for another cookie. "Could be you're right, could be you're wrong," he replied in an attempt to keep the conversation going and the poke near.

"You might recollect German U-boats came over here during the Great War," Phimble added.

Josh knew firsthand that Phimble was correct. It had happened in 1918 and Josh had seen the entire thing from the parapet of the lighthouse. The U-boat had dispatched a freighter with a double shot of torpedoes and then just sat there, daring any other merchantman to try to get past. The Killakeet surfmen pushed out from Doakes, pulling their oars hard to rescue the men off the sinking freighter. They went right past the U-boat as if it weren't even there. The U-boat captain was so astonished, he had taken his hat off to them. The story had even made it into a North Carolina history book.

"You ought to read that article," Phimble said. "I'd say this crop of U-boats are killers."

Josh wasn't a big reader of newspapers, although he made it a point to read at least one novel every year. He especially liked that writer Ernest Hemingway, although he thought Mr. Hemingway was of the opinion he knew more about fishing than he really did. Still, Josh obliged Phimble, borrowing the front page of the paper from Ready and reading it while eating another cookie. The story said a convoy going past Iceland had been attacked by German submarines and the British and Canadians had fought them off in a day-long battle. Six freighters had been sunk but a U-boat had also been destroyed. The convoy had gone on, only to be attacked by another wolf pack of U-boats. The result of that battle was not known.

"Wouldn't surprise me at all to see those old German boys

come this way," Phimble said. He took his poke of cookies and stepped on board the *Maudie Jane* and went to the stern and leaned, significantly, on the empty depth-charge racks.

Josh considered the empty racks, empty because the Coast Guard did not authorize him to have any depth charges. This led him to further contemplate the empty machine gun mount on the bow. Then he looked at the headline on the newspaper again. "Ready," he finally asked, "where's the machine gun?"

Ready looked up from his paper. "In one of the forward lockers, Skipper."

"You ever get it out, look at it?"

Since he was the gunner's mate, Ready knew Mister Thurlow had asked him a fair question. He considered his best answer. "It's clean," he allowed. "I look at it ever so often, make sure it ain't rusty or nothing. But get it out? Never had a reason to. There's no ammunition for it."

Josh was rarely gruff with his boys, reminding himself he was on Killakeet and Killakeeters didn't need to be yelled at to do their jobs. "Tell you what," he said softly. "Why don't you unpack it, then bring it up and at least see if it'll fit in its mount?"

"Sure, Skipper," Ready said and then went back to reading his paper. Ensign Thurlow had not, after all, said *when* to do the work. Ready would get to it, sooner if not later, tomorrow or the next day. That was the thing about life on Killakeet. Time seemed to stretch out pretty much forever, measured by the seasons, not the clock.

Josh waited, saw Ready wasn't moving, then said, in a lower register, "Ready, I mean right now."

Ready put his paper under his arm and went on board, whistling. He went below and looked in a forward locker, and sure enough, the machine gun was there and it still didn't have any ammunition. Nonetheless, he hefted it and headed topside. It fit very well on its mount. The other boys looked at Ready and he replied with a shrug.

Josh boarded the *Maudie Jane* and went over to Bosun Phimble, who was watching a ball of silversides pushing up a disturbance in the water, what Killakeeters called a jerl. "Eureka," he said, "do you think we could fight if we had to?"

Phimble stopped watching the jerl and raised an eyebrow. "Who's 'we,' Skipper?"

"Well, the *Maudie Jane*."

Phimble raised his other eyebrow. "Fight who?"

Josh glanced forward at Ready O'Neal, who was pretending to fire the machine gun while the other boys were firing invisible rifles. They were having themselves a regular little pretend war, more or less like cowboys and Indians. "You know. Like you said. A German submarine, say."

Phimble took his time framing his answer. "Skipper," he said at last in a quiet voice that had the force equivalent of hitting Josh between the eyes with a plank, "this outfit couldn't fight a German ferryboat."

Before Josh could completely absorb Phimble's answer, Once Jackson, half of the Jackson twins, came up and reported. "Mister Thurlow? Can you answer me a question?"

Josh could tell Once from his brother Again only because Once had a dimple in his right cheek caused by a collision with a table corner when he was three. The two teenagers were actually named Frank and Mickey but Doc Folsom had said, "There's once," when he'd birthed the first Jackson baby, "And again," as the second one came into the world. The names had stuck.

"What is it, Once?" Josh demanded, after tearing his eyes from Phimble.

Once had on a big grin, a trademark of both boys. "Can we fish today?"

Josh was pleased to let the boys fish. They deserved to make a little extra money, considering how pitifully small their regular pay was each month, and the fish market was always willing to pay top dollar for tuna, wahoo, and marlin. "After we get out to the Stream and make sure all's well, you can," Josh said.

Phimble shook his head as Once cheerfully went below to bring up the fishing tackle. "We ought to be putting the boys through some drills, sir, not fishing."

"Let me run my boat, Eureka."

"I'm just telling you, sir."

"I know. But look at them! They're Killakeet boys. They're not like the men we had with us up on the ice."

Phimble shrugged. "We weren't men until Captain Falcon made us that way. You remember how he did it, sir. He drilled us until we dropped, pounded us far worse than the enemy ever would. We got so we hated that rat bastard so much we took it out on the poachers. They never had a chance when the ol' *Comanch* hove into view."

"Eureka, I know you mean well, but—Ready, stop playing with that gun! Take it below!—but the Maudie Janes didn't sign on to fight. They're just seagoing surfmen. Their job is to go out and rescue folks, not kill them. You know all that."

Phimble knew and he didn't know, too. Coast Guard was Coast Guard as far as he was concerned. Rescue and killing, it was all part of it. He knew what Josh could do. He had seen the big ensign wade into a band of poachers, swinging that Aleut ax he liked to carry, sending the rascals scattering, those who survived, that is. He had also seen Josh collect a bullet in his leg. God, that had been a bloody fiasco. Captain Falcon had been off his beam that day, for sartain! But it seemed to Phimble maybe Josh had latched onto peaceful ways a bit too hard since they'd come to Killakeet. If the U-boats showed up . . . well, the boys aboard the *Maudie Jane* were going to die and that would be on Josh Thurlow's head. Phimble made up his mind right then to make sure that didn't happen.

On the Stream, all seemed in order, the freighters and tankers coasting by with no problems, so Josh gave the Jackson twins permission and they started fishing and, before too long, so was nearly every one of the boys except Stobs, who kept the radio, and Fisheye, who was left below to watch over the engines. Bets were taken all around on who would catch the biggest fish. There wasn't much money aboard, most of the boys' service pay going to their families as soon as they got it, but what coins the crew had were soon clinking into Millie the cook's biscuit sack as stakes. Millie wrote it all down in a little notebook. When on patrol, the boys liked to bet on lots of things, mostly whatever somebody thought up and sounded good. One time, they'd bet on whether Marvin, their little black-and-white mascot terrier, would next pee off the starboard or the port side. Those who had bet on starboard, which included Millie, started enticing the little dog to that side of the boat with chunks of breakfast sausage. Those who'd bet on the port side cried foul. Marvin, unable to get to either side because of the boys lined up and arguing there, went down to the stern and raised his leg over the transom. After that, he never peed anywhere else and his urinary habits were scrubbed from the crew's games of chance.

"Let's go a bit farther out into the Stream," Josh told Phimble. "Bigger fish out there. As a matter of fact, we'll let the boys fish all night. Then, tomorrow morning, we'll drop the catch off at the fish market. Christmas coming up, they can use the money."

Phimble loved going out into the deeper, tropical water of the Gulf Stream. Out there, he could open the *Maudie Jane* up and let her run, which was not only fun but good for the engines, too. He turned the boat easterly as the boys raised a cheer. Once had already caught a fish, a good-sized wahoo, and Again had something big on his line, too.

Josh stuck his head inside the wheelhouse. "Stobs, call Chief Glendale, tell him to let the boys' kinfolk know we're on patrol tonight."

"Fishing all night, sir?" Stobs asked.

"Patrol, Stobs."

"Aye, aye, sir!"

When the word got around that they'd be fishing the night away, Ready O'Neal got out his fiddle and Bobbie McClung his banjo, and all the boys started singing "Big Rock Candy Mountain." Marvin started howling, his snout to the sky, and Josh clapped his big hands, nearly on the beat. Phimble grinned and pushed the throttles ahead, then tapped his foot to the hobo tune while the *Maudie Jane* bounced across the waves, going out to where the water was blue and deep, and the tropical wind whistled free and clear, and the big fish danced their eternal dance of life and death.

# 5

In a dense, swirling fog, Krebs kept hurling invectives from the *U-560*'s tower. "Come on, you bastards! Show yourselves!"

"We've lost them, *Kaleu*," Max said tiredly. "Let's submerge. The men need sleep. So do I and so do you."

Krebs, his dense beard coated with ice crystals, ignored his second-in-command. "Just show a shadow, that's all I ask," he snarled, but his voice was sucked away by the fog. Even the sea was muffled. He crashed his gloved hand on the rim of the tower fairing and cursed.

Max yawned, as if he were bored. When trying to convince Krebs of anything, he'd learned it was necessary to keep emotion out of his voice and his demeanor. "You know it's tricky business up here," he said reasonably. "The water is cold, and it can fool Pretch's sound-detection gear. Those propeller sounds he heard could have been a hundred miles away. Anyway, that was sixteen hours ago."

Krebs raised his nose to the air. "Can't you smell the ships, Max? I can. They're all around us. I can feel them, too."

Max fell silent. He'd done his best. And he felt nothing except the bone-chilling wind that cut through every seam of his leather coveralls. Only the day before, the *U-560* had been mercilessly battered by a Liberator bomber. After Krebs had come up with a brilliant tactic to avoid the first two depth charges, the next ones had holed one of the U-boat's fuel tanks and blown gauges and air lines apart in the control room. God only knew how they'd survived the attack. Krebs, still gritting his teeth from the pain of a badly twisted knee, had taken hold of the situation and sent the sub on a wild, gyrating descent. More depth charges followed, but an aircraft's advantage was lost after the first attack. If a U-boat could put some water between it and the sky, there was always a chance. With a captain like Krebs, the odds were even better.

To get his blood moving, Max made a tour of the tiny tower, checking to see that each lookout at least had his eyes open. It was probably too much to also expect them to be paying attention since they couldn't see more than a few feet in the damnable fog. They were all nearly frozen by the bone-numbing Norwegian wind.

For his part, Krebs had taken enough aspirin to stop an elephant and drained his private store of schnapps until finally his twisted knee had gone numb. In any case, he wasn't going to let his knee get in the way of his duty. Based on the excited chatter going back and forth from BdU, dozens of small convoys were streaming out of English ports, heading north. The British and the Russians had apparently decided to make a big push to get supplies to the Red Army. Admiral Doenitz had vectored in as many U-boats as possible into the Sea of Norway. Krebs's boat had been kept the farthest south to serve as a trip wire. But nothing, since the first convoy, had been seen. There had only been continued frustration. And now all this goddamned fog!

Krebs sniffed the air. "Wait. I smell something. It smells like . . ." He stopped and considered the odor. It was sweet petroleum, slightly burnt. "There's a destroyer out there," he said, so softly no one on the tower heard him. "Max?" he called.

"Yes, sir?"

"Take the boys below. Chief, take us down."

But it was too late. In an instant, a ship plunged out of the fog, her bow aimed straight at them. One glance was all

Max needed to identify it as a very angry English destroyer. "Chief, down, *down!*" Max roared.

"No!" Krebs barked. He flipped the lid of the voice tube to the engine room. "Hans, give me full turns! Chief, hard to starboard! And send the eighty-eight crew up here. Hurry!"

*"Kaleu!"* Max yelped. "We must dive!"

"Not enough time, Max."

Max took another look and saw Krebs was right. There was a puff of smoke from the destroyer's deck and an explosion erupted behind the *U-560*. Water pattered over the men on the tower. The next shell would probably be on top of them.

The deck gun crew scrambled out of the tower hatch and down to their piece, pulling out the barrel tampion, throwing a shell into the breech, and cranking it around toward the destroyer. These were old hands, practiced and quick.

"Wait, boys!" Krebs yelled at them. "Fire only on my command." Another round whistled past, just missing the tower. The lookouts flattened themselves on deck. Then a few of them raised their heads, astonished that the captain and *Leutnant* Max were still standing as if nothing had happened. "Hard a port, Chief!" Krebs said. He was suddenly exuberant. "I'm going to hug that old English lion!"

Max clutched the rim of the tower fairing. What the hell was Krebs doing? But then another part of his mind, the analytical part, wondered how it was the British had managed to catch them. They'd been on a collision course as if they knew exactly where the *U-560* was. *But how was that possible in this fog?*

Krebs maneuvered until the U-boat was bows-on with the destroyer. The English had stopped firing and Max realized why. Krebs had brought them in so close the destroyer crews couldn't crank their guns low enough to hit them. But the *U-560*'s deck gun was perfectly leveled. Max could count the rivets on the destroyer as it flew past on an opposite heading. Startled faces popped along the rail above them. If any of them had a sidearm, he could have shot the U-boat crew as they sped past. But Krebs had completely surprised the English. The tables had been turned. *He had them!* "Give them hell, boys!" Krebs yelled. "Fire!"

There was only time for one round but it was well placed, pounding the destroyer in its fat stern. Max and all the men on the tower ducked as steel-plate shrapnel burst from the explosion. A man screamed, a lookout, and fell on his back. Max looked to see Winkler with a jagged shard of English steel stuck in his throat, a fountain of blood erupting around it. The other lookouts turned, goggle-eyed, frozen in shock.

Krebs glanced at Winkler and grimaced. "All right, boys," he said as calmly as if it were part of the usual routine. "Let's go below." He called through the hatch. "Chief, take us down." The lookouts pushed to get to the safety of the tower control room, dropping one by one below. Winkler was left lying in a spreading pool of gore.

The *U-560* began to drop by the bow. The destroyer had stopped dead in the water. Her stern was on fire. From the top of her wheelhouse, machine guns opened up. Rounds pounded into the tower. Krebs ducked below the fairing, careful to protect his knee. One of the eighty-eight crew fell clambering up the tower ladder. At first, Max thought the man had slipped in Winkler's blood but then saw he was clutching his arm, blood streaming through his fingers. A ricochet had caught him.

Krebs crawled over beside Winkler. The man's eyes were open, wide and staring, but still had a spark of life to them. When Krebs took his hand, it was soft, and cold. "You did well today, Winkler," he said. "You did your duty." Krebs looked up and saw Max. "Number One, help me with this man."

A shell from the destroyer shrieked over the narrow U-boat stern and exploded. The British, though still adrift, had gotten the *U-560* back into the sights of their big guns. Max and Krebs grasped Winkler under his arms and gently handed him down. Another round whistled in, this one so close Max thought he could feel its hot breath. When it exploded, it sent him flying into the tower fairing. Dazed, he searched for the pain of wounds or broken bones. He looked up to find Krebs beside him. "Really, Max. All those gymnastics at your age!" Krebs dragged him to the hatch.

Dully, Max knew that it must have murdered Krebs's knee to put both their weight on it. "Am I dying?"

"Just the wind knocked out of you, I think," Krebs answered through gritted teeth.

Krebs was the last man down, descending the ladder by hopping on one foot to save his knee. He pulled the hatch shut and threw over the latch just as the water closed over the U-boat. Winkler, lying on the floor near the attack periscope, made a horrible, gurgling sound, then stopped gasping. Men who had knelt around him stood up and moved away. The smell of his blood, like hot iron, filled the control room.

"Down to twenty meters, *Herr Kaleu*," the Chief announced in a formal voice.

"Let's take a look at the enemy," Krebs said. He stiffly lowered himself onto the periscope tractor seat, reversed his cap to get the brim out of the way, and pushed his face into the eyepiece. He swiveled the periscope and ran it up and down. "Fog. It's all I see."

"Engines are up on the destroyer," Pretch called from the sound closet. "She's maneuvering."

"Take us down to sixty meters, Chief," Krebs said. He lowered the periscope and took a towel from someone and wiped his face. The towel came away smeared with the scarlet streaks of Winkler's blood. "We're going to catch hell from that destroyer up there, I suppose." He looked around at the eighty-eight crew. "But our boys gave the English a kick in their ass as we went by, didn't you?"

The deck gun crew grinned at their commander but the others in the control room kept their worried expressions. They anxiously craned their faces toward the surface as if they could make out the destroyer coming after them. All they saw, of course, was grimy, rusted steel.

Max crawled over to Winkler and closed the man's eyes. "We must clean up the blood," he said, but before anyone could respond, the first depth charge detonated. The *U-560* rang as if it were a bell suddenly struck by a great hammer. It lurched over on its starboard side, then rocked violently back. The crew in the control tower shouted and held on as they were lashed and whipsawed by a dozen more explosions. Some men closed their eyes, their lips moving in silent prayer. Others cursed. All found any kind of protrusion, a stanchion or a wheel, and clung to it as if it might save them.

Krebs kept his voice low and steady. "Rig for silent running, Chief, and take us to ninety meters." He took off his white captain's cap, splattered with blood, and ran a hand through his greasy, reddish brown hair, and toted up the odds while hell descended on his boat. Every eye was on him, each man filled with desperate hope that Krebs would come up with something yet again to save them.

Krebs ran his eyes across his boys and saw their fear. Then he had a startling revelation. *Radar*. It had to be aboard that destroyer to find them in the middle of that miserable fog. And if a small destroyer had radar, then that meant the English were putting the sets on every antisubmarine ship they had. If that was so, it was only a matter of time for the *Unterseeboot*. Each of them was going to be picked off, one by one. Radar would seek them out on the surface and ASDIC beneath the waves. There would be no place to hide. The revelation was so startling, it must have registered on his face. *"Kaleu,"* one of eighty-eight crewmen said, "shall we make it this time?"

"We'll make it," Krebs said confidently. "Don't you worry. We'll make it and then I'm going to take all you boys home."

As their U-boat writhed in agony from the bombs exploding all around them, the men of the *U-560* stopped praying and cursing and instead cheered. Max had to smile. Krebs had said exactly the right thing at the right time. Talk about *Fingerspitzengefühl*. "Home" had been the word the crew most needed to hear. All they had to do was survive one more terrible attack and that's where they were going because Krebs had told them so. "Hoorah for our *Kaleu!*"

someone yelled as the word spread throughout the boat. Then the entire crew picked up the cheer and added, "Hoorah for the fatherland! Hoorah for *home!*"

Max did not cheer. Instead, he listened in amazement and smelled blood in his nostrils. *Surely,* he thought, *we are all insane.*

# 6

It was Josh's opinion that there was no better way to start the day than with a cup of coffee properly adjusted with a splash of Mount Gay rum, a heaping tablespoon of sugar, and a dollop of milk from Sally, the Hammerhead's resident cow. It was a recipe that seemed to soften nearly every prospect for the day, even if it included rough weather or unhappy women. Josh called his morning formula Barbados Sunrise.

Josh was having a leisurely Saturday morning breakfast of flapjacks and Appalachian honey and working on his second cup of Sunrise when he heard a most unusual sound, an engine that wasn't a boat engine. And it was just outside the hotel. When he went out to see what it was, he was astonished to find one of the new utility four-wheel-drive military vehicles designated a GP, for general purpose, or jeep. Chief Glendale was sitting proudly behind its wheel. "What do you think, sir? Just came in on the ferry."

"I didn't know we'd ordered one," Josh confessed, which was no surprise to Chief Glendale since he had forged the ensign's signature on the requisition. "How's it take to the sand?"

Chief Glendale was a big, leather-faced man, big in his spirits as well as his voice, which was loud as a foghorn. A Killakeeter, too, though he'd spent nearly thirty years away in one posting or the other, pretty much all over the world.

He was back on the island to finish out his career. He gave Josh a full-toothed grin (courtesy of the Coast Guard, who'd provided him the choppers) and bragged, "She goes like the wind, sir, yes, she does! Like the wind! You want to try her?"

Josh wanted, in fact, nothing more. Queenie and Buckets had come to stand beside him and they were both atremble with excitement at seeing four wheels in Killakeet sand. Queenie wasn't so excited, however, that she did not see an opportunity when it presented itself. "Law, Josh, wait a minute!" she exclaimed, and disappeared through the door. She soon returned holding a basket of fruit—apples and bananas and grapes. "I've made this up for little Dosie. Josh, you could take it down there for me in your new thingamabob."

"It's a jeep, ma'am," Chief Glendale said, tipping his hat to her.

Queenie shot eye-arrows at Glendale, then presented her basket to Josh. "How about it?" she demanded.

"Well, I guess I could . . ."

"Fine." She handed the basket over, then crossed her arms so there was no way Josh could hand it back. Then, just to make certain, Queenie went inside, though she peeked through the windows. She couldn't wait to tell the ladies what she'd done. They'd plotted and schemed on how to get Josh and the Crossan girl together, and now she'd managed it.

Chief Glendale climbed out of the jeep just as Purdy the pelican hopped into the passenger seat. The chief thought nothing of it and neither did Josh or Buckets. Purdy went pretty much wherever he liked. "Go ahead, sir. Take her for a spin," Chief Glendale said grandly.

Josh went upstairs and pulled on his brown leather jacket, climbed in the jeep, and roared down Walk to the Base and across the dunes and down onto the beach. He'd driven a jeep before—the headquarters at Ketchikan had gotten two and he'd stolen one for a ride—and he knew their tricks, which were all wonderful. Why, it would scale just about any sand hill and you could even run her a bit out into the surf without getting stuck. He laid the windshield flat on the hood so that the crisp salt wind whistled past his ears as he barged down the beach, yeehawing at the top of his lungs. When he flashed past the lighthouse, his father came out on the parapet and waved him on. Purdy was having a fine time, too, holding his wings out as if flying low.

The Crossan House was about a mile south of the light-house. It sat alone behind a stretch of sand hills and had a grand vista of the sea. Josh knew the place well, though it had been a while since he'd visited it. During the summers, he had often come up from the lighthouse to play with the Crossan boys—Randy and Bart, those were their names. What great games they'd played pretending to be pirates or cowboys and Indians or soldiers amongst the sand dunes and creeks and woods of the island. Josh wondered what had become of them and supposed their sister—Dosie—might fill him in. He tried to remember exactly what she'd looked like but failed, although he recalled, oddly enough, that she usually had the faint smell of milk about her.

Josh stopped the jeep in the front yard, which was just more sand, and walked up with the basket and knocked on the screen door. The wooden door behind it was propped open by a stack of books. When nobody answered his knock, he hallooed once, waited, then went inside. In the parlor, he saw two small, silver-framed photographs on a table. One he recognized was of Mr. and Mrs. Crossan, the other of the entire family, the boys Bart and Randy when they were perhaps ten and eight years old or so, their arms crossed, looking sternly into the camera. Mrs. Crossan held a little girl, which Josh presumed was Dosie.

Josh left the basket in the parlor and went through the kitchen and looked out and noticed the double doors of the stable were open. There, he found little Herman Guthrie, mucking out the stall. "Missus ain't here," he said. "Gone for a ride toward Miracle Point." He looked suspiciously at Josh. "What do you want with her?"

"I have gift from Queenie O'Neal," he said. "Say, you ever seen a jeep?"

Josh led Herman around to the square little truck and the boy ran around it three times he was so excited. "I'd give just about anything to go for a ride in it!" he cried, but then settled himself down. "But I've got work, promised Miss Crossan to get it done before she came back."

"Well, we'll do it later, Herman, and that's a promise."

Herman nodded sadly, allowed a sigh, and trudged back to the stables. He cheered himself up by remembering he was the richest boy on Killakeet.

Josh climbed back into the jeep. "Well, let's go find her, Purdy, what say?" Purdy lifted his wings, ready to fly as long as he could do it sitting down.

As he drove along, Josh kept his eye out for dead fish or birds that might be hurt, or sea turtles laying eggs, or the remnants of wrecked ships, or trash. All would tell him a story of the sea, how the animals were doing out there, and what kind of people might be coasting by.

Miles of wet sand played out before him, backed by a line of sand hills, topped with waving sea oats. Josh liked the way the dunes changed color as the sun passed through its daily quadrants, a rosy pink in the morning, variations of tan and beige as the day wore on, a feathery blue at dusk. The dunes, sculpted by the wind, were like small mountains and valleys with dips and whorls and hollows. Scattered remnants of whelk and scallop and moon-snail shells littered them, and when the sun caught their pearly remains, they twinkled like stars.

Josh drove past Thurlow's Lump, the highest point on Killakeet, a massive dune near the center of the island. It had been named after Josh's great-grandfather Josiah Thurlow, the first keeper. The story was that a horrendous hurricane had swamped nearly the entire island, and old Keeper Jim had led the survivors to the dune as their last refuge. There, along with wild ponies and raccoons and deer and dogs and cats, all looking for sanctuary, they had dug into the sand for their only protection against the furious wind and raging sea. Not all had survived, people or animals, but those who did had gone on to repopulate Killakeet.

Josh drove on, crossing the dunes and going inland. A mile south of the Lump, he came to a creek curtained by broomstraw rush and joebells. As a boy, Josh had caught snapping turtles from the creek. They'd go after just about any kind of bait tied to a string, and once they latched on, they could be dragged right out. But a snapping turtle was as fast as it was mean. One of them could snip off a finger or a toe in half a second, given the chance. Josh meant the turtles no harm and was sorry they were so cross about it. He just liked to look at them and ponder their cruel eyes and wonder why they were always so angry. Josh got mad sometimes, too, but he couldn't imagine going through life always mad at everything. Keeper Jack had explained it to him. Anger, he said, is sometimes just another way of being afraid.

Josh kept driving until he'd gone as far as he could go, which was Miracle Point on the southwest end of the island. Generations of Killakeet preachers had held sunrise services on Easter Sunday at this extremity of land. It was also a place the wild ponies liked to come to dig for water. He got out of the jeep, looked around, and spotted some hoofprints, not of the ponies, but of a shod horse. He started following them. Across the dunes, on the heap of sand that tumbled down from the edge of Teach Woods to Loon Pond, he came upon a young woman dressed in a checked shirt and khaki jodhpurs and high, brown leather boots. She was sitting on a sand hill, her elbows on her knees and binoculars to her eyes. Tethered to a myrtle bush behind her was a big brown mare who was watching in the same direction as intently as the woman.

Josh followed their gaze and saw three wild ponies, two mares and a colt. He recognized both of the mares. One was called Tawny, based on the color of her coat, and the other was Jezzie, an ancient mare. The colt was surely Tawny's. They all had a good start on their shaggy winter's coat. Tawny was digging in the sand while the colt frisked around. Old Jezzie trotted after the colt and nudged it back to where its mother was still digging. Pony school was in session.

The woman took no note of Josh and kept studying the

horses. Spilling below her straw hat was dark brown hair that draped down to touch her shoulders and a few strands that fell across her face, which Josh found, for some reason, oddly endearing. He might have watched her longer but her mare noticed him and snorted a warning. When the woman turned, she put a finger to her lips, then beckoned him over.

Josh sat down on the sand beside her, a respectable four feet away. He didn't know why but his heart was beating a little faster. There was something lively about her eyes. And, though he sniffed the air, she smelled nothing of milk, just a womanly scent. She said, in a near-whisper, "I think they're teaching the colt how to find water."

"The mares teach the colts everything," Josh said.

The woman put out her hand. "I'm Theodosia Crossan. Everybody calls me Dosie."

Josh took her hand, which had strength to it. "Josh Thurlow."

She gave him a smile, his first. He thought it an oddly poignant smile. "I know who you are," she said.

"I remember you, too, though you were just a little girl."

Her smile faltered but then she found it again. "I was thirteen years old when I last saw you. And I used to follow you around everywhere."

As much as he tried, Josh just couldn't recall her as anything but a girl of about eight. "How are your brothers, and your folks?" he asked, thinking he'd best change the subject.

"Bart and Randy are both on Wall Street, married with kids. Daddy lost nearly everything in 1929 but, thank goodness, never sold our house here. Mama's happy. She's got grandchildren now. And Daddy's back in the money a little. He's a steel man, you know, and steel's coming back."

"Steel and war go together," Josh said. "What brings you to Killakeet, if I might ask?"

She looked him in the eye, as if to gauge why he had asked the question. "You want me to tell you the pretty story or the awful truth?" she asked, finally.

"Well," he said, thinking for a moment, "the pretty story."

"All right. Here it is. I fooled around in college until

Daddy cut me off, worked my way through selling encyclopedias to people who didn't want them, got a good job, fell
in love with a musician—a jazz trumpeter, of all things and,
yes, I should have known better—got pregnant, had a mis-
carriage, lost the job, lost the horn player, started drinking,
fell on and off the wagon, and just a month ago got so dis-
gusted with myself I decided to come down here and see if
I could figure out how to change my life from a living hell
into something a little bit better. Daddy agreed to stake me."

Josh whistled. "I'm glad I didn't ask for the awful truth."

She laughed. Then she moved her boots around in the
sand and watched them, as if fascinated by the marks she
was making. "So what about you, Josh? What have you been
up to all these years?"

"The pretty story or the awful truth?"

"The awful truth. Pretty stories are too sad."

Josh told her a few things, a little of his life in the Coast
Guard, and some of the things about the Bering Sea Patrol.
When he stopped, she seemed to be waiting for him to go
on, but he said, "That's about it."

"And Jacob," she said. "Anything about him?"

He was grateful that she had brought it up. He never knew
how to tell folks about his brother. "No," he said. "Nothing.
Though I find myself still looking for him whenever I'm out
to sea."

"I hope you find him someday." She frowned and shook
her head. "That sounded so ridiculous. Of course, everybody
hopes that." She studied the horses and the sand and the sea,
then allowed a sigh of contentment, at least as near as she
was capable. "It's so good to be back on Killakeet. All my
days here were such good ones. When I came across on the
ferry, I felt as if I had come home." She nodded over her
shoulder to the brown mare. "That's my Genie. She's a comfort. She loves me no matter how stupid I act. Daddy bought
her for me. She's from Kentucky."

"She's a fine-looking horse," Josh allowed. "Did all that
really happen to you? The pretty story?"

"Well, I left out a few things."

"I'm sorry you've had a hard time of it."

"Josh," Dosie said, "I've already figured one thing out. I've had a hard time of it because of the decisions I've made. I plan on thinking things through while I'm here."

"You should talk to my daddy. He's pretty wise."

"I intend to talk to anybody who'll listen," she retorted. "But mostly I intend to talk to myself."

"Queenie O'Neal sent you a fruit basket, by the way. I left it with Herman."

"That's very sweet. I shall make it a point to personally thank her."

"Queenie's been known to give advice, too," Josh warned. "Most times, you don't even have to ask for it." Josh thought for a moment. "That's pretty much true of everybody on the island."

Genie made a low noise in her throat and Dosie looked to see what had disturbed her. "Oh, isn't he magnificent?" she said of a stallion that had stepped from the trees into the broom grass around the pond.

Josh saw it was an old friend. "That's Star," he said. "I'll introduce you."

"Won't he run away?"

"Not from me. When I was a boy, he even let me ride him."

They walked down the dune, Josh holding up his hands so Star could see they were empty. The mares and the colt walked away, then stopped and looked back, curious but unafraid. The stallion lifted his head and then nickered a greeting and trotted over. Josh ran his hand down the stallion's scarred neck, noting a few new scrapes. "Been fighting the young boys, have you?" He rubbed down the horse's nose. "Old man, you'd better start taking it easy." Star bared his teeth at him and Josh laughed.

"Do you think he'd let me touch him?" Dosie asked.

"I don't know," Josh confessed. "Star's not always easy to figure. But give it a shot."

Dosie slowly placed her hand on the stallion's neck. He quivered but accepted it. "I never thought I'd get so close," she said.

"The wild ponies got a sense about people, good or bad," Josh said. "Old Cloud was the stallion of the herd before Star. He used to go into Whalebone City just to chase Doc off his pizer. That was something funny to see. There was just something about Doc he didn't like."

Star, apparently having his fill of humans, walked off to the mares and the colt, which hid behind its mother. "They are amazing animals," Dosie said. "Who could imagine that horses could live on an island where they have to dig for water?"

Josh and Dosie walked back up the sand hill. At the top, she said, "I've been all over this end of the island and I've yet to find a horse skeleton. Where do they go to die?"

"What I've heard is that they go out there," Josh said, nodding toward Pamlico Sound. "When they get lame or sick or just old, the other horses look after them for a while, but then one day they go out into the sound and start swimming for the far shore."

"They commit suicide?"

"Now that's a strong word," Josh said. "The horses just know when it's their time, I guess."

"I wonder where they think they're going?"

"Horse heaven," Josh said, looking across the sound. "You know, I've walked that land over there just straight across from here. It's good horse country just back of the beach. There's lots of grass and even freshwater ponds. To a Killakeet horse, I guess that would be heaven. They just light out for it when they're old and hope for the best."

"I like hoping for the best," she said. "I'm going to adopt that as my personal motto from here on in."

"I guess I will, too," he said.

"Oh, no, we can't both have the same motto. You'll have to pick one for yourself."

Josh gave it some thought. "How about 'moderation in all things'?"

"Terrible. Excess is the purpose of life. I have a degree in philosophy, you know."

"That must come in handy. What do they pay philosophers these days?"

" 'I ask not for wages, I only seek room in the garden of song,' " she said, ending with "Tra-la." Then she said, "Arthur Wentworth Hamilton Eaton, since I'm certain you're agog to know."

"Was he a philosopher?"

"No, far worse. An author and a poet."

Josh tried to catch up. "I like Hemingway, although I think he doesn't know a thing about fishing."

"I met him one time."

"Arthur Wentworth whatever?"

"No, Hemingway. He was drunk but I was drunker, which meant we both found one another fascinating. Do you want to know how I met him?"

"I heard you worked for a publisher."

"No secrets on this island, is there?"

"A few, I expect. But then, if I knew what they were, they wouldn't be secret, would they?"

"You're near a philosopher yourself, Josh Thurlow," she said.

"I'm but an engineer," he replied modestly, "who loves boats."

"Maybe you're more complicated than I thought. How did you get that scar on your chin?"

"From a polar bear."

"It bit you?"

"Not exactly. I was running from it so fast, I slipped on the ice."

She laughed. She had a good laugh, like bells somehow. Josh had not felt so happy since when he couldn't remember. He wanted to keep feeling that way. "I have an idea," he said. "After Sunday services tomorrow, let's you and me go on a picnic. I'll borrow Daddy's horse, old Thunder. How about it?"

Dosie's mouth flew open to accept, then, thinking better of it, she clapped it shut. "I can't," she said uneasily. "It's too soon."

"Too soon after what?"

"You mustn't push me, Josh," she warned.

"I wasn't pushing you," Josh said. "I was just . . ."

"Just what?"

"Nothing. I just wanted to go on a picnic."

"And then what?"

Josh was getting a little flustered. "Well, I don't know. We could—"

"End up in your bed? Is that what you have in mind?"

"Why, no!" Josh exclaimed, although it was, pretty much.

Dosie took a breath. "I'm not going to let any man define me again, not even you, Josh Thurlow. Oh, don't look so coy. Why, a woman would have to be crazy not to want your arms around her. But it isn't going to happen, nosiree. I'm my own woman. I don't need a man. I'm going to find my way in this world just fine without you."

"I didn't say otherwise," Josh said. "I guess I'm my own man, too."

"Well, there it is, then. We're both our own people. How charming. I've got to go." Dosie got up and brushed the sand off her jodhpurs.

Josh stood with her. "Look, I'm sorry. I just thought you'd like to take a ride, see the lighthouse. Nothing more. Honest to Pete."

Dosie tucked the binoculars into a saddlebag. "When I was a girl, I always wanted to go to the top of your lighthouse but you'd never take me." She kept her face hidden, so he couldn't see the unexpected and aggravating tear that trickled down her cheek, but her voice gave her away. "Well, wild horses couldn't make me go with you now."

Josh resisted the temptation to make a witty comment about the wild horses on Killakeet, mainly because he couldn't think of one. "I'm sorry" was all he could think to say, though he wasn't absolutely certain what he was sorry about.

She showed him her face, her eyes gone puffy, the tear joined by another, both coursing down her cheeks. "Why didn't you take me back then? What was wrong with me? Tell me. I need to know."

Josh scratched up under his cap. "Not a thing, far as I can remember."

"If your memory improves, look me up." She climbed on Genie. A touch of her heels and the mare was off like a shot.

Josh watched until Dosie had disappeared behind the sand hills, then walked back to the jeep and sat heavily beside the sleeping pelican. With his hands on the steering wheel, Josh stared at nothing for a long minute, then said, with a great deal of enthusiasm, "Now, that's what I call a woman!" Purdy woke up and spread his wings.

# 7

Doakes Coast Guard Station took up a stretch of the beach next to Whalebone City. It was named in honor of Surfman Phineas Doakes, who had drowned during the rescue attempt of the passengers and crew of the *Frances Clayton*. The installation, however, was older than its name, having first opened in 1885 in response to a howling storm that had flung three ships, one after the other, onto Bar Shoals. One hundred and twenty-nine passengers and crew had been drowned and had washed up on Killakeet for days afterward. Reacting to the disaster, Congress decided to supplement the lighthouse by putting surfmen on the island.

A dozen surfmen, all native Killakeeters, were hired by the Lifesaving Service and provided a house on the beach from which to operate. The house was built of pine planks two stories high. A boathouse was at one end of it and a mess deck and a galley in the other. A lookout tower stuck up through its center. For the next thirty-nine years, the Killakeet surfmen lived in the house and kept an eye on the ships coasting by. Their career would include many rescues in their tiny surfboats on storm-shattered seas.

When engine-powered steel ships replaced most of the wooden sailing vessels along the coast, the days of the surfmen up and down the Outer Banks were numbered. The Lifesaving Service was absorbed by the Coast Guard in 1915, and Doakes was closed nine years later, its surfmen retired.

For two years, Doakes was abandoned, but then the Rum War against the Prohibition-era liquor smugglers heated up, and a small detachment of coastguardsmen moved in and kept it open until 1936, when it was closed again. In 1941, with more Coast Guard cutters assigned up and down the Banks to patrol the busy-shipping lanes, the station was re-opened once more. Josh was assigned as the commander of the station, which now consisted of the old Surfmen's House, two small warehouses, a gasoline-tank farm, and a brand-spanking-new eighty-three-foot patrol boat.

The eighty-three-footer had no official name, only a num ber, 83229. Her crew, however, called her the *Maudie Jane* and had even stenciled that name on her bow. Maudie Jane Cocker had been the Killakeet schoolma'am until she had drowned. She'd been standing on the beach, enjoying a cup of yaupon tea, when a huge wave had rolled in and plucked her right out to sea. Her body had come ashore on Miracle Point. A wild horse, the old mare named Jezzie, was found standing over the body as if guarding it. Josh thought Maudie Jane's name was just fine for his boat. The boys all said she was a good teacher, and kind besides. Maybe her spirit would look after them all.

Fridays were called a Six-Bell Hammock day for the crew of the *Maudie Jane,* thus allowing them to report to the boat at seven in the morning when most of their fathers and broth-ers were already at sea. The day was used for washing and sweeping the decks of the eighty-three-footer, polishing her brass, wiping down her ladders, scrubbing her heads, and generally seeing to her upkeep, including what work might be required on her two gasser engines. Occasionally, some light painting might be done, and for that purpose a pallet of cans of navy gray was kept in the warehouse along with all the attendant brushes and sandpaper and red lead required.

Josh usually did not show until late afternoon on Six-Bell Hammock days and then only for a final inspection. It was Bosun Phimble's time to be in charge. To get the work done faster, the mothers and wives of the Maudie Janes often turned up, going aboard armed with buckets and brooms and squeegees and mops and sponges. By inspection time, there was no boat more scrubbed and sparkling in the service. Josh always had a hard time finding anything wrong, a matter of face for an inspector. At least Marvin could be counted on to leave some hair in his bunk down by the sonar closet, and Josh would dutifully inscribe such on his sheet and solemnly present it to Bosun Phimble, who would salute and promise to "get it cleaned up before the sun's down, *sir!*"

Winks would be exchanged, and all would go home for the weekend with the Maudie Janes prepared to rise the following Monday morning and be at the boat at the required 6 A.M., ready to get out and patrol and rescue if it came to it.

Given the ocean they patrolled, it usually did, and sooner rather than later.

It was on a Tuesday morning in early December when Bobby McClung, a deck crewman, came racing barefoot across the sand, stopped and caught his breath, then reported to Josh. "Skipper, Daddy just got in from night fishing. There's a Beaufort fishing boat out along the ten-fathom line. Adrift, looks like. He didn't have enough gas to get over to it."

Everybody along the dock was listening. The mother of the Jackson twins called out, "Go save 'em, boys!"

"OK, Maw!" the twins bawled back.

Bobby waved to his sweet little mama, who was actually tough as tacks like most Killakeet women, then threw off the lines as Josh ordered the boat off to the rescue. The *Maudie Jane* was a well-designed patrol boat. She had controls in her wheelhouse and duplicate controls topside on a narrow flying bridge. The "stoop bridge," as the crew called it, was Josh's favorite spot. From there, he had a clear view of not only what lay ahead but could take in everything that was happening on deck, too. In just a few seconds, the boat was into the breakers, pushing aside the low waves, spray sent back to spatter the windshield. Leaving Phimble at the wheel, Josh went inside the wheelhouse to have a talk with Stobs.

Stobs, who was Hook and Winifred Mallory's son and

Willow's brother, said, "I'm not picking up anything that sounds like a distress call. Hatteras says there's some traffic up north of us, a freighter named *Walter Terry,* asking directions, but that's it. You want I should use my home brew?"

"Home brew" was what Stobs called his handmade radio set. It was the only way he could talk to the merchant ships. Military radios were set at a frequency too high to communicate with commercial radio sets.

"Go ahead and try," Josh answered. "But likely they don't have a radio."

While Stobs made his calls, Josh went down to the galley to get some coffee. Millie Thompson, the cook, was sitting on one of the bench seats of the mess table. Millie was one of those skinny boys with an Adam's apple the size of a small gourd. He was also Josh's cousin, on his mother's side. He was reading a comic book but quickly put it down and got Josh his coffee. "You want a sandwich, sir?"

"Not right now," Josh answered. "You might check with the other boys."

"Right away, sir," Millie answered and went back to his comic book.

Josh decided to inspect the engine room. It had been a while since he'd looked it over while going full bore. To get to it, he had to first go back up on deck and then aft to the engine room hatch. The roar of twin engines greeted him as he descended into the engine room. Everything was humming right along. Tom Midgette (known as Big) and Troy Guthrie (known as Fisheye) were stripped to their waists, their chests glistening with sweat as they worked with their oilcans and gauges and calipers. At the sight of Josh, they grinned. Big was puckish and short with black, oily hair and a thin mustache. Fisheye was tall, muscular, blond, with a left eye that stayed cocked, thus his nickname. They were good motormen and could take apart their engines and put them together again in three feet of bilge water if it came to it. Most Killakeet boys were good mechanics since they'd grown up fiddling with marine engines.

Josh gave the engine room boys a nod of approval and headed topside. As soon as he was on deck, he savored the feel of the sea. Josh loved being out on the ocean. As was his habit, he scanned from one end of the horizon to the other. There was a distant freighter out there, just a gray smudge, heading north on the Stream. About a mile away, a Killakeet workboat bounced along between the waves, coming in from a night of fishing. It looked like Pump Padgett's boat. Pump was Jimmy Padgett's daddy, Jimmy being designated the sonar operator on board, though he didn't know the first thing about the machine. Like all the rest of the boys, he'd come aboard without benefit of training, a standard practice for Outer Banks boys. Only Stobs had gone anywhere near a Coast Guard school.

Josh took a long minute to think about what would happen if war came to Killakeet. The truth was, he wasn't certain if his Maudie Janes were up to fighting submarines or not. They certainly didn't look very military. Other than their white tub caps, not one of them wore a regulation uniform when at sea. For the most part, they were barefoot and had on a variety of woolen sweaters and cotton knit work shirts that hung loosely over their dungarees, nearly the same thing their fathers and brothers wore on their workboats. On the other hand, Josh considered, it didn't much matter what they looked like as long as they could fight. What he needed to do, he decided, was to get some depth charges for the racks and some ammunition for the machine gun and practice a bit. He should also train Jimmy Padgett to operate the sonar machine, which had never been switched on.

But then Josh reminded himself that he couldn't just go over to Morehead City and requisition depth charges and ammunition, nor could he send Jimmy anywhere, just because he wanted to do it. It wasn't like ordering up a jeep, even though he still didn't remember doing that, either. The *Maudie Jane* was designated a patrol and rescue boat, not a warship, even though it had a sonar machine, depth-charge racks, and a machine gun. Those items were in case of war but were otherwise useless. And even if he got depth charges to put in the racks and machine gun ammunition, it was illegal to fire even a pistol from a Coast Guard boat, even the cutters, without approval from headquarters in Washington, D.C.

Josh went forward to Phimble and told him all that he'd just concluded. Phimble asked, "What would Captain Falcon do?"

Josh had a quick reply because he knew very well the answer. "He'd steal the depth charges and start dropping them on every old wreck out here. He'd blast this ocean into smithereens."

Phimble didn't say anything more. He didn't have to. Josh was looking grim, rubbing the back of his neck the way he did when he was thinking hard.

The *Maudie Jane* was on a southerly heading so as to pass down the likely line of drift. The horizon was clear, except for one thin line of clouds toward the northeast. The weather was holding good. For the next half hour, the *Maudie Jane* droned on until she arrived at a swirl of marbled turbulence that marked an outcrop of Bar Shoals. "There they are," Once said from the bow, and sure enough, so they were.

The lookout masts of the Beaufort fisherman were protruding from the swirl of white water, and bobbing heads to the south presented the crew. Phimble ran down on each one of them, and when a few proved too cold to take a line, Once and Again dived in and kept them afloat until the other boys could drag them over the transom. Soon afterward, the masts fell and the wheelhouse busted loose from the hull below and bobbed to the surface and swirled away. Broken planks started shooting up as if they were coming out of an underwater volcano. "Look at all that lumber," Once said in admiration. "We'll see them on the beach soon enough."

Josh heard Once and went to the bow and watched the planks and the wheelhouse drifting off and his heart sank. Once was surely correct. The debris of the fisherman would soon be caught by the Stream, swept up toward Hatteras, then turned around and brought back to Killakeet by the inner current. That would take about two days, and then most or all of it would be washed up on the beach, probably some-where south of the Crossan House. You could nearly set a clock to it. "Dammit," Josh swore. Jacob and the moth boat should have taken the same trip. *Why hadn't they?*

"Are you all right, sir?" Once asked.

Josh shook his head. "No," he confessed. "I'm not."

"Can I help?"

"Don't you have enough to do?" Josh barked. "If you don't, go see Bosun Phimble."

Once's mouth fell open, but then he saw that Mister Thurlow was in a bit of a state. He crept off, leaving Josh with a harsh recollection seventeen years old that, once begun, was nearly impossible to stop.

After the little boat that contained his brother had come un-tied, Josh had searched across the Stream until darkness had forced him to shore. He was scared but still believed Jacob would be found. Every boat on Killakeet would go out, and with all of them looking, they would find Jacob in no time at all.

Josh had landed the workboat on the beach and raced up the steps to light the lamp just as the sun had set. It was a responsibility he knew he could not shirk, even in those desperate circumstances. When the great light began to make its sweep, he sailed down the circular staircase by sliding his hands over the rails, taking the steps four and five at a time. He hadn't stopped running until he'd reached Whalebone City to spread the alarm. Soon, every boat on the island was out looking with lanterns held high through the abating storm. The grapevine along the Outer Banks was powerful. By morning, nearly every boat from Currituck to Lookout was out searching for a little red boat.

Everyone looked for weeks but nothing was ever found. Not so much as a plank. In the days that followed, Josh sailed up and down the coast alone, tucking into every inlet and coastal town, asking if anyone had seen anything of the little boat. And then the son of a doctor who had a beach house along the coast above Currituck admitted that he'd lost his new moth boat, come untied from the dock, probably due to a sloppy knot. The doctor told Josh that his son's boat had been painted a bright red. Although Josh had discovered who had lost the boat, it didn't much matter. No one ever saw it again. As for Jacob, he was simply gone. And as much as Josh told himself over and over that it just didn't make sense, that it wasn't possible, that Jacob *couldn't* be gone without a trace, he was.

Josh shook off the memory and went aft to see to the rescued fishermen. "Too bad about your boat," he told them. He didn't know what else to say and he'd lost what good humor he'd had, thinking about Jacob.

"Thank you for coming after us just the same," one of them answered, struggling to his feet while Josh gave him a hand. The old man had a scraggly white beard, and a fisherman's deeply lined and tanned face. "Billy Ferguson. Captain of the *Loggerhead,* out of Beaufort. Leastwise, I was. I figgered to get my motor going or put out an anchor if I didn't. What I didn't figger was that blamed little shoal being there. We don't usually come this far north but we heard tell the fishing up here was good." His eyes, red from the seawater, took on a sad, distant look. "Well, the old girl's gone now. A sorry mommick. It's going be a poor Christmas for my crew and their famblies."

"I'm surely regretful, Captain," Josh said, this time in a more sympathetic tone. To lose a boat was a terrible thing, but when it was your living, it was all the worse.

Phimble took the *Maudie Jane* straight back to Doakes, where each of the Beaufort fishermen was adopted by a Killakeet family, to be sheltered until he obtained passage back home. Josh helped the boys clean up the patrol boat, and then headed for the Hammerhead. He was about out of steam. A bottle of Mount Gay in his room definitely had his name on it.

Old Purdy raised his head as Josh came up on the pizer. "How would you like to take some rum with me, Purdy?" he asked. "I'm not a bad sort, you know. Why, we could sit and talk over things, like women."

A voice from a corner of the pizer, a feminine voice, said, "Why, Ensign Thurlow, are you and the bird females? I'm much surprised. I took you both for men."

Josh peered into the corner, and gradually his eyes adjusted to the darkness. "Well, Miss Crossan," he said, "why ever are you in the dark?"

"It's a position I am usually in," Dosie replied, rocking in a rocker. "I am in for a day of shopping and Queenie allowed me to rest up here before going home."

"A day of shopping you say? But there's only one store in Whalebone City."

"I am a thorough shopper, Ensign. Thorough!"

"Then where are your packages?"

"Tied to Genie, who's just around the corner. She likes one of Doc's milk goats. They've become pals."

Josh leaned against a porch post. "I was just on my way up to my room where I have a bottle of Barbados rum, the darkest and richest in the Caribbean," he said. "I have two tin cups. I would be willing to share."

"Here on the porch? That is, I mean, the pizer?"

"If that's your wish."

"Then by all means, mister, let's have a taste of your rum."

Josh swept through the door, nodded to Queenie in the parlor who, for some reason, was looking very satisfied with herself. He headed for his room and soon returned, a bottle of Mount Gay rum in hand and two blue-enameled tin cups hooked in his fingers.

Josh sat in the swing nearest Dosie's rocker. He poured her a finger, then two, and handed it over. He gave himself an equal amount and held his cup out to her. "Here's to blue skies and bowlegged women. That was Captain Falcon's favorite toast."

"Sounds like my kind of man," Dosie said, clinked her cup on Josh's, then knocked back her two fingers. She held her cup out for another. "By God, that is good stuff!"

Josh raised an eyebrow but obliged. "Doc says there's nothing that calms the spirit so much as rum and true religion."

"Him and Lord Byron," Dosie sniped. She eyed her cup appreciatively. "Mount Gay, huh?"

"Finest rum in the world."

"What was the name of the woman?"

"What woman?"

"The woman who taught you to drink Mount Gay. This is good stuff. Guy like you I figure would tend toward the cheaper booze. This is a first-class, uptown kind of drink."

"Thank you for your good opinion of me," Josh said with a wry smile. "Her name was Luzette, if you must know. She was French, more or less, some might call her a mulatto. I just called her one fine woman. She worked at a place on Nelson's Street in old Barbados. She was a pretty good teacher, now that you mention it, and one of her lessons was that good things don't come cheap or easy, be it the ladies or drink."

Dosie raised her cup. "Well, here's to Luzette. I'm encouraged that you could be properly trained, even if it was by a wicked woman."

"Why, Luzette wasn't wicked at all. Just . . ." Josh hunted for the proper word. "Interesting!"

"Save us from interesting women!" Dosie laughed. She took a swig, then seemed to come to a decision. "Look, Josh, I'm sorry I left so suddenly down by the point. No excuses, just an apology."

"Accepted. And I apologize for saying the wrong things, whatever they were."

She gave him a grave look, started to add something, then relented. "I heard you managed a rescue today."

"A small one," Josh bragged. "It will probably only be sung about in legend and verse for a score of years. It's what we do in the Coast Guard, you know. *Semper Paratus*. Always ready."

Dosie thought Josh Thurlow had gotten more witty as the conversation had progressed. This pleased her, even though she was still smarting over his account of Luzette. "Let's see a bit more of that," she said, holding out her cup and slurring her words only a little.

Josh was impressed. He was still working on his second drink and there she was, wanting a third. Then he became cautious. "Maybe you ought to go a bit slower with this stuff," he said, as friendly as can be. "It's good but it's powerful." He mentally patted himself on the back. She would be thankful, him being so concerned for her well-being and all.

But Dosie looked at him and he looked back at her and then he watched her happy face dissolve into something he couldn't quite define. In a second, however, it changed into something he could define very well. He'd made her mad. "I don't need a big, shabby Coast Guard ensign to tell me how to live," she growled. She finished off her cup and tossed it into his lap, then made to whistle. All she could do was spew ineffectually between her puckered lips which made her even angrier. "Herman, where's Genie?" she finally demanded as she climbed unsteadily out of her rocker.

Herman had been sitting in the darkness nearby. He raced around the corner and trotted back with Genie. "Here she is, missus!" he cried.

"We're going home," Dosie said, her voice cracking.

"Is something the matter with you?" Herman asked in a worried voice.

"Not a blamed thing," she answered and climbed unsteadily into the saddle. Then off they went, Herman leading Genie, who left a dump of manure behind to mark her brief appearance.

Josh sat in the swing and smelled the horse pile, which matched the way he felt. He still held his rum bottle in one hand, his cup in the other, and Dosie's in his lap. Queenie came outside. "Well, that was a mommick," she said.

"What happened?" Josh wondered. "Things were going pretty good, I thought."

"What happened, Josh, was that you acted like a man."

"Well, ain't that the general idea?" he demanded.

"Not with this one," Queenie said. She sat down on the rocker and took Dosie's cup out of his lap. She tipped the bottle of Mount Gay still in his hand until it glugged twice, then turned it up straight. "Not with this one," she said, again, her lip over the edge of the cup but a thoughtful expression otherwise.

Buckets came outside and took a breath. "Damn, Queenie. What's that smell?"

"Nothing a shovel wouldn't help," Queenie said and Buckets went off to find one.

# 8

*If they aren't careful, their eyes are going to pop out of their heads.* That was Krebs's thought as he pondered the lookouts on the tower. The *U-560* had reached the Bay of Biscay and the final twenty-mile traverse before reaching its home port of Brest. A warning had come over the wireless from BdU to keep watch for enemy aircraft. Krebs had reminded his boys not to relax. They weren't home yet.

After a month at sea, the *U-560* was going to need more than a little time in the dockyard. Ragged holes on the tower and the deck testified to furious attacks from aircraft and destroyers. A coat of algae shimmered on the wooden slats of the splintered deck. Rust had formed everywhere, even on the attack periscope. The interior of the sub, always malodorous, was enough to make a man puke. Rotted food, piss, shit, vomit, and Winkler's decaying blood slopped around in the bilges. After the boy had died, his corpse had lain in Krebs's bunk for a few days with the thought that he would be brought back for his family to properly bury. It had been a bad decision. After the man had begun to stink, Krebs had him hauled out and buried at sea, tossed off the bow in a weighted canvas bag while Krebs murmured a quick platitude and lookouts nervously watched the skies. Since his bunk smelled like a decaying corpse—even throwing out his mattress and blankets hadn't helped—Krebs had to sleep sitting up, his stiff knee held straight, at the tiny navigator's desk. The crew fought each other to be lookouts, anything to get a breath of fresh air. The Chief did his best to keep the boys in line but only so much could be done. Packed inside a pressure chamber for over a month, they had had enough. Krebs was glad that he had decided to bring them home. Happily, BdU had agreed with his decision.

For his part, Max could think of little other than his wife. He'd already talked it over with Krebs and gotten permission for an extended leave. He was going to Dresden, where, if all had gone as planned, Giesela had secured an apartment. He was ready to dive in and swim to France, if that's what it took. Then he'd be on the first train to Germany.

*"Alarm!"*

Max looked up to see only a flock of birds. He started to laugh and chide the lookout for his mistake, but then took another look. They weren't birds at all. They were airplanes and there had to be at least thirty of them. *Please, God, be the Luftwaffe,* he silently prayed even while he knew it wasn't.

Now everybody on the tower was yelling. The machine gun crew opened up. But the aircraft were too high. They were orbiting like sea hawks, taking their time. The water beneath the U-boat was shallow and the English pilots knew it. The *U-560* was trapped. Max's heart sank and he started to think about how cold the water in the bay was. How long could a man live in it?

"All but the gun crew get below!" Krebs ordered. "Chief, take us down." He explained his plan to Max. "There's a deep spot off to starboard. I marked it as we came out."

How Krebs had marked it, Max had no idea. France was just a smudge on the horizon. But he didn't ask any questions, just kept pushing the lookouts through the hatch. The machine gun continued to bang away as the *U-560* dived.

"Three points to starboard, Chief," Krebs called through the hatch, then ordered the gunners below. Krebs took a last look, just for the log. The aircraft were the type known as Mosquitoes. One of them peeled off, its wings winking with machine gun fire. He heard the bullets splash the water, then work their way toward the tower. He dived through the hatch and waiting arms caught him as he came through.

A lookout pulled the hatch over and latched it to the sound of clanging bullets. His hand slipped and smashed against the rim, tearing away a chunk of flesh. He sank to his knees, clutching the bloody hand to his chest. No one came to help him. All eyes were on Krebs.

Krebs checked his watch and counted off the seconds. "Take us down to thirty meters, Chief."

"There's only fifteen here, *Kaleu*," the Chief replied in a strained voice.

Krebs calmly repeated his order. "Down to thirty meters, if you please."

Multiple splashes overhead told the story. Depth charges had been dropped but Krebs noted they were not directly overhead. They'd been released a moment too soon. The charges went off, and shards of sound pierced the U-boat, some of the men holding their ears and shouting to equalize the pressure. The Chief in happy consternation watched the depth gauge pass twenty meters and keep going. "I wouldn't have believed it," he said.

"God dug us a little hole," Krebs said, smiling.

"Wait until dark before we rise again?" Max asked.

"Yes," Krebs said. "We will slink into Brest in darkness." *Our tails between our legs,* he added to himself.

During every one of the *U-560*'s previous arrivals at base, there had been great ceremony with brass bands, an admiral or two, even movie actresses to greet them. Now, in the inky blackness of midnight, the submarine and its crew were greeted only by silence. Every man aboard was grateful for it. They wanted no attention, nothing to attract night-flying English aircraft their way.

Krebs and Max stood beleaguered on the tower. The Mosquito attack had resulted in the loss of a big section of wooden decking. The eighty-eight millimeter gun was still aboard only by virtue of its base plate, which was exposed, but its barrel was twisted into a surreal angle. For six hours, the Royal Air Force had pummeled the *U-560* in that little hole only Krebs had known about, but the boat had survived until darkness or low fuel had sent the aircraft away. Fifteen extra meters of seawater. That was all that had kept the U-boat crew alive.

A watchman with a dim flashlight waved them past the concrete dock and into a submarine pen. Thirty-one relieved breaths were released by the crew when the reinforced-concrete roof slid overhead. "Engines off," Krebs commanded, then grasped Max's shoulder as the boat was tied up. "Go home, Max," he said. "Kiss your wife for me."

Max felt a surge of gratitude, but then his natural caution returned. "You are sure you will be all right, sir? Will you see to your knee?"

"I will turn myself over to the doctors the very first chance I get. More importantly," he said, raising his voice so every man could hear, "I intend to get drunk and screw every whore in Brest!"

"And the overhaul, sir?"

"That *is* the overhaul!"

The crew of the *U-560* suddenly realized they were alive and were going to stay that way for at least another month. They laughed and slapped one another on the back, their hearty voices echoing through the huge concrete cavern, playing back and forth. All together, it sounded to Max like a pack of howling wolves.

# 9

Just south of the lighthouse was a natural slip carved by a long-forgotten hurricane, and this was where Josh anchored the *Maudie Jane*. He paddled himself ashore in the raft to keep his shoes dry, but the Maudie Janes, save Bosun Phimble, were more straightforward, wading in to shore for a pickup game of straight base. Before he'd gone very far, Josh heard the sharp crack of a bat on a baseball and then the hoots of his boys. He turned and saw Jimmy, his white tub cap flying off his head as he ran for the base, which was actually a bent driftwood stick. Millie was scrambling for the ball in a sand flat lined with saw grass. Marvin, barking, was chasing Millie. That was one thing about Killakeet boys. Give them an idle minute and they could find something fun to do.

The lighthouse seemed to rise up out of the sand to greet Josh as he walked toward it. Beside it was a grassy field with a curved path that led to the Keeper's House and Josh followed it, each step recalling a memory. He went inside, entering through the kitchen, the linoleum on the floor glistening from a recent mopping. He called out a hello but there was no response, no Morehead City fancy girl to answer sleepy-voiced from Keeper Jack's upstairs bedroom. All Josh heard was the steady ticktock of the grandfather's clock in the parlor. The Keeper was in the tower at this hour, polishing the lens. Josh had come to see his father, to discuss the "this or that" he had requested, but first Josh wanted a moment alone in the house. He'd not had one since his return from the Bering Sea.

What Josh most wanted to see was the room his mother had called her art palace. Before she died, her beach-glass and shell jewelry had become popular on the North Carolina mainland, tourists snapping it up. Josh had shown an example of her work, a necklace, to a captain's wife in Anchorage. The woman, a Mrs. Fletcher, who was from a wealthy Seattle family and knew her jewelry well, said it was the finest manifestation of sea art she had ever seen. She also told Josh she would be more than glad to give him $20 for it or, her eyes batting, anything else Josh might ask of her. He had not sold her the necklace, nor asked for anything from Mrs. Fletcher, though she chose to give what she wanted to him, in any case. As a result, Captain Fletcher had threatened to have Josh assigned for life to the one-man weather station on Polar Bear Island. Captain Falcon had interceded by sending Josh off on a mission, one that had nearly gotten him and Bosun Phimble killed, as most of Falcon's missions usually did. In the end, Josh had given his mother's necklace to Naanni. She was buried still wearing it.

Josh looked over the driftwood on the shelves, and the shells and the beach glass stored in cigar boxes. Here was a box marked *moonshells* written in his mother's distinctive looping cursive, and there was one marked *cockles* and there another titled *sand dollars*. There were dozens of the boxes holding about every kind of shell that might be found on a Killakeet beach.

A box marked *This and That* was on her worktable. Josh opened the box and saw, as he very well knew, that it held multicolored beach glass. He remembered how he'd caught Jacob that last morning playing with a spilled box of the weathered glass shards. Josh took that box, marked *Alexander Hamilton,* down from a shelf and opened its lid, finding inside a dozen or so pieces of ruby-colored glass. He picked out a piece and held it up to the light. It seemed to glow, nearly as if it had an inner fire of its own. His mother had said that Rose of Sharon beach glass was rarer than diamonds. Maybe that was why he had fussed so at Jacob that morning when the little boy spilled the contents of the box. *I wish I hadn't been mean to you,* he said in his heart.

Josh placed the box back where he'd found it and left the studio and walked through the house. It seemed unnaturally empty and Josh recalled that when his mother had been alive, it had been filled with cats. Over time, they had all grown old and died. The last of them had died while Josh was in college. Most of the cats were buried, unmarked, near his mother's grave. The Keeper had seen to that.

Josh walked to the tower, thinking of the endless miles of brass and glass he had polished in it while growing up on the island. Even as a boy, he had known it was not just his father's job to keep the light, but the responsibility of everyone in the family. Before the light had come to Killakeet, the Thurlows had been just another family of wreckers living off the cargoes of ships thrown up against Bar Shoals. Some said the Thurlows were a little greedier than average and had even gone so far as to lure ships into the shoals by tying a light to one of the wild ponies and walking it back and forth on the beach as if it were a ship gliding by in safe waters. Whatever the truth, the Thurlow family, like more than a few Outer Bankers at the time, were considered a low and mean bunch who were not above slitting the throat of a wrecked sailor. It was said that when a Thurlow baby was born, the sheriff on the North Carolina coast requested the child's name so he could draw up a wanted poster and save him the time of doing it later.

But when the Lighthouse Service came to Killakeet, the Thurlows were found to be squatting on the land that was placed best for the light. To acquire the property, the service offered the family the job to keep the light, and so it was that Josiah Thurlow became the first keeper. Since then, there had been two more Thurlow keepers, Keeper Jeremiah, Josiah's son, and then Jeremiah's son, Keeper Jack. It appeared, however, that the line of succession was ending. Josh had made no secret of the fact that he would not replace Keeper Jack. When asked why not, he would shrug and say, "I like the feel of a deck beneath my feet," and leave it at that. Although his explanation was truth, there was a greater truth, as there nearly always is. The greater truth was that Josh was afraid of being all alone some fine day at the Keeper's House, perhaps sitting in a rocker and waiting for the time to pass, and then he would see a little red boat go drifting by. He would know that he was insane then, or gone senile. Either way, he guessed it would kill him.

The interior of the lighthouse was cool and pleasant and smelled of wax and soap and paint and tar, a mixture of clean odors that told of ceaseless attention and care. The landing had been laid out in a checkerboard of alternating black and white blocks of marble. Josh recalled how much his mother had loved that marble landing and had often remarked on its simple and elegant design.

Josh climbed the winding iron steps until he reached the lantern room, and there he found his father standing on his tiptoes polishing the glass slabs that made up the great beehive-shaped Fresnel lens. Without looking at him, apparently recognizing his step echoing in the tower, the Keeper said, "Hello, Josh. A goodsome day for December, ain't it?"

Without even thinking about it, Josh picked up a cloth and started to help polish the glass. "When December's fair, January's a bear," he quoted the old saw.

The Keeper gave the lens he'd been working on another swirl of his cloth, then came over and inspected Josh's work. "At least we got past hurricane season without catching one," he said, fishing his glasses out of his pocket. Like all Killakeeters, he pronounced it "herrikin." He peered closely, then gave an extra polish to Josh's slat.

"Did I miss a spot?"

"Not at all."

"Then why did you do it over?"

"Well, that's a good question, Josh. I've invested most of my life taking care of this lens. Sometimes I think it won't shine at all unless I personally polish every square inch of it every day. It's just an old man's conceit. I haven't gone begomered, not yet."

"I guess your Morehead City girls would tell you if you were," Josh said, and then wished he hadn't.

Keeper Jack smiled. "Don't be jealous of them girls, Josh. They're sweet, most of 'em, and they're good company." He peered at his son with a puckish expression. "You ought to go with me sometime, pick one of 'em up for yourself."

Josh shook his head. "I got my fill of that kind of girl in Ketchikan."

Keeper Jack laughed. "Another difference between us, Josh, my boy. I'll never get tired of women of any stripe, even the kind that likes a few dollars for her favors." He regarded Josh for a moment. "I know what you're thinking. Me having those women here is disrespectful of your mama. If she were alive, Josh, I'd not have them, nor want them. But she's not. She's gone and I have to keep living."

"I wasn't judging you, Daddy," Josh replied, though he was.

Keeper Jack shrugged and nodded toward the lens. "Fresnel was a Frenchman, you know, lived in Napoleon's time, but the little tyrant hated him, mainly because Fresnel was a true genius, not some trumped-up short man after glory. I looked him up just recent. You know what he said? 'All the compliments I ever got didn't give me half the pleasure as the discovery of a truth.'" Keeper Jack squinted, as if looking at something far away. "Truth, Josh, that's what this lens is all about. It takes the light, all scattered, and focuses it into a single beam, the way the events of our life, all strewn about, turn into solid truth if we look at them in a certain way. But most people, you and me included, are afraid of the truth so we just let things stay scattered in our mind."

"I plead guilty," Josh said.

The Keeper gathered up his cloths and secured them in a small, battered tin box. He put on his Lighthouse Service jacket and squared away his cap with the lighthouse crest in silver with gold leaves around it. The Lighthouse Service had been absorbed by the Coast Guard three years before, but

Keeper Jack kept to the old uniform, as did most of the old keepers along the coast, who considered the end of their service a foolish decision by the Roosevelt administration. The Coast Guard was not much enamored with big brick towers operated by families. They favored tall, ugly steel structures topped by automated lights.

"I had a drink with Dosie Crossan the other night," Josh said, to alter the subject. "She's a bit crazy."

Keeper Jack smiled. "Smitten already? That'll make Queenie and the other ladies happy. I hear tell they'd like to see you take Dosie as a wife."

Josh's expression indicated his surprise at the news, which amused the Keeper. "The ladies think you need a wife, Josh. Dosie is their candidate."

"Does she know that?"

"Why would she know? How could the ladies do their work if the young couple they were putting together knew what they were up to?" He chuckled. "Let them have their fun. You might enjoy it."

Talking about a wife put Josh in a bit of a sweat. He decided to change gears. "I need your advice, Daddy."

"As long as it's not about romance. I don't know a thing about it."

"How about war?"

The Keeper's expression turned grave. "That I know even less about, but go ahead."

"If German U-boats come over here like last time," Josh posed, "my boys ain't ready to fight them. So I'm thinking about getting some depth charges, and some machine gun ammo, and training them. I suspect their folks won't like it, though. The boys signed up for rescue duty, not to go to war."

Keeper Jack went outside on the parapet and Josh followed, careful to put his hand on his cap to keep it from blowing away. As many times as Josh had seen it, the view was still magnificent. The Atlantic stretched forever beneath them, wild and free. "There's been war along these banks since Blackbeard the Pirate," the Keeper said, lifting his voice above the wind. "But we Killakeeters try not to get involved. We're fishermen or we keep the light by rescuing them what's in trouble. We don't fight."

"Times change," Josh said.

The Keeper nodded. "Yes, they do, more's the pity of it. But you asked for my advice and you got it."

The Keeper pulled a railroad watch from his coat pocket, checked it, then went back into the lantern room and headed down the staircase. Josh supposed his father would keep to his routine even if Blackbeard himself showed up to talk over the events of the day. Next on his schedule was to check the kerosene level in the storage shed. At the landing, the Keeper abruptly stopped and said, "Josh, you've had your this or that with me and now I'll have my this or that with you. My this is this. Pretty soon, I want you to transfer off the *Maudie Jane* to the lighthouse." He held up his hand. "I know. You think you don't want the job. But, Josh, I'm an old man. I don't know how many years I've got left in me. No, I didn't get Doc to write that letter. That was his idea and I regret it, but it happened and that's that. Maybe it's Providence as much as Doc what got you here. You're a hero, Josh, for all that you did on the Bering Sea Patrol. I think the service would let you transfer if you put in your papers. That's the one good thing about the Coast Guard eating up the Lighthouse Service. So why don't you? If not for me, for the family tradition."

Josh shook his head. "I just can't, Daddy."

"Oh, you can do anything you want," Keeper Jack said. "You'll have to do better than that."

His father's insistent tone got under Josh's skin. "Maybe I just don't want to do the same thing over and over again, day after day," he said and, of course, instantly regretted it.

The Keeper's expression darkened. "There's a comfort with routine, Josh, especially if it results in something good."

"You're right. I'm sorry. I didn't mean it the way it sounded."

Keeper Jack found his smile. "Josh, let me ask you something. What do you think of me? Who am I to you?"

Josh gave it some thought. "Well, you're Daddy."

"Yes, but how do you think of me? Mean, angry, stupid, what?"

Josh buckled down to thinking through his father's question, though he didn't much like it. He didn't think a son should go around thinking about his father that way. "Well," he said at last, "you're sure not stupid. You're smart, I guess because you read so much. And you're stern, meticulous, I might say, and your focus is always on the details."

Keeper Jack laughed. "That's because of all that brass and glass I made you polish when you were a boy. But I ain't stern at all, Josh, not most of the time. I'm actually a very silly man, all told. When I play poker with the old surfmen, you should hear me tell a story. Why, they laugh to beat the band. I told Pump Padgett the other day when he was going on about seeing a shearwater that I liked seabirds, too, especially young gulls from Morehead City! Got more than a few groans out of that one. And your mother knew how silly I could be. Why, Josh, right here on this very floor"—he stamped the black-and-white marble squares—"I took her in my arms one time and started singing and we danced all around and she and me just a-laughing. I can still remember the tune: 'Jimmy crack corn and I don't care.' Oh, how she could toss her head back and laugh and laugh when I was at my silliest."

"I guess I never saw you as silly," Josh confessed.

"No, Josh, I guess not. How about you? Are you ever silly?"

After a moment of recollection, Josh said, "When I was with Dosie Crossan the other evening, I think I was silly."

"I should have liked to have been a fly on the wall. Maybe the ladies are right. That girl's the one for you."

Josh kept quiet. He wasn't yet willing to admit such a thing might be possible.

"Well, if you won't do anything else I ask, here's a small, easy thing," the Keeper went on. "I've decided to celebrate the light come January nineteenth. The lighthouse will be fifty years old on that very day. I plan on having some big

doings, food and drink for the whole island. Catch me a big
tuna or two out on the Stream, won't you? And come to the
party and stand up with me as a Thurlow of the Light and
by God, have some fun! Dance, sing, cut a rug, be silly with
that girl!"

"Did you think this up all by yourself?" Josh wondered.

The Keeper chuckled and led Josh outside the lighthouse
onto the grass. "Actually, it was Queenie O'Neal's idea.
Never saw a woman who liked a party more. She's even
invited your boss, Captain Potts, from Morehead City to
share the evening with us. She has it all planned out that
we'll get up on a stage and say speeches, the whole shebang.
Though where she'll get the wood for a stage, I don't know.
Probably somebody will wreck some lumber for her."

Josh thought it over. "I'll get you the fish, Daddy. And
I'll come to the celebration, too. But I don't know about
acting silly. Especially with Captain Potts on the grounds."

The Keeper put one of his big, calloused hands on Josh's
shoulder. "Now, I've got one more thing to say before I
check the kerosene. I've decided to put up a gravestone for
Jacob."

Startled, Josh's mouth fell open. "Why?"

Keeper Jack withdrew his hand. "Because it's been seventeen years and it's past time. I've ordered a stone from
Mallory, engraved and everything. When it's delivered, I'm
going to put it next to his mama's grave and have Preacher
come to say a few words and then we'll both stop looking
for Jacob and worrying about him. He's gone, Josh, and no
amount of wondering what happened to him is going to
change that. We're going to mark that he's gone forever and
that will be that."

Josh looked steadily at his father, eye to eye. "I'll not
attend a sham."

Keeper Jack's eyes blazed, then softened. "Yes, you will,
that's an order. And you will forgive yourself for Jacob. Hell,
everybody else forgave you a long time ago. I never blamed
you, for that matter."

"Daddy, being blamed is not what bothers me about Jacob. It's that it still doesn't make sense that we never found him. Sometimes, I can't stop thinking about it. Why didn't that little red boat end up on Miracle Point?"

Keeper Jack pulled Josh in, held him close for a moment, then released him. "I forget to say my prayers too often, Josh, but when I'm up there on the light and look out and see you go by on your patrol boat, I remember to pray for one thing, that you'll put this awful thing behind you."

Josh didn't know what to say. Too many things were going through his mind: Jacob's headstone, getting ready for the war, and Dosie, too. It all ran together.

Keeper Jack went on to see about his kerosene and Josh went to visit his mother. As always, he found her grave neat and trim. You could tell the Keeper spent some time with it every day. Josh read the words on her tombstone: *Trudelle Thompson Thurlow. A Keeper's Wife and Beloved Mother, 1887–1922.* Seeing her family name reminded Josh that he was a cousin of Millie Thompson, the *Maudie Jane*'s cook. Millie was a good boy. Thinking of that, he said, "They're all good boys, Mama. But I'm going to have to change them." He went down on one knee and smoothed the grass that covered her grave. Then, for some reason, he discovered he wanted to tell her about Dosie. "I wish you could make her a necklace, especially from the Rose of Sharon beach glass," he said. "She would look smart in it."

The wind stirred, and the sea oats around the grave waved in its gentle breath, but it was a northeasterly breeze and Josh wasn't fooled by it. He knew it would soon develop into a goodsome blow that might spell trouble for the smaller freighters skirting too close to Bar Shoals. "I'm sorry I lost Jacob," he said to his mother, as he always did when he visited her. Then he solemnly patted the grass and went back to the *Maudie Jane*.

# IO

The blue-gray mist dissolved before the blunt prow of Krebs's dory as he puttered along, crossing the channel that would take him to a place he'd not seen since he was fourteen years old. He was only vaguely aware of the frothy sea rushing and pitching beneath him. His focus was on the pearly fog that kept wrapping around him, then blowing away. It was as if the mist contained his memories, invisible until he neared them and then becoming transparent as the finest crystal. They were memories of a boy he no longer was, and of a life he no longer knew. Yet, he needed no chart to go where he was going. He could tell the way by feel and smell and sound alone. Above the thump of the tiny outboard, he caught the sound of a bass rumble interspersed with what sounded like a woman sighing, the constant voice of the island, a voice consisting of the surf thrumming on the beach and the higher note of the wind.

The island appeared suddenly, a beige sand patch with gray stones and swatches of bright green moss pushing from the sea's lather. This was the place where he'd been raised, but he had no idea why he'd come back. Yet there was no denying that here he was, drawn by an inexplicable urge the moment he'd signed the papers to turn his submarine over to the dockyard superintendent in Brest. When the Chief had promised to look after the refitting, Krebs had thought first to accomplish all that he'd threatened to Max Hodel, to get roaring drunk, to climb on top of whores; but then, he'd packed a small bag and left for the train station. He'd ridden the train to Hamburg and made his way north and east by hitching rides along the byways and back roads until at last he'd reached the headlands of Schaprode on Rügen, the jumping-off point for the island of Nebelsee.

Krebs was going home and home was Nebelsee. There was no castle in Augsburg, no "von" between his first and last name. His last name was not even Krebs. He didn't know what it was, knew only that it was the one Father Josef had given him.

It was early afternoon when he'd rented the tiny boat. "Are you certain you don't want to wait until morning for the ferry?" the agent at the dock questioned reasonably. "It would be much more comfortable than being out on the open sea in such a small craft."

"Don't worry," Krebs had replied. "I can find my way."

"So you know Nebelsee?"

"I was raised in the *Waisenhaus,*" Krebs answered, the first time he'd told the truth about that in decades.

"Ah. The Dornbusch Schule."

"Call it what you will. It is still an orphanage."

The agent had a form. "I will need your name, sir."

"Krebs. Otto Krebs."

The agent brightened. "The famous U-boat ace!"

"Today, I am just a sailor on leave." He had signed the form and pushed off.

"When will you return the boat, Captain?" the agent called as Krebs sped away.

"When I'm done with it," he had answered over his shoulder.

Krebs turned the little dory westerly to round the southern cape of the island so as to enter the harbor of Fischfang, the only village on the island. The dory was doing well. Krebs had an uncanny ability with all boats, even unworthy ones. He often wondered if a part of his soul was deposited in every boat he'd been aboard. If so, considering all the boats there had been, there couldn't be much of his soul left. Father

Josef wouldn't like to hear that, he mused. The old priest had taught him everything about sailing. That was one thing they'd always had in common, their love of boats and the sea.

Fischfang was a fishing village and it appeared many of its boats were out, although a few of them had been pushed up on the beach for winter maintenance. Krebs eased into the harbor and tied up at a pier and looked around for evidence of a harbor master. What appeared to be a guard shack was at the base of the pier but it was deserted. The whole town seemed empty, not even a dog in the street. He leaned back and inhaled the air coming off the sand and the grass. *My God, it is distinctive*—crisp and tingling, like the scent of the air after a thunderstorm.

Strapping his small duffel bag on his shoulder, he walked to the town square, got his bearings, then struck out along a sandy road that led, he was fairly confident, to the orphanage. A mile inland, he came to a dense wood and a crossroads. There were no signs. The road had changed during the nineteen years of his absence. He was about to turn around and hike back to town when he heard the gentle ringing of a bell and saw what appeared to be a teenaged boy riding a bicycle along the track. The boy stopped and stared at Krebs, then he dropped his bike and came to attention. "Good day to you, sir!"

When the boy stayed at rigid attention, Krebs said, "You may be at ease. Are you in the service?"

"Torpedoman Third Class Harro Stollenberg, sir! Assigned to the Second Flotilla, sir!"

Krebs could hardly believe that this slip of a youth, barely old enough to shave, if in fact he *was* old enough to shave, was a U-boat seaman. But then, they were recruiting them young these days. "Well, Seaman Stollenberg, please stand down. I take it you are on leave."

"Yes, sir. I have just completed basic training."

"What is your boat?"

"Not assigned yet, sir. I am to report to Kiel and from there be assigned."

Krebs thought, *Yes, they will put you aboard a U-boat and send you out half-trained. If you are are lucky, you will go with a good, seasoned skipper and you might survive, at least for a while. If you're unlucky, you'll go with a captain not much older than you and you will die very quickly.* Krebs looked at the boy and imagined he was as good as dead already.

The boy was staring at him. "You are Captain Krebs. I know you from the photographs they showed us at the sea school. They told us how you have the sure touch!"

Krebs waved the comment away. "Do you live here?"

"I grew up in the Dornbusch Schule."

"You're an orphan, then."

"Yes, sir. I came back to say good-bye to the children and, of course, Father Josef."

Krebs smiled. "So he's still with us?"

"Oh, very much. He says he has too much work to do to die. How do you know Father Josef, sir?"

"I, too, was a child of the Dornbusch Schule."

"You, sir? I thought you were an aristocrat."

Krebs shrugged. "Somebody started that rumor long ago when I was a midshipman. They started it to make fun of me because I was an orphan. I went along with the joke then and I still do. Let that be a lesson to you. Don't believe everything you hear, about me or anybody else. The U-boat flotillas are filled with bullshitters!"

"I'll remember that, sir. Are you headed to the orphanage now?"

"To tell the truth, I'm a bit lost."

"I'd be happy to take you, sir."

"A very good idea," Krebs said. "And you can do one thing more for me."

"Yes, sir?"

"We're both on leave so you needn't be so formal. Your name is Harro, correct? All right, that's what I will call you. You may drop in the occasional 'Captain' to me, just so we don't break too many regulations, but not so many 'sirs.' "

"Yes, sir," Harro said, gulping. "I mean . . . sorry, sir. Thank you, sir."

Krebs laughed. "They're going to love you in the U-boats, Harro!"

The sand track led them past the old lighthouse. It was silent and empty and the Keeper's House was a charred ruin. Craters around the house made it clear that it had been bombed. "Why would the English bomb this place?" Krebs wondered.

"Some soldiers were living in the house," Harro replied, stifling the "sir" that almost came out. "They were studying the weather."

Now Krebs understood. It had been a weather station. The English did not like German weather stations even on remote islands. "What about our planes?" he asked. "Did they try to defend the island?"

Harro shrugged. "No, but every day, one of our planes comes over. It waggles its wings to us and we wave at it."

"What direction does it go?"

Harro pointed eastward and said, "Teufel Island. No one can visit that place. There are rumors of scientists working over there."

Krebs looked toward the distant shore. He knew it well, an island of sand and marsh. "What kind of secret installation would be built in such a place?" he wondered aloud.

"I really don't know, Captain," Harro said. "Nobody talks much about it."

Krebs walked away from the broken house to follow the sandy path that led to the tall, eight-sided spire.

Harro followed him. "I wish they hadn't turned off the light. It was beautiful."

"They turned off all the lights, Harro," Krebs replied. There was no lock on the door to the tower. When he pushed against the latch, it swung open.

"We can't go in," Harro said. "There is a sign that says to keep out." He pointed at a small hand-painted sign leaning against the lighthouse.

"And I suppose everyone respects the sign?"

"Yes, of course."

Krebs shook his head. Stay poor, but be honest. It was

the motto of Nebelsee. "Well, Harro, we'll try not to steal anything, OK?"

"Yes, si—Captain."

They climbed the iron steps, listening to the echo of their footsteps. At the top, they found the lamp shrouded by a canvas cover and an ancient brass can that still smelled of kerosene. Krebs picked it up and inspected it. "See the lighthouse insignia on its base? No swastika. It's from the kaiser's time."

Harro took the can reverently. "It is a fine insignia. Are you going to keep the can for a souvenir?"

Krebs laughed. "No, although I'm tempted. Put it back, Harro. We will be respectful."

Harro carefully placed the can precisely where it had been found. "Is it hard out there, Captain?" he suddenly asked. "In the boats?"

Krebs knew why Harro was asking. Young men always wanted to know if they would measure up in combat. "You will do well," Krebs answered.

"I will fight for the fatherland," Harro replied bravely. "And die, if I must."

Krebs smiled benignly. "It would be a crime for you to die so young. What are you, nineteen, twenty?"

"Nineteen, sir."

*Nineteen!* Krebs thought. *What had the U-boats come to, to recruit them so young?* Then he thought, *Of course. The young don't really believe they can die. They make perfect cannon fodder in a war which has already ground up so many of the older men.*

They went out on the parapet and looked across the sea. Clouds covered the sky like a thick, gray blanket that turned into light rain as it touched the water. "For a lookout post, it isn't worth much," Krebs observed. "This fog would never allow much of a clear view. Only in the summer is it ever clear. My God! I'm starting to remember! How I loved to come up here. If I helped the keeper, he let me watch the ships. I imagined I was on every one that coasted by. I wanted to see the world even then."

"And you did, Captain," Harro said.

"I've seen mostly water," Krebs replied. "But I have no complaints."

A distant bell tolled behind them. "They're calling us home," Harro said. "Vespers."

Krebs chuckled. "I don't think I'm up for vespers. I wouldn't want the chapel to fall in because of my presence."

Harro looked nervous but said, "I guess it won't hurt for me to miss one service."

"Brave boy." Krebs studied him. "How is it you came to the Schule, Harro?"

"Father Josef got me from an orphanage in Kiel. And you, sir?"

"I started out in a Hamburg gutter. Probably dropped off by a prostitute. Father Josef plucked me out of an orphanage when I was about six years old. I think I was a bit of a handful for him but he calmed me down by teaching me to sail."

"He taught me, too," Harro said. "I've always loved the water. That's why I joined the navy."

"You joined? And no doubt volunteered for the U-boats, too."

"Oh, yes."

Krebs thought again that the boy wouldn't last long and felt sorry for him.

When they came off the lighthouse and faced the short trek to the Dornbusch Schule, Krebs began to have second thoughts. What was he trying to accomplish? He'd run away at fourteen, after all. Father Josef wasn't likely to be pleased to see his ugly face again. "Harro," he said, "I believe I will go back. It was foolish for me to come here."

"But the ferry only runs in the morning."

"I have my own boat, a dory."

"It will be too dark for you to go across to the mainland tonight in a dory," Harro said matter-of-factly. "Come stay the night with us. The little ones will love it. You are a hero of our country, after all."

"I am not a hero in any way," Krebs said.

Harro looked past Krebs and into the sky. "Look there."

Krebs looked in the direction of Harro's point and saw a two-engined aircraft flying straight for the lighthouse. "Let's get some cover!" he said urgently.

"It's ours," Harro replied. "The one I told you about. He flies over nearly every day at this time."

Against his better judgment, Krebs stood with the boy and watched the aircraft approach. Harro was waving at it. Just before it swooshed past, it waggled its wings. It was on a flight path that would indeed take it to Teufel Island, but why it would want to go to those barrens, Krebs couldn't imagine.

Krebs walked with Harro pushing his bicycle until they reached the orphanage. The structure wasn't anything special. It had begun its life as a small hotel. When it had gone out of business, Father Josef had converted it and built a small chapel alongside. It was as cheerful as it could be made, painted a bright white with a red-tile roof and red shutters to match. Flower boxes attested to spring color, though now they contained only the gray-green vines of past growth.

Harro led the way into a cozy room that was part dining area and part kitchen. A fireplace crackled energetically. The whole room seemed suffused with warmth and light. Krebs heard muffled children's voices and the sound of bare feet running upstairs. The sound of feet on hardwood floors brought back a sudden memory, of a time when it had been his feet on that floor, running with the other boys and girls. He recalled the big room where he'd lived with eleven other boys, and the rows of beds, dazzling white with freshly laundered sheets and snowy pillowcases all lined up like soldiers in ranks. He remembered the meals, always hearty and filling, and the stories Father Josef had told around the fire in the evening. The children of the Dornbusch Schule were lucky, all things considered. Krebs knew now why he had returned. He had never thanked the good priest for raising him in kindness. It was as simple as that.

A young woman came down the stairs. She was dressed

in the old style with the traditional black underskirt that peeked beneath a full skirt hemmed with decorative trim, and a blue vest over a white blouse with puffy sleeves. Black stockings covered her trim legs. When Krebs saw her face, he felt he had never seen a woman quite so beautiful. Her hair was long and golden, braided in the Baltic style, and her face was unblemished, perfect, with a blush of color to her cheeks. Of course, her eyes were as blue and warm as a tropical sky, a gift, it seemed, that God had given to the women of the frigid, northern seas. "Oh, *guten Tag,*" she said, and looked at Harro for an explanation.

Krebs stood mute before this angelic vision. Harro said, "This is Captain Krebs, Miriam. He was once a boy here. Captain Krebs, this is Miriam Hauptmann, the house mistress."

"When were you here, Captain?" she asked while studying him with those wonderful blue eyes.

Krebs finally found his voice. "A long time ago. I left when I was fourteen and now I am thirty-three."

"Krebs. Yes. I know all about you. You ran away to sea. Father Josef often speaks of you."

Krebs could not hide his surprise. "With so many children, I'm astonished he would remember one from so long ago."

She gave him his first smile. "I suppose he thought you were special. I know he'll be delighted to see you. He's on the mainland and won't be back until tomorrow. He's started a much larger orphanage in Kiel. There are so many orphans these days, you know. You'll stay with us until he returns, of course."

Harro said, "I'll take your kit upstairs, sir."

"You are kind," Krebs said to them both, and thought that it had been a long time since he had witnessed kindness. Sacrifice, courage, bravery, all those things that occurred during war, but kindness? He'd almost forgotten it existed.

"Captain Krebs," Miriam said, "would you care for a cognac before dinner? You may need it. You'll be eating with a dozen squirming little girls and boys who will be so excited you're here. I'm sure they'll pester you to distraction." She gave him another glorious smile, his second. Krebs decided to start counting them, like golden coins of a treasure.

"A cognac would certainly be welcome," he answered. "But please, *Fräulein,* it's Otto."

"Then come, Otto, and sit by the fire and I will pour us both a glass. I suppose technically you should call me *Frau.* I am a widow. My husband was a soldier in Russia. But please, just call me Miriam. I was a *Kind* here, too. I stayed on the island after I was married and now I help Father Josef. Do you mind sitting and talking for a while? I imagine you might get bored with a woman who knows so little of your world."

Krebs sat, completely under the spell of this gentle and beautiful woman. "I know enough of my world for both of us," he said. "It will be my pleasure. And I can't wait to see the little ones. They are my brothers and sisters, after all."

For that little speech, she rewarded him with the grand prize, a full grin, before going to the cupboard for the cognac. The war faded in Krebs's mind, the *U-560* all but forgotten. He imagined himself almost happy.

# 11

Krebs woke to a freight train roaring down on top of him. At least that's what it sounded like. Then he recalled where he was, in the guest room of the orphanage where he'd been raised. There were no trains on Nebelsee but there was the noise of boots thundering up the stairs and down the hall. The door of the room burst open and there stood Father Josef, wild-eyed with a great shout on his lips. "Otto Krebs!" With one long stride, he was across the room. He grabbed Krebs and lifted him bodily off the bed and bear-hugged him and swung him around. "My son, you are a grand sight for these old eyes! God bless you, Otto, for coming home!"

Father Josef clutched Krebs's shoulders and pushed him back and forth. Krebs thought the old priest, huge and dressed entirely in black, looked like some giant, run-amok chimney sweep. "Let me look at you!" the priest cried. "Well, a few scars here and there but otherwise a fine-looking man. So, what have you been up to, Otto? Tell me everything!"

Krebs glanced to the doorway and was astonished to find Miriam Hauptmann standing there. He was also embarrassed because he typically slept in the nude when on land and Father Josef had dragged him out from under the covers without a chance to put anything on. Miriam hid her laugh behind her hands and hurried on.

Father Josef had seen Miriam, too, and boomed out his great laugh. "Oh, she sees naked little boys all the time," he said. "Now, Otto, come to breakfast, tell me everything you've been doing." And with that, Father Josef went out, calling to the children to come and eat. "Come on, come on," the priest cried in a great joyful voice. "Food for all my little girls and boys. What a wonderful day it is, children! One of our boys has come home. Oh, you met him last night, did you, Uschi? Well, all right. Lucky little sweet girl. Come on, come on!"

Breakfast was wonderful. Krebs sat at one head of the long table, Father Josef at the other. The priest's great bushy eyebrows danced as he talked to each child. "Now, Gerhardt, that's my boy, eat up, eh? Mrs. Hauptmann said you play too much with your food. You must eat so you'll grow up to be big and strong. Ah, Gerda, you are such a pretty girl. Have I told you that lately? No? Well, your face is like the sun rising, sweetheart. As is yours and yours and yours," he went on, pointing at each child with his spoon.

At last, he reached Krebs. "Here is your big brother Otto. Tell us, Otto, where you have been and what you have done with yourself since you left us."

"I'm a captain of a submarine, Father," Krebs said.

"Yes, yes, so I've heard. But tell us about your wife and your family!"

Krebs was aware that every child had stopped eating and was watching him. "I'm afraid I don't have a wife or children, Father." The children all looked at one another, their little mouths open.

Father Josef frowned. "You have had the opportunity to form your own family, Otto, and you haven't done it?" He looked around at the children. "They are all taught the importance of family. That's why they are looking at you with such surprise."

"Well, you're my family," Krebs said, feeling as if he were a little boy again and mildly angry at the priest for picking on him.

Father Josef wagged his spoon at him. "We need to talk, my son. I can see that." He looked around the table. "Come on, children. Eat!"

The boys and girls, after one last, dubious glance at Krebs, got back to their morning porridge. For his part, Krebs decided he would leave immediately after, perhaps, a final word with Miriam Hauptmann. A week later, he realized to his astonishment, he had gone nowhere. In fact, he wished he would never leave.

"We don't need much, Otto. There is plenty to eat on Nebelsee, as you well know, especially if you like fish, and of course to live here any time at all is to love fish. And our potato cellar is full. We all share here. Whatever one has, all have."

Krebs had just expressed his concern for the well-being of the orphanage and especially for its headmistress, Miriam Hauptmann. "Did they give you anything for your husband?" he asked, meaning the government.

"No. Nothing. There was trouble with my papers as there always is for orphans." She looked down as they walked the path that led along the harbor past the eel smokery and the windmill and the *Bäckerei* just beside it. "Walter tried to straighten it out but he never could. The army authorities are very strict and everything must be just so." Then she raised her head proudly, as if she'd recovered from a moment of self-pity. "Did Harro tell you my husband's profession? No? He was a teacher who taught classical literature in the *Realschule* at Schaprode. He went every day back and forth on the ferry. He loved to teach but I'm afraid he was not very good at it. The boys in his classes often made fun of him because he was so gentle. They would make faces and throw things. They would play tricks on him, put a dead fish in his desk, that kind of thing. It hurt him so much when they were cruel." Miriam was silent for a time and then said, in a bitter tone, "This is the man they sent to Russia to fight."

Miriam's voice turned to one of resignation. "I saw Walter only once after they took him away. Not here. If he had come back, I would have found a way to hide him. I had already talked to Father Josef on how it might be done. Don't look so shocked. I would have seen him off in a boat somewhere. But it was not to be. I visited him in Grafenwöhr when he was training there. Walter told me that he hated what they were teaching him but that his instructors considered him a good soldier. Isn't that odd, that a man can hate something but still be good at it?"

"It is part of our wonderful German character," Krebs said ironically. "Soldiering is in our blood."

"I am worried about Harro going off," she said. "I don't think fighting is in his blood at all."

"He will be fine," Krebs answered, sorry that he had to lie to her.

"He's too young. And so very gentle. I think he will find life in a U-boat very difficult."

"On the other hand, it may be good for him. He will have to work hard."

"They will toughen him, then kill him," Miriam said, her bitter tone returning.

Krebs didn't know what to say since he wholeheartedly agreed it was the boy's probable fate.

"If I could wish this war away, I would wish it a million times," Miriam said. "Even if it were only for a day. Can we do that, Otto? Can we agree between us that there is no war today?"

Krebs tried to imagine life without the war but finally gave up. "The war will not stop just because we believe it has. It's not realistic."

The path was uneven past the harbor as it worked its way around the bay, and she took his arm to help steady herself. It was the first time she had touched him. He shuddered, not because her touch was unfamiliar but because it felt so very right. Their progress was observed by hundreds of swans bobbing in the harbor, their graceful necks turning as they walked past. It all made a kind of sense. Wouldn't even birds watch an angel as she walked by?

Miriam led him off the path, over the grass and into the

sand and down to the rocky beach to a tidal pond. When she released his arm, it felt empty. She knelt at the water and with two fingers plucked something from it that was small and dark. She handed it to him, a proud expression on her face. "What do you make of this?"

He held the tiny, irregularly shaped object. "A stone worn smooth by the sea."

"Hold it up to the sun," she said.

He did and saw that the "stone" was actually translucent, and golden. "Is this amber?" When she nodded, he said, "I would never have spotted it. Isn't it rare?"

"Very. But if you have an eye for it, it can be found all along this coast. A woman in town makes jewelry with gold and amber and shells. Her creations are rather famous. On Saturdays, I clean her house. For my pay, she is teaching me her art."

"It does not surprise me that you are an artist."

She lowered her eyes. "I am not an artist but I wish I could be."

"I suspect you could be anything you wished."

Her smile was proof that Krebs had pleased her. "Silly. Pay attention. Now, look at this shell." She picked a small white shell from the sand and held it out to him. "What do you think?"

"I think you won't fool me this time. It is a common cockleshell. There are a million of them on this beach."

"That's true, but this one is as unique as the amber. Try as you might, you can scour this beach and all the beaches of the world and you will not find a single cockleshell that looks the same as this one."

He smiled. "And your point is . . . ?"

"My point is, Captain Krebs, that there is so much in life that we take as common, yet when we think about it, we realize it isn't common at all. This day, for instance. We shall never know another like it. No matter what we may do, even though we might retrace our steps exactly, another day would not be the same. We therefore must make the most of it, even if it requires that we spin a little fantasy that there is no war."

Krebs came to mock-attention. "You have defeated me, *Frau* Hauptmann. I agree there is no war today." Relaxing, he took the shell and inspected it. "It *is* a beautiful and remarkable shell," he concluded, "but, of course, so is the woman who found it."

"Hush, you," she protested, but rewarded him anew with a glorious smile. "You will have me blushing. My cheeks are always too pink as it is."

"I like your pink cheeks."

"Oh, you are a bit perverted, then. I look like a chapped German pig much of the time."

"If the women in France looked half as good as a German chapped pig, I would have never left."

Her expression clouded. "Don't talk about France. France is for another day. Today, there is only Nebelsee."

"You're right. I forgot. Please forgive me."

Her voice became merry again. "Come!" She put her arm in his again and half-dragged him laughing up the dunes back to the path.

"What's the hurry?"

"Silly! I'm hungry. Do you still like eels? Of course you do! What Nebelsee boy doesn't love eels!"

"It makes my mouth water just to think of them."

"And a good stout Nebelsee beer to wash them down!" she cried to the wind.

*Happy.* He kept thinking about the emotion, getting used to it. *I'm happy.* He let himself be led by the strong, young woman and he wondered if it was possible to always be happy.

They wanted it to happen, of course. That's why it did. Father Josef had taken the children on an outing, Harro going along. Miriam and Krebs sat before the fire. He leaned in close to her and couldn't stop his hands from going around her shoulders. She put her arms around his neck and they shared a kiss. "What is it you want of me, Otto Krebs?" she asked in her direct Nebelsee way.

"I don't know," he answered honestly. "But I seem to be falling in love with you."

She did not smile. "You mustn't. It is too soon, too fast. You have only known me for thirteen days."

"The war demands everything to be in a hurry, even love," he replied, surprising even himself with the intensity of his argument.

She took his hand and led him upstairs. "I don't know about love, Otto," she told him. "But I know too much about being lonely."

Her room was bare except for a rude table and a single chair, and a simple bed, covered by a down-filled comforter. Mounted on the wall was a crucifix. As he knelt on the bed over her and slowly removed her clothes, he discovered she was wearing a necklace with a golden cross pendant decorated with a teardrop of sea amber on each of its tips, and a scarlet gem in its center. It was as unique as the woman who wore it, and the day they had shared. "Did you make this?"

She nodded, her eyes filling with pride.

"You are a remarkable woman, Miriam Hauptmann," he said. "Let me love you, even if it is too soon."

"All right, Otto." She put her hand behind his neck and drew him to her breasts. "All right, my little sweetcake," she said distantly, almost as if she were speaking to one of the orphaned children.

# 12

Miriam and the children had thoroughly decorated the orphanage for Advent. A wreath was on the table with four candles in a nest of fir boughs and two of the candles were lit, signifying the first two weeks of the celebration. In the windows were golden stars hanging by red ribbons. It was the night when Father Josef visited the children, accompanied by the hideous character known as Knecht Ruprecht.

Ruprecht was just as Krebs remembered him from childhood visits. The bent old man was outfitted from head to toe in black and his face was smudged with coal. He rattled his chains and peeked from behind Father Josef, who stood like some grand archangel in the doorway of the orphanage. It was little Gerhardt's turn to come forward. Miriam stood behind the boy, her hand on his shoulders to steady him.

Miriam was dressed in Nebelsee garb: black stockings, a gray smock with a white apron, and a puffy-sleeved, white blouse. Krebs, from his position in a chair by the fire, could not help but recall what a pleasure it was to slowly remove those long black stockings.

Father Josef snapped a look in Krebs's direction as if he'd read his thoughts. Then he cut his eyes back to Gerhardt and said, in a stern voice, "Now, Gerhardt, it's your turn."

The little boy's knees were trembling. "Yes, Father," he said. Ruprecht danced a grotesque dance and shook his chains, muttering. Krebs recognized him as the little man who pushed a cart around the town square, selling fish cakes.

Father Josef held up his hand and Ruprecht stopped his dance. "Gerhardt, Ruprecht tells me you sometimes push the other boys and girls when coming to meals. Is this so?"

"Yes, Father," Gerhardt answered, close to tears.

"Will you stop it now?"

"Oh, yes, Father. I am very sorry."

Ruprecht mumbled something unintelligible, then nodded with a final clink of his chain.

"All right, you are forgiven," Father Josef said. He reached in a sack and brought out a handful of nuts and handed them to the boy. Then he dug a little deeper and brought out a bright red apple. "You are a good boy, Gerhardt. I love you. We all love you."

Gerhardt politely took the apple and managed a quivering smile, then fled when Ruprecht shook his chains at him again. Krebs felt like grabbing the man playing the dirty little devil and tossing him out the doorway.

Father Josef's eyes rested on Krebs. "Otto Krebs," he boomed. "Come you here."

Krebs thought about telling the old man to leave him alone, but for Miriam's sake, he relented. "Good evening, Father," he said, getting slowly to his feet. His knee ached, but he ignored it. Ruprecht leaped, gabbling, shaking his chains.

Father Josef frowned through his beard. "How is your soul, Otto?"

"My soul these days belongs to the *Kriegsmarine,* Father. As you very well know."

"Ruprecht says you do not attend services regularly."

"Difficult to do on a U-boat," Krebs answered.

"Do you recall the significance of Advent?"

"The coming of Christ," Krebs replied.

Father Josef nodded, then dug into his bag and handed Krebs an apple. "If you cannot attend services, at least read from Scripture from time to time. Else your soul will become as shriveled and ugly as this ripe, beautiful apple in a week's time."

"Yes, Father," Otto replied, wondering if he had ever seen a Bible on board the *U-560*. Probably Max had one squirreled away.

"Come, Ruprecht, the other children await us."

After the priest and Ruprecht had gone to minister the same tribulations on the children of the village, Krebs said, "Father Josef can be a gruff old bear."

"I suppose," Miriam replied. "But the truth is the children love him to act gruff at Advent. They know it is all just an act. And, even though he scares them, they'll be giggling about Ruprecht tonight when I put them to bed."

"Will you come and put me to bed, too?"

"Sometimes, you are a silly man, Captain."

"That's what all my boys on the U-boat say, too. Will you?"

"Perhaps. Will you come to the celebration tomorrow? There will be a procession to the lighthouse."

"I wouldn't miss it."

"Good. We shall go together."

"Together. I like the sound of that."

She said, as she allowed him to hold her, "Otto, I have a great favor to ask of you."

"Of course," he said, his hand touching her flaxen hair. "Anything. You know that."

"Will you take Harro aboard your boat?"

Krebs was not surprised by the request. Miriam had been hinting about it, saying how worried she was for the boy. He had already given it some thought. Harro was assigned to the Second Flotilla, the *U-560* was in the Ninth. But things could be arranged if you knew the right people. "I will see what I can do," he told her. "But I think yes."

"You are a good man, Otto," Miriam said.

"No, I'm not," he said reflexively. "I have done many things during my life that would certainly not qualify me as a good man."

Miriam fixed her eyes on him. "Otto Krebs, you are a very, *very* good man."

"Miriam . . ." He hesitated, then plunged on. "You are a woman—"

"Thank you for noticing!" She laughed. "I have never been anything else."

Krebs felt clumsy. He released her and took a step back, trying to clear his head. He had practiced a speech but he'd completely forgotten it. He stumbled over his words. "Listen. I have no need for my pay. There is no place to spend it in a U-boat. I want you to have it."

Those wonderful blue eyes widened. "What are you saying, Otto?"

"That I want to take care of you. That maybe I'm in love with you. That maybe we could . . ."

She put a finger to his lips. "Dear Otto," she said in a sighing voice. "Please be silent."

He gently removed her finger. "I am not like your Walter. But I would make a good husband, I swear it."

"I told you to be silent."

"What are you afraid of?"

"You, of course. What you want is much, much too soon. You are just caught up in the moment."

"I love you, Miriam," he said. "A million moments will not change that."

"One of us must act intelligently," she said staunchly.

"Why? Why must we act in any other way than how we feel? When I am with you, I sometimes wonder if I am in heaven. Perhaps I didn't survive that last depth-charge attack after all."

It was the wrong thing to say and he knew it instantly but it was too late to take it back. Miriam turned away. "We are not in heaven," she said. "And you must live, Otto. You will keep Harro alive, too."

"Oh, I'll live. And don't worry about Harro. I will take care of him."

"I will take that as a sacred promise. Come back to me when you're finished with your next patrol. And bring Harro with you. I will marry you then, if you still want me."

"You give me orders already." He smiled. "I can tell you are used to being a wife."

She grinned at him, a devilish grin. "It is easy to act like a wife with you." Her eyes glanced toward the stairs and she held out her hand. "Come. I will show you what I mean."

Happily, he let her lead him up the stairs to her room.

# 13

The Killakeet Church of the Mariner, built from the planks of a wrecked schooner, began its life in 1908 as a place to store fish meal and the assorted nets and gear of a short-lived commercial enterprise that called itself The Outer Empire Fishery and Crab Pot Company. After the company went bust, the people of Whalebone City simply took over the building, painted it white, and threw open the door for any preacher who wanted to come and preach. The first one who came was a former rumrunner from Mobile who called himself Captain Sam. A good carpenter, Captain Sam added a stunted steeple to the roof of the church and also a brass ship's bell. The bell was rung Wednesday evenings and Sunday mornings for services. If for any reason all the residents of Whalebone City needed to gather, the bell could be rung by any citizen. One would have thought ringing the bell by mischievous boys would have been considered great sport, but the purpose of the bell was respected by everyone.

The interior of the church was plain and functional except for the pews, which were made of a golden poplar with seat backs, end panels, and hymnal racks fashioned from a deep burgundy walnut. They were the pride of every Killakeeter and had been hauled over by boat after Buckets O'Neal, across the sound to gadabout, had spotted them about to be thrown away by a fancy landsmen's church. The preacher's pulpit was constructed from the wheelhouse of the *Cheryl Roberts,* a forty-five-foot workboat swamped by the hurricane of 1913. The cross on the wall was made of driftwood fashioned by Trudelle Thurlow not too long before she died.

It was the first Sunday in December when Preacher, feeling strong and confident, gazed benevolently over his people. The pews were filled, the faithful ready for his sermon, and he had followed Josh Thurlow's advice and gone to sea for a day of fishing on Pump Padgett's boat. He felt now as if he finally understood the people in his flock. It was a pretty morning. The sun was out and angled through the windows in a flush of golden light. Preacher had organized his sermon around the Gospel of Matthew, chapter four, verses seventeen through twenty-one, where Jesus made disciples out of fishermen. But before he got to the Scriptures, Preacher wanted to say a few words about his adventures at sea. Pump Padgett stirred uncomfortably at the reminder. Preacher had been quamished nearly the entire time. Pump had never known a man could throw up quite so violently or for so long. He'd fed the fishes, for sartain.

After his personal chronicle, which left most of the men snickering and the women astonished, Preacher moved on, quoting the account of Jesus accosting the fishermen who were repairing their nets. "How would you feel if a man came along and took your sons away from you while they were fixing your nets?" Preacher asked. "You would not like it, I'd wager, and might have a word to say against it. Matthew didn't write down what Zebedee had to say, but I don't believe he fought too hard. He must have seen that there were greater things for his boys to do, and that was to take up the word of the Gospel and spread it yea across the nations."

"They should have finished mending the nets first," Pump muttered.

"Shut up, old man," his Mrs. whispered in a voice close to a growl. There were similar comments and asides between misters and missuses all over the church. Preacher had indeed hit upon a hot topic that was going to keep the men somewhat awake and the women nearly attentive.

Before Preacher could ratchet up his sermon a notch, the door to the church swung open and he stopped to see who it was that had come in late. So did everybody else on the pews, heads swiveling. Dosie Crossan stood in the doorway, dressed in her riding pants, boots, and a blue denim shirt. When nobody said anything and continued to stare, Dosie said, "I'm sorry I'm late." Then, in the continuing silence, she added, "The tide was high so I had to ride around through the woods."

Josh went up the aisle and escorted Dosie back to sit beside him and the Keeper. "I'm glad you came," he whispered in her ear.

"Well, you promised me a picnic," she whispered back. "So I packed us a lunch."

Josh grinned and gave a hushed introduction to his father while everybody in the church cocked an ear. "We've met," Keeper Jack whispered back, which was news to Josh. "We're neighbors, Dosie and I." They shared expressions of familiarity, which, for some reason, left Josh mildly unsettled.

Five pews behind, Queenie O'Neal caught the eye of as many women around her as possible. There was a triumphant atmosphere inside the church that Preacher took as a response to his sermon. He moved on to what he considered a most appropriate allegory. "You tuna fishermen have to go out a long way to catch the big ones," he pronounced, "just like the Lord God Jesus the Christ had to go into the places of sin to catch his big ones, too. It was why He consorted with prostitutes, thieves, and tax collectors. That's why He said *the healthy have no need of a physician, only the sick.*"

"Amen," Doc Folsom intoned. "Preacher, you're hitting them out of the ballpark today!"

"Never mind baseball, Doc!" Preacher cried in a happy voice. "I feel like a man who just loaded twenty ton of coal and got a 'well done' from his foreman!"

Herman sat beside his brother, Fisheye, completely and utterly miserable and not hearing a word that Preacher was saying. He was in his best Sunday-go-to-meeting coveralls,

and even had on shoes, but it was not his shoes that were
making him miserable. He hadn't expected his missus to
show up at church. That she had not accorded him the common courtesy of apprising him of her intentions was bad
enough. But when he saw her sit beside Ensign Thurlow, a
sudden storm of jealousy struck him like a winter gale. He
sighed so deeply that his brother shot him a look. "What's
with you?" he hissed.

"I'm going to have to fight Ensign Thurlow," Herman
said.

"Why's that, you little snipe?"

" 'Cause he's trying to steal my girl."

"I thought you hated girls," Fisheye said reasonably.

"All but one," Herman replied.

Fisheye realized Herman was talking about the Crossan
woman. "She's too old for you, you moron. You're twelve!
Hell, she's too old for me." Then he grimaced as he received
his reward for cursing in church, a sharp elbow up around
the second rib by Glenda, his pigtailed wife, who was also
the sister of the Jackson twins and three months pregnant.

After an hour, Preacher finally wound down and completed his sermon, which he thought had gone very well.
Many of the men had stayed awake through a lot of it, and
the women kept looking around at one another, no doubt
taken by his allusion to the family being much like the crew
of a fishing boat, all dependent on one another. The collection plate was passed around, getting a nice stack of nickels
and quarters, and then the choir and the congregation stood
up for a final hymn. It was the same hymn they always sang
at the end of the services while the surf grumbled, and the
wind whistled, and the sand stirred outside as counterpoint.
It was the hymn that Killakeeters thought had been written
especially for them:

> *Lord, whom winds and seas obey,*
> *Guide us through the watery way;*
> *In the hollow of thy hand*
> *Hide, and bring us safe to land.*

Outside, Genie stood waiting with saddlebags strapped aboard. She was tied up beside old Thunder, and both horses had taken the time to get to know one another. There had been a lot of nickering and snorting and stamping of hooves, but they had finished their conversation by the time church service was done.

Josh walked Dosie outside, shaking hands with Preacher and introducing Dosie to him. "Glad you came," Preacher said. And then, pointedly: "Services are at eleven o'clock every Sunday."

"I'm sorry I was late, Reverend," Dosie said.

Preacher was so pleased at being called "Reverend," he said loud enough for all to hear, "Miss Crossan, you may come anytime you like, early or late, and you will be most welcome."

Keeper Jack came along and he and Dosie shared another friendly glance. "How is it you've met?" Josh questioned.

"As I told you, Dosie is my neighbor," the Keeper said. "She and I have sat out in her rockers a few times, sharing some coffee and talking about this or that."

"You have a wonderful father, Josh," Dosie said. "He has told me so many stories about you."

"He's been known to exaggerate," Josh replied, frowning.

Keeper Jack grinned. "So I have," he allowed. "But it's all in good fun. Now, Josh, here's Thunder and he's yours for the day. Light the light for me, if you will, then bring Thunder back when you're ready. Pump will be along to spend the night in the lantern room. I'm going to stay here and have Sunday dinner at the Hammerhead and talk a spell with Queenie about the lighthouse celebration. Likely, I'll drink some whiskey, too. Preacher's sermon made me thirsty for it, don't ask me why."

Willow came out of the church, accompanied by her parents, Hook and Winifred Mallory. Her brother Stobs, the *Maudie Jane* radioman, and his wife and baby son were there, too. Willow caught sight of Dosie. "You could protect the sand," she said.

"Beg pardon?" Dosie replied.

"If you are looking for something to do, protect the sand."

Josh introduced Dosie to Willow. "Willow knows things about people," he said.

"Some people say she's a hoo-doo," Hook added helpfully.

"She's not, though," Winifred interjected. "Are you, Willow?"

But Willow walked away without answering.

"Well, that's our Willow," Josh said, and her parents and all within hearing nodded agreement.

Josh and Dosie climbed aboard their horses, leaving the Keeper and most of the island population watching after them with pleased expressions. Herman Guthrie, however, was not among them. He had already made it home and was sitting dolefully in a rocker with his chin in his hands. When Fisheye strolled by, his wife on his arm, he said, "You still plan on fighting Mister Thurlow?"

"I reckon," Herman said.

"Well, don't beat him up too bad. He's my captain, you know. He might take it out on me."

"I'll try not to," Herman replied dolefully.

"You don't look too happy about it. Maybe you ought to give it another think. Mister Thurlow's pretty big. Maybe he won't go down so easy even under the hammer blows of a tough little snipe like you."

"Shut up, Fisheye!" Herman cried, and ran inside the house.

Glenda linked her elbow in Fisheye's arm as they walked on. She said, "That Crossan lady is surely pretty, though a bit cheeky, what with wearing pants to church."

"Kind of hard to ride a horse in a dress," Fisheye replied, wanting to take up not only for Ensign Thurlow's woman but his brother's, too.

"I rode a wild pony in a skirt many a time when I was a girl," Glenda disputed.

Fisheye nodded at the recollection. "I remember that. And you were a sight doing it, too! You could ride like the wind.

We had a time, didn't we, when we rode them old wild things? That's when I first paid attention to you."

"No, that's when I first paid attention to *you*," Glenda teased. "You were as wild as the ponies." Her arm pulled him closer. "You know, I been meaning to tell you. Three months ain't so far along I couldn't use a little ride now and again."

"On a wild pony? Why, you'd be bound to fall off and . . . oh." Fisheye blushed a deep scarlet but his pace picked up in the direction of their little house three streets back from Walk to the Base. Glenda smiled, hugging her husband's arm.

# 14

osh rode along, stealing an occasional glance at Dosie, just to prove to himself that she was really there. Dosie was aware that Josh was giving her the eye. It was a delicious feeling that she liked and mistrusted at the same time. She therefore decided to change the subject, even though there wasn't one. "You're not a half-bad rider," she said.

"Thanks. I learned on the wild ponies. Bareback."

"That must have hurt."

"You have no idea, especially when I got to be a teenager. Where did you learn to ride?"

"Daddy taught me. He was an Olympic rider."

"Olympics, eh? Did he win a medal?"

"No, but he won my mother. Her father was a judge."

The beach stretched before them, lined by dunes on one side and the booming surf on the other. In the distance, as if beckoning, sat the lighthouse. Genie broke into a canter and Thunder, not to be outdone, paced her. "I give you fair warning," Josh said. "Thunder may be old but he's fast."

"Not as fast as Genie," Dosie replied, laughing. "She's a whirlwind!"

"Let's just see!" Josh touched his heels to Thunder, who instantly broke into a gallop.

Dosie yelled, "Let's have a bet!"

"What's the stakes?"

"I'll tell you after I've won!" she cried, and gave Genie the lightest touch with her heels. The big mare lunged ahead.

They roared down the beach. Seagulls threw themselves into the air, then circled and followed, screaming insults. Josh and Dosie were both laughing so hard they were having trouble hanging on. For a hundred yards, the two horses were neck and neck, their eyes alight, coats glistening, frothing at the bit. But then Thunder let off and Genie flowed into the lead. Dosie looked over her shoulder and saw Josh and Thunder recede. She slowed Genie to a walk, then turned her around. "I win," Dosie said as she came alongside.

"Just out of curiosity, what was our bet?" Josh asked, petting Thunder's neck. The old horse was blowing but not too hard.

"That you'd take me to the top of the light."

"I was going to do that, anyway."

"Now you *have* to take me," Dosie said on a note of triumph.

Josh shrugged. "Do you want to hear what I would have wanted?"

"I suppose, even though you never had a chance."

"That maybe you'd learn to trust me," he said, his tone a bit doleful.

Josh's dolefulness did not have the desired impact. "First I have to learn to trust myself," Dosie answered firmly.

They rode on until they reached the lighthouse grounds. The Keeper kept the place like a park with green grass and pin oaks and juniper trees all around. "This is the old home place," Josh said in a hushed voice.

They entered the parlor of the Keeper's House, which was bright and cheerful, the light streaming inside through two big bevel-paned windows illuminating, in prismatic colors, a cherrywood table and chairs, a polished oak floor, and a big hutch filled with bright, silver-rimmed china. When Dosie looked closer, she saw the china pieces were decorated with a crest. When she asked about it, Josh explained that it was the Lighthouse Service insignia. "Daddy got pretty mad at President Roosevelt for merging his service into the Coast Guard," he said.

He took her into the living room, which was spacious and airy with a cloth-covered sofa and easy chairs upholstered in bright, flowery patterns before a big fireplace. Kerosene lanterns stood on the reading tables. Josh wanted to show Dosie his mother's art room more than anything. He swung open the door and Dosie was transfixed by the feeling of welcome she received. She felt an urge to sit down at the worktable and take the beads and shells and beach glass that Josh showed her and make her own jewelry. She had always been good with her hands. When Josh showed her one of his mother's bracelets, an uncompleted piece with green beach glass and silver wire, she wanted more than anything to complete it.

Josh fixed glasses of iced tea, added slices of lemon, and carried them outside. He and Dosie sat in the rocking chairs, shared the sandwiches she'd made, drank the tea, and enjoyed the view of waving sea oats and soft, beige dunes and the rippling, blue sea. After they'd eaten, they rocked for a while longer, comfortable, just being quiet, and then Josh said, nodding toward the lighthouse, "Are you ready to go to the top?"

"Lead on, Hawkeye!" she said smartly, although her heart was in her throat. To her surprise, she discovered she was frightened.

They walked down the path and into the base of the lighthouse and crossed the black-and-white marble squares. Black cast-iron steps wound above them, reminding Dosie of photos she'd seen of the inside of a chambered nautilus shell. Josh led the way up, stopping at each level to let Dosie look through the narrow slits built into the brick walls. Dosie found the ascent disorienting, the interior diameter getting smaller with each step. She was suddenly glad she had not climbed it as a little girl. She knew she would have been even more terrified than she was now.

Finally, they reached the lantern room. There were white curtains around the room and she was glad to get inside them and away from the spiral staircase. She leaned in close to admire the sparkling slats and prisms. The wind blew softly against the surrounding glass. "Can we go outside?" she asked. Her tone was braver than she felt but it was another childhood dream and she was intent on living it.

"You bet," Josh answered, "but let me lead the way and be sure to hold on to the rail. The wind is always strong up here."

Dosie thought perhaps Josh was being too protective, but when she followed him outside onto the narrow parapet, the wind hit her hard, grabbing her hat and sending it sailing away. She grabbed the rail and hung on, her heart pounding. "Oh!" she finally managed to gasp, her voice barely heard above the whistling, grasping wind.

Josh came up beside her. "Are you all right?"

"I'm afraid I might be blown over," she confessed. The wind gusted again and she gripped the rail so hard, her hands turned white.

Josh held her waist to steady her. "Are you sure you're OK?"

"Yes. But don't let go. I'm a bit dizzy."

"I won't let you go," he said in a solemn tone.

Dosie felt as if she were inside a kind of an amazing dream. "I never knew it was so beautiful," she said in a tone much like a prayer.

Josh's voice carried above the river of rushing air in which they were submerged. "See that freighter and that tanker? They're riding the currents. The tanker's on the bright blue water. That's the Gulf Stream come up from the Caribbean. But there, that gray water, where the freighter is, that's the cold current come all the way down from the Arctic Ocean. They're like rivers swiping each other. Up at Hatteras, they sometimes hit head-on. That's a sight, a geyser of sand and shells thrown way up into the sky."

Dosie kept a death grip on the rail, even though she trusted Josh to not let her go. He told her to look at the sky and she forced herself to do it even as her head spun. She saw clouds skimming past, racing one another, so low she felt she could touch them.

"We're going to have a storm," Josh said.

Dosie felt as if she were going to be drawn right up into the clouds. She closed her eyes. "When?" she gasped.

"It's pretty much on top of us already."

"But it was so pretty a minute ago."

"That's the Outer Banks for you!" he cried, then laughed a laugh of pure joy.

They stepped down and down and down the winding iron steps. At the bottom, he told her that his parents had once danced on those very same tiles. "I think I would have loved your mother," Dosie said, her head finally beginning to lose its spin.

"She'd have loved you, too."

Dosie wished Josh would put his hands around her waist again as he had done on the parapet. Maybe he saw it in her face or maybe Josh simply wished the very same. He took a tentative step toward her. She tilted her face. "I hope I find my hat," she said.

His hands went to her waist and drew her to him. "I'll buy you a new one if you don't."

She studied his face, a weathered version of the boy's face she'd sighed over so long ago. Her hands, as if controlled by themselves, flowed across his arms, up to his shoulders, and down his muscled back. Then she closed her eyes and his lips gently touched hers, just a whisper. Outside, the first raindrops of the storm began to fall. "We should dance," Josh said.

And they did. Josh took her into his arms and led her into a waltz. She was a bit stiff at first but she gradually allowed him to lead. Then the wind slammed the door shut and the spell was broken. Dosie took her arms back. "Josh," she said, "I'm sorry. I can't do this."

"It was just a kiss. And a little dance. That's all."

"A kiss, yes, and a dance, and then what?"

Josh put his hand behind his neck and rubbed it, a gesture of confusion. "Dosie, I don't know. It seems to me you kind of look ahead too much."

"You're right," she said after a moment of thought. "I'm

sorry. Why don't we just start over? Just forget everything and act like we just met."

Josh didn't want to start over. He'd told Dosie much of his story, he'd listened to much of hers, he'd ridden down the beach with her and laughed with her and shown her his boyhood home and his mother's art room and then taken her up on the lighthouse. There, the wind had blown and a storm had threatened and then, in the base of the lighthouse on the beautiful marble tile, he'd kissed her and danced with her and he'd thought everything was pretty wonderful the way things were. "All right," he said. "We'll start over." Then he damned himself as the coward around women he'd always been.

"I'm glad you understand," Dosie said, putting her hand on his cheek. Then she lifted her face to his and kissed him again, a long, loving, deep kiss, even more soulful than the one before. Josh was about as confused a man as there could be. He wanted to ask her if the kiss was part of the starting over but didn't dare. Some things, he was beginning to learn about Dosie Crossan, you just didn't mess with.

At twilight, Dosie climbed once more into the lantern room to help Josh light the light. He even let her hold the candle and touch its flame to the mantle. She thought herself happy at that moment, and useful, a feeling she'd missed for so very long.

The rain had stopped and dark was gathering when they climbed aboard the horses. Pump Padgett, who filled in sometimes for the Keeper, waved at them as he walked the path toward the light. "I don't want this day to end," Dosie said. "How about we share another dram of Mount Gay at the Hammerhead?"

"Chief Glendale just brought me a fresh bottle from More-head City the other day," Josh said.

"Then let's go put a dent in it. I'll ride back when Keeper Jack and Thunder are ready to go."

When they rode into town, it seemed very quiet. They found Herman sitting on the hotel steps. Purdy the pelican was sitting alongside him, wearing a grave, long-billed expression. "Why are you here, Herman?" Dosie asked. "Where's everybody else?"

"They're all listening to the radio, I guess," Herman said, looking up. His eyes were puffy and his cheeks streaked with tears. "And I'm here to fight you, Mister Thurlow, for stealing my woman."

"Why, Herman," Dosie said, "do you mean me?"

"Yes, ma'am, I do."

Dosie covered her smile with her hand, but Josh saw that Herman was fondling a hawksbill knife. Josh had fought men with knives up in Alaska and that's what you needed to do, keep your eye on the knife, not the man, and be ready to move when it came your way. Of course, he'd never had to fight a boy before. Herman was fast and would probably nick him a little before he could take the knife away. But then Herman folded the knife and tucked it in his shirt pocket and put his face in his hands. Josh climbed down off Thunder and then noticed the wood shavings around the boy's bare feet. Herman had been whittling at a limb.

Josh sat beside the boy, Purdy moving a step to make room. "I'm sorry, Herman. I didn't mean to steal your woman. You shouldn't cry and I don't think we need to fight, either. You're still in the running, best I can tell."

Herman kept his face in his hands. "I ain't crying about the missus," he said through his fingers. "And I already changed my mind about fighting you."

"Then what's wrong?" Josh asked.

"It's my brother and all the boys, all the boys everywhere."

Josh was flummoxed. "You want to tell me what you're talking about?"

Herman raised his wet face. His hands fell lifelessly between his legs. "It's the damn Japs, Mister Thurlow." He glanced up at Dosie. "I'm sorry for cussing, ma'am." He took a breath. "They just bombed the bejesus out of some place called Pearl Harbor. It's all over the radio. Our whole navy was there and it's been sunk."

Josh absorbed the news while a great weight settled into his heart. "Herman?" he said in a quiet voice.

"Yes, sir?"

"Are we straight, you and me?"

"Yes, sir, we're straight. I guess it's up to the missus who she wants."

"OK. Then do two things for me. First, go find your brother and tell him to round up the other boys and Bosun Phimble, too. Tell him the *Maudie Jane* is putting out to sea."

"Yes, sir. What's the other thing?"

"Take good care of Miss Crossan. Can you do that?"

Herman nodded, and was off like a shot.

# 15

The procession began at the orphanage after Sunday services and wound its way through town and into the heather fields. Townspeople joined Father Josef's children until the narrow, sandy path was crowded with worshipers. Big white cranes wading in the reed flats stood very still as the crowd passed, then went back to picking off fish. The people sang the Nebelsee song of Advent, "Macht hoch die Tür":

> *Lift up your heads, ye mighty gates,*
> *Behold, the King of glory waits,*
> *The King of kings is drawing near,*
> *The Savior of the world is here.*

As the procession approached the lighthouse, Krebs was surprised to see an army truck parked beside the remains of the keeper's house. A tent flapped nearby. Camouflage netting was on the high ground, just to the side of the thornbushes. The soldiers were diligently working on the equipment beneath the netting. A soldier came out of the lighthouse, trailing a wire. Krebs looked up at the parapet and saw that the wire was attached to an antenna clamped to the railing.

Father Josef turned to the assembly and they gathered around him. "It is our tradition to come here each December to recall the days before our Lord came to earth," he said. "Even our fishermen stay in to celebrate. Perhaps," he went on to the approving chuckle of the fishermen and fishermen's wives, "it is because the sea is so cold and fishing is so difficult this time of year, eh? But we gather as a family." Father Josef deliberately sought out Krebs. "There is nothing more important than family."

Father Josef was a great speaker, his voice deep and compelling. Even the soldiers stopped their work and gathered around. Then, when he was finished, he blessed the assembly and the people sang a last hymn and began to disperse to their homes. The children waited patiently to be shepherded back to the orphanage. Krebs saw Father Josef talking to the lieutenant in charge of the soldiers. He caught the gist of their conversation as he approached. "I have my orders, Father," the lieutenant said.

"But your presence is too dangerous for Nebelsee," Father Josef replied. "Please pass along to your superiors my suggestion to put your station elsewhere."

The lieutenant shrugged. "It would be like talking to that lighthouse." He noticed Krebs and came to attention. "Good afternoon, *Kapitän*."

"I'm on leave, Lieutenant, so relax," Krebs said. "What is all this about, anyway? A weather station, I presume?"

The lieutenant nodded. "Indeed, sir. My headquarters wants precise measurements from this site. Wind velocity, temperature changes, and barometric pressures at different altitudes. Those are devices to send up balloons you see just there. Now, I'm sorry but I must get back to work."

Krebs took Father Josef aside. "Miriam and I wish to be married the next time I have leave," he told him.

Father Josef was delighted, though he gave no indication of surprise. "Fine news, Otto," he said. "She is a wonderful woman."

Krebs chuckled. "You knew already, didn't you? There are no secrets from you, are there?"

"Not when it comes to my children," Father Josef replied.

Krebs was distracted by the low grumble of an aircraft

engine. He checked his watch. It was about the right time for the Teufel plane to pass over the island. Still there was something not quite right about the sound of the engine. "Excuse me, Father," he said and studied the approaching aircraft. It was a Ju-88, all right. He could make out its two engines, the flat line of its wing, the vertical line of its stabilizer. But it was coming in very low and very fast. Then he knew it wasn't a *Dreifinger* at all but a plane very similar. "It's a Mosquito," he said, nearly to himself. Then he shouted to the lieutenant, "Get your men away! That's an English aircraft!"

The lieutenant stared, then ordered his men to take cover. Krebs started to look for Miriam and saw her standing beside the lighthouse. "Miriam!" he roared. "Come here!"

The townspeople were running and the troops were joining them, scattering this way and that. Miriam was trying to gather the children. Krebs started after her but his knee suddenly buckled. He screamed at her. "Run away from the lighthouse!"

The airplane flung itself overhead, machine guns stuttering from its wings. It had passed so low that Krebs could make out the rivets on its fuselage. Then he saw people had been shot, their blood spattered across the heather. The Mosquito pulled up and then continued on its course across the island.

Krebs heard another aircraft. Miriam had sent the children running away. She was looking around, apparently to see if there were any more children near the lighthouse. Krebs saw the blur of the bomb falling from the second Mosquito, and then the lighthouse disappeared in a cloud of dust and debris.

When the debris stopped raining down on him, Krebs raised his head. All around him were groaning, wounded, and weeping people. Krebs crawled to the devastated lighthouse. Others came and picked him up, insisting that they were going to take him to a doctor. "No, no, I am all right. Help Miriam Hauptmann. She is beneath this rubble."

Willing hands started tearing into the brick and mortar. Miriam was easily found. She had an arm and a leg ripped off by the blast but was still breathing, her mouth open in shock. Her glazed eyes seemed for just one moment to come back to life, then blurred over. Krebs crawled through her blood and kissed her lips. They were already cold and tasted of brick and dust.

# Part Two

DEATH, I SAID.

# 16

Krebs lay on his back in his filthy bed and groaned, his
head throbbing in painful sympathy with a heavy
pounding at the door. He wanted to scream at whoever was doing it to stop and go away, but all he managed
was a whimper. He reached for the bottle lying beside him
but found, to his disgust, that it was empty. He threw it
across the room where it burst against the door. As if responding to the insult, the door, after a furious kick, flew
open. "Go away," Krebs mumbled, each word like a hammer
on his skull.

Whoever had kicked in the door crunched through the
broken bottle shards and stood over him. Krebs heard a familiar voice, although it was entirely too loud. "*Kaleu,* it's
me, Max. My God, you're stinking drunk! Admiral Doenitz
is here on a visit and is asking for you. The chief told me
down at the boat. You have two hours to get to headquarters!"

"Stop yelling," Krebs growled, "and go away. I'm still on
leave."

"Don't be ridiculous," Max said and grasped Krebs beneath his arms and heaved him to his feet. "Your leave was
over two weeks ago. Pull yourself together."

"Did you kiss your wife for me?" Krebs asked solicitously
while trying to get his legs to work.

Max recoiled from Krebs's breath, which stank of cheap

wine. "Time to talk later, sir. We have to get you ready to meet the admiral."

"Tell him to come here," Krebs blared.

"I don't think that would be wise," Max answered. "If the Admiral came here and saw you this way, he might take you for a drunk."

"Then he would know the true me."

"What has happened to you, sir?"

"Nothing. Everything. Leave me alone."

Sighing, Max put Krebs's arm around his shoulder and supported him. "Come on, let's get a start on your clean-up."

Behind the guesthouse was a garden courtyard with a hand-operated water pump. Max half-dragged Krebs to it. "Stick your head under the spout," he ordered.

Krebs silently knelt and accepted the stream of icy water over his head while Max vigorously pumped. "For God's sake," Max complained. "This isn't for my exercise. The idea is for you to wash your face!"

Krebs's head sank to the rotten boards beneath the spout. The cold water had somewhat revived him, which was something he didn't want. "This is a direct order, Max," he said. "Find me another bottle. I can't be allowed to sober up until we get back aboard the *U-560* and at sea. If I do, I'll prob-ably desert."

"First, you must go and see the admiral," Max answered. "Then you can desert if that's what you want. I would be the last to stop you."

Max dragged Krebs to his feet and walked him back to his room, sat him down, then drew a bath. After the tub was filled, he found Krebs lying on the bed, his arm thrown over his eyes. He had gone to sleep. "No, you don't, sir," Max said, and forced him awake and into the tub. He grabbed a sponge and tossed it to Krebs. "Wash!"

Max sat outside the bathroom on a hard wooden chair and listened for sounds of washing. When they stopped, he peeked inside. Krebs threw the sponge at him. "I don't need a nursemaid!"

When Krebs emerged, naked and dripping, Max found a towel and gave it to him. After much fumbling and complaining, Krebs managed to get himself dry, then dressed in a blue naval uniform that badly needed pressing. He then stood unsteadily for Max's inspection. Max took a look and shook his head. "Your beard looks like it could harbor mice."

Krebs tugged at the tangled, reddish brown bush. "I have decided to look like a Viking." Then he noticed something about Max. "You've shaved off your beard."

"Giesela said I looked ridiculous in it," Max replied stiffly.

"She was right."

Max made Krebs turn around and then shook his head. "Where's your leather jacket?"

"I have no idea."

Max made a search through a pile of dirty clothing and found it near the bottom. "Put it on. At least it isn't wrinkled."

Krebs did, then squinted at Max. "You are the best executive officer a U-boat captain ever had," he said with real affection. "But you are betraying me, Max. You see, I need to stay drunk."

Max saw that Krebs wasn't kidding. "Look, be serious. You must tell me what's happened to you!"

"I've not had enough to drink, that's all."

"I tell you what, sir. I'll buy you some more wine. I'll even drink it with you. But now you must go and see Doenitz."

"Screw him and screw you, too, Max."

"Yes, sir." Max pointed toward the broken door. "Hang on to my arm. Just walk. That's it. Look at you, grimacing from your knee. Did you see a doctor at all?"

"No. I don't need knees to sink ships."

"I thought you were going to desert."

"Did I not tell you to get screwed?"

Max was at least pleased that there was still a spark of life in his captain. "One foot in front of the other," he ordered. "Come on. March!"

Krebs grimaced with each step. As they turned onto one of Brest's cobbled streets, an enlisted man lurched past them, his hat shoved to the back of his head. He held a half-empty wine bottle in his hand. "Officers are shitheads!" he shouted. Laughter erupted from other submariners lounging against a brick wall. Then they joined in. "Screw all officers!"

"I see the men are in a good mood," Krebs growled.

"Well, they're drunk."

"God bless them, then." Krebs suddenly absorbed where they were going. "Is it just me our grand *Befehlshaber der Unterseeboote* wishes to see?"

"I heard five other captains are coming, sir. They are all Type Nine commanders. You're the only Type Seven as far as I know. The Chief said it was concerning a special assignment."

"Type Nines? The big boys! We are in august company, Max."

"Our *U-560* may be smaller, but no boat can match her for durability," Max responded.

"Oh, yes, durable is one thing we are," Krebs replied in a sarcastic tone.

The Ninth Flotilla headquarters building was a grim stone fortress that had once housed the French harbormaster. For all practical purposes, the harbor and the dockyard had become German property in 1940. The guard at the front door brought his rifle up to full port as Max helped Krebs up the steps. "Excuse me, sir," the guard said to Krebs. "Do you have orders to enter?"

"They're with me!" came a deep voice from behind them. Max and Krebs turned to see *Kapitänleutnant* Plutarch Froelich coming up the steps. "Max, you've done your good deed for the day. Go on, I'll take the bastard from here."

"Would you please stop shouting?" Krebs croaked. His hangover was making a comeback.

Froelich laughed and slapped Krebs on the back, nearly knocking him down the steps. Froelich hauled him up with an iron hand on his shoulder. "Come on, man. We don't want to keep Uncle Karl waiting, do we?"

"Be gentle with him, sir," Max pleaded. "He's had a rough go."

"I can take good care of a drunk," Froelich answered in a hearty voice. "Loads of experience. I've been one myself often enough!"

"Yes, sir." Max took another look at Krebs and flicked imaginary lint off the lapel of his leather jacket. "Good luck, *Kaleu*."

"Don't forget to have a bottle waiting for me," Krebs grumbled.

"What an odd duck you are, Otto *von* Krebs," Froelich said, laughing.

Once inside the headquarters, Krebs was surrounded by all the trappings of the *Kriegsmarine* in occupied France. There was an efficient buzz about the place with men in gold braid in abundance. In the anteroom to the flotilla commander's office, four other U-boat captains waited in nervous anticipation as Froelich and Krebs entered. "What do you make of it, Plutarch?" *Kapitän* Simon Vogel demanded of Froelich. Krebs had never cared much for Vogel. He was a nasty little piece of work with a goatee. He was also a rarity amongst U-boat commanders, an avid Nazi. It was said that each morning his men were required to sing a hymn to Adolf Hitler. He had even demanded that the Hitler salute be given aboard his U-boat until one of his men had gotten carried away and nearly punched Vogel's eye out with a stiffened arm in the tight confines. Krebs snickered quietly to himself, recalling the story.

"We're all to be demoted for associating with this Type Seven character, sir," Froelich said to Vogel, nodding toward Krebs.

"You look a bit unsteady, Krebs," Vogel said. "Are you drunk?"

"Not enough."

"If Doenitz thinks you're drunk, he'll have you shot. You'd best make an attempt to sober up!"

"Shot? Delightful. There will be plenty to drink in heaven."

*Kapitänleutnant* Fabian Hoessel chuckled nervously. "You're a U-boat skipper, Krebs. Heaven's not your destination. Like the rest of us, you're bound for hell."

"Some would say we're already there," Krebs wearily replied.

"Perhaps, but to see a tanker burst into flames . . . ," Froelich said.

"And hear the bulkheads collapse as it sinks . . . ," *Kapitänleutnant* Gerhardt Friedeberg added.

Vogel grunted. "To imagine that syphilitic Churchill getting the morning tally of our victories . . ." He stroked his goatee as if he had a vision of the roly-poly prime minister naked and turning on a spit.

"The cheers of the men when at last we make a score . . . ," Hoessel rhapsodized.

"You are all mad," Froelich laughingly accused them all, including himself.

The door to the office swung open. A naval staff officer, all tricked up in gold braid, stepped outside. "The admiral will see you now. This way, gentlemen."

If Krebs wasn't sober before, he was now. Even he had to admit he was scared of Doenitz. He took care to be exceptionally steady as he walked into the den of the man who feasted alike on English ships and German U-boat officers.

# 17

Rear Admiral Karl Doenitz waited for the six U-boat commanders behind a desk covered with stacks of folders. His expression was at once composed and inquisitive. There were upholstered chairs around the desk but no one dared to presume to sit in one. It was said even Adolf Hitler was a little cautious around his intense U-boat admiral. Krebs supposed that might explain the Führer's lack of enthusiasm for U-boats, even though they had provided Germany with her best and perhaps only chance to win the war.

"Gentlemen," Doenitz said in his high-pitched, nasal voice. "Are you well?"

The captains all stumbled over their answer except Vogel, who said, "We are ready to fight for the fatherland, sir. The Führer continues to inspire."

Doenitz nodded, but said, "Inspiration doesn't sink ships, Vogel. Torpedoes do. I could use a few more U-boats to carry them."

Vogel rocked in his shoes, which squeaked. He looked as if he had a retort but then thought better of it.

Doenitz drummed his fingers on the ink blotter, then darted his small, dark eyes at Krebs and apparently didn't like what he saw. "Well, Krebs. You look like shit."

"I feel like shit, too, sir," Krebs shot back.

Doenitz cracked a smile that split his thin face nearly to

his big, flapping ears. "The commander with the sure touch. That's what they call you, don't they? You're a shifty one, Krebs. I'm keeping my eye on you."

"That is a comfort, sir," Krebs replied.

Doenitz's smile faded. "I wish I had more like you, Krebs, even with your smart mouth. You're a bastard who loves to sink ships. God, if I only had another five hundred boats and more Krebses to command them, I could have won this war already!"

Krebs didn't know what to say so he mumbled his thanks. Then Doenitz began a rant all of them had heard before. *If only Berlin would build more U-boats!* Krebs listened and felt a great desire to be drunk again. Before he'd gone off on his binge, he'd at least managed to get Harro transferred to his boat. That's what Miriam had wanted. Now, the boy and he would share the same fate, whatever it was.

Doenitz moved on to the situation now that the Americans were in the war. *They are a soft nation with no stomach for battles,* Doenitz insisted. Krebs believed the admiral was wrong. The Americans had acquitted themselves well in the Great War. After all, hadn't their doughboys chased the German army out of Belleau Wood and pummeled them on a dozen other French battlegrounds? Krebs had never bought into the notion that the Americans were weak and soft. Disorganized perhaps, prone to pacifism, yes, but they were capable soldiers and sailors once they got into a scrap. Of course, it took time for them to work up to it. That was the key. If you wanted to beat them, Americans had to be hit early and hard and never allowed to recover.

Doenitz started complaining about the treatment he had recently received from the high command in Berlin. It was even money on which crowd Doenitz had less respect for— the stupid Americans, the stubborn Englishmen, or what he openly called "the posturing fools in Berlin." Krebs wondered if he was including the Führer himself in that circle. But Doenitz did not elaborate. Krebs glanced at Vogel and found him looking sour. It pleased Krebs to see it.

Doenitz, through with his harangue, beckoned the commanders to a large planning table where he unrolled a chart showing the eastern coastline of Canada, the United States, and Mexico, plus the Caribbean islands. They were sectioned in grid squares that Doenitz himself had devised. Krebs allowed himself a moment to admire a man who had partitioned the entire planet to his own coordinates. What, he wondered, does such a man imagine, that perhaps the world was his to conquer?

The admiral placed a finger on the chart and moved it like a bony stiletto down the American east coast. His eyes were bright. "Gentlemen, here are the most congested sea-lanes in the world. Almost all of the oil the United States requires for domestic consumption and military use is transported along them. If we can stop that movement, America is essentially out of the war. Her cities will freeze, her factories will close, and her armies will be isolated. Your six boats have been chosen for an operation to be called *Paukenschlag*. Do you know what that term means?"

Froelich responded, "It is the orchestral equivalent of a climax. A roll of drums, a clash of cymbals. Boom, crash."

Doenitz nodded. "Very good, Plutarch. I have carefully chosen the name of this operation because it could be a climactic one." He looked at each man, peering into their eyes. When his gaze fell on him, Krebs came to attention. All of the six did. Doenitz had that effect on you. Krebs had the sudden insight that here was a man more dangerous than even the "fools in Berlin." While they were posturing idiots who believed themselves to be savants, Doenitz was actually a true genius with enormous ambition.

"Your orders are simple," he continued in his reedy voice. "Proceed to the American coast and sink every freighter and tanker that passes before your torpedo tubes. And woe to the man who comes back to me empty-handed! Do you understand?"

"Yes, sir!" they all answered in unison.

"Good. Now, where do you think you should put yourselves? Captain Vogel? What say you?"

"Here, sir," Vogel answered confidently, pointing to the

grid square that encompassed Long Island. "I should set up on the approaches to New York Harbor. It is the busiest of all the ports along the American coast."

"Very good," Doenitz said. "I would do the same."

Vogel allowed himself a quick smile. To receive a "very good" from Doenitz was at least as desirable as a Knight's Cross. Of course, all the captains had more than one of those medals already, with clusters.

Doenitz put icing on Vogel's cake. "Captain Vogel, you shall be in charge of *Paukenschlag*. Make tactical decisions based on your observations, place the boats where you will. Keep me informed, of course."

Vogel smiled. "I appreciate your confidence in me, sir."

"Then give me numbers, Vogel. Tons and tons sunk beneath the waves."

"It shall be done."

Krebs was still studying the chart. His finger touched the map, then slid along it until it lingered. Vogel used his new authority. "Captain Krebs? Do you have anything to share?"

Krebs quickly withdrew his finger and clasped his hands behind his back. "Nothing, sir."

Doenitz nodded to each of his commanders in turn. "You are dismissed. Sailing orders will be delivered to your boats. Captain Vogel, you may further meet with your captains in the briefing room." Doenitz waved toward the foyer. "*Leutnant* Mittel will show you to it."

"Just Krebs, sir," Vogel said. "He's never been under my command. The others know how I work."

"Very well. Good hunting, gentlemen!"

In the foyer, Froelich gave Krebs a nudge as if to wish him luck. "Come, Captain Krebs," Vogel said. His voice was somehow threatening. Krebs already detested the man and they'd never shared more than a few words.

The briefing room was dominated by a long, polished table surrounded by dark leather chairs. At the head of the table above a marble fireplace was a huge oil painting of Adolf Hitler, looking angry and determined. He was in a brown uniform, unadorned except for a red armband with a black swastika within a white circle. Vogel took the chair beneath the painting and indicated that Krebs should be seated beside him. Krebs chose to seat himself several chairs away.

Vogel watched him sit. "Of course, I knew in advance about this mission and have been giving it a great deal of thought," he said. "I believe Admiral Doenitz has created a brilliant plan, but I wonder if even he realizes the implications of it. I have come to believe that the success of *Paukenschlag* may determine the fate of us all. Do you love the admiral, Krebs?"

Krebs had no idea how to answer such a question. "I admire him, sir," was the best he could do.

"As do we all. He is a genius and a great patriot. Almost single-handedly, he has created our magnificent underseas force." Vogel eyed Krebs, as if gauging the impact of his comment, then went on, "Did you have a good leave, Krebs?"

"It was tolerable," Krebs answered.

"Tell me about it. I like to hear personal details about my men."

"I stayed drunk most of the time and screwed at least fifty whores," Krebs replied.

"Really? On Nebelsee? I did not realize there were so many whores on such a small island. Perhaps one or two . . ." Vogel consulted the folder. "A Miriam Hauptmann, perhaps?"

Krebs stood. "Listen, you nasty piece of work. I should break you in two just for saying her name."

"Calm yourself, Captain. I was just responding to what you said, after all. Forgive me. Please be seated."

Krebs sat. "Why did you have me investigated?" he demanded.

"I didn't. Admiral Doenitz did. He wanted to be absolutely certain that he was choosing the best commanders for the job." Vogel tapped the folder. "I would say your tragic experience on Nebelsee might have made you a bit unstable."

He sighed. "But, for now, I will adopt the admiral's opinion of you as my own."

"I think you will find me sufficiently aggressive," Krebs said.

"I hope so, Krebs. I really do. You see, that is exactly why I wanted to talk to you in particular. I wanted to be certain you understood the concept of terror that lies behind this mission. Do you understand the concept of terror, Krebs?"

"Not exactly, sir."

"I will explain it to you." Vogel leaned forward, close enough that Krebs could smell his sickly sweet breath. "We in the *Unterseeboote* flotillas do more than sink ships, you see. We also terrorize the enemy, especially their civilians. The mind of a civilian is easily manipulated. If they start thinking of us as a force of maniacs, we become invincible in their minds. What do you think of that?"

Krebs thought it was pure shit but he responded, "I find it interesting, sir," which was his way of saying the same thing.

Vogel sat back and waved his hand dismissively. "Interesting? I should hope you would find it more than interesting. I fear for our country, Krebs, and I perceive only one way to save it, and that is through the application of terror. You and I and the other four commanders of *Paukenschlag* are the instrument to apply that terror. Doenitz's order to sink only freighters and tankers? We will forget we ever heard it. Once we're in American waters, we will sink everything we see afloat, big or small. *Everything!* The war has changed, Krebs, and we must change with it. Terror is what we will bring to the American shore."

Vogel stopped and stared at him and Krebs felt obligated to respond. "I will sink as many ships as possible, sir. I always do."

Vogel leaned forward again, running his tongue along his fat lips. "Listen, Krebs, and make no mistake as to my meaning. The Americans are soft but they are also capable of building up a great war machine that the English will use to pound us into the dust. Then, the cavemen Russians will come in and kill all the German men, then eat our children and rape our"—he hesitated, then said with a curious distaste— *"women."*

Krebs realized that Vogel truly believed every word he was saying. That was more frightening than anything else he had heard.

Vogel went on, "It is imperative therefore that we keep the Americans at bay and scare them so badly they will pour all of their efforts into building battlements from one end of their coast to another."

Krebs nodded. "I understand, sir."

"Do you? What do you understand?"

"I am to sink ships."

Vogel suddenly slammed his fists onto the table. "No, you idiot! I want blood! *Blood!*"

Krebs's face was speckled with Vogel's spittle. It stank and he wanted desperately to wipe it off but he remained still and silent, his lips pressed together so hard they turned white.

Vogel allowed another sigh, then got up and walked behind Krebs. "We must succeed, Otto," he said, placing his pudgy hands on Krebs's shoulders.

Krebs had decided the man was either an idiot or a maniac, and probably both. He shrugged Vogel's hands off, then stood. "I should like to immediately return to my boat, sir. There is much preparation to be done."

Vogel calmly studied Krebs, a wry smile on his lips, then nodded. "Blood, Krebs," he said. "Blood."

"Yes, sir," Krebs replied, and made good his retreat. He couldn't wait to take a shower. He felt far dirtier after a few minutes with Vogel than weeks aboard a miserable, stinking U-boat.

Froelich was waiting for Krebs in the anteroom. "Well, I see you survived."

Krebs was noncommittal. "Yes."

"I don't know about you, Otto, but as soon as I get to

sea, I'm going to give that little bastard the slip. Trust me. You don't want to be near Vogel. His ideas will get you killed."

Krebs plopped his cap aboard his head, then squared it. "I intend to take your advice, Plutarch. Good hunting."

Although Froelich wanted to talk more about *Paukenschlag* over a beer, Krebs turned him down and made directly for the *U-560*. There was much to do. The wheels had begun to turn in his head, and whether he liked it or not, he was excited. He had lied to Vogel, and to all of them. He *had* spotted something on Doenitz's chart. He wasn't going to stop at New York. He was bound for the capes of North Carolina where the Gulf Stream and the Labrador Current squeezed ships together in a blue-water noose.

# 18

For most of December, Josh kept the *Maudie Jane* at sea, coming into Doakes only for fuel and food. There was much to do in the sea-lanes. The war seemed to have tripled the amount of traffic. At any hour, dozens of tankers and freighters were rumbling north and south, and there were many near collisions. Josh kept signaling, using a combination of blinker lamps, signal flags, and Stobs's home brew to demand that the ships spread out. He also ordered them to start zigzagging. Few ships complied or even responded. Most of them pretended not to notice the patrol boat at all. "Let's hope we're wrong about the Germans coming over here, Eureka," Josh said, surveying the chaotic scene from the stoop bridge. "It's going to be a bloody mess otherwise."

"We ain't wrong, Skipper," Phimble said. "It's like it was up on the ice. Remember what Falcon used to say? 'My blood is hot, boys, and my bones are cold! There's a battle coming our way, mark me!' "

"The captain had a well-trained crew and lots of ammunition," Josh said. "We don't have either."

"Past time to start changing that," Phimble replied stoutly.

Josh looked at his innocent boys. Ready and Again were fishing, Jimmy and Bobby were idly watching them do it, Once was napping on the bow with Marvin asleep beside him, Big and Fisheye were probably sharing a joke in the engine room, Millie was undoubtedly in the galley reading a comic book, and Stobs was hunkered down over his home brew, probably listening to juke-joint music from a North Carolina radio station. Josh shook his head. One last moment of innocence, he thought. Then he put the megaphone to his lips. "Man overboard!" he shouted. "This is a drill!"

Phimble grinned. "That's more like it, sir!"

The boys on deck turned their heads in surprise. Marvin scrambled to his feet. "Man overboard, you lubbers!" Josh railed. "Hop to!"

They hopped to, though slowly. Then Josh made them do it all over again. Then again and again. Once couldn't figure what was happening. "Did somebody really fall overboard?" he asked his brother while they scanned the sea from their position on the bow.

Again scratched up under his tub hat. "Beats me. I had me a big old wahoo on the line, too."

"What's gotten into Mister Thurlow?" Bobby asked, after the order finally came to stand down.

"He must think one of us is going to fall overboard, though I don't recall any of us ever done it," Once replied thoughtfully.

"I came close once," Bobby said. "That time we were playing catch with the baseball on the stern and you threw me a high one."

"Oh, yeah," Once said. "I'd forgotten that. That must be the reason. I'll go tell Mister Thurlow I won't do that no more so he don't have to worry."

Although Once did, indeed, tell Mister Thurlow that he was pitching better these days, and not to worry about him throwing too high or long anymore, it didn't make any difference. As a matter of fact, he didn't seem to even understand why Once had told him the good news. Not only were man-overboard drills still being held with alarming frequency, but also fire drills and collision drills and abandon-ship drills and repel-boarders drills and at all times of day and night. General quarters was called nearly every other hour, it seemed, which meant pretending to man a machine gun without ammo and drop depth charges that didn't exist.

Josh also gathered the boys in the galley and showed them a book with silhouettes of German ships, including U-boats, and made them call out which was which when he held them up. He even made Big and Fisheye do it, even though they worked in the engine room. The answer was always negative when the boys asked if they could fish. The only fun they were allowed to have was to step up on the stoop bridge and take a turn at handling the boat. "You have to learn every job aboard," Josh told them over lunch.

"Why's that, Skipper?" Bobby asked, chewing on a ham and biscuit.

"Well, you might get hurt, Bobby," Josh replied. "And Big, for instance, might have to come up from the engine room and take your place. Or the other way around."

At that pronouncement, the boys looked at each other with wide eyes. Getting hurt wasn't the reason they'd signed up for the Coast Guard.

"This war thing's got the skipper all mommicked," Ready muttered at the mess table after Josh had climbed topside to relieve Phimble at the wheel.

"Look what it's done to poor Marvin, too," Millie said. The little dog was lying on his back, his tongue lolling out of his mouth. "He's wored out. He hardly even barks anymore."

"Maybe we should tell our maw how we're being mistreated," Once said. "She'd put a knot in Mister Thurlow's tail."

"Let's tell all our maws," Millie proposed, and the boys all nodded in eager agreement.

Maws were told and Josh heard from every one of them, and still the drills came one on top of the other. "We got to get back to the way we was," Once said to Again while pulling lookout duty on the bow on a cold, blustery day. They'd just finished another man-overboard drill and had gotten soaked doing it. When Once had complained, Josh had replied, not the least bit sympathetically, "I told you to put on your slicker, didn't I? And all you boys better start wearing shoes."

Again looked down at his bare feet, turned chapped and raw in the cold and wet. He hated wearing shoes and had never had to do it on board a boat before. In the past, when his feet got cold, he would repair on down to the galley and warm them up. Now, he had to stand watch on watch and was liable to be rousted out at any time for yet another drill. He pondered a tanker sloshing by and said, "I bet those old boys are staying dry and warm. How do you get out of this chickenshit outfit?"

"I'm ready to quit if they'd let me," Once replied. "I'm colder than a dead mullet."

Bobby joined the brothers. He'd also neglected to put on his foul-weather gear and his teeth were chattering. "Can we quit if we want to?" he wondered.

"We joined because we wanted to," Once observed. "I guess we ought to be able to quit for the same reason."

Ready came up. He'd worn his slicker but his bare feet were still pretty cold. When he heard their idea about quitting, he had to let the boys down easy. "You can't quit the Coast Guard anytime you want to," he said. "It's against the Constitution. But I have a better idea. How about we write down all our gripes and hand them over to Mister Thurlow?"

Once was taken with the idea. "A list might get him straightened out, sure enough. Everybody could sign it."

"It would sure knock Mister Thurlow for a loop," Bobby said, imagining a coil of paper several feet in length.

Word quickly percolated throughout the boat that a list of gripes was being drawn up that would straighten out the skipper and Bosun Phimble, too. It was, of course, to be done in vast secrecy. Josh knew about it nearly before it started. He noticed the furtive looks the boys gave him as they passed by. Then he had to loan Ready a pencil and after that a sheet of notebook paper. He noticed the boys going down into the galley looking unhappy and coming back looking satisfied, as if they'd done something about it. When he descended into the galley for coffee, he noticed Millie quickly tuck away beneath his comic book the sheet of notebook paper he'd loaned Ready. It was covered with pencil scribbles.

"What's going on, Skipper?" Phimble asked as Josh came topside with his cup of coffee.

"Piss-and-moan list," Josh said. Phimble just laughed.

In mid-December, a small gray ship suddenly popped up above the horizon. "A cutter, Mister Thurlow," Phimble announced.

Josh studied the little warship. Her lines and twin stacks identified her as a 165-footer. That particular type of Coast Guard vessel had been designed to intercept booze smugglers during Prohibition. Since the Rum Wars had ended, the cutters had been modified for antisubmarine warfare. "Make a light signal," he said to Once. "Tell them, 'Welcome to the Outer Banks.' "

Once did as he was told and then read the answer that was blinked back. "She's the *Diana,* Skipper. Officers are invited over for a cup of java."

Josh ordered all the boys to put on the shoes he'd bought for them. They were high-top, black-and-white basketball shoes. Mallory's General Store just happened to have had a good stock and Josh had bought them at half price.

"How come the shoes?" Big griped to Millie. Griping was becoming an art form to the Maudie Janes.

"Skipper says we should make a good example to the cutter boys."

"With shoes?"

Millie rolled his eyes. "Chickenshit," he said.

"And how!" Big confirmed.

As Phimble maneuvered toward the cutter, Once peered at a boy on the cutter's bow. "Well, I swear upon a turnip, there's Joe Bird! Hey, Joe Bird!" The other boys picked up the cry.

"Joe Bird's from Killakeet," Josh explained to Phimble. "It's good that they've got a local boy on board if they're going to plow along this bank."

While Josh and Phimble took the raft across to the cutter, the Maudie Janes gathered on deck to look over the *Diana* boys. "Can we feed the seagulls?" Millie asked, coming up with a bag of stale biscuits.

"No," Ready answered. "Mister Thurlow said we weren't supposed to do nothing except work around the boat, give a good appearance and all."

"Well, can we fish?" Again demanded.

"Same story," Ready answered in a grim tone.

Again frowned. "What good appearance does it make if we're out here in the Stream and we don't fish? Seems more foolish than anything else. Millie, write this one down on the list, too!"

Millie disappeared below to take care of it. His list now filled the front of the sheet of notebook paper and he was working on the back.

"Hey, Killakeeters!" Joe Bird yelled. "What's new on the island? Did Judy Jones ever get herself married?"

"She married my brother," Stobs answered. "Why? You still sweet on her?"

"Naw. Just wondering." Joe Bird didn't fool anybody aboard the *Maudie Jane*. Killakeet boys liked to marry Killakeet girls, and with one his age married off, Joe Bird's odds were cut way down.

"Willow's still around," Stobs called across.

Joe Bird pretended not to hear him.

In the cutter's galley, Josh and Phimble took their ease with the *Diana*'s captain, Jim Allison, and her executive officer, Frank Feller. After a few words of greeting, the four officers immediately started to form perceptions of one another. Such stocktaking was the natural preoccupation of men who led other men. Josh determined that the *Diana* officers were a couple of real smart cutter officers, no doubt about it. They wore khakis that appeared as if they'd just been laundered and pressed. The creases were so sharp you could cut yourself on them. It made Josh glad he was wearing his leather jacket so his wrinkled shirt wasn't quite so evident. But though Allison was spiffy, he had an air of calm competence. Josh figured he could trust the man, if it came to it, and with that assessment, he was done figuring him out.

Phimble studied his opposite, too. Feller was a rough plug

of a man, though he had a friendly expression. He was likely strict on the men, Phimble guessed, but fair. He could work with Feller if it came to it, so case closed.

From the other side of the table, Allison and Feller also made their assessments. Allison immediately decided he would not care to have Ensign Thurlow assigned to his cutter. True, he had the weathered look of someone who'd been born to the sea rather than just learning about it through books and lectures. But Thurlow's shabby uniform also indicated perhaps a resistance to strict military discipline. Allison thought an independent command on a small boat was perfect for the man.

From just the few words that had passed between them, Feller took Phimble as quite intelligent and a couple of ranks below where he should have been (probably because he was a Negro). Phimble was a steady man during storms, he'd wager. Feller thought Thurlow was lucky to have such a man. If he could have thought of a way of enticing him over to the *Diana,* he would have done it.

After a Filipino steward served them coffee in fine china with the Coast Guard emblem on the saucers and cups, the next thing the officers did was talk about their boats, another natural preoccupation. Josh and Phimble both admired out loud the *Diana,* her layout as well as her fine-looking and smart crew. Josh especially admired that she had full depth-charge racks.

"But we aren't allowed to drop any," Allison said. "Even with the war on, we can drill all day but no actual expenditure of rounds. I'm of a mind to just go ahead and drop a few, anyway."

Josh asked, "Have you heard anything about U-boats coming our way?"

The two cutter officers exchanged glances. "That's why we've been reassigned north," Feller said. "Word's out a few might be heading this way. We'll be operating out of Norfolk."

"What about the fleet?" Josh asked. "Are they coming out?"

"The Big Bum?" Allison shook his head. "I don't think so. Admiral King is going to keep his destroyers and cruisers all safe and snug in Norfolk until he's ready to go off and fight the Japanese. I'm thinking he'll let us little boys handle any German subs that might come across the pond. But you should be all right this far south. Scuttlebutt is the Jerries will park themselves outside New York Harbor. If so, we'll be ready to run up there."

"If I was a German sub commander, I'd come down to Hatteras," Josh said. "They did in the Great War, you know."

Allison gave that some thought. "Well, nobody I've talked to has mentioned that as a possibility. But I tell you what. You call me if you see a U-boat. I'll come on down to help as fast as I can. That's a promise."

They shook hands across the little table.

Phimble asked Feller, "Do you have a sonar set aboard?"

"Sure," Feller answered. "A QCN-4 Echo Ranging-Listening set."

"That's what we have. Do you have a good man on it?"

"Two good men," Allison answered. "Why?"

Josh filled in. "Our man could use some training. He was never sent to school."

"Have him come across," Allison replied. "We'll send him back in a week all ready to ping."

"We'll do it, sir," Josh said gratefully.

Hands were shaken once more all around.

The appraisals, the coffee, the sitting, the conversation, and the accepted idea of sending Jimmy Padgett off on the *Diana* for training was completed, so the officers went topside filled with a sense of accomplishment. For Josh's edification, Allison ran his crew through a general-quarters drill, and it was impressive to see the *Diana* boys turn to under the sound of a pulsating alarm, each man quickly finding his station, the swift, thrilling rustle of the tarps being thrown off the machine guns topside and the three-inch gun forward, the racks of depth charges unlocked, the calls coming in one after the other to the bridge that all was in readiness.

The Maudie Janes watched the drill. "Damn, they're good," Bobby said.

"But can they fish?" Again demanded.

"Shut up on the fishing, for gosh sake!" Ready said. "We already got it down on our list."

Jimmy was brought across and introduced to the *Diana*'s sonar operators. Josh took the boy aside. "I'll tell your family where you are and what you're doing."

Jimmy looked as if he were about to cry, but said, "Yes, sir." He fingered his tub cap, turning it in his hands.

"Have you ever been away from Killakeet for a week, Jimmy?"

"Never more than two days, sir. When we go into Morehead City to pick up the mail, you know."

"Well, it will be all right. You'll find these boys are fine fellows. There's also Joe Bird. You know him well enough. It'll be like visiting friends and relatives."

"Yes, sir." Jimmy's eyes were large and a little wet. "How am I supposed to get back?"

"How would you do it if you were fishing and your boat broke down in Norfolk?"

Jimmy gave it some thought. "Likely I'd hitch rides on fishing boats and maybe take a ferry or two."

"There you go. Here's five dollars for the ferry boats and the cutter stores if you need anything."

Jimmy took the crumpled bill and then delivered up a brave smile as he went off with one of the *Diana*'s sonar men.

After the officers returned and the eighty-three-footer got under way, the Maudie Janes made a number of surreptitious hand signals, catcalls, and gibes toward the Dianas, who returned them all in kind. Jimmy was seen leaning on the rail of the cutter, looking dismal. "We'll see you in a week, Jimmy!" Josh called across the water. Jimmy responded with a wan smile and a halfhearted wave and the *Diana* sped away.

Josh looked to the horizon where he could see at least a dozen tankers and freighters. "Take us on out there, Eureka," he said, nodding toward the line of merchies. "We'll run along with those big ladies for a while."

Ready was nearby. "We ain't going in, sir?"

"Not for a while."

Ready made an excuse and disappeared below, to add yet another gripe to the list. Two of them, in fact. *Jimmy sent off with strangers* was one. *Stay out too long* was the other. It was going to be a helluva list. Ready wasn't sure how poor Mister Thurlow was going to bear it.

# 19

Christmas Eve found the *Maudie Jane* out on the Stream. Jimmy had still not returned. Some of the crew thought maybe he had been kidnapped by the evil *Diana* boys. Frustration was rife. "Ain't we even going in for Christmas?" Millie moaned to Stobs during a smoke break at the stern. Stobs usually had the straight skinny, being the radioman and all and in the wheelhouse able to hear the skipper and Bosun Phimble talk things over.

"Skipper ain't said," Stobs replied, flipping his cigarette butt into the sea.

"He ain't said much of nothing lately except to call all these damned drills," Ready groused. "I reckon it's time we let loose with our list."

"Poor Mister Thurlow," Once said. "I hope his feelings won't be too hurt."

Millie produced the list. It was covered solid with gripes, front and back. "This is really going to knock the stuffing out of the skipper," he said sadly.

"Well, he asked for it," Ready snapped, then tucked the list in his pocket and climbed topside to ask for a moment of Ensign Thurlow's time.

"What's up, Ready?" Josh asked.

"Serious stuff, sir."

"I see. Well, let's talk over a cup of coffee. Suit you?"

Ready had a stern, no-fooling expression on his face. "That'll do," he said.

They repaired to the galley and Josh asked Millie to take a break, then poured two steaming mugs of hot coffee. Ready took a mug and sat down at the mess table, Josh sitting opposite. "Millie makes a good cup of joe," Josh said, savoring his mug.

Ready demonstrated that he was in no mood for idle talk by drawing out the list and smoothing it on the tabletop. "The subject is crew morale, Mister Thurlow," he said formally, and pushed the sheet of notebook paper over.

Josh took the sheet and put it under one of his elbows. "I see," he said. "Go on."

This threw Ready. He'd expected Mister Thurlow to take a long minute to read the list, then ask Ready how to repair the damage. Instead, the big ensign just sat there, drinking his coffee, the piss-and-moan list firm under his elbow.

"Well, sir," Ready improvised, "it's like this. Our morale stinks. See, we can't take no more of these drills and all of this other bilge you and Bosun Phimble has been laying on us. We're about worn-out and I guess you'd say that's the long and short of it."

Josh made a sympathetic nod. "I had no idea," he said in a soft tone.

Ready thought this was a good start. In fact, he was glad the skipper wasn't looking at the list. The way he was telling it was going to make a greater impact. "Oh, it's awful, sir," Ready went on. "You don't see it the way we do, of course, you being an officer and all. But this running around and getting up in the middle of the night looking for boys what ain't fallen overboard, and dodging colliding ships that ain't colliding, and looking for German subs which ain't nowhere around, and dropping depth charges that we ain't got, and aiming the machine gun what ain't got no ammo! Now that don't make no sense at all, no matter how you look at it. The boys and me, we'd just soon go back to the way we used to patrol, coming in every night except when we fish, which we all agree we need to get back to doing, if you don't mind."

"A Killakeeter that don't fish is liable to miss it," Josh allowed.

"Yes, sir, that's sartain."

There was a moment of silence. During it, Ready began to be afraid he'd hurt the skipper's feelings. He wondered if he should say something to soften his complaint.

"Ready," Josh said, "I'm curious about something. Do you think I'm your friend?"

Ready was relieved. He was going to get to reassure Mister Thurlow that all the boys still liked him. He grinned and nodded eagerly. "Yes, sir, I know you are!" he exclaimed.

"And the other boys, do they think I'm their friend, too?"

"They sure do!"

Josh removed his elbow from the piss-and-moan list. He set down his coffee mug. Then he began to tear the list into tiny bits in front of Ready's startled face. The tatters drifted down like snow on the galley table. "Guess what?" Josh said in a voice that seemed to Ready as if it came from hell. *"I'm not."*

The Maudie Janes, all waiting on deck for the results of the meeting, even Fisheye and Big up from the engine room, saw Ready suddenly tear through the deck hatch as if a shark had bitten him in his britches. Then the skipper came up from below. He caught Ready, dragged him aft, and tossed him down beside the starboard depth-charge rack. The boys all stood frozen, their mouths dropped open.

"General quarters!" Josh bellowed in a voice they had never heard. He caught Once Jackson trying to sneak past him. "Just in case you ain't sure, let me show you where your station is, son!" Josh lifted Once and carried him forward like a rag doll and dropped him beside the machine gun. The rest of the boys tripped over one another to get to their positions. Even Marvin ran down to the depth-charge racks and sat at attention. When Ready got to his feet, he bawled, "Depth charges ready, sir!" He even saluted.

Josh ignored the salute since it was improper. "Listen up!" he roared in his great raspy sea-voice, one he hadn't used

since Alaska. "I am not your friend! I am your captain! Bosun Phimble is not your friend, neither! He is my executive
officer! You will not question my orders or his! You will not
bitch! You will not moan! Any man who does from this day
forward, I will personally lay hold of and throw him off my
boat! Then we'll have another man-overboard drill, only it
won't be a drill. Any questions?"

Not a Maudie Jane said a word. Most didn't even bother
to breathe. "Good," Josh said. "I'm glad we've had this little
talk. Bosun Phimble, you are to keep the men on battle drill
for an hour, then Captain's Mast in the galley. In case you
don't know the terminology, girls, Captain's Mast means a
review of your infractions and subsequent punishment.
We're going to get shipshape on this boat if I have to bust
each and every one of you down to raw recruit. If that
doesn't do it, I will kick your butts up between your ears.
One way or the other, I'm going to get you ready to fight!"

Josh glanced around at each of the boys and they jerked
to attention. He lowered his voice but it still sounded like a
puffing steam engine. "From here on in, if you have any
complaints about the way I'm running this boat, I don't care
to hear them. And don't tell your maws, neither. Nor your
grannies. I'm preparing you for war, boys, and we're in one,
whether you like it or not, whether anyone on Killakeet likes
it or not."

Marvin trotted over and sat down beside Josh and gave
each boy a little stare and a growl of his own. "Attaboy,"
Josh said, reaching down to give the dog a pat on his head.
"Marvin's the best sailor on this pohunkey boat!" he exclaimed.

"The smartest one, too," Ready muttered, entirely to himself.

# 20

osie was furious with herself. She kept thinking about Josh Thurlow, which was precisely the wrong thing for her to do. Her entire reason for coming to Killakeet was to stop being so needy, but here she was, waking up at night thinking about the big coastguardsman and his strong arms around her and how good they'd felt. She hungered to have them around her again. "Dammitohell!" she yelled, throwing her pillow across the room. Then she lay there, morosely listening to the thunder of the waves and whistle of the endless wind. "Shut up!" she yelled at the island. Killakeet responded impishly with more thunder and whistles and even rattled her windows.

It seemed to Dosie that if life were a novel, she was just the romantic character stuck into Josh's plot so he would have a love interest. That infuriated her even more because it wasn't an original thought but that of her musician ex-boyfriend, who was, after all, nothing but a trumpet player in a ridiculous slouch hat worn to hide a bald spot. "Dosie, to you, life is a dime-store novel," he'd told her after she'd once complained about their life in general. "In chapter one, you're the lovelorn and unfulfilled woman waiting for your knight in shining armor. In chapter two, I'm the irresponsible rat bastard who completely fouls up your life. The trouble is you don't have a chapter three where your knight shows up."

The really lousy thing about the son of a bitch was that

he was absolutely right. Well, she was having none of it. She was throwing chapters one, two, three, and all the rest of them out. "I shall never see Josh Thurlow again," she resolved, even though she was on an island nine miles long and two miles wide at its widest, and populated by only 174 people, one of whom was the object of her oath.

Since her arrival, Dosie had kept fighting the empty, hopeless feelings that clawed at her much of the time. She was glad she'd hired Herman, even though he had that big crush on her. He was good company and he also taught her things, like how to prog clams and catch blue crabs with nothing more than an old fish head, a string, and a long-handled net. It made her feel useful if she could help feed herself through her own efforts. Being useful was an idea that kept having more appeal to Dosie. She began to think that maybe it was the root cause of the emptiness in her life. Until then, she had been pretty certain it was all the fault of men.

A few days before Christmas, Herman decided to show Dosie how to gather oysters. He was a bit of an inventor and had devised a special tool, half net, half pry bar, to get them off the rocks down by Miracle Point. While he was showing off, he fell and sliced his arm on the edge of one of the razor-sharp oyster shells. Blood ran down Herman's arm and into the ocean until a thick scarlet stream formed around him. "I'll be fine," Herman said, and then promptly passed out. Dosie pulled him to shore, woke him up, tore off a piece of her shirt and made a tourniquet, and made him climb onto Genie. He passed out again just as they reached her house. She left him there and jumped on Genie and went flying over the sand hills all the way to Whalebone City to get Doc.

Fortunately, Doc Folsom was in his infirmary playing checkers with Pump Padgett and came without delay. By then, Herman had woken up again and dragged himself into one of the rockers in front. Doc took a look at the arm, then opened his black bag and pulled out a big sewing needle.

"What are you going to do with that?" Herman demanded.

"What do you think? You need at least six stitches."

The boy grasped the arms of the rocker. "Do your worst,

Doc. I can take it." But as soon as the needle touched his skin, Herman fainted again. Doc chuckled and got busy with the stitching.

Dosie studied Doc's technique. "Would you like to do one?" he asked.

"I would," Dosie said, surprising herself.

"It's just like sewing up two pieces of cloth. Here. Get to it."

Dosie got to it. She ran the needle through Herman's skin and pulled the thread tight to pull the two sides of the cut together. It pleased her that she wasn't bothered at all by either the blood or the sewing. That could help her be useful, she thought. Maybe she could even be a nurse or something. When she finished with a couple of stitches, Doc admired her work, then took over again.

While Doc sewed and Herman moaned, Dosie looked out and saw the *Maudie Jane* passing by. Since she had decided to never see Josh again, she surprised herself when she waved at him. To her disappointment, he didn't wave back. Crushed, she dropped her hand. Then she got angry for caring. "You ain't chapter three, boy," she growled under her breath.

Herman struggled back from the darkness. "I'm much better," he allowed, even though nobody was paying much attention to him, not even Doc. Doc had joined Dosie looking after the *Maudie Jane*.

"Stay out of trouble," Doc said to Herman after the patrol boat had finished going by.

Dosie smiled down on Herman and Herman thought she looked pretty much like an angel. "He's a boy who's after trouble, I think. But a nice boy for all that."

"I'm not so nice," Herman said, and would have blushed if he'd had enough blood left in him to do it.

Doc plopped on his hat, adjusted it to its usual rakish angle, and retrieved his bag. "Glad to be of help," he said when Dosie asked him how much she owed him.

Dosie, despite her best intentions, kept watching the *Maudie Jane* until she was just a dot on the waves. "Damn you,

Josh Thurlow," she said, then imagined herself sneaking aboard his boat one night, perhaps disguised as one of his boys, and visiting him while the boat sailed beneath the stars. In her mind, his cabin looked like one of those giant rooms they showed in the pirate movies with big back windows that had an ocean view. She then imagined a vast four-poster pirate's bed. "You're disgusting," she muttered to herself, of herself.

Herman healed quickly, the specialty of youth. Then he went back to oystering, just so he wouldn't be afraid to do it. Dosie loved oysters, especially raw. Herman could only eat them steamed. "Raw ones are supposed to put boys in the mood for love," she teased him.

Herman said, "Puts me in the mood to puke." He hadn't learned how to sweet-talk a woman, quite yet. His father hadn't gotten around to that lesson. It was about the last one a Killakeet daddy taught a Killakeet boy.

Dosie began to get up early in the morning, well before sunrise. It was better than lying in bed alone and imagining herself lying in bed not alone. It was interesting, anyway, to walk the beach just as dawn cracked the horizon to see what had washed up in the night. She thought about things as she walked, nothing special, this or that and the other thing, and maybe a little about her being too needy, although the subject had pretty much exhausted itself in her mind. It was being useful that intrigued her now.

At low tide, shells littered the beach and sand dollars were like biscuits strewn across the sand. When she found a broken one, she was delighted to find there were smaller pieces inside like sculpted birds of fine white china. Driftwood, twisted like gargoyles, was left gray and dry before the dunes. A few times, she found some beach glass, mostly green, a few yellows, though none so glorious as the scarlet ones Josh had shown her in the Keeper's House. She carried many of the more interesting pieces back. Pretty soon, she had a good collection and wondered if she might start making jewelry. That would be a good thing to do, she decided.

Even useful. Why, she might even sell her work.

After a while, it seemed every time Dosie sat down to think and worry about herself, she thought of something else better to do. She hung wind chimes made of shells and string on her porch and painted a hand-lettered sign on a driftwood board and nailed it to the gatepost that said *Dosie's Delight*. "*Dosie's Lament* might be more in order," she thought, but she was trying to stay positive. She also put a sign up on the stable that read *Genie's Joy*. It made her laugh.

When she walked on the beach, gulls wheeled overhead and squadrons of pelicans raced down the coast. Little sandpipers played their endless game of tag with the surf, never quite allowing it to touch their feet. What happened, Dosie wondered, to a sandpiper who was ill or simply having a bad day? If the surf touched its feet, was it so mortified that it slunk off to die? One morning, watching the little birds, she had the sudden epiphany that she should write a book about what it was like to live on Killakeet. There were enough interesting characters to fill a book, that was for certain. Josh Thurlow, of course, was one of them. Why, she could interview him and hear all about his adventures up in the Bering Sea and maybe she would even learn more about his Eskimo wife. Dosie realized what she was doing. It was all an excuse to see Josh. She gave up on the book and decided maybe she would take up sculpture.

As December crept on, the wind became a little more insistent at night, rattling the windowpanes of her house, and the rain pattered harder on the roof, and the grumble of the sea seemed a little louder. Though the daytime weather was mostly fair, and unseasonably so according to Herman, cold weather could be all but smelled in the air. Dosie often found the beach enshrouded with a cool fog in the mornings, and she wore a wool, plaid windbreaker to keep the chill away. Strange shapes would sometimes loom up in the fog as she walked along. One day, she found the skeleton of an old wreck. It hadn't been there the day before, yet here it was, exposed by some shift in the current and the removal of tons of sand. It was a testament to the end of someone's dream. She hoped the person had found another dream, or at least survived the old one.

When Christmas approached, she was determined to chase her loneliness away by somehow being useful to somebody, somehow. She baked cookies and took them to Queenie O'Neal, who made her stay to chat over tea. They'd had a fine time of it and Dosie learned more gossip about Killa-keeters than she imagined was possible.

She stopped by to see Keeper Jack, bringing him a big wreath she had made herself out of juniper boughs, seashells, and gull feathers. They hung it on the lighthouse door and Keeper Jack got a little teary-eyed over it, saying he hadn't decorated for Christmas since his Trudelle had died. Herman cut her a little cedar tree and she placed it in the parlor and decorated it with shells and beach glass and put presents under it, wrapped in gaily decorated store-bought paper from Mallory's.

On Christmas Eve, she gave Herman his present, a white Coast Guard tub hat, just like the Maudie Janes wore, pro-cured for fifty cents from Chief Glendale. Herman was thrilled. She gave sugar cubes and carrots to Genie, who nickered her pleasure. There was also a present for Josh, a white silk scarf, but, of course, it remained unopened. There was a letter for Josh, too, that said Dosie would never see him again, that she had to find herself first and she wasn't yet sure where she was hiding. She sent the letter and the present to Josh via Herman. Herman told her he would leave it in Josh's room for when he returned. Dosie cried herself to sleep. She spent Christmas Day all alone, except for Genie and the gulls and the sandpipers.

Queenie showed up the day after Christmas with some johnnycake, and a welcome bundle of packages and letters that had come in by ferry. The packages contained a cash-mere sweater from her mother, and leather riding gloves from her father. Her brother Bart had sent along the latest book by John Steinbeck, titled *The Log from the Sea of Cortez,* and brother Randy had sent powder and lipstick that she knew his wife had picked out. Her horn blower had sent along a letter, which she threw in the trash, then dug it out and read it. It made her mad and sad, both at the same time. He was doing well, he said, though he missed her sometimes. He was seeing the hatcheck girl at the Woodbury Hotel and she was quite the dish. Dosie threw the letter in the trash again. The next morning, she dug it out and burned it in a little ceremony in the sand, and then went for a walk.

She hadn't gone far before something big moved in the fog. Dosie was astonished to see it was Star, the king stallion of the wild horses. The stallion dropped his head, one ear forward, the other back, and stamped his hooves. Dosie took a tentative step toward him, with her hands open so the stallion could see them as Josh had done. Star drew back his head with a snort and regally walked away until he had disappeared into the mist. Seeing him naturally made her think of Josh, even though she didn't want to.

She turned toward the muttering sea and looked out to where the foaming waves disappeared into the shroud of gray. Josh was out there somewhere and she could feel a connection to him, and she found herself wishing and hoping for things with him she had no right to wish and hope for. Then she remembered she had written him the letter and she wasn't ever going to see him again. Suddenly feeling completely useless, she wrapped her arms around herself. "You are a tragic girl," she lamented, and turned back toward the house she increasingly thought of as home.

# 21

The *Maudie Jane* returned to Killakeet the day after Christmas, ending a frustrating patrol. None of the freighters and tankers Josh had tried to escort had paid any attention whatsoever. The merchies not only refused to zigzag, they didn't respond to any amount of light-flashing or flag-waving or even cursing over Stobs's home-brew radio.

As soon as the patrol boat tied up at the dock, the wives and mothers of the crew went aboard to help their boys clean up. The fathers and brothers waited on the dock and talked about fishing and their future plans, which were mostly more fishing. It was believed the war might spur an interest in canned fish and they intended to be ready.

When Etta Padgett, Jimmy's mother, discovered her son had been put aboard a cutter, she went after Josh. "What right did you have to send my boy off?" she cried. Then her lower lip trembled and tears welled up in her eyes. "I should pop you one. If your mother was alive, she'd do it for me."

Josh was respectful of Mrs. Padgett. He could have said that Jimmy was being paid to be a sonar machine operator and should therefore actually know how to operate one. He could have but he didn't. Etta Padgett didn't want or need to understand the real reason and he knew it. "I expect him home in just a few days, Mrs. Padgett," he said to reassure her. "And if he isn't, I'll go get him myself."

Etta wasn't much reassured. "If he gets himself drownded out there with those cutter boys, or if he comes home with the Norfolk clap, it's on your head, Josh," she said, and then fully burst into tears.

"Now, now, Etta," Pump Padgett called over, then went back to talking about a big marlin he'd caught the other day but had slipped the hook before he could gaff her.

Josh went below to hide but he couldn't get away from the women down there, either. Millie's mother was in the galley, scrubbing the stove. "Don't you be sending my Millie off for no training, Josh," Mrs. Thompson warned.

"No, ma'am, Millie already knows how to cook," he said, and fled to the engine room. There he found Big Midgette's mom polishing the brass works. She stopped what she was doing and gave him the evil eye. Josh retreated to the closet that he called his cabin and pulled the curtain shut.

After an hour, Josh came out of hiding, made a fast round of inspections, and then released the crew for a day-late Christmas dinner. The boys were gathered up by their families and escorted home, the women giving Josh a final set of dirty looks over their shoulders. Josh waited until they were well gone. He had half hoped that maybe Dosie might make an appearance. When she didn't, he came off the boat, determined to make an impression on a fresh bottle of Mount Gay, a much anticipated Christmas present to himself.

In his room, Josh discovered a package from Dosie, with a letter propped up on it. He opened the package and found a white silk scarf with a cheery Christmas wish of good tidings. It made Josh feel bad that he hadn't gotten her anything. Then he read her letter and, still clutching it, sat down on his bed. He read it again, then let it flutter to the floor. He gazed longingly at the Mount Gay rum sitting on his dresser, then put the bottle in a drawer just to see if he could keep from drinking it. It remained untouched. It made Josh feel better about himself, even while he felt miserable.

The next morning, Queenie served Josh a big breakfast of a half dozen eggs, over easy, a full basket of biscuits, a slab of fatback, and a mess of tuna hash, all washed down with fresh-percolated coffee. Then she sat down at the table with him. "Now, Josh, talk to me for a little while, won't you?"

"Got to get on down to the boat, Mrs. O'Neal," Josh replied. "There's a war on, you know."

"Well, there sure is, Josh," she retorted. "My gosh, look at me dodging bullets even as we speak."

Queenie had him there. "What do you want to talk about?"

"How are you and that Crossan girl getting along?" she asked, even though she very well knew the answer, mainly because she had steamed open Dosie's letter.

Josh knew whatever he said was going to be reported to every lady in Whalebone City within the hour. He rubbed the back of his neck and thought what he might say, then decided to fall back on the truth. "Well, we're not getting along at all. She's got to find herself."

Queenie managed an expression of astonishment. "I never heard of anybody who couldn't find themself. Yourself is kind of hard to lose."

"That's what she said, Mrs. O'Neal. That's all I know."

Queenie shook her head. "I'm mommicked on this one. It sounds like foolishness."

"Modern women, I guess," Josh replied, then grabbed his cap and made his escape.

Buckets was just getting up, coming down the stairs, tugging on his suspenders as Josh closed the door. "What's for breakfast, woman?" he demanded.

"Whatever you can fix," Queenie snarled, getting up and going into the parlor.

"Is that supposed to be a joke?"

"See if you're laughing at an empty table."

Buckets watched Queenie sit in her rocker by the fireplace. He knew she was thinking and it peeved him because he didn't know what she was thinking about. He came and stood in front of her. "New Year's Eve is coming up," he said. "Are we having a party this year?"

Queenie snapped Buckets a look, then clapped her hands.

"The very thing!" she cried. "Aren't you smart!" She jumped up and hugged him.

Buckets grinned from her hug. He guessed he was smart though he wasn't sure how. "Does this mean you'll fix me breakfast?" he asked.

It did.

The New Year's Eve dinner party at the Hammerhead was a small one, made deliberately so. Doc Folsom was there and so was Keeper Jack and Preacher. Josh was there, of course, him being a resident of the Hammerhead and all. Buckets and Queenie had a cheery fire in the fireplace and a nice spread on the table with fresh duck, cranberries, flounder, clams, oysters, and at least a ton of hush puppies.

The men sat in the parlor and sipped shots of whiskey, courtesy of Keeper Jack, who'd brought a mean supply, while the women bustled in and out of the kitchen and the dining room. Josh heard the jeep outside, and then, to his astonishment and confusion, Dosie Crossan opened the front door and came into the parlor. Taking the opportunity, Purdy the pelican waddled in behind her and took a position in front of the fire.

"Hello, gentlemen," Dosie said. She was dressed in a white frock with blue trim and her hair was up. Josh realized it was the first time he'd seen her in a dress. She looked like a million dollars.

Queenie came hurtling through the parlor. "Oh, how pretty you are!" she exclaimed. "I'm glad Chief Glendale was able to go after you."

"My hair must look a mess," Dosie said. "The chief drives pretty fast."

"Nonsense. Have you men ever seen such a pretty girl in all your life?"

The men all said indeed they never had, except Josh, who was speechless. Dosie glanced at him, then followed the women to the kitchen. Soon, there were peals of laughter. Chief and Sarah Glendale came inside soon afterward. Glendale sat down with the other men and a glass of whiskey, while Sarah went back to the kitchen. There was more laughter.

"What is it women laugh about when we're not around?" Buckets wondered.

"You just answered your own question," Doc said, then laughed and slapped his knee. By the fire, Purdy turned around on his web feet, then tucked in his head to take a nap.

"Do you reckon that pelican thinks he's human?" Chief Glendale wondered.

"If he don't stop stealing fish out of the kitchen," Buckets said, "he's going to think he's dinner."

"Purdy's surely old," Keeper Jack said. "I remember him hanging around the house when Trudelle had her little bird hospital. Of course, back then, he brought his wife. She was a pretty little thing. Don't know what happened to her, exactly, but I guess her passing broke old Purdy's heart. Wonder if he remembers her?"

" 'Lost Angel of a ruined paradise,' " Doc said, toasting Purdy. " 'She faded like a cloud which had out-wept the rain.' Percy Shelley, thank you."

Chief Glendale pondered his whiskey. "A couple more of these, Doc, and I guess I'll know what the hell you're talking about."

Josh helped seat Dosie at the table, then took a chair across from her. Nobody had much to say at first until finally Buckets, who was a retired surfman and also feeling little pain thanks to the whiskey, began to tell stories of rescues on stormy nights.

"We got tossed over by that ol' wave and our boat was filled with water and the boat cap'n, he kept saying, 'Pull, boys, that there ship is sinking fast!' And I said, 'But, Cap'n, we've beat her to it. We're already sunk!' And the cap'n looked around, saw all of us with water up to our necks, and roared, 'Well, hurry up and bail, boys, afore we're seen! It ain't in the reggylations for us to be sunk!' "

Keeper Jack got into the swing of things, too, telling a

story of the dolphin named Killakeet Sue that had befriended the fishermen of the island. "I saw her many times from the lighthouse," he said. "She'd come up and just watch me with that big grin on her face. She used to chase the mullet toward the shore during the season, too, and wind them all up in a ball. Once Pump Padgett fell off his boat and she came up and let him hang on to her, took him right into shore. Oh, that was quite a fish, Killakeet Sue was."

"Sue wasn't a fish, Keeper," Doc tut-tutted. "She was a mammal, like you and me."

"She warn't like you or me, Doc!" Keeper Jack exploded. "She was better!"

"You have me there," Doc acknowledged.

"What happened to her?" Dosie asked.

Keeper Jack sorrowfully shook his head. "Nobody knows, Dosie. One day, she just left."

"I hope she found a mate," Dosie said, "and started a family."

"We all hope that, dear," Queenie simpered.

During the stories, Josh allowed himself a furtive glance at Dosie now and again and she caught him at it, which meant she was stealing glances at him, too. While Buckets was drawing a breath, Queenie brought her into the conversation, asking her how she was doing all alone down there on the beach. "I've fallen in love with Killakeet," she said.

"Well, have you found yourself yet?" Queenie asked.

Dosie eyed Josh, then said, "I think a lot, I sleep, I walk, and I imagine what all the possibilities are."

"And what are they?" Queenie asked politely.

"That life pretty much is what you make it," Dosie said.

"Hear, hear," Keeper Jack said, and tossed back another glass of Tennessee's finest.

"Well said, indeed, Dosie," Doc mused. "I believe, young lady, that by surrounding yourself with the rawness of our island, you are learning that the rules of life are what some call the laws of nature."

"I hadn't thought of it quite that way, Doctor," Dosie answered. "But I believe you may be correct."

Preacher put in his two cents' worth: "The laws of nature are those written by God," he said. "So perhaps you are actually learning His plans for you, Miss Crossan."

"God has no plan for us," Doc stated flatly. "We have free will, Preacher, or have you forgotten?"

Preacher had managed to swallow a good amount of Keeper Jack's whiskey, too. "I haven't forgotten, by thunder!" he roared. "And I don't need a broken-down old evolutionist like you to remind me."

Doc laughed. He'd gotten the reaction he was after.

Queenie worked to get the conversation back to where she wanted it. "How about you, Josh?" she asked, startling him at the mention of his name. He had been wondering if he should just go over to Morehead City and demand depth charges from Captain Potts. When he looked blank, Queenie asked, "What's your opinion of Miss Crossan's quest to discover the meaning of life?"

"I haven't had much time to think on it," he said, tucking into his duck with knife and fork. "There's a war on," he added.

Queenie rolled her eyes.

Keeper Jack found himself strangely affected by being at the same table with Josh and Doc and Queenie. With the whiskey nudging him along, he remembered another time when they were all together, when Jacob had been born.

Nineteen years ago and yet he could recall it so clearly. Doc had come down the stairs, his arms bloody to the armpits. "The baby's stuck sideways, Jack," he said. "And Trudelle's bleeding inside."

Keeper Jack slugged back another whiskey and wiped his mouth, remembering how he had just stood there, helpless, unable to say anything. Then Doc had turned and gone back up the stairs. Presently, there was a smack and a thin wail. The baby had been born. It continued to cry but there were no other sounds from the bedroom. Finally, Queenie, who'd been assisting Doc, came down the stairs and collapsed on the rug in front of the fireplace. "Trudelle's left us, Jack," she said, then began to sob.

Josh had been sent earlier to the tower, to tend the light. By some strange instinct, he came into the house at that very moment. One look at his father's stricken face and Queenie sobbing was enough for him to charge upstairs. He returned, his face flushed, and angry. Only twelve years old, he had walked up to his father and struck him as hard as he could in the face, knocking Keeper Jack down.

Keeper Jack took another drink and discovered he was angry and wanted to hurt Josh. Josh, who refused to be a keeper so as to keep the pride and tradition of the Killakeet Thurlows going; Josh who had knocked him down and then two years later lost Jacob through carelessness. *No, he'd lost Jacob because he had coveted a little boat more than the safety of his own brother!* And now Josh had the gall to say he wasn't going to come to a service honoring little Jacob? Keeper Jack peered at Josh and the anger that he'd bottled up over the years started to come uncorked. He picked up his spoon and wagged it at his only remaining son. "Josh, I've got a bone to pick with you."

Everyone at the table stared at Keeper Jack's flushed face.

"The maws of your Maudie Janes have been complaining about you mistreating the boys," he growled, diverting at the last second his complaint into something not quite as personal. "You work them too hard, they say."

"No more than needed, sir," Josh responded respectfully.

Doc interrupted Keeper Jack just as he opened his mouth to say more. "Do you see a U-boat coming over here as in the Great War, Josh?"

"Yes, sir, I do," Josh said forthrightly. "And more than one."

Keeper Jack put down his spoon and filled his whiskey glass again. "Maybe you're getting too big for your britches," he snarled in Josh's direction. "Maybe you ought to listen to somebody besides that damn Negro."

"Bosun Phimble saved my life more than once in Alaska," Josh replied in a stony voice. "And he's the finest man I've ever known."

Dosie, seeing trouble already brewed, tried to get another

topic going. "Queenie," she said, "how goes the preparations for the celebration of the lighthouse?"

"Why, very well, dear," Queenie answered, although her voice betrayed her, trembling a little. "It should be a grand affair."

"I have been working on the invocation," Preacher said, waving a duck drumstick. "It shall recall how the Killakeet Light is a lot like the Lord's light, illuminating ships, rather than souls."

"Well, Preacher," Keeper Jack rumbled, putting aside his anger with Josh for a second, "it ain't exactly accurate to say my light 'luminates ships.' It shines so that ships might see *it,* don't you know, rather than the other way around."

"I suppose you're right," Preacher said, deflated.

"But I get your meaning, Preacher," Keeper Jack went on. "And while you're at it, why don't you gear up a prayer for my lost son? Get it ready for when we put his marker down. Josh here, of course, ain't coming. Says he don't think it means enough."

Josh said nothing, just sat looking down at his plate.

"Stop it!" Dosie said, snapping her eyes at the Keeper. "Do you think Josh needs a reminder of what happened to his brother? Don't you know he lives with it every second of every day?"

The Keeper shrugged and reached for his bottle. "It's the least he could do," he said, "for all that he did."

Josh and the Keeper didn't look at each other for the rest of the evening. The conversation dwindled to nothing. Chief Glendale sang his rendition of "A Bamboo Bungalow for Two," accompanied by Queenie at the piano, which at least kept some semblance of a party mood alive. Midnight came and Keeper Jack, Doc, and the Preacher repaired to Doc's infirmary to drink some more whiskey. Chief Glendale was staggering drunk and Sarah took him home. Dosie and Josh lingered outside the Hammerhead beside the jeep. "I'll drive you back," he said.

"No, let's walk," Dosie said, kicking off her shoes. "Just to clear our heads."

Josh went up to his room and put on the silk scarf she had given him for Christmas and then they walked down the beach, not saying anything. Finally, the tension had built so much, Josh felt compelled to say, "I read your letter."

"Did you understand it?"

"Not a word."

"How about the part where I said I never wanted to see you again?"

"I took that as sort of vague," Josh said, which made Dosie chuckle.

When they reached the gate of Dosie's Delight, Dosie said, "Sit in the rockers with me for a while and let's talk."

They settled into the rocking chairs. The sea crashed before them, low tide. The lights of passing ships twinkled. The lamp in the lighthouse flashed its great silver beam. Josh's rocking slowed, then he leaned over and let his arms rest on his legs. "Thank you for taking up for me," he said. "Daddy will have a big hangover in the morning."

Dosie bent forward until she could look Josh in the eyes. "I think your daddy just got a little frustrated tonight because you won't attend the service for Jacob. You ought to, you know."

"I want to attend," Josh said. "But I can't pretend that it means anything."

Dosie resisted the urge to pat him on the knee. "Josh, I agree with your father. Go to the service. Give him what he wants. I think he needs it, even if you don't."

Josh knew Dosie was right even though he didn't like it. He studied the lights in the darkness, then said, "I'd better shove off." He wanted to say more but he didn't know how.

Josh climbed down the steps into the sand. "I'll see you, Dosie," he said, and went through the gate, which clacked shut behind him. Dosie's heart, which had been racing, slowed and then she found that tears were trailing down her cheeks. She wiped at them with her fingers, then went into the kitchen and leaned against the kitchen counter, looking through the window. In the darkness, all she saw was her reflection looking back. She was startled when she heard the clack of her gate. Her heart, which she supposed had stopped, started beating again. She went outside, to find Josh on the steps. He was lit by the Milky Way and the moon. "I don't want to go," he said.

"I never told you to," she answered.

He climbed the steps and she met him. She buried her face into his chest and his arms went around her. Dosie took Josh's hand and led him inside. The screen door slapped shut behind them while the lights of the ships, red and green and white, kept moving past, each ship awash in the message from the Killakeet Lighthouse: *Move along. All is still safe along these shores.*

# 22

The *U-560* was caught in a vast and potentially deadly storm. Every few hours, Krebs dipped the U-boat below to let the crew rest from the battering, but the currents, surging eastward, were too strong for the electric motors. After battling for a few miles, the batteries dwindled and he was forced to order the U-boat back to the surface to fire up the diesels and recharge. When he did, Krebs yelled at Hans to not waste a second. To surface without power was to risk being rolled over by the huge seas.

It didn't help that only a few veterans were left on board. During the dockyard refurbishment, the Ninth Flotilla commander had redistributed many of *U-560*'s men to other boats in an attempt to put experienced men with all the recruits flooding in from the training centers. The fuzzy-faced replacements, most of them nineteen or twenty years old, had trooped aboard the freshly painted *U-560* with the enthusiasm of children off on a trip to a museum. Krebs had watched them, thinking they were indeed clambering inside a museum, but one of death and destruction. Now, most of them were deathly ill, too sick to rise from their bunks except to puke. Only a few of them had strength enough to moan, but those who did managed to make up for the rest. "For God's sake!" the Chief finally roared down the pressure tube. "Stop all that howling!" The moaning stopped for a few minutes, then started up again. "Babies!" spat the Chief.

"They send us babies!" He filled his ears with cotton.

The Chief had other concerns beside the crew. He was proud of the work he'd overseen in the shipyard. A new deck had been laid in, and the bullet holes in the superstructure repaired and painted over. The engines had been overhauled and the drive machinery taken apart, inspected, and put together again. Even the symbol of the *U-560*, the grinning white shark, had been repainted on the conning tower. But now, after four days of continuous storm-toss, there had come an ominous thumping in one of the drive shafts. It only made its noise at low revolutions and the Chief had no idea what was causing it. If the drive shaft was out of round in some way, it could come apart at any moment. If it had been up to him, he would have turned the boat around and headed back to Brest. But it wasn't up to him. It was up to Krebs, who showed no inclination to do anything but beat westward.

When the batteries were drained, Krebs signaled the chief to bring up the boat again, then climbed onto the conning tower. He was struck by a shrieking wind that clawed at his face like an angry banshee. Three days into the journey, dead reckoning told him he was about halfway across the Atlantic. He crawled along the tower through the horrific wind until he could grasp a safety tether and strap himself in. After closing the tower hatch, Max crawled up beside him and did the same. No lookouts followed. There was no need of them, not in this weather. Even the Canadians wouldn't be out in such conditions.

Krebs stared morosely at the thick, dark clouds sweeping past so near they seemed to be combing his hair. "What a shitty day," he grumped.

Max thought he saw something. *Yes!* It was a small freighter, its lights defiant in the storm. It was atop a huge wave, then disappeared behind it. He tapped Krebs on the shoulder and pointed to where it had been. They watched and then saw the freighter's twin stacks appear, only to disappear once more behind a mountain of water. "Separated from a convoy, I'll wager!" Max yelled over the shriek of the wind.

"She won't make it," Krebs replied. The water ran down his face into his beard. His eyes were red-rimmed from the salt water being blown into them. "She'll be sunk within the hour."

"Poor souls," Max replied.

An enormous wave reared up in front of them. Max only had a moment to duck behind the fairing before it broke over the tower. When he opened his eyes, the tower was completely underwater. Then, abruptly, his head was clear and the wind was howling in his ears while he gasped for air.

Krebs signaled Max to go below. He followed, slithering through the hatch. Max caught him, then the Chief dogged the cover. "Take us down, Chief," Krebs ordered, kneeling in a lake of water and foam and hoping he was going to vomit. He'd swallowed at least a liter of seawater. His stomach lurched and up it came in a greenish spew.

The Chief averted his eyes from Krebs and complied, sending the signal to the engine room. The diesels whined down to let the electric motors catch up. As they did, the deep, ugly beat of what sounded like a bass drum thumped through the submarine. "That damned shaft," the Chief muttered.

Krebs mopped himself as dry as he could with a damp, sour towel, then sat on the cushioned bench behind the tiny navigator's table. Max came back from the galley carrying two mugs of luke-cold coffee. Krebs gratefully took one of them, sipped it, then screwed up his face. "This tastes like shit," he said, putting the mug down.

Max took a healthy swig. "Really? I thought it was closer to cold piss."

Krebs allowed a smile, then unrolled a chart on the desk. "Well, Max, here's my plan. Have a look."

The chart was of the American east coast. Max noted the line that Krebs had drawn tucked into New York harbor and then down the east coast. "Our orders are to operate only off New York, sir," he said.

"So I heard," Krebs replied. "But once a cruise has begun, a commander has to take initiative based on the situation.

Admiral Doenitz himself has said this many times."

"And what is the situation?"

"I think we'll be the first of the six boats across. And therefore we are duty-bound to visit New York. But as soon as we attack there, the Americans will probably be down our throat. So we will let the Type Nines handle the United States Navy and go to where the pickings should be sweet. South. Right here."

Max studied the chart. "Cape Hatteras," he said.

"Or a little farther south." Krebs touched the islands below Hatteras one by one. "Right about here."

"Why there?"

Krebs ran his finger alongside the islands. "Here the Gulf Stream starts its sweep. The Labrador Current is pinched until it's just a sliver. Ships riding north and south come together. It's a choke point."

"What about Vogel? You know he'll be looking for you."

"Who?" Krebs asked, and smiled.

In the bow torpedo room, Harro and the other torpedomen blessed Captain Krebs for taking the *U-560* under. Immediately, the pounding of the waves and the tossing of the boat stopped. After the strange thumping noise passed, the only sound was a few last moans from the boys still desperately sick and the dripping of water from one of the torpedo tubes. The leak wasn't believed to be serious but the steady dripping was annoying. Everything the torpedomen had done to stifle it hadn't worked. "Go and lie under it, Harro," his mate Joachim Felcher told him. "Open your mouth and drink it as it comes out. That will stop its tedious noise."

"You should use it to take a bath, Joachim," Harro answered with a laugh. "You could use one."

"Couldn't we all?" another boy said, and all agreed. Less than a week out of Brest, they were already foul with sweat and grime.

The *U-560* steadied and began what everybody hoped would be an hour of smooth underwater sailing. "Enjoy the quiet time," the Chief said, coming forward to stretch his legs. "We'll be back on the surface soon."

Harro asked, "Chief, have you ever been to America?"

"I was second mate on a freighter that used to go to New York every year or so. We also sailed to Charleston to off-load iron ore we picked up in Africa. Someone told me it was bound for Alabama, which is somewhere out west. Indian country, perhaps. I think the Grand Canyon is there."

"America is a big place," Harro said. "I always wanted to visit it."

"Well, here's your chance," the Chief gibed. "Only I don't think you're going to be very welcome."

"I have relatives in Milwaukee," Joachim said. "They used to write and ask my family to come and visit all the time. If only they knew one of their cousins was on his way!"

"Where is Milwaukee?" Harro asked.

Joachim gave it some thought. "Not too far away from New York, I shouldn't think."

"They haven't asked you to visit lately, I don't suppose?" the Chief asked.

Joachim shrugged. "Since the Führer took power, we haven't heard a word."

The torpedo tube's drip had filled the can beneath it and was slopping over. Harro looked around to see if anyone was going to do anything about it, but apparently no one was. He was one of the few new recruits who hadn't gotten seasick. Sighing, he crawled out of his bunk surrounded by live torpedoes and got the can and replaced it with an empty one. Then he went back into the engine room and poured the water into the bilges. Hans, the ghoulish engine-room officer, glanced at him with disinterest. Hans was mostly deaf after three years of living in the nearly constant clatter of his beloved twin diesels. Harro was a bit afraid of him but other crew members said he was harmless, just driven a bit mad by his job. "Well, the quiet is nice for a change," Harro said to Hans, raising his voice to overcome the man's deafness.

"What do you mean?" Hans demanded. There was a wildness in his eyes.

Harro indicated the diesel engines. "I mean with these two shut down."

Hans lunged for him, grabbed him by his shirt, and slammed him against the air lines that ran along the bulkhead. "You will not speak of my girls this way!"

"Hans!" It was the Chief. He grabbed the man from behind and threw him to the deck plates.

"Get out of my engine room!" Hans blared. He got up on his knees and screamed, "Get out before I throw you out!"

"Calm down, Hans," the Chief said. He nodded to Harro. "Go on, boy. Get back where you belong."

Harro ducked forward through the hatches until he got back to the safety of the bow torpedo room to lie amongst the groaning boys and the thousands of pounds of high explosives. An hour later, the boat rose again. Everything was level and quiet until the deep thumping began that announced the sickness in the drive shaft. Then came the plunging and rolling of the *U-560* on the surface and the din of the diesels raising hell. "At least crazy Hans is happy now," Harro muttered while burying his head under a pillow that stank of hydraulic fluid and his own homesick tears.

# 23

On the first morning of the New Year, Josh and Dosie sat with cups of coffee and looked out across the brightening sea, the sky behind it resplendent with the scarlet and yellow glory of a Killakeet sunrise. After admiring it properly, Josh said, "There's a dance Saturday at the Hammerhead. Why don't we go?"

Dosie set her cup down and leaned over in the rocker as if her stomach hurt, which Josh suspected was not a good sign that she wanted to go to the dance. "Josh, this is so hard for me," she said, after sitting back. "Last night was swell. Real romantic and all. It's what I've been wanting ever since I laid my eyes on you down on Miracle Point. But I keep coming back to the fact that I'm just doing the same thing I've always done, latching onto a guy and then letting him take care of me. I've got to learn to take care of myself. Another time and another place, you and I . . ." She shook her head. "I have to be alone, mostly. Do you understand?"

"Well, mostly you would be, Dosie," Josh said. "There's a war on, you know. I'll be at sea a lot of the time. Hell, I might even get myself killed."

"Don't say that!" she snapped.

Josh's lip went out. "I don't mean to say that I will," he muttered, "just that I might."

"Look, Josh, there's more to that pretty story I told you.

If you knew it all, you'd jump up from that rocker and you couldn't get away fast enough."

"There's a lot you don't know about me, either. For instance, I was married to an Eskimo woman. Of course, they don't say 'Eskimo' in Alaska. She was an Aleut."

Dosie hid her face in her hands. When she parted them, he saw, to his consternation, that she was laughing. "Oh, Josh, everybody knows you were married to a woman named Naanni in Alaska, married according to her tribe, that is." Her expression sobered. "I even know she was killed by renegades and you went after them and killed them one by one."

Josh was astonished. "I didn't think anybody on the island knew all that except Bosun Phimble!"

"I knew it almost from the first day I was back."

"Who told you?"

"Everybody!"

"And you've still had anything to do with me at all?"

"Poor man. You have no idea how a woman thinks, do you?"

Josh hung his head. "I guess not. Are you going to tell me?"

"No. I can't give up the secret. I would be drummed out of the sisterhood."

"Look, Dosie," Josh said, "I don't care about any of that. I mean, we could be friends, couldn't we?"

That struck Dosie as insincere, although she couldn't put her finger on the reason why. "Friends, is it? Like rolling in bed real friendly-like every time you came in from patrol? Yes, I can see me now, me sitting here on this pizer—why the hell do you call a porch a 'pizer,' anyway?—looking out to sea thinking, 'Oh! I can't wait until my lover sailor boy Josh comes home and takes care of little me.' Well, no thank you."

"You drive me crazy," Josh said truthfully.

"Well, I like the hell out of you, Josh Thurlow, and that scares the shit out of me, so there. We've had our tumble and I'm done with you. Good-bye."

Josh jumped up from the rocker. "Fine with me, sister! You've seen the last of this sailor boy."

Dosie's expression dropped and then she threw herself into Josh's arms. "Josh," she said, "hold me."

"I've got you, Dosie," he said.

Then she pushed him away. "No, you don't. Nobody's got me."

"That's it!" Josh cried, and stomped down the steps.

Dosie called after him, "You want to know more of the pretty story? I'll tell you. It wasn't just the trumpet player. I let myself be passed around the entire band. How do you like them apples?"

Josh just stood in the sand, his mouth open. "Apples is not what comes to mind," he said at last. Then he asked, rubbing the back of his neck, "How many were in the band?"

"Six. Seven, counting the manager. You better run, Josh Thurlow."

"That's the first thing you've said all day that makes a lick of sense," he replied, then came back up on the porch and snatched her before she could get away. "I don't care. I ain't no angel, either."

She kissed him so hard their teeth clicked together. Then she tore his shirt open, the buttons flying. "Ah, Josh, you crazy, crazy boy."

He reached under her sweater and drew it over her head, then threw it into the yard where it snagged on her sign, *Dosie's Delight*.

They both nearly tore the screen door off getting it open.

# 24

Cowboy Rex Stewart, carrying his pants, shirt, and boots, gratefully sat down in the chief medical officer's office of the Los Angeles Armed Services Recruiting Center. For the last four hours, he had been poked and prodded until he felt as if the next thing would surely be a brand on his butt. The chief medical officer, whom Rex had been told was the last doctor he would see, was a chubby little man with thick glasses who wore a white lab coat over a brown army uniform. Rex thought he looked a bit like Oliver Hardy, or maybe Fatty Arbuckle. Rex had worked with both of the movie comedians, one time or another.

The doctor tapped Rex's paperwork with a stubby finger and made an observation. "According to this, you've broken nearly every bone in your body."

Rex scratched his head, losing the grip on his boots, which fell to the floor with a double thump. "Well, you work the rodeos and do the flicks, that's pretty much what happens, Doc. All them bones are healed, though."

"What do you do in the flicks?"

"Stuntman, trick rider, gags, you know."

Rex picked up his boots, an ornate, carved pair he'd got down in Arizona while working on *Stagecoach*. John Wayne, the kid who had been the star of the flick, had given the boots to Rex as a gift on wrap day. Rex figured he'd earned them. In a scene where Wayne's character was dragged beneath a wagon behind a thundering team of horses, the director, John Ford, had insisted on take after take. Rex had been the stuntman, and it was only after he was pretty much beat to death that Ford, the fat bastard, finally declared himself satisfied. He had come over and pondered Rex lying in the dirt, groaning. "Get him a drink, he'll be fine," the director snapped, then stalked off. Rex's back had been broken.

The doctor's eyes drifted away from Rex to look out on Hollywood Boulevard. Sports cars were driving up and down and the occasional big Rolls. "I used to work for one of the studios," he said wistfully.

"Yeah? Which one?"

"MGM. I was the physician on call for all the Marx Brothers movies."

Everybody in Hollywood had a story. Rex didn't mind hearing one more, especially if it meant he could sit for a while longer. All the standing in line had been hard on his knees. "So what happened you stopped?"

The doctor shrugged heavily. "One of the brothers came down with the clap. I treated him but then I asked him how he got it. That's the law, you know. Next thing I knew, I was out on my can."

"Let me guess. The producer's wife."

"Close. The director's girlfriend."

"Well, it's a dirty business, Doc," Rex said, and then remembered the real purpose of his visit. "The marines is my first choice, Doc, but I'll be just as happy with the army. Which one am I going to get?"

The doctor sighed, still apparently thinking of his studio days. "Well, you can't be in the marines or the army. And not the navy, either. You can't be in the military at all. You're beat to death. Why, you can hardly walk." He studied Rex's file. "Rex? Is that your real name?"

"It used to be Frank but I got it changed, all legal. I figured Rex had more of a ring to it. But, Doc, never mind about my name. It don't make sense what you're saying. Why, I'm sound as a dollar. I can still ride a bronco with the best of them, lasso a lizard if I had to, and even shoot the eye out of a gnat from a hundred paces. I'm from Montana where they grow us boys tough. Why, surely you can see I can fight, can't you, Doc?"

The chief medical officer could see no such thing. What he could see pretty clearly was the stunt cowboy breaking down in a trench somewhere and two healthy boys having to carry him back to the hospital tent. The doctor took a rubber stamp and inked it on a pad and applied it to the top document in Rex's stack. He gathered the papers and put them in a manila folder. "Go in there"—he indicated a door—"and get dressed. Leave this folder with the clerk just outside. I've stamped you 4-F, unfit for military service."

"Well, damn, Doc, that's a pisser!"

"A lot of men would be happy to be 4-F," the doctor replied amiably. "Go back to work in the flicks and enjoy yourself. I wish I could do the same."

Rex could hardly believe what he was hearing. "Look, Doc, I got to go fight. It's my patriotic duty!"

The doctor shook his head. "Well, you can't and that's that."

Rex got to his feet, although slowly. The doc was right about his bones being broken and all. And he had this trick knee, too, which he'd failed to mention. He carried his clothes inside the little toilet, got dressed, and went on past the doctor, who was talking on the telephone while looking out the window. A lot of folks tended to look out the window in Hollywood, recalling what they'd once been, and they talked a lot on the telephone, too, mostly about nothing. Hollywood was filled up with people who'd once been one thing or another and now talked on the telephone about nothing. Rex stepped out of the office and was about to drop the folder on the clerk's desk and go about his business when a man dressed in a dark blue uniform came up to him. Rex guessed he was in the navy.

"You Rex Stewart?" the man asked.

Rex said he was. "What of it?"

"The doc in there called me. I work in an office right around the corner. I hear you're a stuntman."

"You ever hear of Gene Autry?"

"Sure."

"Well, he ain't never done a thing on the screen what I ain't actually done it."

"So you can ride a horse?"

Rex thought maybe the man was a bit slow. "Before I started doing gags for the studios, I was a champ rodeo rider. But that don't seem to cut much ice around this place. They say I ain't good enough to fight."

The man indicated the manila folder in Rex's hand. "Could I see that, please?"

Rex didn't see the harm in it so he handed over the folder. The man looked through his papers. "Did you ever think about joining the Coast Guard?"

Rex rubbed his jaw. "You mean like with boats?"

"Pretty much."

"I don't know nothing about boats. I'm a trick rider, mister."

The man—he had some stripes around the sleeve of his jacket that made him into an officer, Rex supposed—nodded toward two chairs along the wall. When they sat down, the man said, "Look, Rex, my name is Captain Phil Revelez, United States Coast Guard. I'm on the scout for boys just like you. The Coast Guard's organizing horse troops to patrol along the coast. How'd you like to join up?"

Rex never liked to give a quick answer to anything. He mulled it over and came up with a question. "What the hell does the Coast Guard know about horses?"

Revelez shook his head. "Not a blamed thing. We're looking for someone like you to help us out."

"Would I carry a rifle?"

Revelez shrugged. "I don't know."

"Well, what *do* you know, Cap'n?"

"I know that we've got a couple thousand miles of coast to guard and we need boys on horses to do it."

Rex chewed on that one for a second. "What kind of horses?"

Captain Revelez shrugged again. "Do you have a horse?"

"Sure. His name's Joe Johnston, named after the Civil War general. He's a trick pony."

"Could you bring it? That would save us having to get one for you."

Rex liked the idea of keeping Joe Johnston with him. Joe was a smart horse, although he was from Texas, which accounted for the fact that he could get sullen from time to time. "I reckon I might. But if I did, I'd want to carry my rifle. I've got a good one, a Winchester ninety-three. I can hit a fifty-cent piece a hundred yards away backwards over my shoulder using a mirror."

"I'll make a note of that. So, are you and Joe Johnston going to join up?"

Rex looked around, saw all the other boys, children really, walking around in their Skivvies and bare feet. They would soon be slugging it out with the enemy, teeth and toes. He was being offered a beach to ride along where there probably wouldn't be anything more than seagulls to watch, but it was helping out the war and it was better than nothing. "I reckon we might be," he said before he could think of a reason why not other than the likely boredom.

Revelez gave Rex a document to sign. Rex signed it without reading it. He never read his contracts with the studios, either. There had to be a little trust in the world and nobody trusted others like a cowboy, for good or for evil.

"There's something else, Rex. I have a little boy . . ."

"You want Gene Autry's autograph, don't you?"

"Yes. Yes, I do."

"What's your boy's name?"

"Uh . . . Phil."

"It's for you, isn't it?"

"Yes."

"Just don't forget I'm going to carry me a rifle."

"I won't."

Rex thought it was time for more particulars. "When will I leave and where will I go?"

Captain Revelez took the form with Rex's signature and put it in his inside jacket pocket. "We'll send you a letter with a train ticket for you and Joe Johnston," he said. "It could be a week from now or even a month. Where? Well, one coast or the other, I guess." He stood and helped Rex to his feet when he saw the cowboy was having trouble with his knee. "Welcome to the Coast Guard, Rex."

"So I just wait?" Rex asked.

"Yes. Your pay and allowances won't begin until you get that letter and you go on active duty."

"What do I do until then?"

Captain Revelez handed Rex a card. "That's got my address and phone number on it. If you know of any other stuntmen or trick riders or cowboys who might want to get in on this, send them my way, especially if they've got their own horses. Otherwise, you can keep making movies until you hear from us. Oh, and get that autograph, please. Just send it to the address on the card."

"When do I get a uniform?"

Revelez looked embarrassed. "I don't know. It would help if you got your own."

"OK. I supply my own horse and rifle and uniform. This Coast Guard's a pretty cheap outfit, Captain. Sort of like one of those independent producers, I reckon. Can I wear cowboy boots?"

"I don't see why not."

"Chaps?"

Revelez thought it over. "That might be pushing things."

"OK." Rex put on his hat, a big white one like Gene wore, shook the captain's hand, then clomped through the recruiting station and headed home, which was a little place he had over in the San Fernando Valley. Some youngsters were sitting around waiting for their physicals. When they saw the bowlegged man with his ornate leather boots and tall white cowboy hat, they were stirred with curiosity. "Say, mister," one of them called, "you join the cavalry?"

"Naw," Rex said. "The Coast Guard. Don't I look like a sailor?"

The puzzled expressions of their faces told Rex they didn't think he looked like a sailor at all. "Well, damn," he said as he went out on the sunny street. Of all the things he'd figured would happen when he'd come down to the recruiting station, this sure wasn't one of them. Then he got excited about his uniform. It had been a while since he'd seen Cindy, the costume lady over at Columbia, and now he had a good reason for a visit. She was a sweetheart. He'd even offered to marry her once. She'd laughed in his face and then taken him to her bed and kept him in it for a day and a night. What a sweet little place Hollywood was, all in all, filled with pretty swell folks. He'd miss it and them, a little bit than more. *And wait'll Gene hears what I've done,* he said to himself, and it made him laugh. *Ol' boy will have to do some riding on his own for a change!*

# 25

The conning-tower control room of the *U-560* was silent except for a few clicks and whirs emanating from the periscope gears. Krebs pressed against its eyepiece and surveyed the night sea above. Though the sun had set, it wasn't dark. A carnival of lights from the tall buildings and the buoys and the ships at anchor lit everything in a dazzling yellowish glow. This was the entrance to the harbor of New York City. Krebs had never seen anything like it. He offered the periscope to Max. Max looked for a moment, then shook his head. "Maybe the war's been called off," he said.

"No. The Americans just haven't figured out they're in one," Krebs said. "We beat all the Type Nines across."

A lookout reported, "A big freighter standing in, *Kaleu*."

Krebs watched the freighter coming closer, then said, "The water's too shallow here for us to attack. The Americans might be asleep but we'd surely wake them up with a torpedo. Let's get a little sea room."

The Chief put the *U-560* into a slow turn. The freighter wallowed past, heading in. It took no note of a German U-boat passing just a hundred yards away even though the harbor lights made it completely visible. "I could hit that tanker with a rock," one of the lookouts murmured.

"Sir," Max said, "it is my duty to remind you that the operation isn't supposed to begin until tomorrow."

"Thank you, Max," Krebs replied. "But this is too good to wait. Nobody's expecting any German submarines around here. Let's make some noise."

An hour's run and they were in deeper water. They had never been out of sight of a freighter or a tanker during the entire time. Krebs felt the old excitement stir his heart. "Well, let's pick one out," he said. "How about that big one over there?"

Max thought it seemed wrong to determine whether men would live or die on a whim, but Krebs was right. There were so many targets, there was no other way. "I agree, *Kaleu*," he whispered. The lookouts had put down their binoculars and had their arms draped over the fairing. Max thought the youths had no sense of danger whatsoever. In truth, neither did he. Everything was tranquil.

*This is it,* Krebs thought. *The start of the American campaign.* He called down his calculations to the bow torpedo room. The report came back that all was in readiness. "Tube one," he called. *"Los!"*

The torpedo leaped from the tube with a spew of bubbles, its electric motor zinging. Krebs watched its white trail disappear into the gloom and counted off the seconds. But nothing happened. Krebs heard one of the lookouts whisper, "He missed her."

"Shut up, you," Max ordered.

Krebs found himself shaken. He had never missed such an easy shot before. He used the torpedo aimer again, called down the numbers to the chief, who reported that another eel was in tube two. He ordered, *"Los!"* and there was a spew of bubbles forward. Finally, orange flames blossomed on the side of the big freighter and thunder rolled across the placid water. "I think we just woke America up," the Chief said.

Krebs nodded, though he was frowning. He was still trying to figure out why it had taken him two torpedoes to do it.

# 26

The *Maudie Jane* eased along the Stream. Sunrise was still a few hours away. Josh came up on deck with a mug of hot coffee that Millie had thrust in his hand as he passed through the galley. He was feeling pretty good. Jimmy had returned home the day before, fully trained on the sonar and filled with excitement about the new friends he'd made aboard the *Diana*. Now, he was below in the sonar closet, his earphones clamped on, as happy as a boy with a new Lionel train set.

Josh gauged the movement of the sea by the feel of the deck. There was a bit of a chop but a glance to the northeast revealed a star-littered sky. There was no storm coming, at least not right away. He went inside the wheelhouse and found Phimble sitting on a stool with one hand on the wheel, keeping the boat meandering generally north. Stobs was bent over his radios.

Phimble glanced over his shoulder. "Good morning, Mister Thurlow. Stobs has been picking up some interesting traffic."

"Some merchie ships have been blown up," the radioman said. "They've been screaming their heads off about a minefield. They say the navy's strung one off New York and New Jersey and not told them a thing about it."

Josh and Phimble exchanged glances. "What's the navy say?"

"Nothing," Stobs said. "Coast Guard, neither."

"Call Doakes. See what they know."

"Stobs has been trying that, Skipper," Phimble said. His voice was weary. "They don't answer. Chief Glendale's probably working on the lighthouse celebration."

Josh sipped his coffee while he thought things over. He supposed it was possible a minefield might have broken loose and drifted into the sea-lanes. Possible, but not likely. He took the wheel from Phimble. "Go get some rest, Eureka. It could be a long day."

Krebs still didn't know what to make of it. Since the *U-560* had reached American waters, it was as if it had entered an alternate universe. Even though he had torpedoed two freighters, no one onshore seemed to care. There was no evidence that the United States was at war. Cities and towns were lit up like Christmas trees. Cars could be seen moving along coastal roads. Buoy lights danced everywhere. Lighthouses threw their beams in grand strokes. And ships! The ships were cruising with full running lights on, and not one of them zigzagging. They were all going straight as ducks in a shooting gallery.

The thing that worried Krebs most was running out of torpedoes. The *U-560* had headed across the Atlantic with fourteen, the usual complement for a Type Seven boat. A bit unnerved after missing the first shot, he'd attacked the next two ships with a spread of two torpedoes apiece. All four eels had struck home and sent the targets to the bottom, but that left him with only eight for the remainder of the patrol. He began to think about using his deck gun or perhaps the tactic sometimes used by U-boats during the Great War: stopping ships, boarding, and scuttling them. There didn't seem to be anybody around to stop him.

The lookouts reported that more ships were dying out on that inky sea, all burning like bonfires. Obviously, some of the other U-boats had gotten in on the carnage a day early, too. Although strict radio silence was being observed by the boats, BdU sent a message to the *Paukenschlag* boats to rendezvous with *Kapitän* Vogel at a point thirty kilometers northeast of Montauk Point. Krebs pretended he hadn't received the message. He suspected all the other commanders were going to do the same. Vogel would be incensed, but Doenitz would forgive them when they reported spectacular success.

After each attack, Krebs had cautiously ordered the boat to submerge. When no warships showed up, he had brought the *U-560* back to the surface. By then, the torpedoed freighters were settled low in the water, and the lookouts were entertained by the American crews trying to get their lifeboats launched. They were apparently ill-trained to abandon ship. Usually only a few of the boats got swung out before the freighters sank, leaving the sailors floundering in the water. Since no one came out to rescue them, many men drowned while the Germans watched. One lookout was brave enough to ask Max why they didn't try to rescue the Americans. "Couldn't we take them aboard, sir?"

Max reminded the lookout there was little room on a U-boat for prisoners. He also nodded toward the sky. "You're new so you have no concept of being attacked from the air. This close to shore . . . they could be on us in seconds if we stopped to take aboard survivors."

"But there are no aircraft, sir," the lookout said, pointing to a sky empty of everything except the stars, the moon, and a few clouds.

Max had no answer to the lookout's correct observation. "There is something very odd going on here," Max told Krebs.

"Yes," Krebs replied. "Perhaps we have died and gone to U-boat heaven."

Krebs ordered the *U-560* to continue south and went below. He sat on the navigator's couch and tried to make sense of it all. Max, standing nearby with a mug of coffee, said, "Don't they understand that they're in a war? I expected to see convoys, at least. But single ships going back and forth fully lit up without a care! It's amazing."

"I think Admiral Doenitz is going to be very happy,"

Krebs replied. "But the Americans must try to stop us, eventually. If they don't, we're going to knock them out of the war. Even they can't build ships faster than we're sinking them." Krebs crossed his arms, marveling. "We're like wolves let loose in the flock while the sheepdogs are asleep."

"And the sheep don't even recognize us as wolves," Max added.

Krebs bent over the chart of the American Atlantic coast. "The second happy time of the U-boat brethren," he mused. "But how long will it last?" He pondered the chart, then put his finger on Norfolk. "Here's the key, Max. Will the Atlantic Fleet come out or just sit and do nothing?"

"They have to come out, sir."

"Then what's taking them so long?" When Max didn't answer, Krebs said, "If they do, they'll likely head north toward New York. That's why we're going south. We'll motor right past Norfolk and set up station below Hatteras. Before the fleet can turn around, we'll have bagged our limit and be halfway back to France."

"The boys will be pleased to hear it. This will be our shortest and most successful cruise."

Krebs rolled up the chart. "I screwed up that first shot, Max."

"It happens, sir."

"Not to me."

"Is there something wrong?" Max asked gently. "Did something happen while you were on leave?"

Krebs was tempted to unburden himself to his second-in-command. Max was the kind of man who could be sympathetic without condescension. But Krebs could not bring himself to do it. Too many years of habitually keeping his personal life secret from the men in his command overruled the nearly overwhelming urge to share his aching heart. "Another time, Max," he answered but then surprised himself when he added, "And I promise there will be another time."

Although disappointed that Krebs had again chosen not to confide in him, Max didn't force the issue. He did, however, begin to worry. It seemed peculiar to think that Krebs, of all people, might crack, but it was not unknown for the most stalwart of commanders to suffer a sudden mental breakdown. He decided he had better watch Krebs carefully for the rest of the cruise. As much as he liked and respected him, Max had no intention of dying under a mad commander.

The *U-560* ran on the surface through the night, crossing the placid New Jersey waters and on down the Maryland coast. Krebs and Max came up on the tower and saw the lights of dozens of freighters and tankers coming at them like auto headlights on a main Berlin *Strasse*. Krebs wanted a tanker and kept telling the lookouts to find him one, though he doubted if the children he had aboard would know one if it ran them down.

Around two in the morning, a lookout called Krebs's attention to a ship with a high bow, an indented stern, and masts hinged with booms fore and aft of the wheelhouse. Her running lights were ablaze and her name on the bow could clearly be read: *Metropolis General*. She was a tanker, and all alone. The Chief looked her up in the ship's register. "Eight thousand and forty-six tons, owned by General Oil."

Since the tanker rode low in the water, she had to be filled to the brim with petroleum. "Let's go after her," Krebs said to the Chief. And then to Max, "Why don't you take over? It'll be good practice."

Max's face registered surprise. Krebs had never passed up such a juicy target before. "Me, sir?"

Krebs took Max aside. "Just do it, Max. I don't want to miss this one. Put your first torpedo in her bow. If she spots it coming in, she'll try to turn away but you'll still catch her. And loaded as she is, she'll burn."

Max started to say something encouraging to Krebs, then thought better of it. If Krebs was unsure of himself, anything Max said would be an insult. "Chief, hard aport," he ordered, "and maintain an easterly heading."

Max went to the torpedo aiming device, thinking through each step as he peered through the special binoculars set atop it. It was a textbook situation: clear skies, a placid sea, the target in front of him lit up like a beer tent at *Oktoberfest*. He could almost imagine the crew aboard the tanker sitting around the mess table singing, laughing, drinking, having a wonderful time. There appeared to be no lookouts at all. Max entered the numbers, then called for a spread of two torpedoes to be launched from the bow tubes. *"Los!"* he barked, and watched as the first and second torpedoes he had ever launched sped straight and true. He discovered that he was thrilled.

"Chief Glendale's on the horn, sir."

Josh was still at the wheel. "Ask him what he wants."

Stobs told him and then put the Chief on the speaker. "Tell Mister Thurlow his daddy said not to forget the celebration nor the fish. Two tuna."

Josh had forgotten the tuna. Ready O'Neal was in the wheelhouse as lookout. "Roust out the Jacksons, Ready. Get them to catch me a couple of big tuna for the lighthouse party."

Josh started the *Maudie Jane* on a slow turn toward a more southerly direction. They'd run along and let the Jacksons catch their fish, then head west to Killakeet. As Josh had predicted, the Keeper, after sobering up, had come to Josh on the military dock after patrol and apologized for his outburst at the Hammerhead. "The thing is, Daddy, you're right," Josh had replied. "I'll attend the service for Jacob. The only thing I can't do is be the next keeper."

Josh recalled with a pang of conscience how the Keeper had wearily shaken his head. "I won't condemn you for it," he said, "but God knows, Josh, it is a bitter thing to be the last Thurlow of the light."

Ready interrupted Josh's unhappy recollection. He had been listening to Stobs's radio and the merchies crying for help. "I meant to tell you, sir. Chief Glendale gave me a rifle to put on board. It's an old Enfield from the Great War. He gave me about twenty rounds for it, too."

"Good old Glendale. Well, roust it out and keep watch. It's better than nothing."

Ready headed below, to get the Jacksons to catch fish, and to bring up the only working weapon aboard, a World War I rifle and twenty bullets, this to defend the east coast of the United States of America.

The tanker burned furiously. Men on fire twirled and danced on her deck. Some of them leaped into the sea, puffs of smoke marking where they hit. Only a few lifeboats were in the water and they were on fire, too. Max's skin crawled at the sight. He had caused the carnage. During all his years at war, he'd never seen anything like these burning men. Their screams carried across the water, hideous, wretched wails.

Radioman Pretch came up. "Sir, shall I signal BdU?"

Krebs lowered his binoculars. "We're supposed to maintain radio silence for another day."

"I picked up a signal from *Kapitän* Froelich. He's claiming three sinkings. He's already received a congratulations back from Admiral Doenitz."

"The bastard," Krebs growled, then laughed. "Good for him! Anything from Vogel?"

"Yes, sir. He's complaining to BdU that no one showed up at his rendezvous."

"What rendezvous? I must have missed that message."

"Yes, sir."

A ball of flame, looking like a bright orange cauliflower, rose from the stern of the tanker. The flames had breached the last bulkhead. "What signals from this tanker?" Krebs asked Pretch.

"They say they think they hit a mine."

"We're sitting here in plain sight. A blind man could see us!"

Pretch shrugged. "That's what they're saying."

A deep rumble thrummed across the gap of ocean between the U-boat and the tanker. Then the crackle of flames. More men on fire leaped overboard like falling meteors.

"Another tanker, *Kaleu!*" a lookout called, his youthful voice cracking. It was Harro. Krebs had studiously ignored the boy during the voyage across the Atlantic. He didn't want any rumors of favoritism to get started, especially since he meant to implement a little of it. He had in mind to take the boy out of the torpedo room and make him into a radio and sound-detection operator. He knew Miriam would have liked the idea. In any case, Pretch could use the help.

He savored a pleasant memory of Miriam while glancing at Harro. The boy's face was even thinner than he recalled, and very pale. "Well done, Seaman Stollenberg," he said.

"Thank you, sir," Harro replied.

"Did you hear that?" Joachim whispered to Harro. "The captain knows your name!"

"We grew up in the same place," Harro whispered back.

"In a castle?"

"No, an orphanage."

That left Joachim confused. "Von Krebs grew up in an orphanage?"

"I'll explain everything later," Harro said importantly.

Pretch was still waiting for an answer on whether to transmit to BdU. "Go on, Pretch," Krebs said. "Transmit our news. Two freighters and one tanker sunk. Estimate a total of eighteen thousand tons."

Another explosion aboard the tanker caused all the lookouts to gasp in unison. A wall of fire seemed to be walking up the deck pushed by a boil of smoke. Men were running away from the wall but they had nowhere to go.

"I wish it would go ahead and sink," one of the boys on the machine gun crew said in a small voice.

Krebs looked toward the thin, brown smudge that marked the coast. There was still no sign of a single ship coming out to help. Max was also looking around, in the air, along the eastern horizon. "Nothing," the Chief said, also taking a look around. "No aircraft, no destroyers, not even a rowboat from the United States Navy."

Krebs lowered his binoculars. "Come on, boys. Let's sink this next tanker coming up on us, then we'll ask for news from BdU. Perhaps we've won the war and just don't know it."

"I wish that was the truth," Max muttered. "We could end this and go home."

Krebs could not let the comment pass. "The only home we have right now, Max, is the *U-560*."

# 27

January 19 finally arrived. Paper lanterns hung all around the lighthouse parapet. More were hung from the pin oak and juniper trees and on the Keeper's pizer. A wooden stage, built out of planks from the wreck of the Beaufort fishing boat *Loggerhead,* was at the base of the light and decorated with the hand-painted insignia of the old Lighthouse Service. The *Loggerhead*'s flotsam had come washing up not more than a hundred yards south of the lighthouse, which made it easy for the volunteer carpenters to build the stage. No one thought much about the coincidence. It was expected that the sea would provide for the celebration. A band played, Ready on the fiddle, Bobby on the banjo, Again on the harmonica, Once on the washboard, and Millie on the jug.

It was a glorious night, the skies clear, the Milky Way like a silver river meandering across the heavens. The moon was a bright yellow crescent, looking so close that a long-armed man might think to touch it. There was a breeze from the southwest, but just enough to rustle the needles on the juniper trees and waft along the delicious aroma of the big tuna slow-roasting over an open pit of charcoal. A long table, also built from *Loggerhead* planks, was laden with hush puppies, oysters, clams, slaw, and gallons of punch. More than a few bottles of hooch, both legal and illegal, were making their way into the punch. Everybody was getting happier by the minute. Off the coast, in the darkness, lights moved steadily past, the great ships carrying their cargoes north and south, unaware of the celebration of the sweeping beam that was keeping them safely away from Bar Shoals.

Josh stood on the beach and worried over the running lights of the ships passing by. Dosie strolled up to join him. She was wearing a flower-patterned, ankle-length, silk-and-nylon frock with a pin-tucked bodice that showed her off in spectacular fashion. She was carrying a glass of punch. "What's wrong?" she asked.

"Ships are dying out there, Dosie. Up north."

"Can you do anything about it?"

"No."

"Then have a drink. Try to enjoy yourself for an evening. This is a celebration of your family as much as the lighthouse."

Josh had a flask filled with Mount Gay in his leather jacket. He pulled it out and took a hit. "Did you miss me while I was out patrolling?"

"Not a bit. I told you I don't need you."

He smiled. "Why don't we go inside the lighthouse and you can show me how much you don't need me? There's a lock on the lantern room, you know."

"Can you turn the light off, too?"

"Why would I want to do that? I'd love to see you lit up by eighty thousand candlepower."

"You really know how to sweet-talk a girl, don't you?"

"It's part of our training. *Semper Paratus* is our motto, you know. That means—"

" 'Always ready.' You told me that at the Hammerhead, remember? You Coast Guard boys need to get another line. Anyway, I made an A in Latin. But don't get yourself all pumped up, mister. I'm just here to celebrate the lighthouse, not the lighthouse keeper's son."

"Did I tell you how great you look tonight?"

"No, but I'm listening."

"You're gorgeous. I love that dress."

"All the ladies tonight are knockouts," Dosie replied. "All

the orders to Sears Roebuck came in just in time. I noticed Amy Guthrie even wearing white pumps."

"They're all jealous of you."

"Not Willow. Now, there's a pretty girl."

"Pretty but not right."

Dosie's smile faded. "You know what she told me the other day when I was in to see Doc?"

"Why were you in to see Doc?"

Dosie snickered. "I'm not pregnant, if that's what you're worrying about."

"Not a bit," he lied. "I just hope you're not sick."

"I'm not sick. I just went in with Herman to get his stitches out. Do you want to hear what Willow said?"

"If I said I didn't, I bet you'd still tell me."

"You're right. Do you remember she said I ought to protect the sand?"

"Something like that."

"Well, this time she said I would find him in the sand."

"Him who?"

Dosie finished her punch and borrowed Josh's flask. She took a long drain. "My, that'll put hair on your chest."

"I sure hope not, in your case. Him who?"

Dosie whistled out a breath. "You know Willow. That's all she said."

Josh and Dosie fell silent and watched for a little while longer the shipping lights sliding past. Then Josh said, "We'll be fighting soon, and just out there."

Dosie was a little drunk. She shrugged, then put her arm around Josh's waist. "That's what you've been training for, I guess," she said. "Give 'em hell."

"I guess I might," he said, oddly encouraged even though he still didn't have any depth charges or ammunition for the machine gun.

"You know," Dosie said, "if you had something with a picture of a Trojan warrior in your pants pocket, I might consider seeing if that lock on the lantern room works."

"Who told you?"

"Mrs. Mallory saw her mister slipping you certain supplies."

"You women think you're pretty smart, don't you?"

"No. We *know* we are. Eighty thousand candlepower, you say? That would shine right through your clothes, I'll bet."

Josh grinned and draped his arm around her shoulders while she leaned in tight. "It might, but if it doesn't work, I have another solution."

"You have a dirty mind, Josh Thurlow," Dosie said. "It's one of the things I like about you."

Preacher was first up on the stage to give the invocation. He had managed to get a snootful of the doctored punch and some folks would later say that it made him a bit resentful as a result. He'd also been spending a lot of time out on the Stream aboard this workboat or that and had developed a great empathy for the hardships of fishermen. A bandage on his thumb indicated a recent accident that probably wasn't helping his attitude. Whatever the reason, his invocation was a bit testy.

"Dear Lord," Preacher said, "on this island, we are ever mindful of your miracles because they are always near us. We go out each day and dodge your storms and try to make a living, hard as it is at times. We fish for your fish and You knock us around to make us earn them. Your clams we go stomping for and sometimes you have a stingray throw a barb in our legs. We catch Your crabs and they pinch us."

Preacher continued, "We thank You for all of it, don't think we don't, the days of clear skies that you occasionally give us and the days of storms that are Your usual. All of it fits within Your plan, yea, we know that well enough, though we might not understand any of it, including that sometimes an unworthy preacher hits his thumb with a hammer while trying to patch up *Your* church. All is according to Your design, I'm sure, and we humbly accept it, I swear we do.

"But we ask You, dear Lord, to bless this assembly as we celebrate something we did pretty much by ourselves some fifty years ago by the piling up of bricks to make a light that shines across Your tossing seas and Your awful shoals. All we wanted to do was keep those ships out there safe. That's not too much to ask, is it, Lord? I hope You don't think so. So bless us, dear Lord, and stave off the other things You like to test us with, at least for this evening. In Jesus' name we pray, amen."

Somebody helped Preacher off the stage and the church choir came up and Queenie O'Neal came out and stood in front of them. "Next thing we're going to do is sing the national anthem," she said.

The choir began to sing. Everybody joined in except for the little boys and girls who were mindlessly playing tag on the fringes of the crowd. Josh and Dosie sneaked back during the anthem, having finished their tour of the lighthouse cupola. Josh climbed up onstage and sat beside his father.

After the choir filed off the stage, Captain Potts, the commander of the Coast Guard patrol boat squadron in Morehead City, stood up and gave his speech. Captain Potts was a spiffy little officer who strutted around like a banty rooster. He had an elfin face that, under the dim glow of the lanterns, made him look thirty years younger than he was, which was forty-four. He extolled the virtues of the Lighthouse Service and all the good work it had done before being absorbed by the Coast Guard, which, according to him, had been a good thing because there was no better service than his.

"Now we are here to celebrate the Lighthouse Service's finest moment," Captain Potts said from his boy's face. "That was when it built this grand edifice behind us, the Killakeet Lighthouse. The Killakeet Lighthouse has a magnificent record of service." Then Captain Potts went on a lot longer, into the history of the lighthouse and a lot more besides. The crowd became a little restless. He sensed it and ended his speech by saying, "But what do I know? I'm just a dit-dot begomer." Because of his last reference, he got not only tremendous applause but a chorus of agreement.

Captain Potts sat down and Keeper Jack stood up. "Fellow Killakeeters," he said. "I am honored by all of you today, especially my good friend Captain Potts, who is not a begomer or scarcely a dit-dot, either. We agree with him on how important it is to protect this coast, and to rescue those who find misfortune along it, and to maintain all the equipment necessary to keep the lanes open and the ships moving so that disasters can be avoided.

"You know the history of the Thurlows. We've been on this island for two hundred years and maybe more. We were wreckers at first, like most of your families were, and were considered outlaws. But when the Lighthouse Service came, it changed us. It made us into better people by offering us a chance to serve, and by God, we've served ever since.

"My family are the keepers of the light on this island. But every man, woman, and child who lives on Killakeet is a keeper of the light, too. You keep the light when you're at sea in your workboats, watching what's going on and reporting what you've seen. You keep the light when you look out your windows while you're washing the dishes or when you're hanging out the laundry and take note of what's happening in our front yard, which is the ocean. This light"—the Keeper raised his arm in the direction of the lighthouse—"as magnificent as it is, is merely a symbol of the greater light, the light of the people of Killakeet . . ."

Phimble appeared out of the darkness, crept up to the back of the stage, and tugged on the cuff of Josh's pants. Josh looked down between his knees. "Whatever do you want, Eureka?"

"Sir, something to see."

Josh slipped off the stage and followed the bosun to the lighthouse and up the spiral staircase, emerging on the parapet. Phimble didn't have to tell Josh where to look. There was what appeared to be a fire on the sea. While his father was talking about everybody on Killakeet watching the ocean, only a Hatterasser had actually been on the job.

Josh looked down at the glowing lanterns, the people clustered around the stage. There was applause at something the Keeper had just said. At sea, the fire suddenly flared, followed by a long rumble.

"She's been hit again," Phimble said.

At what sounded like a thunderclap, Keeper Jack stopped talking and everyone stood still for a moment, then moved toward the beach. A fire seaward burned bright, then was seemingly quenched, only to brighten again. Preacher stumbled through the crowd and fell to his knees. The flames jumped before his eyes and he called out in a wailing voice: " 'And I stood up upon this sand, and saw a beast rise up out of the sea. And all the world worshiped the beast, saying, Who is able to make war with him?' "

While everybody looked at Preacher in shocked silence, he tore open his shirt as if daring the beast to plunge its fangs in his chest. "The revealed truth," he said, then pitched face-first into the sand.

# 28

As soon as the *U-560* arrived off Cape Hatteras, it caught a freighter slipping past Diamond Shoals. Krebs turned over the attack to Max, who used a single torpedo from the stern tube, and the freighter went down fast. When a double explosion was observed west of the island marked on the chart as Killakeet, Krebs crept in closer. After idling the diesels, the tower watch began to hear terrible screams, different from the ones they'd heard coming from the merchant sailors. These were the cries of women and children.

Krebs leaned on the fairing of the tower and listened across the dark water. "What do you make of it, Max?"

"A passenger vessel, *Kaleu*," Max said in a grim voice.

There was another flash of light and then more thunder. Just for a moment, Krebs thought he could make out the silhouette of the ship being attacked, a sleek ocean liner. "Whoever did this is still working her over."

"Look there, sir," Max said, pointing. "A light coming from shore. Let's hope it's a rescue vessel. It is a terrible thing a German U-boat has done this night."

"Unless it carried a neutral flag, it was a fair target, Max," Krebs observed.

"Maybe so, *Kaleu*. But there are so many other targets! Why a passenger ship?"

Krebs said aloud his suspicions. "*Kapitän* Vogel may have his own reasons."

"Vogel," Max said with distaste. "He should be brought up on charges for this."

Krebs rounded on Max. "Keep your voice down," he hissed. "Or it could be you who's brought up on charges." He nodded toward the lookouts. Although their posture indicated massive indifference to what their Lieutenant Max had just said, who knew their true feelings? The potential for party spies amongst a crew always existed, even though it was unlikely, considering the death toll aboard U-boats. Why bother to ferret out disloyal U-boat men? They were all eventually going to die, anyway.

"You think Vogel found out we were heading down here?" Max asked.

"No. I suspect it was his intention all along. The others will probably end up down here, too. It's an obvious choke point."

"But Doenitz approved Vogel's idea of concentrating on New York."

"The Admiral has always recommended flexibility. He won't complain when he sees the score."

The Chief brought up the shipping register. "I'd put her as the *Lady Morgan,* sir. A Canadian passenger ship."

"Unforgivable!" Max snapped.

Krebs started to reprimand Max again, then decided it didn't much matter. If a Nazi informant had heard, the damage was already done. He went back to studying the light coming out from the island. "It may be a rescue ship," he said. "But it may also have teeth. In any case, there's no reason for us to stick around. Chief, take us out a few miles. Let's see who we can catch coming around Hatteras or up from Lookout."

The Chief had a bit of bad news. "Hans wants to inspect the coupling on the port shaft before we move again."

"Dammit! Can't you fix that thing?"

"We don't even know what's wrong with it," the Chief replied with a shrug.

Krebs sighed. "All right, Chief. We'll sit here for a while. But keep the electric motors on-line. I want to be able to maneuver if necessary. I don't trust that vessel coming from shore."

The screams across the water suddenly increased. "She's going down," Max said of the *Lady Morgan*.

The boys of the *Maudie Jane* toiled on the heaving, oily sea. Although she was dead, lying spent on a bottom of sand at twenty fathoms, the remains of the *Lady Morgan* kept surfacing. Deck chairs, life rings, coils of line, and bodies popped randomly to the surface. Nearly everything that floated had to be inspected to make certain it wasn't a survivor or a body. Bobby manned the searchlight but the narrow beam barely penetrated the smoke that covered the sea.

At Josh's order, Ready began to fire a Very gun every ten minutes, lofting a flare into the sky to burst into a bright ball of light before falling back. The smoke hindered the effect of the flares, and the result was a confusing kaleidoscope of shifting light and shadow patterns across the choppy sea. Most of the boys were spaced around the deck with boat hooks, all straining to see.

Phimble slowly maneuvered the *Maudie Jane*, placing her alongside each bobbing piece of debris, lifeboat, or floating body that the boys called out. The eighty-three-footer was not a stable platform. She dipped and wallowed at slow speed, then rocked and pitched when stopped.

Over and over, the hollow thumps of boat hooks striking the gunwales were followed by the sound of water falling back into the sea as something was hauled out. Bodies were laid out between the two empty depth-charge racks. At first, blankets were used to cover the bodies, but they were soon needed to warm the survivors huddling in shivering clumps. When a woman became hysterical, Josh sent Again to take care of her. Talking to her all the while, the Jackson twin helped her below. The galley was filled with men, women, and children, all soaked and miserable and some of them groaning from wounds and broken bones. Millie had his first-aid bag open, doing what he could do, which wasn't much.

The first of the rescued had established the identity of the torpedoed ship and the sad news that she was a Canadian passenger vessel out of Caracas. Although her captain was among the lost, the first mate, found clutching a life ring, told Josh what had happened. A thin, hook-nosed man, he kept his tie knotted primly and his navy blue wool suit buttoned even while he dripped seawater on the *Maudie Jane*'s deck. The *Lady Morgan* was riding the Gulf Stream off Killakeet looking to round Hatteras, he said, when a torpedo had arrived off her starboard side. It had started a fire amidships. The captain had immediately ordered the engines stopped and the lifeboats lowered. Just as the first boat was being let down the falls, another torpedo had struck the stern. Then a third torpedo caught them amidships again.

"That was when the carnage truly occurred, Captain," the mate said as he gratefully accepted a blanket and a steaming mug of coffee from Fisheye. He wrinkled up his nose. "I would have preferred tea," he said, and then went on, "If we could have pushed away while the old girl sank, all would have been well. But the U-boat skipper wanted to make sure of his kill. The lifeboats were still hanging in their davits when he struck us again. All we could do was jump. I was lucky to come up near a life ring."

"How do you know it was a U-boat?" Josh asked.

The mate gave Josh a petulant look. "What else could it be?"

"A mine? Explosions from your boilers or cargo?"

"Don't be ridiculous, Captain. I saw the second and third torpedoes coming in. What I can't figure is why the U-boat attacked us. There was a tanker not a thousand yards away, a much better target, and more coming up behind. We had our running lights off, too. No, I'll tell you what I think, strange as it may seem. I believe we were chosen. Somebody out here likes the idea of killing women and children."

The mate craned his neck as Ready fired the Very gun from the bow. "I must say your light discipline here leaves something to be desired. The U-boat that sank us can't be far away. What would happen if a torpedo hit you?"

Josh thought about it. "You wouldn't be able to find us with a microscope."

"I daresay."

Stobs stuck his head out of the wheelhouse. "Chief Glendale is bringing the Doakes workboat out, Skipper."

Josh nodded, then took a tour of the deck. It was covered with the stink of oily seawater and the sharp metallic odor of blood. The smell, combined with the low groans and whimpering of the suffering, made the deck a nightmarish place.

Josh saw Millie come up for a tour of the passengers, then kneel to peel a man's oil-soaked coat away. A bone, slick and pinkish white, pushed through a tear in the bloody sleeve of the man's shirt. "Jesus H. Christ!" Millie exclaimed.

Josh knelt beside him. "What do you need?"

"Doc Folsom."

"You're going to have to do your best until we can get back to Doakes."

"I could use a splint, I guess."

Josh saw Again turn away from something mushy and red dangling from his boat hook. "Again, go see if you can come up with a splint for Millie to put on this man's arm. Look forward in stowage."

Again gratefully threw down his boat hook. "On my way!"

Millie drew a morphine Syrette from the canvas medical bag. He spoke to the passenger. "Sir, I can't set your arm but we'll splint it. I'm going to give you some morphine, which should keep you until we get to shore."

The man, his face pale and scared, nodded.

Millie bit off the plastic tip and plunged the needle into one of the passenger's legs. He squeezed out its contents and the man's eyes fluttered. "I'm down to six Syrettes, Mister Thurlow," Millie said.

Josh was tired. He thought Millie was whining and it made him a little angry. "Use them sparingly, then," he snapped, then headed back to the wheelhouse just as the Doakes workboat came alongside.

"How many survivors?" Chief Glendale called over in his foghorn voice.

"Maybe thirty," Josh replied, "and I don't know how many bodies."

"Mister Thurlow!" It was Ready.

"What is it?"

"Dawn coming, sir."

The eastern horizon looked as dark as ever, but then Josh saw Ready was correct. There was a faint but glimmering bright yellow line marking the far eastern horizon.

"Can you see them yet, sir?" Ready asked.

"See them who?" Josh replied in a weary voice. Then he started to make out images on the sea, bumps rolling with the waves. The horizon grew brighter, then the red ball of the sun broke through, bringing everything floating into bleak relief. "My God . . ."

In a vast, undulating field all around the *Maudie Jane,* floating bodies of men, women, and children, their arms and legs akimbo, their heads thrown back in openmouthed, sightless stares, drifted like gruesome flower petals strewn across the sea.

The Chief gave Krebs his report. The port drive shaft seemed to be holding together. The *U-560* could go back on the attack. "Chief," Krebs asked, "what do you make of those American rescue boats?"

The Chief thumbed through his book of American naval vessels. "The larger one is an eighty-three-foot patrol boat, I believe. The other appears to be a motorized launch."

Krebs used the powerful Zeiss binoculars to examine the patrol boat. "I believe those are depth-charge racks on the stern, but no sign of the barrels themselves."

The Chief took a lookout's binoculars and made his own observation. "There is also what appears to be a machine gun on the bow, sir. It's a belt-fed gun, I'm certain. But I see no belt leading into it. Still, I think this boat has the potential to make trouble. Shall we sink it?"

Krebs contemplated the situation. It was apparent the

Americans were going about rescue duty. Bodies were being lifted out of the water, one by one. Yet, it was a warship, even though it appeared to be unarmed. On the other hand, he didn't care to waste a torpedo.

A lookout reported, "*Kaleu,* a ship to the south coming very quickly!"

Krebs aimed the Zeiss binoculars at the ship. "Good spotting. It looks like another tanker."

Before Krebs could comment further, a plume of steam rose up the side of the tanker, followed by the low thrum of torpedo thunder.

"Vogel," Max said as if cursing. "He beat us to it."

"Let's get out there, anyway," Krebs said. "I expect there will be another tanker before long."

"What about the patrol boat, sir?" the Chief asked. "It's a warship."

"It's an unarmed rescue vessel," Max retorted.

Krebs's instinct was to call up the eighty-eight crew and blow the Americans to bits, but he said, in deference to Max, "We'll let it go."

"Thank you," Max said in an aside.

"You may not thank me," Krebs answered, "if that unarmed rescue vessel grows teeth and claws."

The first mate of the *Lady Morgan* came to stand beside Josh. "There's our killer, Captain. A Type Seven German U-boat. See that gun forward of the tower? That's an eighty-eight-millimeter gun. If the captain wanted, he could blow you out of the water with one shell."

Josh observed the submarine through his binoculars. There was something painted on its tower fairing. "See if you can make out the insignia on that U-boat," he said to Once, tossing him the binoculars.

"It's a shark, sir. I can see men on the tower, too, sir. One of them has a white cap."

"That would be the kraut captain," the mate said.

Josh looked around. His boys had stopped their work and were staring at the U-boat. He heard Ready say, "Do you think it'll come after us?"

"Our father who art in heaven," Bobby began, "hallowed be thy name . . ."

The other boys bowed their heads and prayed with him. To Josh, it appeared as if they were submitting to the Germans. "Bobby!" he bellowed. "Belay that prayer. Ready, bring me the Enfield. We're going to get into this war."

Ready brought up the rifle. "I had to use five rounds to sight it in, sir."

"I'll just need one to kill that son of a bitch," Josh said.

"What's the skipper doing?" Bobby wondered to the other boys.

"I guess he's going to attack that U-boat," Again answered.

Bobby, his knees trembling, started to say his prayer to himself.

"All right, boys, go below," Krebs ordered the lookouts as he took a completed message form from Max. Pretch had alerted Krebs an hour before that a signal was coming through, a long one that would take some time to decode. Krebs glanced at it. It was a list of instructions from BdU to all U-boats at sea on how to save diesel fuel. Krebs knew it was just Uncle Karl reminding all his commanders that he was thinking of them. Krebs chuckled, and prepared to go below.

Josh propped the Enfield on the railing aft of the wheelhouse and took a long sight. He could see only one man left on the tower, but it was the one he wanted, the captain of the U-boat, identified by his white cap.

"Whatever are you doing, Captain?" the Canadian first mate asked.

"I'm going to kill that son of a bitch."

The mate's eyes bugged out. "They will slaughter you."

"I had an old captain up on the Bering Sea," Josh said, sighting in, "who taught me you can't win unless you fight."

"Even against impossible odds?"

"Especially then." Josh took a breath, then held it. The

front sight lined up with the *V* of the rear sight, centered on the white cap. Josh squeezed the trigger and the Enfield barked.

Krebs put his hand on the tower hatch cover to steady himself as he started below. Above and behind him, there came a metallic *ping* and then immediately, a second one. Paint flew off the hatch cover. Startled, he dropped Doenitz's message. The form, caught by an eddy of wind, flew off the tower, fluttered down to snag on the traversing wheel of the deck gun, then floated off into the sea. Krebs stared at a dent in the sky periscope where his head had just been a moment before. *Unbelievable!* A rifle shot had struck the periscope and apparently the ricochet had hit the hatch. He took off his cap and raised his head just enough to squint over the fairing. On board the patrol boat, he saw a big man dressed in khakis and a brown leather jacket standing with a rifle in his hand. "You're brave, my friend," Krebs said, "I'll give you that."

The U-boat began to move away in a southeasterly direction. "I admire your spunk, Captain Thurlow," the mate of the *Lady Morgan* said. "But that was a foolish move."

Josh handed the rifle to Ready. "You'll notice he's leaving."

"Yes, to sink more ships. How many destroyers are on their way to get after these buggers?"

"None, as far as I know," Josh answered.

The mate shook his head. "The U-boats are going to cut you to pieces."

A thunderclap seaward caused everyone to turn in time to see a second boil of smoke rise from the tanker that had been attacked minutes before. Then a sudden release of bubbles from the *Lady Morgan* brought up a dozen bodies.

"What are we going to do about this, Mister Thurlow?" Phimble demanded.

"We're going to take these folks in to Killakeet," Josh said, indicating with a nod the survivors and bodies littering the deck.

"Let the dead bury the dead. We've got to get us some depth charges."

Josh didn't reply. The U-boat with the white shark on its tower had disappeared. Maybe it wouldn't return. Maybe there was just going to be a day of carnage and then it would be over, just as in 1918 when the old surfmen had gone out and the U-boat captain had lifted his cap in respect to them. *Maybe it's all over.*

"It ain't over," Phimble said.

"You in the business of reading my mind now, Eureka?"

"No, sir. I'm just telling you. Captain Falcon—"

"Is not here. I am. End of discussion."

Phimble opened his mouth to argue, then clapped it shut. "Yes, *sir,*" he said while providing a sharp salute that Josh knew very well meant *Up yours, sir!*

# 29

By the time the workboat was tied up at the military dock, nearly all of Whalebone City was waiting there, summoned by the clanging church bell. Chief Glendale came ashore followed by the mate of the *Lady Morgan*. "I'm sorry," the mate said to the assembly. "I'm afraid we were torpedoed."

"We're right sad to hear that, sir," Queenie answered. There was a mumble of sorrowful agreement from the assembly. "What can we do?"

"My passengers," the mate replied, his voice choking, "they should come ashore."

"Preacher," Chief Glendale said, "can we put them in the church, do you think?"

Preacher was nearly sober by now, though he still had sand on his face. "It would be an honor, Chief," he said.

Keeper Jack was the first aboard the workboat. He knelt beside the body of a young woman whose eyes were open, fixated, as if she was startled to discover herself dead. He gently closed them, and lifted her into his arms. The people of Killakeet quietly followed his example and soon a line of people carrying bodies wound from the military dock to the church.

"Where was God last night, I wonder?" Queenie asked as she and Amy Guthrie struggled to carry a young woman off, Queenie lifting under her shoulders, Amy at her bare feet.

"Bible says a bird don't fall what God don't know about it," Preacher said between gritted teeth. He had a dead woman in his arms, and his ruined shoulder was killing him. "God knew all about this. You can be certain of it." It sounded like an accusation.


Harro and Joachim were released from the bow torpedo room to take their turn at lookout duty. After receiving permission to climb the rungs of the ladder to the tower, the two boys took up their station and cocked their ear to the conversations of the officers.

"I should like to use the eighty-eight against this one, Max," Captain Krebs was saying.

"Against a tanker?" *Leutnant* Max shook his head. "It's not feasible." He snapped a look at Harro and Joachim. "Why are you staring at me and the captain? We're not the ones you're supposed to see! Keep your eyes peeled out there!"

"Yes, sir!" Harro yelped, and threw his binoculars so hard to his eyes, he knocked himself back a step.

The Chief came up. "These boys are full of piss and vinegar, sir."

"If they don't pay attention, they'll find themselves full of extra duty," Max sniped.

"I can't believe I looked so stupid," Harro whispered to Joachim.

Joachim chuckled. "You always look stupid to me."

Harro gave his shipmate a surreptitious elbow and Joachim responded in kind. For their efforts, they got a rap on the back of their heads by the Chief. "Look, you two, you keep skylarking and I'll have you down with the stokers scrubbing the engine-room deck plates. You understand?"

The boys started looking as hard as they could. Before them lay three burning and sinking ships. The *U-560* had bagged one of them. Other U-boats had gotten the other two. Harro noticed a glint off something to the south. "Tanker, sir!" he squeaked.

Max replied tiredly, "Yes, boy. We've been watching it

for the last fifteen minutes. Concentrate on the sky. Let us know if you see any aircraft."

Harro and Joachim got busy with the sky. They saw seagulls and pelicans and a few puffy clouds, but that was all. Furtively, Harro swept his binoculars across the smudge of land to the west. He had heard they were lying off an island that had a lighthouse. If so, it was too far away to make out any details.

"Send up the eighty-eight crew!" Krebs suddenly barked, startling Harro so much he nearly dropped his binoculars.

"We're in for some action now," Joachim said, nudging Harro.

The eighty-eight boys scrambled to their artillery piece, pulling out the tampion and unlocking the ammunition boxes. The eighty-eight was a wicked-looking cannon with a long, narrow tube and traversing wheels to adjust its aim.

"Chief, fall in behind that tanker and get us as close as you can," Krebs ordered.

Harro sneaked a peek at the officers. *Leutnant* Max was saying something to *Kaleu* Krebs. Harro couldn't hear what he said, but Krebs responded by saying, "Well, let me prove it to you, Max."

The *U-560* picked up speed, leaving behind a blue-white trail of frothy turbulence. Forgetting the sky, Harro swept his binoculars to the stern of the tanker. There were men standing on it, pointing at the *U-560*. The tanker was putting out its own wake of blue-white froth, really churning up the sea. "They're making a run for it," Harro whispered to Joachim.

"Are you ready, Beeker?" Krebs calmly asked the gun captain.

"Ready, *Kaleu!*"

At Krebs's nod, Beeker pulled the lanyard and the big gun erupted. Harro caught the blur of the shell as it raced out of the tube, then lost it against the sky. He started looking at the stern of the tanker again. The men standing on it were suddenly enveloped in a blossom of flame and smoke. He saw a legless torso thrown high in the air, then watched it all the way down until it splashed into the sea. Harro felt a bit sick to his stomach.

"Good shot!" Krebs congratulated Beeker, then slapped Max on his back. "You see, Max? We don't need torpedoes. Beeker, put another round into her."

The eighty-eight gun fired again, but this time the shell fell short, producing a plume of water. The tanker was starting to pull away. Beeker adjusted his aim and the next round caught her on her superstructure and a fourth round burst again on her stern. An oily smoke cloud began to trail behind her but the tanker plowed on, leaving the *U-560* rocking in her wake.

"She'll burn," Krebs said, satisfied. "Well, what do you think now, Max?"

"The deck gun was more effective than I thought," Max confessed.

Joachim saw the masts of a ship poke up along the southern horizon. He watched it, then cried, "Look, sir, another tanker!" and proudly pointed toward his discovery.

Max took a look. "It's no tanker, you idiot. It's just a small freighter. Probably a banana boat."

Banana boat or no, the U-boat curved south, running down on the little freighter. The Chief identified it as the *Dona Marta,* owned by the Tropical Fruit Company of Tegucigalpa, Honduras, 1,026 tons.

"Fire at will, Beeker," Krebs ordered.

"Why waste shells on a banana boat, sir?" Max asked.

"Doenitz loves tonnage," Krebs answered with a shrug. "He doesn't much care how we get it."

The eighty-eight boomed, striking the small freighter and leaving a big hole on her port side. Some crewmen could be seen scrambling aboard the single lifeboat hanging from its falls. It fell and turned over, men swimming from beneath it. Other men, clinging to life jackets, jumped overboard. The freighter, drooping into the water, released a flood of green bananas from her hold. The Chief sent a few men forward to hook the lifeboat, flip it over, and bail it out. "Give them some food and water, too, Chief," Max said.

The Chief called down through the galley hatch and soon a jug of water and a package wrapped up in brown paper

Embry-Riddle Aeronautical University
CheckOut Receipt

Customer ID: 21932000389949

Title: One six right [DVD]
ID: 31932000656428
**Due: Tuesday, March 15, 2011**

Title: The ghosts of Sleath
ID: 31932000359338
**Due: Tuesday, March 15, 2011**

Title: The keeper's son
ID: 31932000548179
**Due: Tuesday, March 15, 2011**

Total items: 3
2/22/2011 3:44 PM


Thank you for using the
Express Checkout machine

was handed up. The Hondurans were also plucking bananas from the sea. The Chief pointed to the west and made rowing motions. The freighter crew waved and began to pull their oars.

"It's a long haul," Max said. "I hope they make it."

"Well, anyway, we have made the fatherland safe from bananas, Max," Krebs said with an impish grin. "Let's go a bit farther south and see if we can catch another tanker."

"I wish I could be on permanent lookout duty," Joachim said enthusiastically. "This is fun!"

"Not to me," Harro mumbled. He kept thinking of the bloody torso he'd seen thrown high into the air off the tanker.

"You'll be on permanent shit detail if you don't shut up," the Chief said, coming up on the tower and rapping them both on the backs of their heads again.

Both boys instantly threw their binoculars to their eyes, but all they saw was a spreading pool of bananas and a rapidly sinking rusty, old freighter.

Bodies were laid out on the pews and up and down the aisles of the Church of the Mariner. When Josh came in, the first thing he saw was a little boy, which immediately made him think of Jacob. He stifled the ridiculous urge to look closer, to make certain it wasn't his brother. He felt a touch on his arm. It was Dosie, splattered with blood. She had changed out of her party dress and was in her riding outfit. "I could not possibly say what I feel," she said. "The closest I can come is that I hate this. It's senseless."

"It made sense to the men who did it," Josh replied. Then he fought an overpowering urge to take her into his arms and let her comfort him. Instead, he said, "Dosie, you need to leave Killakeet. On the next ferry. This is a battleground now."

"I'm not going anywhere," Dosie said. "This is my island, too. Where's Preacher? That's why I'm here. Doc sent me to get him."

Josh nodded toward the altar. Preacher was on his knees, his head bowed. "Preacher," Dosie said, "Doc needs you in the Surfmen's House."

Preacher raised his head. "I am praying for the dead," he said. Then he added with a sneer, "Just in case God might be listening."

"Doc says the survivors need you. Most of them are Catholic and they're asking for a priest."

"I ain't no priest."

Dosie had a roll of white hospital tape. She tore off a strip of it and wrapped it around the preacher's neck. "You are now," she said, buttoning the top button of his black coat.

Dosie seemed to have a power over Preacher. She led him to the Surfmen's House and Josh followed. Dozens of survivors were lying or sitting on the floor. Doc was tending to them with Millie assisting. Off to the side were those who had recently died, covered with blankets and waiting to be carried to the church.

"You'll find them by the supply cabinets," Doc said when Dosie asked about the ones needing a priest. "Some are dying for certain, some of them are hurt enough that they might die."

Preacher went down on his knees beside a woman who clutched her stomach, her face pinched with pain. She was bleeding from her nose and her ears. "Hear my confession, Father," she said.

"I don't know what to say," Preacher whispered to Dosie, who was kneeling beside him.

"You'd better figure it out," she hissed.

He looked to the ceiling as if praying.

"Father, confess me," the woman said again.

"Yes, my child," the preacher said. "*Montani semper liberi.* I will hear your confession now."

" 'Mountaineers will always be free'?" Dosie whispered. "What's that?"

"The West Virginia state motto."

The woman gasped a few words and Preacher made a clumsy cross over her. "The Lord God Jesus forgives you."

The woman subsided and seemed to go to sleep. Her hands fell away from her stomach.

Dosie said, "Keep going, Preacher. You're not done yet."

She rose to find Josh watching her with a proud expression on his face.

Josh said, "You are one hell of a woman, Dosie Crossan."

"Dosie," Doc called. "Need some help here with this one." Dosie, after a grateful glance at Josh, went flying.

Josh spotted Captain Potts. He'd taken off his coat and his hands were bloody from helping to move the dead. He waved Josh over. "What's the toll?"

"Sixty-one survivors, sir. I don't know how many dead. We've brought in seventy-five bodies. There's a lot more still out there. I saw the U-boat that did it. It has a white shark painted on its conning tower. I also observed three other ships out in the Stream that had been attacked. As we came in, we saw a big tanker heading north on fire. We saw another plume of smoke a little after that but couldn't tell what it was."

Captain Potts absorbed the information. "You're planning on going back out, I presume?"

"Soon as I get some diesel in the *Maudie Jane*," Josh said. "Request permission to go over to Morehead City and arm the boat from your warehouse, sir. Depth charges for the racks and ammunition for the fifty caliber."

Captain Potts thought it over. "I haven't received orders to attack U-boats."

"They've received orders to attack us, sir. I have to defend myself."

"As long as you are on a rescue mission, I don't see why they would bother you."

Josh worked to keep his voice low and steady. "I will tell you why. We're at war, and the *Maudie Jane* is a warship."

Captain Potts raised his index finger, covered with dried blood, and shook it in Josh's face. "You're a rescue vessel, Mister Thurlow. *Rescue!* And that is what you will remain until I receive orders to the contrary."

Captain Potts went off to join his wife, who was comforting the injured. Preacher, on his knees and holding the hand of a dying boy, looked up. "Josh," he said. " 'He that killeth with the sword must be killed by the sword. Here is the patience and the faith of the saints.' "

Josh went over the words. "Preacher, that's the first thing I've heard today that's made any sense."

Josh found Phimble and Chief Glendale fueling the *Maudie Jane*. Phimble gave him a sour look. "Wipe that ugly look off your face and listen up," Josh said. "We're going to cross the sound, find Potts's warehouses, and get what we need to fight."

Phimble brightened all the way to a grin. "I just happen to have a key to those warehouses, sir."

"Bring it."

They waited until dark, then coasted the *Maudie Jane* next to the warehouses at the supply depot. A guard in sailor blues came out. He was just a boy but he had a pistol on his hip. "What's going on?" he nervously inquired.

Josh came off the patrol boat, followed by the Jackson twins, Ready O'Neal, and Bosun Phimble. The guard gave a sloppy salute. "Excuse me, sir. The warehouses are closed."

"You ever hear of a midnight requisition, sailor?" Josh asked.

"Yeah. It's called stealing."

"You have bullets in that thing, bub?" Ready asked, pointing at the pistol.

The guard heard the menace in Ready's voice and shrugged. "Naw."

"You have your key, Eureka?" Josh asked.

Phimble produced a ball peen hammer. "Sure do, sir."

"Step aside, son," Once said to the guard. Then they all pushed past the boy.

The guard kept turning around. "Y'all better stop!" he protested.

The last boy off the boat was Millie. He handed the guard a sheaf of requisition forms. "Here. This makes it legal."

"You should've give me these first!" the guard cried. He shuffled through the forms and hoped they really were legal.

"This is the one, sir," Phimble said, as the gang of Maudie Janes trotted up to a big wooden warehouse.

"Use your key, Eureka."

Phimble slammed the hammer down.

# 30

Krebs took his ease on the tower. Darkness had come in like a cloak. To the east, the lighthouse began to flash. It was an odd comfort to see it. There was a chill in the air but it was crisp, not bone-cutting, and the sea was as flat as a mountain lake. He puffed at a cigar, savoring the taste, letting it transport him back to another, better time. He had picked up the habit of smoking cigars during a tour of duty in Cuba as the naval liaison to the German ambassador. That had been a sweet assignment. He'd been twenty-three then, barely out of officers' school. It had been his job to keep an eye on the shipping going in and out of Havana, but mostly he'd enjoyed sailing along the coast, usually with a special young senorita.

He lingered over the memory for a while longer, trying to square its pleasure against the now painful memories of Miriam. His mind wandered on. The English pilots who had strafed the crowd of Advent celebrators just to knock out a weather station had accomplished their duty. Likely, when they got back to base, they'd celebrated. But Krebs wondered what they would have done if they had known someone beneath their guns. He suspected they would have been enchanted by Miriam. And likely, they would have given money to the orphans and Father Josef. England, of course, was a seafaring nation. The Britishers in those cockpits probably had relatives who were fishermen, just as the people of

Nebelsee. How easy it was to kill when you didn't know
whom you were killing. That's what made war so insane,
yet paradoxically so easy.

Krebs was unsettled and he was trying to grasp why. In
American waters, merchant ships had lined up like bowling
pins, almost impossible to miss. But he had missed. He was
wondering if there was something about his experience with
Miriam that had changed him, had taken away his sure touch
for battle.

He touched Miriam's cross beneath his shirt. It was the
only thing of her he had left. But was that true? Had she
somehow placed in his heart something that was growing,
something greater than duty? *Family.* That's what Miriam
had kept talking about, and Father Josef, too. There was
nothing more important than family. Krebs decided that if he
survived the war, he would go back to Nebelsee and do what
he could for Father Josef and the orphanage, and if God was
so kind, perhaps he could find another good woman like
Miriam and have a real family, too.

Krebs flicked his cigar overboard, watching its glow fall
into the sea. A glimmer of lights to the north was an indication of the island that had sent out the rescue boat observed
at the *Lady Morgan.* He thought of the big man in khakis
who'd shot at him. For a reason Krebs couldn't discern, he
thought he'd like that man, that they would be friends if the
circumstances were different.

The lookouts had reported the name on the rescue boat's
bow was *Maudie Jane.* It seemed an odd name for a warship.
Then again, *was* it a warship? It apparently had no working
weapons beyond a rifle. The crew aboard hadn't looked military. They were in all kinds of clothes, a patchwork of different shirts and caps. Some of them even appeared to be
barefoot. The *Maudie Jane,* Krebs concluded, was probably
used mostly for rescue. Still, the depth-charge racks, though
empty, on her stern were a worry.

Reluctantly, Krebs came to the conclusion that, should he
meet her again, he would need to sink the *Maudie Jane,* just
to be cautious.

Cautious. He'd never thought that way before. He shook his head. What was happening to him?

"*Kaleu.*" It was the Chief calling up through the hatch. "Signal from BdU. *Leutnant* Max is decoding."

"I'll come down." Krebs took a last look around. The wind on his cheek seemed different, a little insistent. Then, he heard the Gulf Stream sigh in an odd way. He glanced at the lighthouse and saw it dim, then go out. Then he saw a diffused flash. No, the light had not gone out. A fog or a cloud had covered it. But what kind of cloud moved in so quickly? Then he remembered something he had read about this sea. It was called the Graveyard of the Atlantic and for a reason. Besides the shifting shoals, there were huge waves that could come out of nowhere.

Krebs dived for the hatch, scrambling headfirst through it, grasping the rungs and dangling from them. "Close the hatch!" he roared to a startled helmsman.

The boy lunged for it just as the vast wave struck. A spout of seawater came surging inside, knocking the helmsman down. Others rushed to close the hatch as the *U-560* was lifted up and up, then flung down on its side. Pots, pans, wrenches, food, garbage, bedding, and men went flying.

The *Maudie Jane* was coming out, this time to fight. Josh studied the water and the sky. He didn't like what he saw. "Watch for rogue waves, Eureka."

Phimble peered ahead and took a breath. "It smells right airish to me, too, Skipper."

All the boys aboard the *Maudie Jane* sensed a change coming. They knew these waters and could feel danger, even when everything looked normal. "It'll be breezing up right quick," Stobs predicted, sticking his nose out of the wheelhouse.

"Well, I know you'll keep yourself high and dry, Stobs boy," Bobby said, padding by. "How about we join you in the wheelhouse come the blow?"

"Just don't be dripping on my floor if you boys get too mommicked," Stobs replied, grinning, and slapped the wheelhouse hatch shut.

Below, in the forward compartment, Ready and Big worked over the fifty caliber, getting it ready for its first belt of ammunition. They could also sense the change in the motion of the boat. "Ever been caught by a rogue?" Big asked.

"No, but my daddy was," Ready said. "He said it was as tall as the lighthouse."

"What happened?"

"He drowned!"

Big scratched his head. "Did you have another daddy besides the one you've got now?"

Ready rolled his eyes. "It was a joke." When Big didn't respond, just stood there with a questioning look on his face, Ready said, "He didn't die. I just made that up."

"How come?"

"Just help me with this gun, you goober."

On the stoop bridge, Josh felt the bow rise, then plunge steeply. "Here it comes," he said. The first drop of rain hit him. There had been stars across the sky only minutes before but now they were gone. Josh glanced over his shoulder. There was no sign of the lighthouse. Then the wind howled.

Josh yelled to the deck crew. "You boys make sure the hatches and vents are sealed. Tell all the other boys to hang on!"

The deck crew scampered off as a torrent of rain hit the boat.

"What do you think?" Phimble asked, pulling on his slicker.

"We've got about fifteen minutes, I figure. I'm going below to talk to Jimmy, see about the sonar."

Phimble nodded, then went into the wheelhouse to take the wheel there.

In the sonar locker, Josh found Jimmy hard at it, the sound-phones clamped to his ears. Josh leaned inside. There wasn't room for two people in the tiny closet. "Anything?"

Jimmy shook his head. "Nothing solid, sir. I think I'm getting a lot of fish echoes. It's there and then it's gone. When it's like that, the boys on the *Diana* taught me it was probably a school of fish or a whale or maybe layers of water all different temperatures."

"How about propeller sounds?"

"I've been listening. All I can hear is us."

"We're going to get knocked around in a few minutes," Josh said. "Go ahead and turn your set off and get yourself wedged in. Afterward, we'll drift some with the engines off. That should help your listening. Do you think you'd know the sound of that white shark U-boat if you heard it again?"

"I ain't about to forget that bastard, sir. He had kind of a rattling sound to him as he started up. I'll bet it's his propellers or drive shaft or something."

Josh patted Jimmy on his head and then went topside and into the wheelhouse. "What's the word, Stobs?"

Stobs lifted the phones away from one ear and shrugged. "Morehead City keeps calling, sir. Captain Potts got back and learned about our midnight requisition."

"That figures. Listen, Stobs, here's what I want you to do. See if you can get hold of the *Diana*. Tell Captain Allison we need help down here."

"Yes, sir, I'll try, but in the last few hours, there's been a lot of traffic on CG frequencies."

"What are they saying?"

"All in code and we don't have a codebook."

"Why don't we have a codebook?"

Stobs's face clouded over. "Radio school said headquarters would send one out to Doakes if we ever needed it. I guess nobody ever thought we did."

"Try to squeeze our signal in. Send it in Morse."

"What about Captain Potts, sir?"

Josh resisted an inclination to ignore the good captain but then decided to get it over with. "Call him up."

Stobs made the call and Morehead City answered. It didn't take long before Potts was yelling. "Thurlow, this is a direct order. You will turn around and bring my depth charges back! Do you understand?"

"I can't do that, sir," Josh replied. "We're in a bit of a storm. If I turned around, I might get rolled over. You'd best batten down your hatches, too. This looks to be a big one and it's headed your way."

"Don't change the subject. You have destroyed and stolen government property. I'm writing up the charges against you now. A court-martial will be assembled within the week. Your career is over."

"Yes, sir. Thank you, sir. I left the necessary requisitions with your guard. I destroyed nothing that I know about."

"You busted a lock!" Captain Potts yelled. "And you don't have the authority to sign requisitions for ammunition and depth charges!"

Josh heard somebody in the background: "I'm not so sure of that, sir." Josh recognized the voice.

"Shut up, Glendale! I'll deal with you later!" Captain Potts snarled.

Josh grinned at Phimble, who was looking over his shoulder. "The good ol' chief went over to make it right." Then Josh keyed the microphone and said, "Captain Potts, I know you're mad and I guess you have a right to be. But my priority is to rescue survivors. I'll only defend my boat and my crew if I have to."

"It's not your boat, Ensign," Captain Potts growled. "It's the Coast Guard's boat."

"All right, sir. I'll defend the Coast Guard's boat."

"I can't talk to you," Captain Potts said. "You are the most insolent officer I've ever had the misfortune to command."

"I'm sorry you think that, sir," Josh said in a sorrowful tone. "I really am."

There was a pause, then Glendale came on. "Good hunting, Mister Thurlow. I wish I was out there with you. When do you figure to come in?"

Josh hadn't thought about it. "I guess when I'm out of depth charges, Chief."

"Attaboy, sir. Go get 'em. And don't worry about no court-martial. Captain Potts was just huffing and puffing. He'll get over it."

Josh handed the mike back to Stobs and peered through the salt-streaked windows at a gray-and-white sea gone wild. The *Maudie Jane* mashed through the waves, spouts of froth flung across her bow to slam against the wheelhouse, its bronze shell rumbling like a kettledrum.

Then something huge and dark, lifted by a mountain of water, loomed in front of them. "What's that?" Phimble yelled.

Though he could scarcely believe it, Josh knew exactly what it was. "Brace for collision!" he yelled.

Krebs and Max were the only men on the tower, the lookouts kept below after the rogue wave had battered the boat. The rain and wind beat on them. Only their safety harnesses kept them from being flushed overboard. "One minute there was nothing!" Krebs yelled above the raging thunder of sea and wind. "Then this! Out of nowhere!"

"It's the currents, *Kaleu!*" Max yelled. "Mix all that hot and cold water and it can blow up in an instant!"

They ducked beneath the lip of the tower fairing to get out of the gale. "What's the bill?" Krebs asked.

"A broken arm. One of the boys in the bow torpedo room. We were lucky the torpedoes didn't come loose and crush them."

"It wasn't the boy Harro Stollenberg, by any chance?"

"No, sir. Torpedoman Dumbacher."

"I want to make Stollenberg into a radioman, Max. See to it, will you?"

"Of course. But why Stollenberg?"

"I was going to tell you what happened on my leave," Krebs said. "Stollenberg played a part in it. But later, Max."

Max frowned, but nodded dutifully.

The *U-560* crashed through the waves, shuddered, then plunged into a trough. "We are probably the most seaworthy craft out here," Krebs commented, rising up to peer through the cascade of torrential rain. For his trouble, he was smashed in the face with what felt like a bucket of cold water. He dropped back down and wrung the froth from his beard.

Max peered over the fairing. "What's that?" he suddenly shouted.

Krebs rose to look. A gray shape was riding atop a giant

wave. It was the patrol boat, being flung directly at the
*U-560*. "Get down, Max!" he yelled. "Brace yourself!"

The great wave roared and the *Maudie Jane* rode its lip, then
slid down its back side. Beneath the wave sat the *U-560*.
Both craft were helpless in the grip of such awesome power.
Josh, hanging on to the instrument panel, watched the
U-boat tower loom at them like a blunt spear. But then the
giant wave tossed the eighty-three-footer as if she was as
inconsequential as a gull feather, sending her sailing over the
U-boat. The *Maudie Jane* landed with a crash, her bow dis-
appearing underwater before she popped up, her propellers
biting into the sea. Finally, she steadied.

Josh and Phimble had both been thrown to the deck. They
crawled to their feet, then stared at each other. They had
missed the U-boat by a matter of inches. Had they struck it,
the *Maudie Jane* would have been torn to pieces. "All this
ocean," Phimble marveled, "and we almost hit the bastard."

Josh chanced going outside. He gripped the railing while
the wind and rain brutally tried their best to throw him overboard. He ignored the murderous effort and peered into the
storm, trying to see the submarine. The Germans had disappeared. Josh could only hope the Graveyard had sunk them
and saved him the trouble.

# 31

For twelve days, the ocean from Nags Head to Lookout battered everything on it, be they U-boats, tankers, freighters, banana boats, or the *Maudie Jane*. Then, at dawn on the thirteenth day of the January blow, which by then was actually in February, the skies turned a crystal blue and the wind subsided into a gentle, though chilly breeze. The Atlantic had become so placid that a stone dropped into it would have shimmered to Bermuda. In the Stream, two U-boats came together while a freighter slowly settled nearby, rolling heavily toward a ragged, charred torpedo wound in its side. Ignored by the German sailors, lifeboats were being lowered off the stricken ship and the men aboard them were manning oars, their frightened faces turning occasionally to consider the enemy submarines.

One of the two U-boats was the *U-560*. Krebs was on the tower, and his knee was bothering him. It was terribly stiff. He tentatively flexed it. It hurt like the devil but still worked. A lookout reported another U-boat had surfaced about a mile away. Krebs hauled out the powerful Zeiss glasses to study it. It was a big, black Type Nine. "*Scheisse,*" he cursed. "Vogel."

The sub next to the *U-560* was Froelich's Type Nine. "Our glorious leader," Froelich confirmed.

"Well done, by the way," Krebs gibed. "I'm glad you found a vessel going slow and straight enough for you."

Froelich allowed a grin. "It was not one of those amazing torpedo shots for which you are so justly famous, Otto, but it will do. Happily, it was my last torpedo. We will soon be on our way home. How about you?"

"I have two left," Krebs answered. "It shouldn't take too long to find targets for them and then we'll head back across the Atlantic. I think the boys are ready to see France."

Both crews, except for the necessary watches below, were on their respective decks, stretching their legs for the first time since the long, violent storm had struck. A buzz rose from the crew of the *U-560. France!* "Ooh la la!" someone shouted.

The three lifeboats off the sinking freighter milled around aimlessly until one of them straightened itself and began to pull in the direction of the U-boats. A man with a trimmed white beard, perhaps the captain as he was the only one in a uniform jacket, stood anxiously in the bow.

"You should try your deck gun on a few ships before you leave," Krebs said, looking askance at the approaching lifeboat.

Froelich lowered his binoculars. He'd been watching Vogel's sub, still determinedly plowing toward them. He pushed his cap to the back of his head. "I'm too low on diesel to give any kind of chase. No, another wave of boats are probably on their way over here even as we speak. It's time for me to take my boys home."

The lifeboat from the sinking freighter crept in behind Froelich's submarine. The man in the bow took his cap off and clutched it to his chest. His men all had their heads down. "Good morning, *Kapitän,*" he said in Spanish-accented German. "I am Captain Castro. Could you direct me to the coast?"

Froelich looked the man over. His chief came out with the marine registry in his hand and demanded, "What ship?"

The merchant captain answered, *"San Paulo.* Out of Havana."

"What cargo?"

"Sand."

Froelich's expression was comical. "Sand?"

"We were in ballast, senor," the captain replied, shrugging heavily. "That's why we were heading south, going back to Cuba for more bauxite."

Krebs laughed. "You have interrupted the supply of sand to the Cubans, Plutarch. Well done!"

"Tonnage?" Froelich's chief droned.

"Two thousand six hundred. The coast, senor?"

Froelich waved distractedly to the west. "Follow the setting sun, you fool. Don't you even know where you are?" Then he quieted his embarrassment and became solicitous. "Do you need water? Food?"

"*Sí*, we have nothing."

Froelich sighed at the lack of preparation by some men who went to sea, then gave instructions to his chief to see to it but to be quick. He looked anxiously toward Vogel's U-boat. Its engines could be heard clearly now. Vogel and his officers could be seen riding atop the conning tower. "As soon as you're done," Froelich called after the chief, "prepare to head home."

"Give our regards to the ladies!" crazy Hans called from the deck of the *U-560*, and all the boys around him picked up the shout. Froelich's crew laughed and made rude gestures to the effect that they meant to give more than regards to the women of France.

"I wish we were going home, too," Harro said in a gloomy voice to Joachim.

Joachim shrugged. "It won't take us long to use our remaining eels," he said. "Of course, now that you're being trained on the radio, you don't have to sweat loading them in their tubes. Girls like radiomen, for some reason," Joachim added authoritatively. "It'll be easy for you to meet girls back in France. Don't forget me when you do."

"I've already met one," Harro said proudly. "I think she likes me."

"A girl? This is news! What's her name?"

"Yvette, of the Crazy Dog Bar. I have twelve letters to her in the mailbag."

"Yvette of the Crazy Dog!" another boy exclaimed, standing nearby. "I am writing to her, too!"

"And I!" somebody else said. There was in fact a chorus of youths confirming that they were all writing to Yvette of the Crazy Dog Bar in Brest. The Chief scratched his head. He was writing Yvette's mother.

Harro reddened, then hung his head. "It was different with me and Yvette than those others."

Joachim patted his friend on the shoulder. He knew Yvette pretty well, too, but he would never tell his friend that. "I am certain you are right," he said.

Vogel's U-boat moved in alongside with Vogel scowling from its tower. When he saw Froelich's cook bring out tins of food and jugs of water for the men in the lifeboat, he reacted with a shout. "*Kapitän* Froelich, it is against my express orders to assist enemy crewmen!"

Froelich nodded to the cook to keep handing over the supplies. "They're just Cubans, sir."

Vogel said something to one of his crewmen, who went down on the deck of the long, black submarine. He had a sidearm. He aimed carefully and shot once. A Cuban passing back a jug of water fell, a red stain on his back. The others shouted out an angry torrent of Spanish. The wounded man flopped over like a hooked fish, then quieted.

The captain of the Cubans whipped his cap off again. "Sir," he implored Vogel, "please! We are just merchant sailors. We are not at war with you."

Vogel ignored him. "So what's your plan, Froelich?"

At the moment of the shooting, Froelich had turned pale but now he was crimson with anger. "I intend to return across the Atlantic, sir, where I will report what you've done to the first military lawyer I can find."

Vogel laughed. "I act with the authority of the highest command, Froelich. The highest! We are here to bring terror to these shores, not just destruction."

"Why doesn't Captain Krebs say something?" Harro whispered to Joachim. Joachim shushed him.

At Froelich's command, his crew filed into the U-boat.

Froelich pointedly ignored Vogel and spoke only to Krebs. "Well, we're off. Anything you want us to carry back?"

"The mail, sir," the Chief said, hoisting the sack.

Krebs was so angry at Vogel for ordering the shooting of the Cuban that he did not yet trust himself to speak. He waved approval to Max. "Throw it over," Max said, and the Chief did. Froelich's chief caught the bag and disappeared through the galley hatch with it.

"Anything else? Any messages to BdU?"

"No, nothing, Plutarch," Krebs replied. "With any luck, we'll soon be on your heels. Good luck and remember the Biscay escape hole I told you about."

"I will. Godspeed, you men of the *U-560*." And with that, Froelich disappeared below and his U-boat began to move toward the east, submerging quickly, leaving the *U-560*, Vogel's submarine, the nearly sunken *San Paulo*, and her lifeboats the only vessels in a vast blue circle.

"Are you ready for new orders, Krebs?" Vogel called.

"Orders?" Krebs responded in a stony voice. "I have two torpedoes left and not too many eighty-eight-millimeter shells. I will be leaving soon."

"No, you won't. You are to stay in the area until you hear from BdU. You will be given new coordinates for further deployment."

"What can I do without weapons?" Krebs asked reasonably.

"You can wait until you're told what to do." Vogel made to leave the tower of his boat but he stopped and came back. "You were supposed to rendezvous with me off Montauk Point. Failure to comply with my orders again will . . ." He seemed to suddenly become conscious of the crew of the *U-560* all watching him, their ears well cocked. "I want your radioman punished. He clearly did not properly relay my orders."

"I shall have him flogged immediately, Captain. How many lashes do you think would be best?"

Vogel gave Krebs a long, threatening stare, then disappeared below. Soon, his U-boat was moving eastward.

Max said, "What good does it do for us to stay here without torpedoes or eighty-eight rounds? Vogel is playing us for a fool."

Krebs privately agreed but said, "Get the boys below, Max."

As his crew filed through the tower hatch, Krebs contemplated the lifeboats and noticed that they were already angling off to the northeast, the Stream clutching them and shoving them along. The best strategy to use one of his remaining torpedoes, he thought, might be to track the lifeboats and see if the *Maudie Jane* might come out to rescue them. It would be a fine ambush. After more consideration, he looked to the west and said, "Let's lay off the island just there."

Max was surprised by the order. "May I ask why, sir?"

"I don't want to use our eels until we discover what BdU has in mind. I've heard the boys talk about the island. We might as well play the tourist. We'll post extra lookouts so every man can get a chance to have a look at America."

The lifeboats of the *San Paulo* kept pulling away. Krebs wondered what it would feel like to be in their situation. The Chief and some of the other hands had been merchant sailors before the war. The Chief apparently was thinking along the same lines. "Those men," he said wistfully, "are us."

# 32

D osie rested her face in her hands and slowly shook her head. "I will surely go insane," she said between her fingers. She was sitting in her parlor before a crackling driftwood fire on a glorious Killakeet morning. Sunshine shot through the shards of beach glass she'd hung in her windows, playing delightful rainbow patterns across the walls. Dosie knew it was beautiful but she couldn't enjoy it. She'd been thinking about Josh and missing him. Even though it was still an hour before noon, she was also seriously thinking about opening a bottle of wine, just to soften her mood. Instead, she abruptly reached for her boots, pulled them on, and strode through the kitchen and out the back door, heading for the stables. "To hell with all men," she said to Genie, who gave her a querulous nicker, as if to say, *What, again?* Every time Dosie had gotten lonely for Josh, or morose about the possibilities of her future and the particulars of her past, she'd saddled up Genie and gone flying into the storm.

Though Genie bared her teeth and stamped her hooves, Dosie told her to stop acting silly. "Come on, don't act all mehonkey," she said, tossing the saddle on the mare's back. Then she said, "Well, listen to my Killakeet vocabulary, why don't you? Danged if I ain't mommicked for a dit-dot. But I ain't quamished, not by a sight. Even though I do long for that puck, Josh Thurlow. For sure, don't you know, that wampus cat." She laughed at herself, and it felt good to do it. "Yep, insane, for sartain, cattywumpus, that's me."

It had been too wet to ride on the beach during the long January blow, so mostly Dosie had taken Genie through Teach Woods and across inland tracks to Whalebone City. But with the clearing skies and the gentle breeze and the bright sunshine, she decided to go south along the beach to see what she could see. Once on the sand, littered with shells and driftwood tossed ashore during the storm, Genie took a few quick steps, then slowed to a walk. Dosie felt the mare's unhappiness and allowed her to set the pace. "I'm sorry, girl," Dosie said. "I have no right to wear you out just because I can't face life." She sighed heavily.

Genie also sighed, then plodded on, her head low, taking little note of the sandpipers scurrying ahead of her dragging hooves. A fussy seagull settled in on her haunches for a ride and, for the trouble, got a beakful of Genie's swished tail. It flew to a sand hill and complained, though none of the other gulls much listened. Gulls tended to be complainers, Dosie had noticed, but not much interested in complaints other than their own. In that, they were like a lot of people she knew, including herself.

Dosie was so lost in her thoughts that she failed to see the circling seagulls ahead, or the objects of their attention. She was nearly on top of them when she saw what appeared to be sodden cloth bags. Genie stopped short, and the seagulls flew off, screeching. Then Dosie saw that the "bags" were not bags at all but coats, shirts, and blouses covering the backs of drowned human beings. As if she were coming out of a dream, other objects began to coalesce before Dosie. There were heads protruding from the sand, and hands, arms, and legs.

Dosie fought both the urge to vomit and also to wheel Genie around and go flying back up the beach. She waited herself out until her stomach calmed down. The tide was coming in. Soon, the people would be covered up. She had a responsibility to report what she'd seen, then bring others to recover the bodies. She turned in her saddle. She could still see her house less than a mile to the north.

She clicked her tongue. "Walk on, Genie," she said. Shoes by the dozens had been cast up, along with life rings, shattered decking, oars, and—*there!* A complete lifeboat. Dosie steered Genie to it but it was empty. A white square, cast ashore by a rough wave, caught her eye. At first, she thought it was a handkerchief but then she saw it was a sodden sheet of paper. Hoping it might identify the ship the bodies were from, she dismounted and carefully plucked it from the murmuring sea. To her surprise, the handwriting on it was in German. A notation along the top edge said *"560"* and *"Krebs."* She pressed the paper against Genie's saddle to wring out a little of the water, then inserted it carefully into her saddlebag. "They'll want to see this, Genie," she said, not exactly sure who "they" were. Perhaps Josh, when he came in. Or at least Chief Glendale.

"They're resting," a voice, like soft wind, said.

Dosie nearly jumped out of her skin. A figure rose from a sand hill. It was Willow. She reminded Dosie of a wisp of smoke, the way she nearly floated when she walked. She wore a white dress and her red hair rippled like a Russian flag in the breeze.

Dosie was also surprised to see Jezzie, the old mare, come up behind Willow. "We been watching them all day," Willow said. "They're resting."

"They're dead, Willow," Dosie replied.

" 'Rest in peace,' they say over the graves," Willow replied. Then, she hopped aboard Jezzie. The mare trotted toward Miracle Point, Willow hugging her close.

Dosie, shaking her head at crazy Willow, turned Genie toward Whalebone City. As she did, she was surprised to see another mounted figure coming down the beach. At first, she thought it might be Keeper Jack aboard Thunder, but as she got closer, she saw it was a man in a big white cowboy hat riding on a large brown stallion with a saddle glittering with silver trim. He looked like something right out of the movies.

Rex Stewart, the best trick rider in Hollywood, and Joe Johnston, the best trick horse, trotted down the beach toward what appeared to be a woman mounted on a big mare. "Maybe we'll find out where we are now, boy," Rex said. He was dressed in the very same uniform, only tailored a little in the shoulders, that Gary Cooper had worn in *The Lives of a Bengal Lancer,* a crisp khaki jacket with epaulets on the shoulders, and tight, white pants that ran down into knee-high, brown leather boots. He was also wearing the big white hat Gene Autry had given him after they'd wrapped *Springtime in the Rockies.* A Sam Browne belt, taken from his work on *Mounties to the Rescue,* completed the ensemble, from which hung a holster filled with an ivory-handled Colt forty-five revolver. Joe wore a saddle studded with silver conchas that Roy Rogers had awarded him for stunt work on *Wall Street Cowboy.* For that one, they'd painted Joe yellow to match Trigger's color because Roy's big palomino was having an off day. A Winchester 94 carbine also dangled from Joe's saddle in a silver-studded holster.

Rex and Joe had come across on the morning ferry from Morehead City along with other riders and horses of the newly formed Coast Guard Beach Patrol. The pair had been let off on the island called Killeykeets, or some such, with the rest of the troop taken on up to Ocracoke to leave a few men and their mounts, and thence to Hatteras and Currituck for the rest. Rex's only order, received from a Coast Guard officer before going aboard the ferry, was to report in to somebody at Doakes Station. He had asked the folks at the ferry landing where he might find Doakes. After they were through staring at him and Joe, they had pointed across the island. Rex had ridden through a dense woods and then through a cut in some high dunes that led to the Atlantic Ocean. He wasn't sure where to go from there but he spotted the lighthouse and headed for it to get more directions. The lighthouse and the house beside it were empty, so he and Joe had continued on down the beach toward a house a mile or so farther. It had also proved empty, although they had found a stable. Rex started following the hoofprints leading out of it.

The woman and the mare came up to them. Rex doffed

his hat. "Afternoon, ma'am," he said. "Is this the way to Whalebone City?"

"Exactly the wrong way," Dosie answered. "If you turn around and go about three miles, you'll be there. If you don't mind me asking, who and what are you?"

"Sergeant Rex Stewart of the United States Coast Guard Beach Patrol, ma'am," Rex said, sweeping his hat. "This is my horse, Joe Johnston. Come to keep this island safe from Nazis."

Dosie introduced herself. "Miss Dosie Crossan. I live in that house just there. I didn't know the Coast Guard had sergeants. Isn't that the army or the marines?"

Rex plopped his hat back on. "Well, they said I could call myself pretty much what I wanted to. What should be my rank, do you think?"

"I guess you can be a sergeant," Dosie said. "I'm not an expert on the military."

"Have you seen any suspicious activities?" Rex asked.

"I was just going to Doakes to report bodies washed up on the beach."

Rex was astonished, then made more so when Dosie told him about the sinking of the *Lady Morgan* and all the dead and wounded brought ashore. She also told him a bit about Josh and the *Maudie Jane,* which was even at that moment out hunting U-boats. Rex patted his Winchester. "Guess I might need ol' Winnie here."

"Do you want to see the bodies?" Dosie asked.

Rex guessed it was his duty to see them so he agreed and Dosie turned Genie around. Genie seemed reluctant to break the nose-to-nose contact that she was having with Joe, who, after all, was a handsome stallion.

At the site of the bodies, Rex dismounted and tried to come to grips with the situation. "Damnedest thing," he said. "Who would've thunk it?"

"I found some more," Willow said.

Reflexively, Rex filled his hand with his revolver, but then he saw it was only a girl riding bareback on a shaggy pony. They had both appeared like a puff of wind. Rex holstered the Colt, doffed his hat, and swooped it politely. "Afternoon, little lady. Who might you be?"

"Her name's Willow," Dosie said. Then she whispered in Rex's ear, "Some people say she's a hoo-doo."

Willow said, "I am not a hoo-doo. I found some more and they're not resting." She pointed to the south.

"I believe Willow's found some men in a lifeboat, Sergeant Stewart," Dosie said, squinting in the direction of her point.

Rex climbed back aboard Joe. "Let's have us a look," he said.

The lifeboat was from the tanker *Esso Salt Lake City*. There were six men aboard it, one of whom was badly burned. Rex and Dosie helped them to the sand hills above the beach. "I don't even have so much as a first aid kit," Rex said. He was starting to realize his job might be less fighting Nazis on the beach and more helping poor sailors stranded on it. "What do you think we should do?"

Dosie gave it some thought, then said, "Use a blanket from your bedroll to cover the burned man. Then, if you head that way across the sand hills, you'll come upon a path that will lead you to a pond of fresh water. I noticed a bailing bucket in the lifeboat. Take it and bring back water for these men. While you're doing that, I'll go up to Doakes, borrow the jeep, and come back with Doc Folsom. One way or the other, you wait here until I get back."

"Say," Rex said, "you're not in the Coast Guard, too, are you?"

"No, why would you say that?"

"Well, you seem to know exactly what to do."

Dosie puffed up, just a little. "I was always a good organizer," she said.

"Maybe you ought to join the patrol. I mean this looks like a lot of beach to cover all by myself. You and Genie would be a big help to me and Joe."

*Dosie of the Beach Patrol.* She liked the sound of it. "I wouldn't mind being in this war," she said.

"I was told by an officer I could recruit some help on the

island as long as they didn't care to get paid."

"I'll think about it," Dosie said, even though she was already inclined to do it. Then, to the stranded sailors, she said, "You just wait here. Rex is going to get you some water and I'm going to fetch back a doctor."

"Bless you, little miss," one of the sailors said. "You are like unto an angel."

Dosie leaped aboard Genie and went off on the gallop.

# 33

The *U-560*, going in to lie off the island, caught the little freighter steaming along as if it had all the time in the world. "We'll use the eighty-eight millimeter on it," Krebs decided.

Before the gun crew could get into position, the freighter suddenly sped up and away. She was a fast little thing. Krebs was reluctant to order Hans to use full turns to catch her. "Load the G-7 in the stern torpedo tube," he said, referring to the old-style steam-driven torpedo. It was, in fact, the only torpedo left in the stern. The old design, however, was best for what he needed, a long-distance shot at a receding target. The G-7s could go long and fast, though they produced a large amount of bubbles. Krebs doubted if it mattered whether the freighter could see the torpedo or not. Her master was not taking her on a zigzag course. He was just moving her as rapidly away from the *U-560* as possible.

Krebs accomplished the calculations and launched the torpedo, expecting to catch the freighter in the stern. But she zigzagged at the last second and was struck broadside. The explosion lifted her nearly out of the water and broke her in two. Within a few minutes, the bow went down. Krebs ordered the *U-560* in closer while the Chief made an identification, then watched the freighter crew row off in lifeboats.

There didn't seem to be any casualties unless men had been trapped in the bow. "I put her as the *City of Tallahassee,* sir," the Chief said. "Five thousand four hundred and forty-six gross tons carrying general cargo."

Krebs saw a glint of sunlight reflecting off a boat coming their way. "I think it's the patrol boat from the island."

Max took a look through the Zeiss glasses. "It is. They're coming to rescue the crew," he concluded.

Krebs wasn't so sure. "Chief, take us down. Let's take a closer look."

The stern of the freighter lolled in its half-sunk position, the placid sea lapping against its rust-pitted hull. She had been broken in two, the bow drifted off or sunk. "I think it's the *City of Tallahassee,*" Phimble said, after a study of the shipping registry. "Five thousand four hundred and forty-six gross tons according to this. General cargo. Look there on the stern. It's hard to see for all the rust, but its number is the *Tallahassee*'s all right."

Josh was at the wheel, idling the *Maudie Jane* around the ragged stern. There was charring on the exterior of the broken wheelhouse, indicative of an internal fire that had spread from below. A lifeboat hung awry on its davit fall, perhaps stranded when the freighter had rolled toward the torpedo hole, a wound that looked as if a giant hammer had beaten a huge hole in its side. Upwind, the sharp odor of ammonia pierced nasal passages. "Refrigerant," Josh commented to Phimble. "I hope the crew got well away before it was released. I've heard of men being asphyxiated by it even out on the open sea."

The Maudie Janes were looking hard for bodies while hoping they wouldn't find any. "Hey, a contact!" Jimmy called from the sonar closet, his voice shrill with excitement. "About five hundred yards dead ahead, Skipper!"

"Remain calm, Jimmy," Josh replied through the voice-phone after handing over the wheel to Phimble.

"Yes, sir!" Jimmy shrieked.

Josh grimaced and held the receiver away from his ear. "All ahead," he said to Phimble. Phimble pushed the throttles to the stops and the *Maudie Jane* roared.

Jimmy called out, now a bit calmer. "Still good contact. It's running from us, whatever it is. Thirty degrees to starboard."

It was a good feeling to have a U-boat running from them. "Go help Ready with the depth charges, Eureka," Josh ordered. "Set two charges at sixty feet. I'll give you the signal when to let them go."

Krebs let Max take a turn at the scope. "She's got depth charges in her racks," Max observed.

*Pok! Pok!*

The sonar echoes striking the *U-560* were startling. No one had been expecting them. "She's also got ears," Krebs said. "That settles the issue, then. Let's get rid of this nuisance." He took back the periscope. "Chief, is our last torpedo ready?"

"Yes, sir, ready!"

Josh took the wheel again and Phimble scrambled back to the racks, told Ready to set the depth on the next charges, and pulled the safety pins. Josh raised his hand, then let it drop. "Pull!" Phimble yelled at Ready on the starboard rack, then followed his own order on the portside one. The depth charges rolled overboard and splashed into the wake. A few seconds followed, and then a thunderclap shook the *Maudie Jane,* followed by twin geysers of foamy white seawater spewing high into the sky. Sunlight flashed through them, producing a million sparkling rainbows.

"Why, that's right pretty," Again said to his brother at their stations on the bow. Marvin was with them, thumping his tail on the deck. He had an eager grin on his face. "You like chasing U-boats, don't you, Marvin?" Again asked, squatting to pet the dog.

"Dammit, Again, stop petting Marvin and get on that machine gun!" Josh yelled.

• • •

"Here they come," Krebs said, his eyes melded with the periscope eyepiece. "Chief, take us down ten meters and then hard aport."

The *U-560* painfully throbbed as the electrics spun up to speed, then they heard overhead the splashes of two depth charges. "Push it, Chief!" Krebs yelled.

"It's still moving, sir," Jimmy said over the speaker. "Sixty degrees to port. About a hundred yards away."

Josh cut the eighty-three footer in that direction, signaling Phimble and Ready to get prepared for another drop. He thought to himself, *I should slow down, wait until we get right over the target and then drop the charges*. He drew back on the twin throttles and the *Maudie Jane* dipped her bow, friction slowing her down. Jimmy yelled, his voice back up to shrill. "We're right over it, sir!"

Josh gave the signal and Phimble and Ready pulled the levers and the barrels rolled in. "Uh-oh," Ready said at that instant. "I forgot to set the depths."

"Oh, shit," Phimble groaned just as a volcano of blue-green water roared up under the *Maudie Jane*. When she came down, her transom disappeared underwater, and what looked like a tidal wave flushed Phimble and Ready nearly halfway to the wheelhouse.

On the bow, the men hung on to the railings except for Once, who held on to Marvin. Somehow, they all managed to stay on board. Below decks, Fisheye and Big went tumbling past their engines, which, after a moment's hesitation, fortunately kept chugging.

On the stoop bridge, Josh had been knocked flat on his back. *My God*, he thought as he got up. *I've sunk my own boat!*

Pretch announced, "Hydrophones are quiet, sir. The Americans are dead in the water."

Krebs ordered a return to periscope depth and took a look. The patrol boat was just sitting in front of the

freighter. Some of the men aboard her seemed to be getting
to their feet. "Looks like she took a hit from her own depth
charges," Krebs said, grinning. "We've got her now." He
called out the numbers for torpedo guidance. "All right,
Chief! *Los!*"

The crew of the *U-560* held their collective breaths at the
spewing noise of their last torpedo leaving its tube.

"Torpedo!" Again yelled, and pointed to starboard.

Josh looked after the point and saw, not more than a hundred yards away, the unmistakable track of a torpedo streaming straight for them. He jammed the throttles forward and
the engines stuttered. "Come on, baby!" Josh yelled. "Oh,
come on, you sweet *Maudie Jane!*"

Krebs saw a sudden boil of white froth at the stern of the patrol
boat as she began to gather way. In disbelief, he watched the
torpedo sizzle past and keep going, striking the freighter. The
crew of the *U-560* misinterpreted the resulting explosion and
raised a cheer. "Hoorah for our captain!"

The Chief gleefully added, *"Fingerspitzengefühl!"*

Then came the sound of the American sonar, its thump
on the hull like the rap of ghostly knuckles. The cheering
abruptly stopped.

"I missed her," Krebs announced.

The faces of the men in the tower control room first registered disappointment, then turned to fear.

*I should come to the surface and fight it out,* Krebs
thought. *Lay into them with the eighty-eight.* Then he decided
he had taken enough chances. "Chief, get us out of here,"
he said. "Flank speed. Let's get some room."

"The sub's moving west, Skipper," Jimmy advised.

Josh had no choice but to let it move anywhere it wanted.
The *Maudie Jane*'s engines needed to be inspected. Fisheye
had already come up and said he was worried that one of
them might be a bit mommicked.

"Eureka, let's get out of here."

"This one's a draw, eh, Skipper?"

"This one was just practice. Next time, we'll get him."

Max found Krebs in the bow torpedo room, looking at the empty racks. He'd sent the torpedomen back to the galley to be given a cup of beer apiece. It hadn't been their fault that their last torpedo had missed.

"*Kaleu,* are you all right?"

Krebs pretended to be inspecting the leaky torpedo tube door. "What do you think, Max?" he asked almost idly.

"I think anybody can miss a torpedo shot on a moving target, especially if you don't know it's going to move."

"I should have anticipated it."

"The Americans were lucky."

Krebs wheeled on Max. "We've always been the lucky ones, Max. If we've lost our luck, we are in trouble."

"It hasn't been luck that's kept us alive, sir. You've always seen a way to get us past our scrapes. I'm confident you will continue to find a way."

Krebs shook his head. "I wish I was as confident as you."

Max started to serve up a platitude, then realized Krebs wasn't looking for consolation. He was looking for something inside himself, the thing that had made him love matching his wits against the enemy. If he had lost that, then perhaps the *U-560* was indeed in trouble. "I have hidden away a respectable bottle of schnapps, sir," Max said. "Perhaps you would care to join me in its destruction."

Krebs smiled, then gripped Max's shoulder. "What would I do without you, my friend?"

"Today, you'd miss out on a good drink," Max said modestly, then led the way astern to find the bottle.

Phimble moved the *Maudie Jane* eastward, deeper into the Stream. A subdued Ready was acting as lookout. He had been thoroughly chewed out by both Phimble and Josh for forgetting to set the depths on the charges. To make up for it, he was determined to see everything. When he caught sight of something bobbing on the ocean off to the north, he called it out even if it was small. It proved to be a tiny boat, very low in the water.

Josh took a look through the binoculars that hung around his neck. It was, indeed, a tiny boat, too small by far to be this far out. "Eureka, head over to whatever that is," he called over his shoulder.

A few minutes later, the *Maudie Jane* closed to a hundred yards of the odd little boat. Josh had nearly screwed his binoculars into his eyes. It was what it was, whether he believed it or not. It was a moth boat, its hull painted a bright red, and its mast lashed to its deck.

Josh's mind swirled with possibilities. Abandoned wrecks off the Outer Banks, if they were placed just so, were sometimes carried north by the Gulf Stream, then sucked south by the Labrador Current, only to be caught in the Stream again, looping around.

*But, my God, seventeen years!* Surely, in all that time, the little moth boat that had held Jacob, even caught between the two currents, would have been sunk by a storm or put down by a rogue wave or simply spotted and picked up. But there was no denying that it was there, bobbing placidly. Waiting.

Phimble idled the *Maudie Jane* to drift in on the tiny boat. Once was on the bow, closest to it. "There's something moving in it!" he called out. "And it's whimpering!"

Josh let loose of the binoculars, which fell to dangle from the strap around his neck. His vision went a bit fuzzy and then he went down on one knee. He felt as if he were suffocating. Ready reached down to help him. Phimble saw what had happened and would have come to help, too, except that there was another problem. A ghost ship had suddenly appeared, reared up on the distant horizon, and it had turned in the direction of the *Maudie Jane*.

# 34

osie arrived back with the jeep and Doc in it. Doc slogged up the dune to where Rex and the men of the *Esso Salt Lake City* were waiting. "I'm Doc Folsom," he said, resting his black bag in the sand. "How you boys doing?"

"Most of us is fine, Doc," one of the men replied. "Sure glad to see you. Ed's burned up pretty bad."

Doc knelt beside the burned man and lifted the blanket covering him. He looked, then slowly lowered the blanket.

"Can you help him, Doc?" a crewman asked.

Doc shook his head. "Let's get him in the jeep. Then all you boys pile in, too. We'll get Chief Glendale to carry Ed across to Morehead City aboard the workboat. They'll fix him up there."

Dosie said, "I'll walk back, if you don't mind. I have a few things I want to talk over with Rex here. You can drive."

Doc said he'd do it, and he, Rex, and Dosie helped the sailors into the jeep. Somehow, they all squeezed in, with Ed laid across their laps. Dosie remembered she hadn't formally introduced Rex to Doc. She corrected the oversight. Rex once more swooped his big white hat.

"That's a fine uniform you have there, Sergeant Stewart," Doc said.

"Thanks, I kind of came up with it myself. What part do you like the best?"

"The whole thing in general. You look like a Bengal Lancer, I'd say, except without a turban."

"By God, you're a smart man, Doc. This is the very same uniform Gary Cooper wore when he played the part."

"If every soldier was dressed like you, we'd have this war won in a week," Doc swore, then climbed in behind the wheel of the jeep and sped off with the merchant sailors toward Whalebone City.

Dosie and Rex and Joe Johnston started walking. "Doc seems like a good guy," Rex said.

"He has his ways," Dosie said. "You're about to find out that everybody on this island has a pretty strong personality."

"Well, I ought to fit right in," Rex said, then gave Dosie a glance. "Are all of the girls on this island as pretty as you?"

Dosie nearly blushed. The cowboy was pretty smooth. "Why, I'd say they're mostly pretty," she answered, "but they're also mostly married or spoken for."

"How about you? Married or spoken for?"

"I've pretty much sworn off men except for one. I'd swear him off, too, if I could."

Rex was mildly disappointed but not much. He had what he figured was about a twenty-year head start on Dosie, after all. "Why don't you swear him off, then?"

"Good question."

"And the girl, the wispy one?"

"I guess the only one who speaks for Willow is herself."

They silently walked past the bodies on the beach. "Chief Glendale and Keeper Jack and a bunch of men are coming to get them," Dosie said.

"Who's Keeper Jack?"

"The keeper of the lighthouse." Dosie nodded toward the distant spire. "He's also the father of my honey, the one I should swear off."

"Is everybody related to everybody else on this island?"

"Except for me and you, I expect that's about right. Oh, Bosun Phimble, he's a Hatterasser."

"A what?"

"That means he's from the island of Hatteras."

"Hark!" Rex called. "What's that?" He looked over his shoulder.

Dosie heard it before she saw it, a low drumming sound. Then she saw a long, thin boat with big bulge in its center sailing up the coast not more than a football field from the surf line.

Rex said, "That's an odd-looking craft."

Dosie squinted, then her expression turned angry. "Not so odd if it's a German U-boat!" she cried.

Krebs had been shaken by the encounter with the patrol boat. Why, he wondered, had he decided to run away? The *U-560* was out of torpedoes but it still had its eighty-eight. He could have risen up and pummeled the patrol boat until it was nothing but splinters. Perhaps, he had finally been worn out by the war. That was the only explanation, that and the way Miriam had changed him. *I've become soft,* he griped to himself. *I am no longer fit to command.*

And that, Krebs deduced, was the situation. He was quite calm about it. Sooner or later, it happened to every captain. It was an accumulation of events or simply getting older, and it meant he was a danger to himself and, more importantly, his crew. Krebs suddenly made up his mind. As soon as he got back to Brest, he was going to request to be relieved. He contemplated taking the *U-560* back that very minute. Who cared what Vogel might have to say about it? Who cared, for that matter, what Doenitz might say or do? What *could* he do? Hang him for ignoring a verbal command from Vogel shouted across the water? It could have easily been misunderstood. Anyway, Krebs sincerely doubted the navy would hang a U-boat captain who reported in with six freighters and two tankers hanging like scalps from his belt.

It was a pretty day. The sky was blue, the breeze warm for February, and the island with its stately lighthouse was a glorious sight. Krebs suddenly felt very free. "Max," he asked lightly, "what do you think? Are we safe here?"

Max had been badgering the lookouts to scour the skies. They'd seen only birds. "It looks safe enough," he said. "I don't think the Americans have any aircraft around here. The water is too shallow for us to maneuver, though."

"We'll chance it," Krebs said. "Let the boys come up for a look. They can air their bedding, too."

Max called through the hatch to the Chief and soon a dozen men who were off watch came up, to see the island they'd heard so much about, to gawk at the distant lighthouse, and the beige piles of sand, and the maritime forest, and also to hang out their mildewed blankets. Sliding past them was a little piece of the United States of America. "Look, horses!" one of the boys cried.

Krebs smiled. There were indeed a number of horses gathered on the beach. "They're probably the wild horses I've read about," Max said. "Look how shaggy they are."

"There's a girl on one of them!" another boy whooped.

A cheer amongst the crew went up. Krebs peered at the girl with the Zeiss glasses. She was a pretty girl, dressed in a wispy white dress, her red hair rippling as her horse trotted along.

The herd of wild horses and the girl were soon left behind and some of the men stripped off their shirts and stretched out on the deck to sunbathe. Krebs saw Harro was amongst them. The report he'd gotten from Pretch was that the boy was turning into a pretty good radioman. It was bound to mean a promotion. Harro looked up, saw Krebs watching him, and nodded. It was as much thanks as a greeting. Harro knew very well that the captain had been behind his reassignment.

"Look, another horse," Max said.

Krebs saw the horse, this one not wild like the others. Two people were walking beside it. One of them was wearing a khaki uniform and a big white hat. The other one was a woman, dressed in tall boots, jodhpurs, a checked shirt, a straw hat, and a red bandanna around her neck. "They're a colorful bunch around here," Krebs said.

"The man with the white hat has a pistol on his hip," Max observed through his binoculars. "He looks like something out of a Gary Cooper movie."

Krebs laughed. Neither he nor Max nor any of the crew saw the woman draw the Winchester lever-action rifle from its sleeve on the silver-lined saddle.

"Whoa there, little lady," Rex said when he saw what Dosie was up to. "That's a dangerous weapon."

"I hope so," Dosie said, tossing it to Rex. "See that bastard on the tower in the white cap? He's the captain. Shoot him."

Rex just stood there, holding the rifle in one hand. He'd never shot a human being before. A rabbit or two, over the years, but that was about it.

"What are you waiting for?" Dosie demanded. "Can't you hit him?"

"From this distance, I could put a bullet through his eyeball," Rex said. "But it don't seem sporting, somehow. I mean he's just riding along. And there's all those others. Looks like they're sunbathing and I'd say that was their blankets and mattresses and whatnot. Must be laundry day."

"You saw those bodies back there. Who do you think killed them? And who do you think burned up poor Ed? Shoot the bastard!"

Rex looked a little closer. "I believe that's a machine gun they've got there. And that's a mighty big gun up front, too. It's artillery, I'd say."

"Well, for the love of Franklin Delano Roosevelt," Dosie snarled, and snatched the rifle from Rex. She propped it over Joe Johnston's saddle and took careful aim. With his tangled reddish brown beard, the captain of the U-boat reminded her of a Viking warrior. Just as she started to squeeze the trigger, he disappeared behind the fairing of the tower. "Dammit!"

"Look, Dosie," Rex said. "I don't think this is a real good idea."

"Shut up."

"OK," Rex replied, putting his hands in his pockets. He whistled and Joe Johnston pranced around, throwing off Dosie's aim.

"Hold still!"

Rex whistled another combination and the horse bolted and ran up to the sand hills. Rex didn't want Joe to get hurt.

Without the saddle to steady her aim, Dosie wasn't sure she could hit anybody in particular, so she shifted her aim to the group lounging on the deck. She cut loose in their general direction. "Take that, you lousy Nazis!" she yelled at the same time.

Harro and Joachim were having a fine time. They'd enjoyed looking at the wild horses and the girl, and at the sand dunes and the forest behind it, and the squadrons of pelicans going overhead, and the seagulls making lazy patterns in the sky. Now, they'd seen the most remarkable sight, a cowboy in a white hat with a good-looking woman walking beside him and a big brown horse with a saddle all decked out in silver trim. "America is a strange and wonderful place," Joachim decided and said so.

"Look," Harro said, "the horse is prancing around and now it's running up into the forest."

"I bet it's a trick horse," Joachim said. "Cowboy horses usually are."

"Take cover!" *Leutnant* Max suddenly yelled from the tower. "She's got a gun!"

Some of the men dived under their mattresses. Others ran to hide behind the tower. The men at the machine gun jacked back the handle and swiveled their wicked double snouts toward the beach.

The woman's bullet struck the deck and ricocheted off. Krebs came up to see what was happening just as she fired again. He looked toward his boys and saw Harro fall.

"I got one!" Dosie said. Then her expression changed from exultation to grief. "I got one," she said again and a big tear welled up and rolled down her cheek.

Rex took back his rifle. "I think we'd better run for it."

The Germans were crawling out from under their mattresses. The man who'd fallen was being helped up. The machine gun on the tower was aimed directly at Rex and Dosie. "I think it's too late," Dosie said.

Rex took a look at the machine gun. "I see what you mean." He considered raising his hands to surrender but decided not to give the Germans the satisfaction. Nonetheless, the thought crossed his mind that he sure wished he had that boy John Wayne doing this particular stunt.

Krebs shook his head. "What is it with these Americans and their rifles?"

"Do you want me to kill them?" the machine gun captain asked.

"I suppose not," Krebs replied, and went down the tower ladder to see about Harro. Joachim was bending over him. Harro was bleeding profusely from the side of his head. "Can you speak?" Krebs asked him, fearing the worst.

"Yes, sir," Harro said. "I tripped on one of the mattresses and hit my head on the deck."

"The boy's got a hard head," the Chief said, coming up for a look. "He'll be all right."

Krebs was relieved. The boy's survival had become important to him. "Go on below, get cleaned up. Pretch can give you a stitch if you need it."

"I hope I don't need it, sir," Harro said, touching his head gingerly.

"Go on, now." Krebs said. He patted the boy on his shoulder as he went past. Then he cupped his hands and yelled in English to the woman and the cowboy, "You missed!"

Dosie wiped away her tear, then shouted back, "You're a bunch of murderers!"

The U-boat captain seemed to consider that charge for a moment, then yelled, "We are at war, *madame!* We do our duty!"

Rex said, "Boy, his English sure is good. But maybe we shouldn't be talking to him. There's probably a law or a regulation against it. Loose lips sink ships and all that."

"I already told you to shut up," Dosie growled.

Rex wiped his nose with the back of his sleeve. "Yes, ma'am."

Dosie went back after the U-boat captain. "You're still a bunch of Nazi rat bastards!"

"Are all Americans as brave as you?" the captain called. "I have a machine gun, you know. You would not stand a chance if I gave the order to fire."

"This is the home of the brave, bub!" Dosie cried. "And the land of the free, too, and don't you forget it! Why don't you go back to Germany and stay there?"

Dosie was astonished when the men on the U-boat's deck cheered her.

"I think you have put forward a popular proposal to my men," the captain said, then tipped his white cap to her and went back up to the tower. Apparently, he'd barked a command, as the other Germans followed him, carrying their bedding with them. Quickly, the deck was cleared, and the U-boat curved out from the beach and headed for deeper water. Soon, it had submerged, leaving only a froth of bubbles to mark its passage.

Joe Johnston came plodding down from the dunes, nickering. "You're a good boy," Rex told him.

"You're a trickster is what you are," Dosie complained. She looked at Rex. "I'm sorry I told you to shut up. But what got said needed to be said."

It wasn't the first time a woman had told Rex to shut up so he wasn't particularly upset. "Do you realize you just had a conversation with a U-boat captain?"

Dosie gave that some thought, then shrugged and asked, "If I join the beach patrol, do you think I'll need a uniform?"

Rex appraised her. "Well, your jodhpurs and boots are a good start, already. How about a shirt or some such that looks sort of military?"

Dosie snapped her fingers. "I could borrow one of Josh's khaki shirts and cut it down! I'm pretty handy with scissors and thread."

"Josh?"

"Mr. Sworn Off. He's in the Coast Guard."

"Do you think he'll miss a shirt?" Rex asked.

"No," Dosie said. "As far as I can tell, he wears one until it completely wears out, and then and only then puts on another."

"I like him already," Rex allowed. "I've got an extra Sam Browne belt and holster. We just need to get you a sidearm to put in it."

"Oh, I have a pistol back at the house," Dosie replied. "Daddy gave it to me since I live alone and all. It's a Smith and Wesson thirty-eight. Daddy also has a thirty aught six deer rifle locked up in the attic."

"That should do it. I think you and I are going to make quite the team. Of course, like I told you, there's no pay involved."

"I'm not looking for pay," Dosie said, "just a job that means something." She hadn't realized how true that was until that very moment. It perked her up. "What do I have to do to join?"

"All I did was take an oath."

"Give it to me, then."

"Raise your right hand. Do you swear to uphold the Constitution of these United States pretty much forever and die doing it, if you have to?"

"You bet," Dosie replied.

"Welcome to the Coast Guard Beach Patrol. You can put your hand down now."

Instead, Dosie snapped a salute. "Thanks. What's my first order?"

"Don't take my rifle away from me again. Also, don't salute me. Salutes are for officers."

Dosie dropped her salute. "What's my rank, by the way?"

"What's below sergeant?"

"Corporal, as far as I know."

"OK, you're an unpaid corporal for the duration."

Dosie was thrilled. She couldn't wait to write her parents and her brothers and tell Josh. In the space of one afternoon, she had rescued stranded sailors, shot at a U-boat, called its captain a rat bastard to his face, and joined the United States

Coast Guard Beach Patrol. Any way you measured it, Corporal Dosie Crossan of Killakeet Island was doing an important job. She was in this war with both feet, both legs, and all that came afterward.

# 35

The ghost ship was coming on fast, but first the little red moth boat had to be understood. As Josh shook off the shock and got to his feet, a teenaged boy popped his head up from the cockpit, then disappeared and then reappeared, this time with a teenaged girl. To the general amusement of the Maudie Janes, both of them were hastily rearranging their clothes. Phimble shook his finger at them. "What in the blue blazes are you two doing this far out? Don't you know there's a war on? Even if there wasn't, a freighter could run you down, wouldn't even know it."

Josh was concerned about the girl. "Are you all right, honey?"

The girl, furiously blushing, finished buttoning her blouse and pushed her blonde hair back from her freckled face. She was cute as a button. "I'm OK," she said. "Are you going to tell my parents?"

Josh ignored her question. "Where did you come from?" he asked the boy.

"Ocracoke, sir," he answered, his voice an adolescent screech. "This morning. Guess that old current got us."

"You might have done better if you'd put up your sail," Phimble said, grinning now like the others.

"Let's get you two on board," Josh said, trying to keep a straight face. "We'll take you to Killakeet. You can catch the ferry home."

"What about my boat, sir?"

"We'll take it with us."

After the couple was aboard, the Maudie Janes clustered around the girl. She seemed to like the attention, blinking her eyes hither and yon, and smiling as demurely as anyone just caught in the act of smooching on the high seas might manage. The moth boat was set between the depth-charge racks.

"Skipper," Phimble said, "we got another kind of company. See that smoke? That there is a World War I, four-stack navy destroyer. Seeing her is like seeing a ghost. I didn't know there was any still in service. If she's here, maybe it means the fleet's been let out of Norfolk."

Once read the destroyer's light signal: "She's the USS *Piper,* sir, and she's telling us to heave to."

"The *Piper.* I know something about her," Phimble said. "Kind of a hard-luck ship. She rammed a cruiser on her maiden voyage. Later, she ran aground. Some folks say she's got a hoo-doo hex on her. I was sure they'd scrapped her and every last one of those old things."

"Those four-stackers might be old but they're fast," Josh said. "Thirty knots on a head of steam."

"She's just a tin can," Phimble replied, unimpressed.

For a tin can, the four-stacker came down on them very businesslike, continuously blinking her signal. "Get those children below!" Josh barked when he saw the teenagers gawking at the destroyer. Millie coaxed them along with promises of biscuits and honey. A tarpaulin was thrown over the moth boat.

The *Piper* was ugly, not a smooth line on her. Her wheelhouse was a box stuck in front of four huge vertical stacks, all blowing a foul black smoke. The greasy cloud from her oil-fired boilers streamed behind her like a black river in the sky. She was well armed, with three-inch guns, torpedoes, and multiple depth-charge racks. The designation on her sharp, gray bow was painted big, bold, and white: *DD731.*

The men aboard the destroyer were lined up at the rail with few smiles amongst them. In fact, they looked positively grim. The Maudie Janes for the most part were grimly looking back at them, too, as if they were foreigners. There was a palpable tension between the crews. "Damned evil-looking thing," Again said of the *Piper*. "Don't like the look of her boys, neither."

"Navy sailors," Ready said, "what the hell do they know?"

"Hush up," Phimble said. "I'll tell you what they know. They know how to operate that big old ship, don't think they don't. You boys could take a few lessons, I'd warrant."

The Maudie Janes exchanged doubtful glances but chose not to argue with the bosun lest they get extra duty or a rash of drills.

Several officers of the *Piper* came out of the wheelhouse and stood on the bridge. They were smartly turned out in blue winter coats. The senior amongst them turned out to be a Captain Dekalb, a stout man with piercing dark eyes and a bulldog jaw. "What boat are you?" he called, even though Ready had nearly worn out his arm signaling their designation.

"We're a Coast Guard eighty-three-footer, number eight three two two nine, sir," Josh called over. "I'm Ensign Josh Thurlow. We operate out of Doakes Station on Killakeet."

"Where's that?" Dekalb demanded. His officers registered surprise at his question, then pretended deafness.

Josh pointed westward. "See that lighthouse, sir? That's Killakeet."

Dekalb didn't bother to look. "My orders are to patrol from Hatteras to Lookout. I'm also supposed to chase U-boats. Damn if that won't be like hunting hornets all over the farm. I need a man who knows these waters. Send one across."

Josh and Phimble shared a glance. "For how long?" Josh asked.

"Until I let him go," the captain replied brusquely.

Josh knew he had no choice, other than to make a run for it. Dekalb outranked him and didn't look like a man who cared to debate an order. "Who do you think should go, Eureka?"

"Maybe it should be me." Phimble said. "If they try to shanghai me for too long, I'll figure a way to jump ship."

"No, I need you," Josh said. "Hell, I need all of you," he said to the listening deck crew. After a few seconds of consideration, he said, "Once and Again, I'm going to send one of you because you know these waters backwards and forwards, considering all the fishing you've done up around Hatteras. You pick between you."

"I'll do it, sir," Again said before Once could answer. "I allus wondered what it would be like to be in the blue-water navy."

Josh walked Again to the stern where they could have some privacy. "Listen," Josh said. "Don't let them put you to work doing anything else other than piloting. They start giving you a hard time, you get word to me one way or the other and I'll chase that old four-stacker down and get you off. In any case, I intend to tell them you can stay aboard for one week and that's all."

"Sounds good to me, sir."

While Once prepared to paddle his brother across on the raft, Josh went back to conversing with Captain Dekalb. Josh suspected Dekalb was impatient because he yelled, "Hurry up, damn you!"

"Captain, I'm going to send you over one of my best men," Josh replied in a measured voice. "I would like to have him back in one week."

"And I told you you'll get him back when I'm done with him," Dekalb snapped. Then he said, "You haven't heard about the *Jacob Jones,* have you?"

"She's another four-stacker," Phimble advised Josh.

"No, sir," Josh replied. "I'm afraid we haven't gotten much news down this way."

Dekalb gripped the rail of his bridge and his voice shook with outrage. "She was sunk off New Jersey, Mister Thurlow, by a U-boat. Of her crew of two hundred, only eleven men survived, which did not include her captain, a classmate of mine at Annapolis." He clenched his bulldog jaw, then slapped his gloved hand down on the rail. "No, I wouldn't call her sunk. She was *smashed,* swept aside like a paltry nuisance by some arrogant son of a bitch Nazi U-boat captain. I will take my revenge, sir, where I find it. And I *will* find it. Your man will help me in that cause."

"I'm powerfully sorry to hear about the *Jacob Jones,* sir," Josh answered sympathetically. "We've had our losses, too. There have been eight freighters and tankers sunk not more than a few miles from this very spot. We even had a U-boat fire a torpedo at us."

"The *Jacob Jones* was a warship of the United States Navy, Ensign!" Dekalb roared. "Not a merchantman or some piss-pot Coast Guard boat!" He scowled at Josh, then barked. "Send your man over!"

"One week," Josh insisted. "One week or I'll be coming after him."

"You're impertinent, Mister Thurlow," Captain Dekalb said. "We shall see what we shall see." With that, he turned on his heel and went inside the wheelhouse.

Josh saw Again off. "Remember what I told you. You stay on the bridge and advise the captain and the navigator. Keep them off the shoals as best you can. But don't let them put you to any other kind of work. That's a direct order from me to you. Got it?"

"Got it, sir," Again said resolutely, then climbed down into the raft and let Once paddle him across.

"Enjoy the Big Bluewater Bum," Phimble called after him, then said to Josh, "I don't like this, Skipper. I see Captain Dekalb mad and scared, both at the same time. God only knows what he might do if he gets attacked."

Josh agreed. He stuck his head in the wheelhouse to talk to Stobs. "Stobs, make a signal to the *Piper*'s sparks. See if he'll answer with something personal."

"Already done it," Stobs said. "I asked him what his skipper was like. He answered in Morse. I wrote it down."

Josh read Stobs's note: *Vengeance is mine. I will repay.*

Josh handed the note to Phimble, who took a look, allowed a low whistle, then said, "He left off the 'saith the Lord' part."

"Saith Captain Dekalb, looks like," Josh said. Then he thought of all the sailors who'd died aboard the *Jacob Jones.*

"A big old bucket like that is one hell of a juicy target."

"You think she's going to collect a torpedo, Skipper?" Stobs asked.

"I don't know, Stobs. But Mrs. Jackson will have my hide if anything happens to Again."

Later, when the *Piper* had disappeared beneath the horizon and the *Maudie Jane* was halfway back to Killakeet, Phimble took Josh aside. "Skipper, about the moth boat, the way you almost passed out. You got to get over it. You and me, we don't have time for anything but fighting this war right now."

Josh was taken aback by Phimble's concern. Sure, he'd felt a bit woozy when he'd seen that little red boat right about where Jacob had been lost. But what did Phimble expect, that such a coincidence wouldn't mean anything? Josh thought he'd handled it pretty well. "I'm doing my best," he answered in a calm voice, though he got a little pink in the face. "Anyhow, I don't reckon we'll happen upon any more red moth boats out here."

Phimble wouldn't let it go. "No sir, but it just ain't right, you still getting torn apart this way. Let little Jacob rest. Go with Keeper Jack and put up that headstone and be done with it. You got to have your mind on your business, to keep all our boys safe."

Josh still didn't see what the bosun was so concerned about but Phimble had rarely steered him wrong. "Maybe you're right, Eureka," he allowed. "You usually are."

Phimble was embarrassed by Josh's response. "Now, sir," he said to his friend and commander, "why don't you figure out how we can catch us a submarine? If there's anybody who could figure it out, it'd be you."

Josh gave Phimble's suggestion some thought. "I've been kicking something around," he said. "We might get court-martialed for it, but it might just work."

"Let's hear it," Phimble said. After Josh voiced his idea, the bosun grinned. "You are a devious man, Mister Thurlow."

Josh took it as a compliment.

# 36

It had been two of the most frustrating and degrading weeks of Krebs's life. First, he'd let a woman chase him away from a small island, then he'd skulked out to deeper water to wait until Vogel or BdU made up their minds what they wanted him to do. Waiting was the only choice he had. The *U-560* barely had enough fuel to get back across the Atlantic, its torpedoes were gone, and there were only enough eighty-eight shells to defend the boat in a scrape.

During the day, Krebs kept the boat resting on the sand in about one hundred feet of water. Propeller sounds overhead never stopped as freighters and tankers continued churning back and forth without any idea that they were passing over a German U-boat and its thirty-two-man crew. Sharp, hollow thumps followed by the shriek of rending steel told of other U-boats attacking successfully in the area. Thunderclaps told of depth charges in reply. It was apparent some Americans were fighting back. But neither Pretch nor Harro on the sound-detection gear reported the huge gush of released air that would indicate a destroyed U-boat. The *Unterseewaffe* boys were still winning, but Krebs was no longer part of the battle. He just sat and waited.

At night, he brought the boat up to air it out and let some of the boys get some time on the tower. The Killakeet Lighthouse flashed its signal, and moving lights marked individual ships running the gauntlet. Sometimes, there was an orange blaze marking the strike of a torpedo, followed by flames and smoke and the cries of dying men. Once, Krebs had been surprised to hear the whooping alarm of a warship. Moonlight showed a long, low ship with four stacks cutting rapidly through the water toward what appeared to be a torpedoed tanker. The Chief identified it as an old destroyer, built for duty during World War I.

"But what's she doing?" Krebs wondered. "Look at her. She goes south for a mile, then heads west, now she's going back north."

Max had been studying the destroyer through the Zeiss glasses. "I see something like bedsprings on her mast. I think that's radar, and unless I miss my guess, she's running a search pattern with it. There must be something wrong with it or she'd have picked us up by now."

Krebs's imagination was stirred by the sight of the old destroyer. What if he let her find him, perhaps even turn a light on to help? Most likely, based on her frantic movements, she would steam right at him, and alone as she was, Krebs could easily turn that into a fatal mistake. He would submerge at the last possible moment, let the destroyer pass overhead, too fast to drop her depth charges with any accuracy, and then he would rise and slam a torpedo in her stern. Since that was where she stored her depth charges, there wouldn't even be a splinter of her left. It was an interesting thought but all theoretical, of course, since Krebs had no torpedoes. He had no choice but to watch the destroyer run her idiotic patterns and the tankers and freighters steam back and forth while he gritted his teeth in frustration.

Nearly everyone aboard had managed to catch a cold. Krebs had one, too. During the day, the *U-560* sat on the bottom in the tropical wash of the Gulf Stream with most of the crew coughing, wheezing, and sneezing in a miserable chorus. The temperature rose inside the submarine throughout the day. If anyone tried to nap, he had to lie in a puddle of his own sweat. At night, when Krebs brought the boat up and threw open the hatch, a cloud of fetid, human-derived steam escaped. Cold air flushed through the interior, chilling the sweaty men. Since there was no fresh water for laundry, clothing was washed in the ocean by putting it in a net bag and tossing it overboard at the end of a line. The bag was then pulled the length of the U-boat by a crewman designated the laundry officer for the day. A "two-pull" wash—that is, walking the bag from the stern to the bow and back again—was used to get the sweat and general grime out of a shirt. Pants and underwear took a "four-pull." The clothes, still wet, were returned to their owners. Since there was no way to dry them, they remained damp. Most of the men broke out in rashes and sores. Krebs considered the misery and ordered a ration of beer for everyone.

Pretch and Harro started tuning their radios to American broadcasts when the *U-560* was surfaced at night. The Big Band sound reverberated throughout the boat when they put the music over the internal speakers. They also started listening to the short-range-radio voice communications of what was probably the patrol boat that had nearly rammed them and then dueled with them around the sinking freighter. The shore radio was being manned by someone who called himself "Glendale" and sometimes "Chief." He always called the patrol boat *Maudie Jane,* the name that had been stenciled on the bow of the boat. Every night, Pretch and Harro, both of whom were better than fair with their English, wrote down what they heard and sent it to Krebs. One of the messages from Glendale seemed good news:

> TELL ENSIGN THURLOW (SPELLING?) CONGRATS FOR
> GETTING HIS LIEUTENANT'S BAR. JUNIOR GRADE BUT
> WHAT THE HELL.

From the radio traffic, Krebs was starting to get a picture of the foe he faced, this Lieutenant Thurlow. Most likely he knew these waters as well as Krebs knew those off Nebelsee. He also was apparently a good ship-handler. Probably, he had been the big man in officer's khakis who had shot at the *U-560* with the rifle. Once again, Krebs wished he'd sunk the patrol boat when he'd had the chance.

Sometimes, during the interminable hours waiting on the bottom of the ocean, Krebs imagined what he might do to sink a U-boat if he were Lieutenant Thurlow. To do it, he would have to conjure a way to lure one into a patch of the ocean where it was too shallow to dive and maneuver. Krebs gave it a great deal of thought, imagining how it might be done, but finally concluded the U-boats had too many cards for a small patrol boat to do much. There were so many targets, a U-boat could simply choose to hide while an American warship, including the little patrol boat, was around. Although it was an interesting mental exercise, Krebs concluded that all Thurlow could do was what he was doing, going out to the sinking ships, picking up the dead and the wounded, and carrying them to shore. He imagined how frustrated the American must be, nearly as frustrated as Krebs.

Every other night or so, a message from BdU was received that said essentially the same thing: The *U-560* should remain off the American coast and be prepared to follow *Kapitän* Vogel's orders. Krebs knew the messages quickly filtered throughout the boat. He supposed his crew wondered why he didn't try to get the orders changed so they could head back for France. After all, wasn't he the famous commander with the sure touch? *No, I'm not,* Krebs thought wearily. *Not anymore.* He recalled a U-boat captain who had signaled Doenitz that he was mentally ill and had handed over his command to his executive officer. Krebs astonished himself by thinking maybe he ought to do the same thing. He went to Pretch and asked for sleeping pills. He got them but could never quite bring himself to take one.

Sometimes, he'd lift Miriam's cross from beneath his shirt and just stare at it, trying to read in its design her mind. He had written Father Josef asking if he knew the significance of the amber pieces and the gem in its center. But mail from Germany was slow and no answer had come before the *U-560* headed across the Atlantic.

With so much time to think, Krebs began to wonder if perhaps he was getting religious. He tried a prayer and found himself asking God to provide him with more torpedoes. He could imagine Miriam laughing into her hands at the idiocy of such a prayer. *I have gone insane,* he concluded. Then, after he thought about it, he changed his opinion. *I have been insane and now I'm sane.* He preferred the former state.

The days dragged on. Another way to pass the time was to simply talk. Everyone on board talked and talked and then talked some more, and Krebs and Max were no exception. Usually they went up in the tower control room to have lunch, the standard fare of boiled sausage, bread hard as rocks, and a short beer, and there they would have their conversations. Eventually, since there was time to do it, Krebs went ahead and told Max everything, how he'd adopted the lie of being an aristocrat for his own purposes to spite those who had made fun of him for being raised in an orphanage. He also told him of Father Josef, and sweet, lost Miriam, and how it was that Harro had come to be a member of the *U-560*'s crew.

Max, for his part, was not much surprised. Krebs had never had the lack of imagination he associated with a Junker. He'd seen them strutting around his father-in-law's shoe shop, demanding service, using High German when they talked amongst themselves, laughing up their sleeves at others. They might have money but they were generally dull.

Although they rarely discussed the situation at hand, one afternoon Max asked, "What do you think Vogel has in mind for us, sir?" At the time, he and Krebs were dining on something that had perked up their spirits, fresh Gulf Stream wahoo caught by the cook and fried in flour, supplemented by one of the last bottles of Krebs's personal stock of wine.

Since Krebs was feeling fairly expansive with the tasty fish in his stomach and more than a drink or two of the wine, he said, "I believe it has something to do with terror."

Max didn't understand and said so. Krebs took another long swig of wine straight from the bottle, then poured some in Max's mug. "He wants to accomplish something spectacular, that's all I can tell you," Krebs said.

Max sifted the answer through his brain, a bit fogged due to the high alcohol content of Krebs's special wine. "*Kaleu,* let's head back," he urged. "We have a sick drive shaft. It's excuse enough."

Krebs shook his head, then upended the bottle and finished it off. He wiped his mouth with the back of his sleeve. "Not yet, Max. We have our duty to accomplish."

"I doubt that our concept of duty compared to Vogel's would be a close match."

Krebs could not argue with Max's opinion so he didn't bother. "Well, there it is" was all he said. He balanced the empty bottle in the palm of his hand and considered it. "I wonder if we could convince that woman who shot at us from the island to buy us a few bottles of wine?"

Max laughed. "I doubt it. She does not seem to have a high opinion of us."

Krebs laughed, too, and it felt good to do it.

"It was a beautiful island," Max went on, staring at the steel bulkhead in front of him as if it were a window. "I should have liked to walk its beaches."

Krebs took on a distant expression as well, as if he were seeing the island on the other side of the tiny tower control room. "It reminded me a bit of Nebelsee. Miriam would have liked it." Because he was feeling warm and generous, Krebs drew out the chain that held her cross. "This is all I have of her."

"I wondered what you were wearing," Max said. "I could see the chain but not the pendant."

"Miriam designed it," Krebs replied, suffused with pride.

"It's beautiful. And most unusual, if I may say so."

Harro poked his head through the hatch. "Coded message just in from BdU, sirs."

"I'll be right down, Harro," Max said. As the executive officer, one of his duties was to go through the laborious effort of decoding transmissions on the Enigma machine in the main control room. The machine required setting wheels to a code, then turning them for each letter.

Harro started to drop below but noticed a golden shimmer against Krebs's shirt. "Miriam's cross," he said. Then his eyes widened as he realized he had said something of a familiar nature to the exalted captain. "I beg your pardon, sir."

Max eased past Harro on the ladder. "Go on, boy. Have a word with the captain if you like. He's in a talkative mood."

"Permission to come up, sir?" Harro nervously asked Krebs.

Krebs replaced the cross beneath his shirt, then gestured with a wave of his hand. "Come."

Harro squatted near Krebs, as near as an enlisted man dared to be to the captain of his U-boat. "I want you to know something," Krebs said. "I'm proud of the way you've handled yourself aboard my boat."

"Thank you, sir."

"In a way, I suppose you and I, we're nearly family. Like stepbrothers."

Harro didn't know what to say to that so he didn't say anything, although he felt very proud.

Krebs smiled. "Don't let it go to your head. I'll still let the Chief skin you alive if you foul up."

Harro looked relieved. "Thank you, Captain. Permission to go back to duty, sir?"

"First, give me a rundown of those duties."

"Yes, sir. Sending and receiving of radio traffic, coding and decoding radio messages, and using the hydrophone devices."

"What else?"

"Well, we have the medical kit and we also make entries into the daily log."

"Are you proficient with the wireless key?"

"Not yet. But I'm working on it every day."

"Practice will make perfect. On your way, Harro."

The boy disappeared through the hatch and Krebs leaned back against the cold, gray steel of the bulkhead. Every minute seemed an hour, every hour a day. He prayed that the message Max was decoding was something that would send the *U-560* somewhere—it almost didn't matter where as long as it was anywhere else. After what seemed an interminable age, he climbed below to see how Max was doing. Max looked up from the decoding machine on the navigator's table. "Well?" Krebs demanded.

Max pushed a paper across the tiny desk. "Looks like more U-boats are coming across."

"But nothing for us?"

"No."

Krebs sat down heavily on the couch and, in case any of the men were noting his reaction, did his level best to look bored and not, in any way, agitated. Inside, however, he was seething. He heard the rumble of a marine engine and then the dull swish of the propellers of what sounded like a small freighter passing overhead. He briefly considered surfacing and chasing her down, boarding her, and opening the sea cocks to scuttle her. But, no, it would use up valuable fuel.

"Another message, sir," Harro said, bringing in the coded text.

"I'll take this one," Krebs said, just for something to do. Max moved over and let Krebs position himself behind the Enigma. Krebs worked for a few minutes, writing down each letter as it was produced. Finally, he had it. He allowed himself a brief smile. Immediately, whispers went all through the boat. *The captain has decoded a message and is smiling!*

"Well, Max, this is the one we've been waiting for," Krebs said, after allowing Max to grind his teeth a bit. Ears close to the hatches of the control room perked up.

"Back across the Atlantic?" Max asked without any real hope.

"No. Something much more interesting. We're to catch a whale."

# 37

Keeper Jack, Buckets O'Neal, and Hook Mallory leaned on their shovels and surveyed the makeshift cemetery behind the lighthouse grounds. So many dead merchant sailors had washed ashore, it was impossible to wait for the ferry to transport them across the sound. Until help could come, the bodies would be buried there. Doc accomplished what identification could be done and kept a record on each man for the authorities whenever they might show up. To date, there seemed little interest on the part of Morehead City to do anything although Chief Glendale continued to call in the daily body count of poor, drowned merchant sailors found on the beach.

Josh, Bosun Phimble, and most of the Maudie Janes including Marvin came walking across the sand hills for the service. Amy Guthrie and the women from the fish market in their leather aprons gathered around. Preacher, in his long black coat, stood clutching his Bible. Dosie and Rex came riding up from the beach, rifles slung on their backs. Queenie O'Neal led a contingent of Whalebone City ladies, all wearing black armbands. Chief Glendale drove the jeep and Doc Folsom and Purdy the pelican rode with him. Overhead, gulls wheeled and banked and called their high-pitched yelps above the everlasting rumble of the Atlantic and the low whistle of the never-ending breeze. The skies were overcast, a watery light drenching the makeshift cemetery.

Atop a sand hill stood Willow and Jezzie. Willow was not looking at the gathering at the graveyard but out to sea. Jezzie stamped at the sand, then quieted.

Preacher was bareheaded, his long brown hair wild in the wind. When the assembly was fully gathered, he asked for a bowing of heads and began speaking in a fierce tone:

"Dear Lord God Almighty, what is there to say except to quote your own good Book, that which you bid to be written down in the Psalms? 'Those who go down to the sea in ships, who do business on great waters; They see the works of the Lord, and His wonders in the deep. They cry out to the Lord in their trouble, and He brings them out of their distress. He calms the storm so that its waves are still, and so he guides them to their haven.' "

Preacher clutched his Bible and shook his head. "But these men you did not guide to a haven. Though they cried out, no storm was calmed, and neither were any waves stilled. The Germans raised hell while You watched and these poor men drowned. What are we to make of this?"

Preacher petulantly kicked at the sand. "I have to hand it to you, Lord. I am lost from your thoughts these days, and your ways. We need help, Lord, and that's what I'm saying as best I can."

Amy Guthrie came over and put her hand on Preacher's arm. Her touch seemed to calm him, although he started to weep. Keeper Jack cleared his throat. "Now, Preacher, those are good words, but might I say a few as well?"

Preacher hung his head and nodded. Tears dripped off his nose. He dropped his Bible. Amy picked it up and then kept patting his arm.

Josh had gone over to stand by Dosie, who remained astride Genie. She reached down and playfully ran her hand through his hair. He held her hand briefly, then let it go. She was smiling, just a little.

Keeper Jack said, "These merchant seamen did not wish to die. But we must remember that to God our bodies are only temporary. It is our souls that are eternal. I'm certain these men had faith in God and they reside with Him now and that's all we need to know. Preacher here is having a trial of faith, you might say." Preacher raised his head at that, then lowered it again. "I guess we all might have our own trials of faith before this is over. It's hard to believe God would let a thing like this happen. But we trust things will work out according to His plan and we'll just do what we can in the meantime." The Keeper cast his eyes around the group until they landed on Josh. "Josh, do you have something to say?"

Josh felt the eyes of the assembly move to him. "Up on the Bering Sea," he said, "one of my men kind of rewrote the Twenty-third Psalm. I always admired it and I think it might be good to say it here and now over these poor men. It went more or less like this: 'The Lord is my Skipper, I shall not drift. He guides me across the dark waters. He steers me through the channels. He keeps my log. Yea, though I sail amidst the tempests of the sea, I shall keep my wits about me. His strength is my shelter. He prepareth a quiet harbor before me. Surely the sun and the stars shall guide me and I will come to rest in heaven's port forever.' "

Eureka Phimble, his wife, Talkie, on his arm and his little boy, Josiah, holding his hand, said, "One thing you all need to know. The *Maudie Jane* is out there every day and we've been chasing those U-boats as hard as we can. We're going to get one of them Germans, too, don't think we won't."

"You boys get 'em!" Buckets said fiercely.

Keeper Jack had something else to say. He pointed at the grave of his wife. "Folks, you'll note there's a little headstone beside Trudelle's resting place. It's for my son Jacob. Just as these men, Jacob met his fate on the waters of our Father who is known as the Atlantic Ocean. We know he is in heaven with his mother, and the stone beside her grave is a mark of that."

The Keeper looked across the graves at Josh. Dosie, still on Genie, had her hand on Josh's shoulder. Josh's face was stricken. "God bless you, Son, for all that you're doing for us out there against them damn submarines. If all that I've said today constitutes a prayer, then I'm going to say amen."

"Amen," the assembly said in response.

"Amen," Josh also said, and just like that, he felt free. His father and Bosun Phimble had been right. Although Jacob wasn't really there, the headstone by his mother's grave had been what Josh needed to finally let his brother go.

But then a movement down the beach caught Josh's eye. Willow had climbed aboard Jezzie and was looking hard in his direction. It shook him a little and he didn't quite know what to make of it.

# 38

Its crew called their Type Fourteen submarine a *Milchkuh*, but to Krebs, the supply submarine reminded him of a big, fat whale. Whatever it was called, it was well designed for its mission. Within three hours of rendezvous, its crew had filled the *U-560* with diesel fuel and sent across four torpedoes and a dozen cans of eighty-eight-millimeter rounds. Next came crates of fresh food, and above all else in importance to the crew, three sacks of mail. The men kept making excuses to tuck up to the tower control room, just to eye the sacks while the Chief stood guard over them. "Soon enough, children," he said to each of them, although truth be told, he was as anxious as all the rest to dig into the letters.

Vogel's boat sat nearby, after completing its own provisioning. The stubby *Kapitän* was apparently below, probably consulting with the officer who had come off the supply submarine and crossed over in a raft. The officer had worn the green-and-brown uniform of the *Marine-Infanterie*. The marines were used primarily as guards on naval bases. Krebs expected to be called by Vogel at any moment to cross over and receive orders, and perhaps then he would discover the purpose of a German marine officer off the coast of the United States. Even as he speculated what that purpose might be, the signal lamp on Vogel's U-boat flashed a message. Harro was on the tower to translate. "Captain Krebs, it is a request for you to come aboard, sir."

"Request, is it? Or a demand?"

Harro gulped. "It says you are ordered, sir."

Krebs glared at Harro and watched the boy melt. "Here is your lesson for today, Radioman Stollenberg. Never change a message in any way. A single word can cause a commander to completely misinterpret important information. Do you understand?" Before Harro could reply, Krebs snapped, "Confirm receipt and say I will comply. Be damned quick about it."

Harro, wounded, furiously started blinking the return message. Max rolled his eyes at the exchange, knowing that Krebs was being deliberately tough on the boy in case any of the crew thought he might be playing favorites. "Chief, send up someone to take the captain across to Vogel's boat," Max called through the tower hatch. "Make sure they can handle a paddle." He glanced at Krebs. "Wouldn't want you to get swept away by the currents, *Herr Kaleu*."

A stout seaman was given permission to come up on the tower. He reported. "I will paddle you across, sir."

"Ready the raft," Krebs replied, "and stand by. I want to get the report from the diver first."

The paddler went off to accomplish his order and Krebs went down on deck and joined the others perusing the bubbles coming up from the stern. A hard-hat diver from the supply submarine was working back there. It was the result of an idea of the Chief's, that the persistent problem of the rattling port drive shaft might be a defect in the propeller it drove. Some of the men were also fishing. It was a pleasant day but Krebs had become all too familiar with the insidious nature of the place. He looked to the northeast and saw a few gray clouds rising along the horizon. In about three hours, he thought, there would be a heavy wind coming from that direction and a sea rapidly going to hell.

The diver finally rose and was pulled aboard the milk cow. "Well?" Krebs called across the water after the man was led to a chair and his diving hat unbolted.

The diver called back. "Captain, I have bad news. There is a crack in one of the blades of your portside propeller. It is approximately one-sixteenth of an inch wide, perhaps six inches long starting from the outer tip."

Max had joined Krebs to hear the report. "There's probably been a hairline crack for a long time, but too small for the shipyard to see, even if they'd been looking for it. The storm coming across the Atlantic must have opened it up."

"So what can we do, Max?"

"Nothing, except to baby the portside drive. The crack could easily get worse if we put a lot of pressure on it. The entire blade might shear off. Then we'd really be in shit up to our necks. If we didn't shut it down fast enough, it might even tear the packing out and cause a flood in the stern."

Krebs nodded agreement. "You'd better let Hans know, even though it will make him even crazier." He climbed into the raft. "You have the boat until I return, Max."

"I shall take good care of it, sir."

"Don't leave for France without me."

Max didn't reply. The thought had occurred to him, don't think it hadn't, a delicious but impossible proposition.

Krebs was received in what he considered a nonchalant manner by the lookouts on Vogel's boat. "No need to go below," an ordinary seaman snapped when he'd climbed up on the tower. "Captain Vogel said he would come up to give you your orders. I will inform him you are here."

"I will inform him you are here, *sir*," Krebs growled.

The lookout shrugged. *"Sir,"* he added without enthusiasm, then went below. It was clear to Krebs he was not popular on this boat. Vogel must have made a habit of saying uncomplimentary things about him where anyone could hear. The other lookouts got busy with their binoculars scanning the horizon, empty of everything except the building storm clouds. Krebs, simmering at the insult, went down on the Type Nine's deck and calmed down by looking across the water at the *U-560*. It was interesting to see his boat as others did. It was an ugly duckling, for certain. The rust had burst through on its tower again, the grinning white shark apparently afflicted with reddish brown measles. The crew of the supply submarine had battered the deck with one of the torpedoes during the loading, splintering some of the planks so much they had been removed and tossed into the sea. The cracked bronze of the portside propeller blade was hidden beneath the sea, but it was all part of the weariness of his old boat. At least, the interior was in good shape. With all the time available during the last two weeks of waiting around, the Chief had formed teams to scrub down the walls, grease every hinge, swab every deck, even pump out the bilges and scrub them clean. With nearly all the food eaten, the second water closet, usually used as a food locker, had been made operational, which kept the air fresher. Rotten food had been tossed. The cook had caught baskets of fresh fish every night. Except for the cold symptoms, which seemed to have run their course, the crew was in decent shape, ready for another campaign, whatever it might be.

Krebs went back to contemplating the crushed decking from the torpedoes, then recalled the prayer he'd flung up to heaven that he might receive more eels. Had God answered his prayer by providing the milk cow? It made him uneasy to think about it.

"Captain Krebs," Vogel said, coming up behind him. Krebs turned to find Vogel accompanied by the marine infantry officer observed earlier. "Let me introduce you to Lieutenant Schlake, fresh from Germany. Lieutenant, this is the famous von Krebs, the commander renowned for his *Fingerspitzengefühl*." The compliment was delivered in a subtly sarcastic tone.

Schlake was not at all what Krebs had expected. There was nothing villainous in his aspect, only a pleasant, pink-cheeked face that beamed cheerfully, as if he'd looked forward to meeting Krebs for ages. Give him a year or ten, Krebs thought, and he would make a good mayor of some Bavarian mountain village, all corpulent, filled with beer and hearty heigh-ho's. There was, however, more than enough villainy in Vogel's expression. "The lieutenant comes with good news," Vogel said. "My plan has been approved at the highest level." He placed a finger to his lips, an indication that the news was to be kept secret. "The *highest* level," he repeated, this time with great emphasis on the adjective.

Krebs assumed Vogel was referring to Hitler. Still, he kept his expression bland and waited to hear what came next.

Schlake clicked his heels. "Captain, it is an honor."

"Welcome to America, Lieutenant," Krebs replied.

Schlake was a spirited man. "I find this sea air *most* invigorating!" he exclaimed. "Especially after a week inside a submarine smelling farts. I must say I was terribly seasick until I managed to get my sea legs. I cried out to Neptune more than once!"

Schlake opened his mouth to go on but Vogel interrupted him. "Let us review the plan. Lieutenant Schlake, I have already selected the men who will go ashore. They are men loyal not only to the fatherland but especially the party. However, they are sailors, not soldiers. How much training do you anticipate they will require?"

"Did you say go ashore?" Krebs asked.

Vogel had gotten Krebs's attention. His reply was a satisfied smile. "Go on, Lieutenant," he said.

"Well, sir, training will be minimal," Schlake replied through his goofy grin. "I assume your sailors are familiar with the rifles. It was required of them during basic training. The machine guns we can set up on deck and fire off a few rounds for practice. The main concern I have is that they will respond quickly to my commands once we're ashore. It is one thing to study a map and quite another to put a plan in practice. There will always be surprises."

Vogel nodded. "You have my permission to work the machine gun. Brief the men thoroughly and I am confident they will follow your orders. The operation will occur one week from today. Krebs, your boat will take up a station so as to block off interference seaward. Lieutenant Schlake and his party will make the landing at midnight, local time."

"Perhaps you would be so kind as to explain the ground operations to me, Captain Vogel," Krebs interjected. "Then I might understand the blocking operation you have in mind."

Vogel studied Krebs, as if looking for treachery. After a few uncomfortable seconds of silence, he said, "We are going to land a dozen men ashore on Killakeet Island, specifically at the Coast Guard station known as Doakes. We will blow up the facilities there and take over the town."

Krebs had to admit he was impressed by the audacity and ambition of Vogel's vision, except he immediately saw a flaw in it. "Why don't you just sit off the island and fire your deck gun into the base? You could destroy it with just a few rounds and not have to risk a landing."

"I have orders to search the base for intelligence information, documents, perhaps a decoding machine," Vogel replied.

"I see," Krebs said. "But why are you going to take over the town? It is only a fishermen's village, according to my understanding of the place."

"And here I thought you had such a great imagination, Krebs." Vogel shook his head as if he considered it quite sad that Krebs couldn't figure it out for himself. "Destruction and intelligence are two of the objectives of this raid. But terror is its primary purpose."

Krebs had a sinking feeling but he kept his expression bland, his voice relaxed. "And how will this terror be accomplished?"

Vogel's expression was triumphant. "What I intend to do, *Kapitän* Krebs, is to invade the United States." He paused to let his utterance sink in, then nodded toward Lieutenant Schlake, whose round, pleasant, somewhat goofy Bavarian face brightened at the attention. "And utterly destroy an American town."

Homer Hickam

studded Kmrs, as if looking for trcacts. A lit

# 39

The first night in the mess room aboard the *Piper*,
Again had to get a few things straight with a sailor
the others called Mudball. Mudball shoved up next to
the mess table and said, "I ain't sitting down to eat with no
boy what takes orders from a nigra."

It took Again a few seconds to realize Mudball was talk
ing about Bosun Phimble. "Then don't sit down with me,"
Again said to Mudball, hoping that Mudball would see the
logic of it.

Mudball, however, was a disappointment. He apparently
wasn't much interested in logic. All he said was "Coast
Guard boy, I guess I might have to whack you good." Mud
ball was an ugly man with a scar that went across his forehead and down his cheek. Again wasn't much impressed by
the scar, but he was pretty sure he would be impressed by
the man who'd supplied it.

A bosun's mate by the name of Cracken said, "You boys
want to fight, take it outside."

"I don't want to fight," Again said.

"Nigras are cowards," Mudball sneered.

Again doubted that Bosun Phimble would approve his
fighting over such a stupid statement, so he said, "I tell you
what. I'll take my plate to my bunk and eat my chow there."

Even that, for some reason, did not satisfy Mudball. He
said, "That sure is a pissy-ant boat you came off of."

Again had already picked up his plate to leave the mess room, but now he put it back down. "What did you say?" He hoped he'd heard Mudball wrong.

"That boat of yours looked pissy-ant to me. And all those boys on it looked like piss-ants. And your cap'n, there's a piss-ant if ever I seed one. Not to mention that piss-ant nigra bosun."

Again had no choice in the matter now. He walked around the table and stood close to Mudball and waited. Mudball raised his fist and threw it at Again's head. Again easily dodged it and then socked Mudball as hard as he could. He knew a glass jaw when he saw one, and sure enough, Mudball fell like somebody had kicked his feet out from under him. He lay flat on his back on the steel deck until Bosun Cracken threw a pitcher of water on him. Mudball sat up and shook his head, throwing out spray like a wet dog.

"I thought I told you boys to take your fight outside," Cracken said mildly.

"I didn't want to fight at all," Again pointed out.

"I'm glad you didn't," Mudball said, looking up from his position on the deck. "I'd hate to take you on if you did."

"Well," Again said, "I just didn't like much what you said, about Bosun Phimble and about piss-ants and all."

Mudball nodded. "Now that I think on it, that bosun of yours sure seems like a good one to me."

"How about the piss-ant thing?"

"Your boat don't look like no piss-ant, that's for sure. Nor your crew or your skipper much like piss-ants, neither."

Again, a stubbornly friendly and forgiving boy, reached down and took Mudball's hand and helped him to his feet. He sensed that Mudball hadn't really wanted to fight, either. It was just something inside him that made him have to say what he'd said. Now, all his confusion had been cleared up by a sock in the jaw. That's what it took with some fellows.

Since they'd already gotten their fight out of the way, Bosun Cracken assigned Mudball to take Again under his wing and show him around the destroyer. One thing Again noticed was that everybody was always drinking coffee. "We stand so many drills, we have to, just to stay awake," Mudball said. He was drinking a cup himself at the time.

"Guess everybody's pretty jumpy with all that coffee," Again said.

"Oh, we're jumpy," Mudball agreed, "but nothing like the old man. He's been scared out of his wits since the *Jacob Jones* got sunk up by New Jersey. Her depth charges went off when she sank. All her crew was in the water and the explosions busted them up inside. Must have hurt like hell, dying that way."

"I guess your captain's got a right to be nervous," Again allowed.

"I guess so but he's wearing us out. Every time sonar gets a hit, he calls general quarters and starts dropping depth charges. I bet we've blown up every sandbank and old wreck along this coast."

Just as Mudball said it, the alarm rang. *"General quarters, general quarters, this is not a drill!"* came the tired voice over the loudspeaker.

Again had headed for the wheelhouse for that first general quarters just as Ensign Thurlow had told him to do and had continued to go there every time it was called over the next two weeks. It seemed as if every hour, the alarm sounded and the call was made. Nobody was getting any sleep, too much coffee was being drunk, and nerves were raw. There were a lot of fights amongst the crew. Again managed to stay out of them, mostly by sneaking off on his own to catch naps here and there. He was a good sleeper, a habit acquired by a lifetime on bouncing Killakeet workboats. As soon as he would lay himself down, and it didn't much matter where, he'd be snoring. One of his favorite places was on top of the wheelhouse, curled up inside a lifeboat near a big searchlight.

After Again had been sixteen days on board the destroyer, he came to the conclusion that he might be there more than a week. He had hoped Captain Dekalb would take him back to the *Maudie Jane,* but it didn't happen, wasn't even brought up. Again assumed that he'd been permanently shanghaied. Other than he was somewhere he didn't want to be, he didn't have much room to complain. He had no real duties on the *Piper* and could pretty much come and go as he pleased. Captain Dekalb chose to ignore him, as if he didn't exist, even though he stood on the bridge in front of God and everybody, ready to offer advice. The only officer that paid any attention to him at all was the executive officer, a Lieutenant Flagston, who was a decent sort.

Again noticed that as long as Flagston was on the bridge, everything went along pretty smoothly. But when Dekalb came up, everybody would get tense, and pretty soon he would squawk general quarters. That meant the crew had to stand at their stations for at least an hour and sometimes longer.

It was Again's opinion that Dekalb was falling apart. His skin was sallow, and great, fleshy bags hung beneath his blood-rimmed eyes. He looked like a sick bulldog. He also slurred his words as if he were drunk, but Again didn't think he was drunk. There was something else wrong with him. After listening in to the conversations between Lieutenant Flagston and the ship's doctor, Again came to realize that Dekalb's problem was that he needed sleep. In fact, the doctor allowed as how he didn't think Captain Dekalb had slept much at all since the *Jacob Jones* had been sunk. "He's grieving for the *Jakie,* Doc," Flagston had said. The doctor replied that he'd given Captain Dekalb some sleeping pills and that was all he could do. Flagston suggested whiskey and the doctor went away, shaking his head.

On his seventeenth night aboard the *Piper,* Again was in the wheelhouse for the lack of anything better to do. Lieutenant Flagston had the bridge. It was near midnight and the *Piper* was steaming off Nags Head when the radar operator yelled out a report. The big, clumsy radar machine was in a corner of the wheelhouse with a curtain drawn around it. Again had looked at its screen a few times, but all he could make out of it was a bunch of humpy lines, sort of what you'd expect static to look like. The operator had claimed, however, that he could tell what they meant.

"There's a solid contact here, Mister Flagston!" the operator said.

Flagston had been jawing with one of the chiefs but he immediately became all business and went over to the radar machine. "Where away?"

"It's just ahead of us, sir. It's about as solid a return as I've ever seen. It's dense but not too big."

And just like that, Lieutenant Flagston had said, "It's a U-boat conning tower," and set the *Piper* after it. He called Again over. "Go up on the wheelhouse and tell the boys to turn on the searchlight."

The chief the lieutenant had been talking to asked, "Ain't you gonna tell the captain, sir?"

"No, let him rest until we're sure what we've got." Flagston left unspoken what everybody was thinking. As scared as Dekalb was of U-boats, who knew what he might do?

Again went outside into the cool night and climbed up on the wheelhouse and told the boys there what Flagston had said. They switched on the big light and its beam cut through the darkness beyond the destroyer's sharp bow. Before too long, Again saw what appeared to be the phosphorescent wake of a small boat. "A workboat, that's all it is," he told the searchlight boys. "Some Hatterassers doing some night fishing."

But then the wake started to twist and turn. "It's running from us," one of the searchlight boys said. And then the light picked up another track, this one coming in. Somebody yelled out what all of them were thinking: *"Torpedo!"*

Lieutenant Flagston had apparently seen the torpedo. The *Piper* turned aside and then got back on track. Five minutes later, the spotlight lit up a U-boat. It started to turn and the *Piper* turned with it.

Again thought he might be useful to Lieutenant Flagston. As he came down, he saw Captain Dekalb barge into the wheelhouse. "What the hell is going on, Lieutenant?" Dekalb cried while pulling on his jacket. His thin hair was a mess of gossamer white strands.

"I was just going to call you, sir," Flagston lied. "We've run down a U-boat."

"The hell you have!" Dekalb's eyes bugged out. Again

had never seen a man look so terrified. The captain croaked, "General quarters!"

The alarm sounded, the this-is-not-a-drill command was made, and the 206 men of the destroyer struggled wearily to their assigned positions. Some were putting on their life jackets as they went but many already had them on. A lot of *Piper*'s men had taken to sleeping in the damned things to save the trouble of having to put them on and take them off again. Mudball was the captain of one of the three-inch guns, and Again thought that might be a good place to see the action. He sensed it was best to stay as far away as possible from Captain Dekalb. He raced down and stood behind the big gun, figuring to act as an ammo carrier if Mudball needed one.

Mudball looked over his shoulder. "Hey, Again, another damn crazy nothing call."

"Not this time," Again replied. "There's a U-boat out there. It already shot a torpedo at us!"

"No shit!"

As if in confirmation, the U-boat suddenly appeared, lit up by the searchlight and directly in front of Mudball's gun. Mudball yelled for his boys to load a round, then cranked the barrel down, aimed, and fired, all in the space of less than ten seconds. Mudball was a good marksman. There was an explosion right in the middle of the conning tower, a big burst of yellow and red flames gushing from the resulting hole. Then the most amazing thing happened. Men started pouring off the U-boat tower and jumping into the ocean. The destroyer crew cheered.

The searchlight stayed on the U-boat until it disappeared beneath the waves. The *Piper* came about, then stopped dead in the water. There was a lot of mumbling amongst the crew. "What the hell are we doing?" Mudball demanded. "We got to make sure that sumbitch is sunk."

"I'll go find out," Again said, and sprang up the series of ladders to the wheelhouse. He sneaked inside the open door to find Captain Dekalb nose to nose with Lieutenant Flagston.

"You may write it down if you like, Flagston," Dekalb was saying, "but my order stands. We will make a depth-charge run on that U-boat."

Flagston said his piece. "For the record, here is the situation as I see it. The U-boat is sunk. Its crew is in the water. If we drop depth charges, they will likely be killed."

"Just like the boys aboard the *Jacob Jones,*" a chief said bitterly.

A bosun's mate said, "They deserve it, those kraut bastards."

Dekalb pointed a trembling finger at Flagston. "Follow my orders!"

Flagston's lips were pressed together so tight they'd disappeared into a straight line. Finally he opened them and said in a bitter tone, "Ahead one-half."

"Ahead one-half," a seaman replied in a mechanical voice, and threw over the annunciator lever, ringing its bell. Shortly, another ring announced the order had been received below by the engine crew.

Flagston picked up the internal-communication microphone. "Drop a diamond pattern, set at eighty feet, on my command," he said. Then he turned and faced forward, staring into the bow portals. His reflection revealed his thin face held taut, as if he had to make every muscle strain to keep it from crumbling.

The *Piper* began to move, at first slowly, then picking up speed. Clouds of smoke poured from her stacks. Again left the wheelhouse and went back down to Mudball's gun and saw him and all the others just staring out to sea. There were a lot of glowing shapes in the water. He worked his way forward to the bow and then he saw that the shapes were men, their frantic movement stirring up the phosphorescent plankton that thrived in the Gulf Stream. The spot of the searchlight played over them. The *Piper* kept coming and then Again heard the Germans start to scream. He looked over the rail and saw one man clawing at the *Piper*'s side as she passed. A voice carried across the water in perfect English: "Save us! We are just sailors like you!"

No one answered. Depth charges rolled off the *Piper*'s stern and her Y-guns discharged more. The Germans quieted as if waiting, and then the charges detonated in great turquoise sheets beneath the sea.

The *Piper* turned around and stopped. The old destroyer's stacks belched smoke, an orange glow swirling up from them like embers tossed up from hell. Then she began to move again. Another diamond pattern was dropped, and multiple deep thumps and flashes of underwater lightning left behind pools of blue-white foam. She turned and stopped once more, her old boilers seething.

Again had closed his eyes after the first run. Now he opened them and listened. All he heard was the low moan of the wind across the destroyer's bow cable. He could still see Germans in the water but they were quiet. They all looked as if they were resting, some on their stomachs, some on their backs, their arms spread wide, just drifting peaceably across the waves.

Again made his way back to Mudball's crew but they weren't at their gun. It was as if everybody aboard was in some sort of trance. General quarters had not been suspended, but the sailors were leaving their duty stations. They weren't talking. They were just wandering around or looking out at the floating bodies.

Again went back up to the wheelhouse to find it was also eerily quiet. Captain Dekalb was slumped in the duty officer's chair. Lieutenant Flagston stood nearby, his head bowed, his hands in a clenched knot behind his back. The radar operator had switched off his set. A bosun's mate, the one who'd said the Germans were going to get what they deserved, was staring at the deck, as if there were something of great interest there amongst the steel plates and rivets.

Captain Dekalb finally stirred. "Call it in. We have sunk a U-boat which attacked us first."

"Aye, aye, Captain," the radioman on duty replied without enthusiasm.

"And tell them," Lieutenant Flagston said, his hands working behind his back, "that we will be bringing in the U-boat crew."

"Who drowned," Dekalb said immediately, staring defiantly at his executive officer.

A staring contest ensued until Flagston finally gave in. "Who drowned," he said with resignation.

When the *Piper* stood into Norfolk the next day, she was met by four Naval Intelligence officers who ran up the gangway to inspect the Germans, all of whom had been piled on the bow and covered with a big square of canvas. After they were finished, soldiers with stretchers came to carry the Germans off. Armed troops ringed the dock, their backs turned to the scene. Two covered trucks waited. As soon as the bodies were loaded, the trucks sped off. At a command, the troops formed up and marched away. Soon, the dock stood empty except for *Piper* hands who'd come down in an undisciplined mob. Again found Mudball. "I'm leaving, Mudball," he said.

"Without orders?" Mudball asked.

"Mister Thurlow told me to come home in a week. It's been two weeks plus three days."

Mudball frowned, then a tear welled up and trickled down the man's ugly face. "I think we did a bad thing last night," he said, his lips twisted.

Again looked around and saw a lot of other stricken faces. He didn't know what to say except what he said. "I guess it was wrong what happened but I'm not sure how. It's war and those Germans tried to kill us but we killed them instead." He tried to think his way through it. "Of course, they were trying to give up. Maybe that's what was wrong with it."

Mudball's tears increased. "Do you think I could go with you? I don't want to be on the old *Piper* anymore. Our captain is sick and I think so's the rest of us, too."

Again shook his head. "Naw. They'd track you down and probably hang you for treason."

Mudball wiped the tears off his cheeks. "But I'd be working on a Coast Guard boat!"

Again smiled sadly. "That's the main reason they'd hang

you. The Big Bum, he don't always care much for his little brother, you know."

Mudball dug into his pea coat and handed Again a round medallion on a chain. "You want this? One of the guys what went out to pick up the bodies took it off the U-boat captain. I knocked him down and took it for myself. Now, I don't want it no more. I don't never want nothing to remind me of last night ever again."

Again didn't want the thing, either, but he took it, anyway, just to be polite. Mudball nodded, then turned away to join his fellows still milling about on the dock. Again suddenly felt a surge of pure joy. He was through with the blue-water navy! He glanced at the medallion and determined that it was actually a German-navy version of a dog tag. He read the name on it: *KL Plutarch Froelich.* "You poor dumb son of a bitch," Again muttered, then tossed the tag into the water.

# PART THREE

## BUT THERE
## THE SILVER ANSWER RANG . . .

# 40

The *Maudie Jane* hugged the starboard side of the tanker SS *Orville Stokes,* which was slogging north, fully laden, at the western edge of the Stream. Josh worked the wheel of the patrol boat, staying just outside the water churned up by the ponderous ship, though catching the flowing pressure wave off her bow for a boost. Millie and Fisheye were at the depth-charge racks. Preacher, taken aboard as an auxiliary, was manning the machine gun, which had moved to the top of the wheelhouse. Ready was the gun captain and Bobby the crew of the retrofitted three-inch gun bolted on the bow. Only Jimmy, on the sonar, and Big, in the engine room, were below.

Bosun Phimble had transferred aboard the *Stokes* and was at her wheel. Once was on the outer bridge of the tanker, scanning the water toward Killakeet. They were all part of a trap designed to catch a U-boat. Rex Stewart had spotted the U-boat with the white shark painted on its tower earlier in the day sniffing around Miracle Point. So had several island workboats making short runs out to fish. Chief Glendale had found Josh at the Crossan House, sitting with Dosie sipping yaupon tea. It had been the break Josh had hoped for.

Josh, for all his focus on what was about to happen, still couldn't help but smile when Dosie crept into his mind. She had been so excited about her new job. Lounging in bed, she'd teased the curls on his chest with her finger and looked so pleased with herself. "What is it?" he'd asked.

"Nothing. I'm just happy, that's all."

At first, Josh thought she meant he had made her happy, but then she had gone on to explain herself. "Do you remember Willow said I should protect the sand? Well, I guess I am."

Disappointed, Josh came close to sulking. "Willow also said you'd find *him* in the sand," he pointed out. "Found any 'hims' yet? Maybe they're 'hymns,' like to sing."

Since he thought he was being clever, Josh felt better, not that it mattered. Dosie wasn't paying any attention to him, anyway. "My land, I nearly forgot!" she exclaimed, and sprang naked from the bed to dig into her pants once she found them on the floor. She produced a scrap of paper, then bounced back on the bed. Josh was more interested in her than the paper, so he wrapped his big arm around her waist and brought her down for a kiss. "Stop it. This is important!" she said, although she allowed a long smooch and added to its warmth considerably.

After a while, they broke free and Dosie convinced Josh to have a look. He perused the wrinkled paper. "Damn!" he exclaimed. "Dosie, this is a radiogram off a U-boat! It's even got the name of the U-boat captain on it. His name is Krebs! We should be able to find out more about him, maybe figure out what he's up to, or his tactics, or something." He looked at her disapprovingly. "You should have turned this in sooner."

Dosie pouted, then pulled Josh back down beside her. "I've been busy, bub. You know, protecting the sand. And I guess I found *him*, didn't I?"

Josh took Dosie into his arms. He just couldn't get enough of her. "I've been wondering what kind of schedule you've been keeping," he said. "Guess I was lucky to catch you at the house tonight."

"You surely were. Rex and I go twelve hours on and twelve hours off for six days, and then on the seventh day, whoever's still riding after midnight extends three more hours. That way our shifts move round the clock."

Josh didn't think much of their schedule. It was his experience that after six hours, lookouts weren't worth much. But it was Beach Patrol business so he wisely stayed out of it.

"Sometimes Willow shows up and rides along," Dosie added. "She's good company except she doesn't say much."

"What does she say when she says it?"

Dosie thought for a moment. "One time, she was looking out to sea and she said, 'And then the silver answer rang.'"

Josh pondered the words but nothing came to mind. "Does that mean something to you?"

Dosie shrugged. "I've heard it somewhere but I can't quite place it."

Josh kissed Dosie on the nose. "You have a cute nose. I like the way it has a little turn-up at the end of it."

"It's my absolute worst feature," Dosie complained. "So's your nose, knocked all askew. How'd that happen, anyway?"

"Some woman in a bar in Ketchikan," he said. "I forget which one."

"Woman or bar?"

"Both."

"Wait a minute," Dosie said. "I remember where 'the silver answer rang' comes from. A college education is a wonderful thing, ain't it? *Sonnets from the Portuguese*. It's an Elizabeth Barrett Browning love poem and the silver answer part is about when a ghost grabs her. She's sure it's the grim reaper. Only it turns out to be a love spirit instead."

Josh was far more familiar with the Browning automatic rifle than Browning poetry. "I don't know about love spirits," he said, "but they say old Blackbeard's ghost still walks up and down the beach in these parts. You ever see him out there carrying his head under his arm, Corporal Dosie Crossan of the Coast Guard Beach Patrol?"

"No, but if I did, he'd absorb some lead from my trusty Remington thirty aught six rifle."

"You're a feisty girl, ain't you?"

"Feisty enough to handle the likes of you, Josh Thurlow."

"Well, let's just see about that," he said and grabbed her just as she grabbed him back.

· · ·

A few hours later, Josh and Dosie were on her pizer, rocking placidly, when Chief Glendale arrived in the jeep, Purdy sitting alongside. "News, Mister Thurlow!" the chief cried. It was news, indeed, of the white-shark sub nosing around Miracle Point.

Josh had given Glendale the radiogram, asked him to find out what he could about this Krebs character, then hitched a ride back to Whalebone City to gather up the Maudie Janes. He was ready to put into play the plan he'd outlined to Bosun Phimble some weeks before. To prepare for it, they'd taken the patrol boat over to Morehead City, bowed and scraped to Captain Potts and made their request for a three-inch gun to be bolted to the bow. This time, Potts had been more accommodating, although he made Josh sign another requisition with an official stamp on it. Josh would have been happy to sign a hundred of them.

Preacher had caught Josh on Walk to the Base. "You going out to sea?" he asked.

"Sure am, Preacher," Josh said, looking the man over. His shoulder seemed to be drooping more than ever and there was a hangdog look about his entire aspect. Josh was direct with his question. "You still struggling with your faith? Lots of people are worried about you."

"So many poor dead men," Preacher said angrily, "and no answer from God."

"We Maudie Janes are about to give our own answer, Preacher," Josh said, then had an inspiration. "I'm going to be a little short-handed. You know anything about guns?"

"What West Virginia boy don't? I was hunting nearly afore I could walk."

"Can you cook?"

"You should taste my corn bread."

"You want to come along, man the machine gun sometimes? You could also help Millie in the galley and with the first aid kit."

Preacher raised his shoulder and put his Bible down on the church steps. "I'm your man," he said fiercely, and so it

was that Preacher joined the Maudie Janes as an unpaid auxiliary coastguardsman, assigned as a machine gunner, assistant cook, and back-up pill-pusher.

Josh cleared his mind and got back to business. He had to
maneuver the *Maudie Jane* carefully. In order for the ambush
to work, the patrol boat had to stay completely hidden behind
the tanker bulk. Finding the tanker had been a piece of luck.
Josh had moved the *Maudie Jane* south, hoping to find anything big. When they'd spotted the tanker lumbering along,
Once blinkered a message for her to heave to. When she
didn't, Josh ordered Preacher to fire the machine gun across
the tanker's bow. He did a good job of it. The captain of the
*Stokes* immediately cut her engines. Phimble and Once had
then gone across in the raft and clambered up a side ladder
to secure the tanker's bridge.

In the wheelhouse, Phimble had to deal with a very upset
tanker captain. "This is a Panamanian ship, mister," he railed.
The captain had a white beard, a pink face, and was dressed
stiffly in an old-fashioned blue uniform with lots of brass
buttons. He also had an accent that sounded a lot more Yankee than Panamanian.

"I don't care about your papers, Captain," Phimble retorted. "You're American and so is most of your crew.
There's a U-boat up ahead waiting to sink you and we're
going to do something about it."

The tanker skipper replied that he hadn't heard anything
about U-boats along the Outer Banks. Phimble shook his
head. Was no one in the merchant marine paying attention?
He informed the captain that there had been sixty ships sunk
off the Outer Banks in the months of January and February
and no let-up in sight for March. "You might survive," Phimble said, "if you do exactly what I say. What's it to be?"

After considering the statistics of the sinkings, the captain
became more agreeable. "I reckon we'll do what you say,"
he said. "What do you have in mind?"

"We're going to make you the biggest, fattest target any
U-boat ever saw," Phimble replied, and for some reason the

captain went back to being disagreeable, not that it mattered. Once came inside with the Enfield, patting it like he knew how to use it, which he did. The merchant crew and the captain looked at the rifle, then meekly started taking orders. The trap was set.

# 41

The *U-560* sat brazenly on the surface a mile off Miracle Point. Its crew moved freely about its conning tower and its deck. They owned this sea, and now that their U-boat had four torpedoes aboard, they were confident they would soon claim more victims.

Krebs, Max, and the lookouts were studying a tanker trundling up from the south. Even in the dim light provided by a pink sunset over their shoulders, the tanker was clearly a big one, heavily laden, and almost begging to be torpedoed. It was not only completely lit up, it was also swinging in close to shore. This was more than a little peculiar. To avoid the U-boats, most tankers had been going farther out, some of them as much as two hundred miles offshore. It hadn't helped. A few U-boats had parked themselves that far out, too.

"Look how big she is," Harro said to Joachim, both lookouts. The two friends didn't get to see much of each other these days with Harro mostly in the radio room, so they enjoyed it when they got to be lookouts together. They talked too much, however, and were often reprimanded, not that it stopped them.

"We have three eels forward and one in the stern," Joachim said. "I bet the captain uses the one in the stern. It's an electric and won't make any bubbles."

"No, he won't," Harro said. "He'll use a bow torpedo. He

likes to keep a stinger, just in case he has to make a run for it."

Joachim chuckled. "Run from whom? Nobody around here to chase us."

"Hush," Max said, walking behind the boys. "The captain is making his plans."

"Yes, sir," Harro and Joachim whispered in unison.

The tanker plowed on. Very soon, it would be broadside to the bow of the U-boat, as simple a shot as there was to make. Krebs watched it coming almost as if he were in the middle of a dream. More than anything, he wanted to read and reread the letter that had come from Father Josef. The letter made him feel so close to Miriam, almost as if she had written it rather than the old priest. In it, Father Josef had written that Miriam had told him how much she was in love with "her U-boat captain." There was so much more, about Miriam's childhood in the orphanage, her marriage, her life as the housekeeper, how she was so artistic, even the purpose of the design in the cross she had made. The letter was all that Krebs had thought about since he'd received it. He kept it in an inside pocket of his leather jacket. As soon as he got another chance, he would read it again. Krebs suspected he would be reading it over and over for the rest of his life.

Max touched Krebs's arm. "Sir? She'll be past us soon."

Krebs tried to focus on the tanker, then gave up. "You take it, Max," he said.

Max was not surprised. Krebs had become increasingly detached after receiving a letter from the priest on Nebelsee. He leaned over the tower hatch. "Chief, ready one of the bow torpedoes. Fire on my mark."

Harro elbowed Joachim. "You see? I told you he'd use a bow eel."

"It wasn't the captain. It was *Leutnant* Max."

Another lookout hissed at them, "Pay attention. You're supposed to be watching for airplanes."

Joachim and Harro reluctantly turned their eyes away from the rapidly approaching tanker to look skyward. The sun was low and the evening star had popped out, bright against the blue-black bowl that stretched forever above. Harro suddenly felt very small, caught beneath heaven and the sea. When he considered it, the arguments of men against other men that had caused this war seemed ludicrous. He had a sudden longing for peace, and for a reason he couldn't quite discern, he thought of the strange but beautiful girl on the wild horse.

Pretch poked his head through the tower hatch. "Message coming in."

Max sighed. "Another postcard from BdU. I'll go decode it."

"No," Krebs said. "Bag the tanker. Pretch, decode the damned thing. We're a bit busy at the moment."

Pretch shrugged and disappeared below.

The tanker kept angling toward land, causing Krebs to pay more attention. "She's going to hit the shoals if she keeps coming," he said to no one in particular. He thought perhaps coming in close to shore was a new strategy to avoid U-boats. If so, it wasn't going to work. He puffed into the voice tube. "Hans, slow ahead. Easy on that port drive."

Hans answered, testy as always, that he knew very well to go easy on the port drive. The *U-560* went through its usual shuddering as the propellers took hold. Everyone on board held their collective breath but soon the drives evened out and the U-boat moved steadily ahead.

Max bent over the torpedo aimer. "Variation is zero. Open the torpedo door, Chief."

"Which one, Max?"

"As long as it's in the bow, I could not possibly care less."

The Chief chuckled. "How about number one?"

"That will do."

Harro nudged Joachim. "Here we go."

Pretch reappeared. "I think you should see this, *Kaleu*."

Krebs took the radiogram Pretch was holding and used the faint light coming from the tower hatch to read it. "Froelich," he said after a moment, then straightened up. "And by an American destroyer."

"Not Froelich!" Max said, looking up from the torpedo aimer.

"Every hand believed lost."

The lookouts were listening. "One of our boats got it," Joachim whispered to Harro.

Krebs handed the message back to Pretch and went to stand beside Max. "Are you ready?"

"I should make one more check, sir."

"Get on with it."

Max made his check, then announced in a subdued voice, "Chief. Let the eel go."

The familiar release of bubbles announced the launch of the torpedo from the tube. Krebs watched it speed away, then lost interest. He leaned against the tower fairing and thought instead about Plutarch Froelich and hoped he had died quickly.

"Here it comes!" Once yelled from the port bridge through the open door of the tanker wheelhouse.

Phimble threw the wheel hard over and the *Stokes* rolled into a ponderous turn. The tanker captain and his men scowled. "You'll tear the rudder off her!" the captain snapped.

"Better than getting it blown off," Phimble replied merrily, and kept cranking the wheel. He gave the engineer a significant look. "Full ahead, mister, all engines cranked as far as they go."

The engineer glanced at his captain, then shrugged and pulled over the annunciator. The answering bell was evidence it was heard. The tanker began to whip up the water behind her into a froth, then bore into the turn like a huge locomotive accelerating along a curved track.

"What the devil?" Krebs was looking with disbelief at the tanker as it turned toward the torpedo.

"She's dodging it," Max said.

Krebs couldn't believe what he was seeing. It was most unorthodox. A little alarm went off in his mind. "I would have turned away and headed for deeper water," he said, the alarm getting shriller.

The torpedo sped past the tanker and still she kept turning until she was bows-on with the *U-560*. That was when the real reason for her turn was revealed. There was a small shape behind the tanker, hidden until the last possible moment, and it suddenly burst forward. A searchlight flashed across the sea, catching the U-boat in its bright yellow beam. "The patrol boat!" Max gasped.

Krebs was startled enough by the ambush that, for just a moment, he could not think of the proper order to give. "Bravo," he said under his breath. "Very well done, Lieutenant Thurlow." Then he roared at the machine gun crew, who were all gaping at the onrushing American boat. "Fire, you idiots! Chief, tell Hans full turns! And forget about babying anything!"

"It's jammed, sir!" the machine gunner yelled. The oncoming patrol boat was clearly better prepared. The machine gun atop her wheelhouse opened up, a barrage of lead peppering the tower. The machine gunner and his crew were struck in the first burst, blown away in a spray of blood and bone.

Harro heard Joachim scream, then saw him fall off the tower. Harro started after him but was stopped by Max. "Help me with the machine gun," he ordered.

Max settled in behind the gun and swiveled its twin snouts while Harro fiddled with the ammunition belt. He got it back in place and snapped the cover shut just as Max pulled the triggers. Harro thought his eardrums were going to burst when the gun started rattling. It was so loud!

Then the machine gun jammed again and no amount of banging on it would dislodge its cover. "Get below!" Max ordered Harro.

There was a flash of light and a peal of thunder from the patrol boat's bow. It had a cannon! A round whistled over the tower and detonated, throwing up a geyser of gray water. "Chief, take us down!" Krebs yelled. "I don't care if we hit sand, dive deep as you can!"

Harro looked down and saw Joachim clawing at the ladder, trying to pull himself up. "Help me, Harro!" he groaned.

Harro couldn't leave his friend. He climbed down the ladder but slipped in Joachim's blood and fell to the deck. Suddenly, the sea flushed across the deck, carrying both boys overboard. Harro caught Joachim by his jacket. Then a gush of air from the *U-560*'s buoyancy tanks pushed them out of the path of the American patrol boat, which charged past, firing its machine gun and its cannon.

"Swim, Joachim!" Harro begged. But Joachim couldn't swim. His head lolled backward, and there was a pink froth flowing from his mouth. He was dead and Harro had no choice but to let him go.

How much time had passed, Harro couldn't say. It could have been hours or minutes. There was a chop to the sea. Every time he looked up, Harro got a faceful of salt water. The *U-560* was gone but he heard the grumble of the patrol boat's engines, although they seemed far away. Harro knew Captain Krebs would take the *U-560* as rapidly as possible into deeper water. Some time later, he felt the thumps of explosives in the water, a slight pressure, almost a tickle. The patrol boat was dropping depth charges but far away.

Harro started to swim toward the lighthouse since it was the only thing he could see. He had no idea if it was a mile away or ten. He just kept swimming. A cold current clutched him with an icy hand, and he thought about giving up. But then he saw the light and was inspired to fight his way toward it. When he heard a noise like rolling thunder, he stopped and listened, afraid that they were depth charges. Finally he realized it was the sound of waves crashing on a beach. He tried to swim but he couldn't feel his arms anymore. Maybe he wasn't swimming at all. Maybe he was only dreaming that he was swimming.

Then there was a terrible roar and it felt as if the ocean was sucking him down. His head struck something, and he was pushed up, then drawn down again, tumbling. Then the tumbling stopped and he didn't feel the icy hand of the sea anymore. He felt as if he were in a woman's warm arms, being cradled and gently rocked. But that changed suddenly when he was slammed against something gritty and hard. His hands dug into it. It was sand.

He crawled across the sand while the ocean beat on his back. He felt so heavy after being buoyed for so long by the water. It was very dark. He couldn't see anything except, far away, the flashing lighthouse. He felt the water recede from around his legs. He crawled a little farther until he was completely out of the water, then collapsed. He was tired and cold. He had never been so tired and cold in his life. He put his aching head down on his arms and watched the lighthouse until he couldn't watch it anymore. Then his eyes closed.

When he awoke, there was sand in his mouth. He spat it out and raised his head. His eyes were bleary with salt water but he could see that the lighthouse was still there, only it wasn't flashing anymore. The rising sun had turned it into a distant alabaster spire, like a white needle. Harro wiped at his eyes with his fingers to clear them.

Then he was aware that he wasn't alone. He looked up and saw a girl kneeling in front of him. She had wild red hair and the most amazing eyes Harro had ever seen. They were the color of the French lavender that Father Josef grew in his greenhouse. He realized she was the girl he'd seen on the wild horse. He wanted to say something to her but he didn't know what to say. He was lost inside those eyes. Then she said something very strange. She said, "Hello, Jacob. I've missed you."

# 42

The *U-560* had been ravaged. Its deck gun was gone, ripped off by a well-placed depth charge. One of its saddle tanks had been ruptured and a stream of diesel fuel followed behind like a rainbow-hued ribbon. The Chief was frantically working to pump the fuel out of the holed tank into the others. The conning tower had taken a hit, the sky periscope was bent and probably unusable. The torpedo aiming device was gone. The railings around the tower were missing, and a large steel plate that formed the forward part of the fairing was hanging by a scrap. Two of the bow torpedo tubes had sprung leaks and were spewing seawater faster than the bilge pumps could keep up.

There was another, even greater problem. Both of the electric motors had been knocked off their mounts and their cabling torn loose. Hans had reported to the Chief that not much could be done. The Chief thought otherwise and told Hans to come up with a plan to fix them. At least the diesels were still working, although, with the loss of the saddle tank, they had a lot less fuel to burn.

Krebs found Max in the bow torpedo room, supervising the emergency packing of the leaking tubes. "It's a hell of a mess, Max," he said.

Max was covered with sweat and grime. "As soon as we can, *Kaleu*," he said gently, "we need to bury the gun crew. The boys don't like it, having them lying topside."

Krebs knew Max was right. During the first few hours after getting away from the patrol boat, all he could do was bring up the machine gunners and lay them, covered with blankets, on the splintered deck. They were too ripped apart to keep below. But as soon as possible, they needed to be put over the side with all the attendant ceremony. Sailors, even young U-boaters, were superstitious and needed sacred words read over their dead fellows and the bodies consigned properly to the deep. Max, thank God, had brought along a Bible.

Despite the deaths and the battering the *U-560* had taken, and the bodies lying topside, morale was still holding. Perhaps it was because the crew was too busy keeping the *U-560* afloat. At first, Krebs had put the loss of Harro and Joachim out of his mind. Now, when he had a moment to catch a breath, he gave them some thought. Joachim had been observed struck by one of the fifty-caliber bullets from the patrol boat, but Harro had reportedly not been wounded, just washed off into the sea. Maybe he was still alive but, if so, he wouldn't last long. The water in the Gulf Stream was warm and tropical, but closer in, where Harro had been lost, the water was cold. Krebs considered the unthinkable.

"I do not know how to advise you, sir," Max said when Krebs voiced aloud his thought. "It is completely unprecedented."

"Tell me what harm it would do," Krebs pressed. "If it will endanger the crew, I will not do it."

"Pretch must be quick. Very, very quick, that's all I am saying."

"But am I wrong?"

"Would you do the same for another of your men? That's a question only you can answer."

"I don't know if I would or not," Krebs replied.

Max gave Krebs a long look, then snapped, "If you're going to do it, then do it quickly." Then he left to go back to work on the leaking torpedo tubes.

Krebs felt oddly forlorn. Max had not given him the absolution he had hoped for. Nonetheless, the advice he'd given was sound. Krebs had to do this thing right away or not at all. He found Pretch fiddling with his radio. "Can you still communicate?"

Pretch nodded. "The antenna took a beating during the attack but I'm receiving."

"Can you transmit?"

"I think so."

"Then I want you do something for me. Should trouble come from it, I will claim that I forced you to do it. Do you understand?"

The look on Pretch's face told Krebs that he didn't understand.

"The patrol boat that nearly sank us," Krebs said, "can you contact it?"

Pretch raised his eyebrows. "Yes, as long as the Americans are monitoring the usual frequencies. Morse or voice?"

"Morse, I think."

"I have heard their radioman use Morse." Pretch took on a worried aspect. "Sir, we would have to be quick. They have direction finders. If we transmit too long, they'll be able to find us. What is it you want to say?"

"I want to ask them to look for Harro and Joachim."

Pretch looked relieved. "I was afraid you were going to surrender."

"I would hope you would know me better than that, Pretch. Here, I will write the message down for you. Remember, should there be trouble, I will swear that I made you do it."

Pretch opened up the box that contained the old telegraph key. He looked over the message Krebs had written and then began tapping:

WHITE SHARK TO PATROL BOAT. TWO BOYS IN WATER.

Pretch looked up. "I will send it again in fifteen minutes, sir."

"Good. Thank you."

Krebs started to climb the ladder to the tower control

room but was stopped when he heard Pretch's telegraph key start to click. Pretch took down the message:

COAST GUARD TO KREBS. WILL LOOK.

Krebs read the answer with some astonishment. "They know my name." He scribbled a reply. "Let's return the favor."

KREBS TO THURLOW. THANK YOU. THEY ARE GOOD BOYS. ONE WOUNDED.

A reply came clicking back within seconds.

T TO K: UNDERSTOOD.

"Dammit!" Josh growled after Stobs had relayed the reply from the U-boat. "How does Krebs know my name?"

What made the whole thing frustrating was that until the moment Stobs received the first message from the U-boat, the crew of the *Maudie Jane* had been convinced they had sunk the damned thing. The evidence was everywhere in the form of a thick pool of diesel fuel and splintered deck planks. All night, after the attack, Josh had kept the patrol boat beside a buoy thrown into the slick. Since sunrise, they had gone back and forth over the site with a grapple, hoping to snag a very dead submarine. Then Stobs stuck his head out of the wheelhouse and announced he'd received a message from the Germans.

"I think we beat Krebs up pretty good, Skipper," Phimble offered. "He's probably lost half his fuel load, based on this slick. He'll have to head across the Atlantic."

"I don't want him to go anywhere," Josh griped. "I want to sink him so Killakeeters can fish on his bones for the next one hundred years."

"What about the two krauts you promised to look for?"

"I said we'd look for them and we will."

Josh was furious with himself. His answer to Krebs had

been a reflex, a courtesy from one seaman to another. Now, after thinking about it, he knew he shouldn't have answered at all but kept hunting. He shook his head. What was done was done. He guessed his word was worth something, even if it was to a U-boat captain.

"I think I know how he got your name, sir," Stobs said. "Chief Glendale's dropped it a few times calling out here."

"Damn Glendale," Josh griped. "He don't know the first thing about radio discipline."

"That German radioman's real good with his Morse code," Stobs said. "Not a bit of hesitation. I'd like to race him, see who could tap the key the fastest."

"Don't get too familiar with the son of a bitch, Stobs," Josh replied crossly.

"Yes, sir," Stobs said, ducking back inside the wheel-house, always a good idea when Mister Thurlow was building up to a foul temper.

The girl went away for a while, then came back carrying a cloth satchel over her shoulder. She gave Harro water from a metal canteen and then she built a fire with a match taken from the satchel. She used dry weeds to start it and then fed the fire with driftwood. While he dried his coveralls by turning around in front of the fire, she dug clams from the beach and cooked them in their shells on a piece of old tin propped up over the flames with empty conch shells. She briefly disappeared again, returning with a slimy-looking green plant that she proceeded to chop up on a rock with a hunting knife. She also used the knife to cut the clams open at their hinges and sprinkled the chopped plant over the creamy meat inside. Harro ate them from the shell with a sharpened stick she gave him. The taste was tangy and sweet, both at the same time. He thought it was the best food he'd ever eaten in his life. Warmed by the sun and a full belly, he sat with her on a sand hill. The girl, he thought, smelled like sunlight.

Harro realized he was happy, though he had no right to be. Joachim, his mate, was dead, and his home, the *U-560*, might be sunk and all his mates with it. But then he thought—no, Captain Krebs would get the boat through somehow. He squinted out to sea but saw nothing but a pod of dolphins working their way down the coast, and a trio of pelicans flying across the beach, and a shimmering layer of fish in the shallows attracting the interest of a few gulls, kewing to one another anxiously before plunging like darts into the ocean for a meal. He felt confused, as if his world had turned sideways.

"I'll take you home now," the girl said.

"I must find my boat," Harro replied.

"Your boat?" She canted her head and those glorious lavender eyes lit on his face. They were somehow warmer on his skin than even the sun. "You should go home," she said. "Your father will want to see you."

Harro knew she had him confused with someone else but he didn't want to hurt her feelings. "My name is Harro," he said. "What is your name?"

Now she canted her head in the other direction. "I am Willow, of course. Don't you know me, Jacob?"

"My name's not Jacob. It's Harro."

She frowned, but then something seemed to dawn on her. "It's because you've been gone for so long. You've forgotten your name." She nodded toward the distant needle of the lighthouse. "That's where you live."

Harro allowed a sad smile. "I have always liked lighthouses." He shook his head. "But I must find my boat."

"Let me take you home," she said.

"I don't live at the lighthouse," he insisted.

"Yes, you do. You will remember when we get there." She stood and held out her hand. "Keeper Jack will be so happy to see you."

"Who's Keeper Jack?"

"Your father."

Harro took her hand and stood but resisted when she started to take him across the beach. "No," he said, pulling away. He took the tin off the fire and blew on the coals, then added driftwood. "I must make a big fire. Then maybe my boat will come for me."

"Oh, Jacob," Willow despaired.

"Willow, I—" Harro began, but she placed two fingers on his lips and pressed them closed. She slipped into his arms, then she kissed him on his cheek.

"Even when we were little children," she said, "I knew we were meant to be together."

The girl was frightening Harro now. He pushed her away and went back to the fire, pulling up tufts of grass and throwing them into it to make smoke. Willow watched him with tears trickling down her cheeks. Harro kept looking over his shoulder at her. A storm of emotion, like flashes of sheet lightning, struck his core. He fought for rationality and made himself think of his duty to Captain Krebs, to his crewmates, to the fatherland itself.

But then a shadow fell across him, and her. He looked skyward. A cloud, its rim etched in silver and gold, had drifted across the sun. When he lowered his gaze, he saw the *U-560,* come to rescue him. But then he saw it wasn't the *U-560* at all, but the black U-boat of *Kapitän* Vogel. There were men on the tower and one was behind a machine gun. Harro heard a call from Vogel, followed by the hard metallic click of the charging handle of the gun being ratcheted back. *"Nein!"* Harro screamed, waving his hands. *"Ich bin deutscher Seemann!"*

The gunner swiveled his sight from Harro to the girl. Harro ran toward Willow, to throw himself in front of her, but then came the sound of hoofbeats. A man in an odd uniform on a great brown horse came charging down the beach. He was holding a rifle to his shoulder and fired a single shot. Vogel's gunner snapped backward, his forehead spurting blood.

# 43

The sea off Killakeet always revealed its secrets, if only one knew where to look. Preacher helped Once pull the dead German boy out of the water and place him gently on the deck. Once took the boy's name tag from around his neck and carried it to Lieutenant Thurlow. Preacher couldn't stop looking at the boy's innocent face. Except that his skin was wrinkled from immersion in seawater, he might have simply been asleep. Preacher crossed the boy's hands on his chest. He wanted to pray but he couldn't find the words. What Preacher couldn't understand was why God would crush his shoulder in the coal mine, and then bring him to this sorry state. Why not kill him outright? "Who are you?" Preacher inquired toward heaven. "I mean, really? I would like to know."

Phimble came over and squatted beside him. "What did you think war was all about, Preacher?"

"I killed this man in a righteous wrath," Preacher said miserably.

"So what?" Phimble retorted. "Mister Thurlow swore you in and you did your duty. It's like Joshua in the Bible killing those cretins on Jericho's wall. Or David smacking Goliath upside the head with a rock. God's partial to warriors, if you ask me, especially if they're on his side."

Preacher could not take his eyes off the dead boy. "He probably thought he was on the side of the Lord, too."

Phimble lifted Preacher to his feet. "Here's what's going to happen now. You're going to get your skinny tailbone on top of the wheelhouse and get behind the machine gun. And if we see any more Germans around here, you're going to blast them, see? The Coast Guard says there's only one God on their boats and that's the captain it puts there. Don't make me have to smack you."

Josh was in the wheelhouse, unaware that the Coast Guard had made him God or anything else other than one angry lieutenant, junior grade. In fact, he was fit to chew on nails, mostly because he'd found the dead German boy so quickly, right where he thought he would be. Josh kept his expression stoic but inside he was howling the old and terrible question: *Why had he not been able to find Jacob?*

Josh's fixed expression did not fool Stobs. He knew the lieutenant was just this side of exploding. "Sir?" he asked warily. "Do you want me to tell the Germans?"

"Tell them what?" Josh snapped.

"About finding the boy."

Josh fumed. "I don't care."

Stobs transmitted.

T TO K. ONE FOUND DEAD. JOACHIM FELCHER. WILL
BURY KILLAKEET.

As if the German radioman had been waiting on the other end, the response was nearly immediate.

RECEIVED.

"Received," Josh growled at the one-word reply. "These krauts ever hear of 'thank you'?"

"It's not the same radio operator as the last time," Stobs said. "His rhythm was different."

"I guess they've got more than one radio operator," Josh grumped.

"You want to reply?" Stobs asked, his finger poised over the key.

Josh's expression darkened even more. "Tell that damn Nazi I mean to sink him!"

Stobs's finger remained poised. "He probably knows that, sir."

Josh ignored Stobs and slammed the wheelhouse door behind him, bellowing orders. "Man's in a state, that's what he is," Stobs said to himself. He saw Once run past the wheelhouse, then Jimmy in the other direction. He heard scratching on the door and got up and let Marvin inside. The little dog dived under the table. "You're smart, Marvin," Stobs said. "I'd like to crawl under there with you!"

Another gunner jumped behind the machine gun on the black U-boat. Harro grabbed Willow and flung her down behind a sand hill. The big bullets ripped across the beach, throwing up smacks of sand.

Rex fired another round at the replacement German gunner, a fraction of a second before Joe Johnston caught a slug in his chest. The great horse faltered, but kept going. The gunner, hit by Rex in the mouth, pawed his face, then collapsed. The other men on the conning tower ducked out of sight. Then the diesels roared and the submarine sped up, curving seaward.

Rex leapt off Joe and took his reins. Blood spouted like a fountain from Joe's chest, bathing Rex in it. Then the big horse began to tremble and made a awful groan. He tried to walk, but fell abruptly on his side, wailing and kicking. "Joe, Joe," Rex cried, letting go of the reins, throwing down his rifle, and dropping to one knee at the head of the stricken animal.

Joe's eyes were wide. He whinnied once, as if asking a question, then laid his head in the sand and shrieked. Rex sat down and lifted Joe's massive head into his lap. The horse was trembling and his legs were jerking. His great breath was ragged. Rex knew he should pick up his rifle and shoot Joe in the head but he couldn't do it. "Oh, Joe," he said. "Good old horse."

Joe blinked his eyes, turned huge and glassy, then a quiet nicker escaped from him. "I'm here, boy," Rex said. "I'm here." But Joe's nicker was meant for someone else.

Harro couldn't stop Willow. She struggled from beneath him and climbed on her hands and knees to the top of the dunes. "He's coming," she said. Harro crawled up beside her. The cowboy soldier who'd shot with such expertise was sitting in the sand, holding his wounded horse's head. But then Harro saw a big gray horse plodding up the beach. His head held low, the horse walked up to the cowboy and his bleeding horse and stood over them.

"It's Star," Willow said. "He's come to help Joe Johnston cross over."

Rex had seen the stallion before during his patrols but never so close. Star lowered his nose until it was only inches from Joe's nose. The two horses breathed the same air, back and forth, their nostrils flaring. Rex could feel and smell their warm breath, like fresh-cut grass on a summer's day. Then Joe made a long, low moan, and Rex felt only the wild stallion's breath. Star raised his head, then dug at the sand. Then he walked away, back where he'd come from. Rex watched him for a time, then eased from beneath Joe's head, resting it gently on the bloody sand. He brushed the sand as best he could off his blood-drenched pants and shirt. Then he picked up his rifle and knocked the sand off it. In the best Hollywood tradition, he'd not lost his hat during the entire ordeal.

Willow led Harro down from the dunes. Rex eyed Harro, took in his gray German coveralls, then leveled his rifle chest-high at the boy. "Say something," he demanded. "And it better not be in German."

"He's Jacob," Willow said. "He's come home."

Rex ignored Willow and narrowed his eyes at the boy. "Say something, you son of a bitch!"

"My name is Harro Stollenberg," Harro said in accented English. "And I am a sailor in the *Kriegsmarine*."

"That's what I thought, you rotten Nazi bastard. Put your hands up where I can see them."

Harro raised his hands, then clasped them on the back of his head. "I am sorry about your horse. That was not my boat."

Rex wanted to shoot the German so bad he could taste it. This was one of those bastards who had killed all those poor people washed up on Killakeet's beaches. And now they'd killed the best trick horse that had ever taken a turn before the cameras in Hollywood. About the only thing that stopped him was poor, simple Willow, who was standing so close to the boy, hanging off him, nearly.

Rex waved the barrel of his rifle up the beach toward the lighthouse. "Go on," he growled at Harro. "March! And do me a favor. Try to make a break for it. I'd like nothing better than to plug you."

Harro shrugged. "Don't worry. I know I wouldn't have a chance. You even chased away a U-boat all by yourself."

Rex barked a harsh laugh. "Me? I guess you missed something." He nodded his head seaward.

Harro looked toward the ocean and saw the cowboy soldier was correct. He had indeed missed something and it was rather large. Easing in beside the beach was the patrol boat, the *Maudie Jane* herself.

Krebs found Pretch on the ravaged tower erecting a makeshift radio antenna fashioned from wire wrapped on a diamond-shaped wooden frame. "The antenna shorted out," Pretch explained. "Hans and the Chief keep turning the batteries off and on and I think they finally overloaded a relay. I'm trying to fashion something that will at least let me work short-range."

"Before you lost contact, did you hear anything more from the Americans?"

"No, sir. Sorry."

Krebs went below, to see how the Chief and Hans were doing on the electric motors. "We'll be ready to test them in a few hours, *Kaleu*," the Chief said. The motors were back on their mounts and the Chief was untangling the wires leading into a breaker panel.

"We must start immediately for a shipyard," Hans snapped, throwing down his wrench, which clanged against the deck plates. "To even attempt to operate my electrics in this condition is unacceptable." He rounded on Krebs. "You caused this. Why were we in such shallow water?"

"Hans, this is the captain," the Chief cautioned. "Be careful what you say."

"It's all right, Chief," Krebs said. "Hans, you're right. I was careless. But we are not going across the Atlantic. You are going to get your motors operational again. We have a duty to perform here. Until we do it, we will stay."

Hans's expression, already sullen, turned darker. He stood rigidly, breathing heavily, his hands knotted in fists. The Chief took Krebs aside. "Give us another hour," he said.

"An hour!" Hans screamed. "We need to be in a dock-yard!"

"Shut up, Hans!" the Chief snapped. "One more word out of you and I will beat your brains out with your own wrench!" He turned again to Krebs. "One hour, sir, and we'll be ready to make a test dive."

"Thank you, Chief. I'm going to have a ceremony for those boys laid out on deck. Then, when you're ready, we'll make our test."

The Chief, weary to the bone, nodded and went back to the ravaged breaker panel while Krebs went to see Max to borrow his Bible.

Josh and Once climbed out of the raft and came trudging up the beach. "What you got here, Rex?" Josh demanded.

"A damn Nazi, Josh. You just missed his friends. They killed Joe Johnston."

"It was not my boat," Harro said.

"Shut up," Rex snapped.

Josh called over his shoulder to the *Maudie Jane*. "Tell Stobs to send a signal to Krebs. We found his other boy."

Harro was so astonished, he lowered his hands. "You send messages to my captain?"

"Get your hands back up, boy," Rex warned.

"Leave him alone," Willow said. She hugged Harro's arm. "Don't you recognize him, Josh?"

"Why would I recognize him?" Josh demanded.

"Because he's Jacob."

Josh felt as if he had been kicked in the stomach. "That's an evil thing to say."

"Can't you see it in his face?" Willow asked.

Josh stared into the boy's face and was met by steady, blue eyes. Even while he was doing it, he knew it was crazy but he tried to read into the German's features his own, or his father's, or . . . *my God, was that his mother's face? Perhaps. Maybe. It could be.* Josh shook his head. "Willow, this is cruel."

Harro was irritated that no one would pay attention to him. "The girl is confused," he said. "I am Harro Stollenberg."

Josh still couldn't tear his eyes from Harro's face. "Where did you grow up? Who are your parents?"

"I do not have to answer you," Harro snapped.

"Answer the lieutenant or I'll bust your skull," Rex huffed, raising the butt of his rifle.

Harro looked at the rifle butt and raised his chin. "Go ahead. Hit me. I will not answer your questions."

"Skipper!" It was Phimble from the deck of the *Maudie Jane.* "Stobs says he's got a fix on the U-boat!"

Josh kept staring at Harro until Once tugged at his arm. "Did you hear Bosun Phimble, sir?"

Josh nodded. "Can you handle the prisoner, Rex?"

"Count on it."

Josh took another look at Harro. "You are not Jacob," he said, and then headed for the raft.

# 44

Harro was very tired. After all, he'd swum for miles and hadn't slept much. If he could only rest, he thought, he might make some sense of what was happening. But the cowboy soldier kept prodding him along the beach. Willow followed, her arms crossed, her head down. When they reached a lone house on the beach, a woman, wearing a uniform nearly as odd as the cowboy's, came out. Then Harro recognized her as the woman who had shot at his U-boat.

Dosie saw the blood on Rex's uniform. "What happened, Rex?"

"Got ourselves a Nazi, Dosie," Rex said. "But, dammit, he killed Joe Johnston."

Dosie gasped in horror. "Not old Joe!"

"I did not kill his horse," Harro said wearily. He was so terribly tired.

Willow came sobbing and threw herself into Dosie's arms. "Why, Willow," Dosie gasped in surprise. She had never seen the girl with any emotion, beyond a certain petulance, and here she was crying on her shoulder, of all things.

Willow lifted her head, her face wet with tears. "This is Jacob, Josh's brother. And Rex wants to shoot him."

"I am not Jacob," Harro said, weaving from fatigue. He was having trouble staying upright.

"He's forgotten who he is," Willow explained.

"Josh saw him earlier," Rex said. "He ain't his brother. But Willow's right about one thing. I'd like to shoot him."

Dosie stroked Willow's hair. "We'll go see Keeper Jack, honey. He'll know what to do."

Willow tore away from Dosie and began to dance. "Yes! Keeper Jack! He'll know!" She danced around Harro. "Your daddy will know you!" Then she sprinted on ahead.

"Crazy as a betsy bug," Rex said, watching Willow run, her bare feet kicking up the sand.

"I agree," Harro said.

"Shut up and keep moving," Rex growled.

Ready was at the wheel and the *Maudie Jane* was rumbling toward the Stream. Josh and Phimble read the U-boat's latest message. "They stayed on for about three minutes, sir," Stobs said.

> PLEASE YOU TO CALL IF HAVE FOUND OUR CREW BÓYS. WE ARE LEFT WHEN YOU GIVE US THIS.

"This took three minutes to receive?"

"No, sir," Stobs said. "But they kept sending it over and over. When I realized they were going to keep sending it, I fired up the direction finder and got a bead on them."

Josh scratched Marvin's head when the dog came out from beneath the table. "Which operator sent this?" he asked Stobs. "The first one or the second one?"

"Second one, sir."

"His English is pretty bad."

"Yes, sir."

"You smell a trap, Skipper?" Phimble asked.

"I don't know," Josh said, after a few seconds thinking about it. "Go make sure Jimmy's got the sonar fired up. Tell him I want to know everything he hears, even if he thinks it's just a fish jerl."

"Aye, aye, sir," Phimble said, and headed below.

• • •

Harro stood before the lighthouse. He had never seen anything quite so beautiful as the tall black and white spire.

"There's the Keeper," Dosie said.

Harro looked across the grass to the house built beside the lighthouse. Willow was on the porch and with her was a man dressed in a dark blue uniform. She was clutching the man's hand and began to pull him up the sandy path. He walked with a stiff authority, yet Harro sensed the man's gentleness. As he neared, Harro saw he was older than he'd looked from a distance, his beard gray against a sun-browned and deeply wrinkled face.

The Keeper stopped and looked into Harro's eyes. He did not acknowledge the cowboy soldier or the woman. Harro saw that the Keeper's eyes were blue-gray, and he saw the pupils in them suddenly enlarge. "Who are you?" he demanded in a strained voice.

"I told you who he is, Keeper Jack," Willow said.

Harro identified himself once again as a German sailor. "And you, sir?" Harro asked politely.

"I'm Keeper Jack Thurlow," he answered, continuing his scrutiny. "Who were your parents?"

Harro saw no harm in answering the old man's question. In any case, he was too tired to argue with him. "I am an orphan. I was raised in a *Waisenhaus,* an orphanage."

"Where was that?" the Keeper asked.

"*Deutschland,* of course."

The Keeper put out his hand and Harro, tentative at first, took it. The Keeper's grip was strong. "I understand why Willow has you confused with my son. You see, he was lost at sea seventeen years ago when he was two years old, which means you would be about his age. And you favor my wife—his mother—in the face. Willow is a very smart girl. She remembers things and sees things the rest of us don't, or can't."

Harro took back his hand, wanting to rub it to bring some blood back after the wringing it had taken. "I understand, sir."

"Please, come inside. Rest for a bit."

"Josh said I should take him to Doakes," Rex interjected.

"Let the boy rest and get something to eat," Keeper Jack replied. "He looks like he's at the end of his painter."

Dosie decided the matter. "I think that would be fine, Keeper."

Keeper Jack led the way and Harro followed, Willow beside him. "Don't you recognize your father?" she whispered in his ear.

"Please stop saying these things," Harro begged.

Rex came kicking along behind, with Dosie beside him. "Well, ain't this something?" Rex spat. "Now, we're going to let the Nazi rest up a bit. Hell of a way to fight a war."

"He's just a boy, Rex," Dosie scolded.

"And boys just like him killed Joe," Rex said. "Not to mention all them poor dead sailors."

Harro entered the Keeper's House. He felt its snugness and imagined it would be a cozy place during a storm. Keeper Jack waved him and Willow into a large room where there was a fireplace. There was a fire going, and some comfortable-looking chairs set before it. Old-fashioned kerosene lanterns sat on tables made of driftwood. Harro's eyes wandered over the room and then a question came out of him, completely unbidden: *"Wo sind all die Katzen?"*

Keeper Jack came inside from the kitchen with a tray of johnnycake and coffee. "What did you say?"

"He said," Doc Folsom answered, as he let himself in through the front door, " 'Where are all the cats?' "

The Keeper dropped the tray, and the mugs and dishes smashed on the floor.

"I think we are ready for a test, sir," the Chief told Krebs. Krebs and Max were on the tower after completing the burial ceremony for the dead boys and committing them over the side.

"All right," Krebs said, still low from the funeral.

The Chief dropped back down the hatch and the diesels were abruptly shut down. Krebs kept his eye on the stern, then was pleased to observe a froth of pale blue and white bubbles flush to the surface. The *U-560* began to make headway. "The electrics are working, sir!" Max cried. Then he added, "Let's keep going. There's no telling how long this fix will hold. Every fuse in the boat could blow at any moment. Not only that but we have no communications. How can we accomplish our mission if we can't communicate?"

"Pretch assures me he'll have the radio operational once he has consistent power," Krebs replied.

"And if he can't?"

"You must stop being so negative."

"And you must stop being so foolhardy with our lives," Max snapped. Then he sighed and shook his head. "I'm sorry, *Kaleu*. I'm a little tired."

"As we all are," Krebs calmly answered. "Get some rest."

"What about Vogel's operation?"

"To hell with Vogel and his operation. We'll use up our torpedoes and go home."

For the first time in days, Max felt as if he might survive this patrol after all.

Josh pulled back the curtain from the sonar closet. "What do you have, Jimmy?"

Jimmy lifted an earphone. "Something big and dense, sir, and it ain't moving. But I was on to something smaller before."

"We're near the *Lady Morgan*. It could be her you're pinging."

"Could be. But I'm sure I also heard propellers."

"The white shark boat?"

"I'm not sure. Just a constant swishing sound. Then it stopped when this big old thing started echoing back."

Josh was uncertain of his next move. He was fairly certain that Jimmy was presently bouncing his propagation wave off the wreck of the sunken passenger liner. But it was also possible that the U-boat had parked itself nearby.

Phimble came down. "Skipper, not much current here today. We can shut down and maintain our position."

Josh made his decision. "We're going to stick around, then. You keep pinging and listening, Jimmy."

Jimmy clapped the earpiece back on and hunched over his set, the posture of the sonar warrior.

Keeper Jack asked Harro to sit down and took up an opposing chair. Willow perched on the armrest beside Harro. Rex and Dosie sat on the couch, Rex still cradling his rifle. The driftwood fire was going strong. Doc, who had come to return and borrow a book from Keeper Jack's library, stood before the fireplace, warming his back.

"All right," the Keeper said to Harro. "Tell me why you asked about the cats."

Harro pointed to a portrait on the wall. It was of a young woman in an ankle-length, gray dress with a white collar. Her hair was tied back in a tight bun. She was seated in a wooden chair with a black-and-white cat in her lap and another, this one tabby-striped, at her feet, playing with a ball of yarn.

"I see." Keeper Jack sounded disappointed. "That is a painting of my wife. Jacob's mother. She loved cats. Maybe you can see that you favor her a bit."

"Favor her? I don't understand."

"Look like her."

Harro peered at the portrait. "No. I'm sorry. I don't see that at all."

"Why is your English so damn good?" Rex demanded. "I'm starting to think you're a spy."

"Father Josef spoke perfect English," Harro explained. "He ran the orphanage where I was raised. He taught all of his children to speak English. He said it was the language of the world, that no matter where we went, we would be able to find someone who could speak it." Harro looked at Doc Folsom. "How do you know German, sir?"

Doc shrugged. "German is the language of medicine, as is Latin. I have made a point to study them both."

Keeper Jack bent forward. His expression was intent. "Harro, tell me what you first remember of your life."

Harro shook his head. "All I know is that I was in an orphanage in Kiel. Father Josef came and took me, as he did many children. I remember none of this."

"How old were you when he came and got you?"

"I'm not sure."

"The first thing you remember," the Keeper prompted again. "Try. See what you recall. You may surprise yourself."

"I am very tired," Harro confessed, rubbing his eyes. The hot fire was making him even sleepier.

"Tell me the very first thing you remember," Keeper Jack insisted.

Harro rubbed his temples, trying to think. If nothing else, he wanted to please the old man. "The very first thing," he mumbled. After a few moments he said, "Sand. I think I remember sand."

Keeper Jack frowned. "Jacob loved to play in the sand."

Doc said, "What boy raised on an island doesn't?"

Harro thought some more. "The sand was dry and I remember piling it up, although I don't know why."

"Josh taught Jacob how to make a fort out of sand," Keeper Jack said, smiling at the memory. "He had little soldiers and they used to play war together."

"Hell, I played soldiers in the sand and I'm from Montana," Rex said. "This don't prove nothing except this kraut might be a pretty good liar, trying to fool us."

"Keeper," Doc said, "you sound like you hope the boy here is Jacob. You keep throwing him clues."

Keeper Jack gave Doc's comment some thought. "I guess you're right, Doc."

"I am not your son," Harro said. "I mean, I don't see how I could be."

"I know," Keeper Jack replied softly.

"How was he lost, sir?"

Keeper Jack told Harro of the tragedy, and how the last ever seen of Jacob had been in the tiny moth boat. "We never found a single trace of him. That was more than peculiar. The way the currents work here, we nearly always find something of those lost off our island."

Harro shook his head. The sad story had added to his misery.

"I've thought about this for a long time, Harro," Keeper Jack said. "Out on the Stream where Jacob was, there are always many freighters and tankers. What if one of them stopped to investigate a little red boat and picked up its cargo, a baby boy? And now, seeing you, I wonder what if that freighter or tanker was German or headed to a German port?"

"Surely, in the name of common decency, they would take a baby into the nearest port," Doc argued, "or at least radio in a report."

"Some freighters are always filled with contraband, especially ones coming up from the Caribbean," Keeper Jack explained. "Rum, drugs, guns, silver, gems from Brazil, could be just about anything. The crew of one of those contraband-runners could have found Jacob and been afraid to notify anyone of it, lest they call attention to themselves."

"But the idea of Jacob returning on a German U-boat is ludicrous," Doc insisted.

"God plays with us," Willow said. "Don't you know that, Doc? God plays with us all."

Doc stared at her for a long second, then nodded. "You humble me with your wisdom, Willow. Though is it God or mere fortune that plays with the affairs of men?"

Keeper Jack looked at Doc. "Doc, you have records on every baby born on Killakeet since 1919, don't you?"

Doc's usual composed expression faded. "See here, Keeper, those records are my research materials. They're confidential."

"You've taken fingerprints of the children, right?"

"Not always—"

"But you might have Jacob's fingerprints," Keeper Jack insisted. "You saw him several times after he was born for one thing or another. I remember it."

Doc shrugged. "I suppose I did."

"Then," Keeper Jack said reasonably, "go back to your office, dig Jacob's file out, and see if you took his fingerprints on one of those occasions. If so, we can discover the truth of this matter."

Harro no longer cared. It was all a philosophical question, after all. He was not this lost boy, although he felt profoundly lost. He sagged into the chair. He was, within a second, fast inside a deep, dreamless sleep.

# 45

The electrics were holding and Max was whistling with relief. *Thank God for German engineering!* Krebs ordered the *U-560* to surface after a look around with the attack periscope, the sky periscope left useless by the attack of the *Maudie Jane*. Krebs swept the horizon toward the sea, then swiveled toward land. The setting sun, a glorious scarlet orb amidst orange and pink streaks, greeted his eye. He saw no ships of any kind. "Surface, Chief," he said.

As the U-boat came up, the deep thumping of the port drive announced a spinning up by the diesels. Pretch called down the corridor from the radio closet, "*Kaleu,* the radio is working!"

"Good. Send Vogel a message. Tell him we were attacked and have sustained damage. Also tell him we're operational and are going back to hunting."

"Signal coming in from BdU, sir," Pretch replied.

"Go see what it is, Max," Krebs said in a voice as tired as he felt.

Max went below while Krebs waited for the lookouts to open the tower hatch. The fresh air that blew in was warm and tangy, Gulf Stream air. Krebs climbed onto the mangled tower and noted that the bow was riding low. "More buoyancy forward, Chief," he called.

"I think we have a leak in one of the forward buoyancy tanks, sir," the Chief replied.

Max came up. His face seemed paler than usual. Silently, he handed the message over and Krebs read it carefully. " '*Kapitänleutnant* Krebs relieved of command for unauthorized contact with enemy,' " he quoted. " 'To be placed under immediate arrest and delivered to the proper authorities upon return. Rendezvous with U-Vogel and take on new commander.' "

"Vogel must have picked up our transmissions to the Americans," Max said. "A fucking disaster, sir."

Krebs folded the message and tucked it in his jacket. He allowed a weary smile. "I am not functioning well these days, Max. I should have known Vogel's radio operators would be listening to the patrol boat, too."

"There is a way out." Max lowered his voice to a whisper. "Surrender to the Americans. After the war, we won't find the present government in power."

"Be silent! That's treason. I will surrender to Vogel. You and the other boys will perform in your usual professional manner during his operation. It will be proof of your loyalty and perhaps all will be well for you."

"Think about it, sir," Max said, then headed below to find the manual that would tell him how to sink the *U-560* and test the mercy of the Americans they had drowned so liberally over the past six weeks.


Josh came awake and found Marvin sitting on his bunk beside him. That had never happened before. He quickly sat up, bumping his head on the wooden locker placed perfectly for just such an eventuality. Marvin growled at him. "What's your problem, Marvin?"

Marvin jumped down and clambered topside. He was the only dog Josh had ever known who could actually climb a ladder. Sighing, Josh got up, tucked his shirt in his pants, and looked unsuccessfully for his shoes. He went forward and found Fisheye bent over the sonar screen, his eyes closed. "Wake up," Josh said, putting his hand on the boy's shoulder.

Fisheye's eyes flew open. "I am awake, sir, just resting.

*Ping, pock. Ping, pock.* Over and over. It's enough to drive you daffy."

Jimmy was curled up in the corridor, lightly snoring. Josh woke him and told him to replace Fisheye, then sensing trouble, went back to his bunk and opened the locker on which he had bumped his head. From it, he removed a small ax. It was an *anautaq,* as the Aleuts called their battle axes. He had brought it back from the Bering Sea Patrol. He'd learned to fight close-in with it in several pitched battles against renegades. The blade was of the finest American steel and was honed sharp as a straight razor.

Josh slipped up on deck and froze until his eyes adjusted to the darkness. He listened but heard only the Stream bubbling against the *Maudie Jane*'s hull. Maybe his unease was not warranted, he thought. Maybe Marvin had just gotten hungry and that was why the little dog had decided to come below. But why had Marvin awakened him and not Millie? Marvin knew very well who was the cook and who was the captain.

There was a glow around the edges of the wheelhouse hatch, emanating, no doubt, from the dials of Stobs's radios. Josh crept past the wheelhouse, glancing inside through a portal. Phimble was at the wheel, his head slumped forward. Atop the wheelhouse, he could make out the shape of Preacher slumped against the fifty caliber. The Stream had lulled them all asleep, except for Marvin. Josh thumped a knuckle on the portal glass and Phimble jerked upright. Then Josh climbed up to Preacher. "Wake up," he whispered, nudging him. Preacher grunted. "Hush," Josh hissed.

Josh eased back down the ladder to the deck where he nearly tripped over Marvin. Josh stared at the dog, then slowly turned in the direction he was looking. Josh tightened his grip on the ax when he heard something squeak against the hull. Suddenly, there was a blaze of light high in the sky. *Flare!* Josh found himself standing in front of a man dressed in gray fatigues and holding a machine pistol. His face was covered with black grease, a face that Josh would later reflect had a goofy expression. Beside him stood another man, dressed the same, but holding a rifle. Josh saw the rafts the men had arrived in. For a split second, they were all frozen in place. *"Surrender or you dies!"* the man holding the machine pistol cried out, and pointed it at Josh.

Josh lashed out with his ax and the man fell backward, his nearly severed neck spewing blood. Another swipe with Josh's ax sent the second man down, clutching his stomach. Josh struck a third man as he came on board, the axe this time embedded in the man's chest. Then from the tower of a U-boat not more than a hundred yards away, a machine gun erupted. Preacher immediately fired back, more flares began flying, and the deck was suddenly awash with light and blood.

Phimble ducked as bullets blew out the starboard portals of the wheelhouse in a shower of glass and bronze splinters. He started the engines and pushed the throttles forward as far as they would go. The big diesels howled and the *Maudie Jane* responded, pulling away. Josh had slipped and fallen in the blood from the three men he'd killed with the ax. One German remained, standing all alone. Josh took his rifle away from him and tossed him howling into the sea.

The rest of the Maudie Janes came up through the hatches, scattering in the face of the wild machine-gun fire coming from the receding U-boat. Ready had the Enfield and began cracking away. Josh yelled at the boys to get back below. Preacher was still firing, pounding the U-boat and exploding its searchlight. Still, it came on, launching flares. Tracers from its twin-barreled machine gun and Preacher's crisscrossed. Phimble began to weave the patrol boat back and forth, but the U-boat easily turned with it. Its rounds began to chew up *Maudie Jane*'s deck. Desperately, Josh armed the depth charges and sent them rolling overboard.

The submarine turned away before the charges went off, huge sheets of turquoise lightning flashing beneath the sea. Then it swerved back into the *Maudie Jane*'s wake.

Josh saw Preacher go down. Josh dragged him to the galley hatch, yelled at someone to take him, then dodged inside the wheelhouse. "We can't outrun it, Skipper," Phimble called over his shoulder. Phimble cranked the wheel over to put the patrol boat into another wild turn.

"The Beaufort fishermen, Eureka," Josh said. "The *Loggerhead* went aground near here."

Phimble understood. He slammed the wheel hard over to starboard, then bent forward to catch sight of the Killakeet Light through a shattered portal. The wheelhouse suddenly erupted in another storm of glass and splinters as the U-boat gunners found their range again. Josh snarled as something hit his back. Stobs went down on the deck, holding his hands over his head. Phimble, the backs of his hands bleeding, kept the patrol boat speeding ahead. The pounding of the machine gun bullets into the deck and the hull was tearing the boat apart.

Phimble studied the dark sea until he saw a hint of luminescence in the water. The U-boat came alongside, then slammed into the *Maudie Jane*'s bow. Phimble threw the wheel hard over and tore away, slashing within a few yards of the swirl of white water. The U-boat followed, plunging across the swirl.

The machine gun on the U-boat abruptly stopped firing. Josh crawled out of the wheelhouse and looked aft. The flares were receding. The U-boat had turned nearly sideways and was leaning over, as if a giant hand had reached up and snatched it. It had struck the same shoal as the *Loggerhead*.

Millie and the other boys climbed to their feet in the galley and found that they were standing ankle-deep in water. Once went forward and threw open the hatch to the head. A flood of water hit him, spinning him down the corridor. He ran topside, where, dripping, he made his report as succinct to Mister Thurlow as possible: *"Holy shit, sir! We're sinking!"*

Josh ran below and forward, peering into the head where the planking was punched inward, sheets of seawater spewing through the cracks. "Get mattresses and start piling them in here," he ordered.

Once and several of the boys started pulling up mattresses from their bunks and rushing them forward. "Are we done for, sir?" Millie asked. He had Preacher stretched out on one of the tables.

"Not by a long shot. How's Preacher?"

"Bullet in the gut."

A bucket line was organized to assist the bilge pumps. Phimble kept the throttles full ahead. "Try for Doakes, Skipper?"

"No," Josh said with an eye on the boys in the bucket line. They were young and strong but he knew the water was coming in faster than they could bail. "Head straight in. We'll beach her."

Straight in it was, and straight in took them directly to the beach just south of the Crossan House. Dosie was just starting her patrol. "Look," she said to Genie. "I do believe there's the *Maudie Jane.*"

The patrol boat plowed through the outer line of breakers and kept coming. It was an amazing sight to see, as if a crazed whale had decided to hurl itself out of the ocean. Genie started bucking at the sight. The *Maudie Jane* came on, flying through the waves until she struck the beach. Then, with a noise like a million fingernails dragged across a chalkboard, she shrieked across the sand, plowing a furrow until she bashed into a line of low sand dunes, a spray of sand sent flying as she climbed atop them, quivered for a moment, then subsided.

Dosie calmed Genie down and rode to the boat. She saw heads begin to pop up from the deck. Josh crawled from the wheelhouse and pulled himself to his feet by clinging to a rail. "G'morning, Dosie," he said, as if he'd just encountered her during a leisurely stroll.

"Damn, Josh," Dosie said, gasping. "What happened?"

Josh looked around as if he needed to confirm his answer. "Well," he said at last, "I guess you might say we've been wrecked."

# 46

The Keeper sat in a hard-backed chair, a book balanced on his knee, and watched Harro asleep in Josh's boyhood bed. He watched with an attentive expression, at once suspicious, yet concerned, as if the boy was nothing of what Willow claimed he was, and everything. Willow was sleeping downstairs on the couch before the cooling embers in the fireplace. Doc Folsom was gone; so was Rex, having borrowed Thunder to go into Whalebone City and bring back a party to bury Joe Johnston. Dosie had left on patrol.

That the boy had a certain resemblance to Trudelle, there was little doubt. The set of his mouth, the cheekbones, the high forehead, all could be rearranged in the Keeper's mind to form into his wife's gentle and patient face. Yet, those same features might be formed in other ways, too. If this was Jacob, it was a vastly improbable coincidence, but then again, Keeper Jack had seen too many instances of such coincidences occurring, especially when it came to the sea giving up its secrets. Had not, after all, Mrs. Donley found her husband Brick in the marsh three weeks after he'd fallen from a fishing boat in the Stream? Had not a plank containing the shipping license of a freighter washed ashore at the lighthouse, a freighter that had been lost off Hatteras the year before and included six Killakeet boys aboard her? Had not, in every instance he could think, the sea and the island somehow eventually provided an answer to what had happened to

those who went out and, for one reason or another, not returned?

The Keeper allowed a sigh. What if there was never anything that could confirm or deny who the boy was? What if,
instead, no proof at all ever came, one way or the other
beyond Willow's belief? What would happen then? Would
Josh, who after the placement of Jacob's headstone seemed
to have finally come to terms with the tragedy, revert to his
continuing torture? It had driven him away from Killakeet
once. Likely, it would again, even if the war didn't do it. *It
would have been best if you hadn't come,* the Keeper thought
as he kept studying the boy.

Yet . . . here he was. He was the right age and had the
frame and the features of the young man Jacob might have
grown into. He was an orphan without knowledge of his
parents. And it was not outside the realm of possibility, after
all, that Jacob might have been found on the Stream by men
too kind to let him drown but selfish enough not to endanger
themselves. And if that had happened, it was perfectly feasible that Jacob might have ended up in Germany and grown
up to join that country's navy. After all, men without family
or money gravitated toward military service, no matter what
country they lived in.

A chain of circumstances, Keeper Jack considered, each
one feasible, each linking to the other. If such links had been
forged, then one could easily see the next link, that the
German navy would bring the boy across the Atlantic, a natural occurrence considering the high probability of war that
had existed between Germany and the United States ever
since the Nazis had taken power. And even if there had not
been war, might not the boy have eventually ended up as a
merchant sailor? And any seaman who came to American
waters would eventually sail the Stream that washed past
Killakeet. If one could accept all the links, a case could be
made that it was almost inevitable that, had he survived,
Jacob would have returned as a young man just like Harro.
The more the Keeper thought of it, the more his hopes rose
that, indeed, his lost son slept before him.

He had gone to Emerson, who always seemed to have an answer. He opened the old book and let his thick, calloused finger trace the message: *A sublime hope cheers ever the faithful heart, that elsewhere, in other regions of the universal powers, souls are now acting, enduring and daring, which can love us, and which we can love.*

This is a boy who needs love, Keeper Jack thought. And if he is Jacob, he shall have it. But if he is not, then perhaps he should have it as well.

He closed the book, and inevitably the arguments in his mind started anew. *No, this can not possibly be. This is hope gone wrong.*

Shaking his head, Keeper Jack placed the book on the floor and wearily rose from the hard-backed chair. He did not even have to take note of the dim light at the window to know dawn had come and it was time to climb the tower and douse the light. He found Willow still asleep on the couch, the quilt that usually draped its back pulled around her. She was so pretty lying there, her face angelic in its sweetness. Certainly, Willow had taken to the boy upstairs. Maybe, he thought, this had all happened so that Willow would find the love she deserved.

But that was not clear thinking. Harro was headed for a prison camp for the duration of the war, a place where he would be subjected to disease and privation. Once he was gone from the island, it was likely no one would ever hear from him again.

Willow stirred beneath the quilt, then opened her eyes. "Keeper," she said. "Is Jacob awake, too?"

Keeper Jack sat on the coffee table beside the couch. "No. He was very tired from yesterday, you know. I think he may sleep for a while longer."

Willow stretched beneath the quilt embroidered with colorful whales and dolphins. Trudelle had sewn the quilt for the baby and Keeper Jack had kept it all these years. "Willow, may I ask you something?"

"Yes, Keeper."

"Are you going to talk so easily now? All these years,

you would not even look me in the eye when I spoke to you. And when you did speak, you spoke sort of . . . well, peculiar. You made sense but it was more as if you were talking to yourself than anyone around you."

"Was that wrong? No one ever told me that I was being bad."

"It wasn't bad, dear girl. Just different."

"How should I talk?"

"Well, honey, I guess any way you want. But it's best to have a back-and-forth, like we're having now. And it's just nice if you look at the person you're talking to. Do you understand? But you haven't been bad at all."

"I guess I never wanted to talk much," she said, "not after I couldn't be with Jacob anymore. That made me mad and then I got in the habit of not saying anything except what I wanted to say when I wanted to say it."

The Keeper touched her cheek. "You are a remarkable girl, Willow."

"I love you, Keeper," she said. "Everybody loves you."

"I don't know about that," he replied, but he was all but simpering at the compliment. "Why don't you sleep some more? When"—he nodded toward the stairway—"when *he* comes awake, we'll have breakfast together and talk some more."

She snuggled back beneath the quilt and in a moment was sound asleep. The Keeper envied her innocence, and her peaceful slumber, unmarred by doubts. He went on to the lighthouse and climbed the old iron steps with a heavy pace. At the top, he swung over the door to the lamp, then crouched behind it to turn the valve that pinched off the gas. The flame went out with a gasp. It always seemed to Keeper Jack that the light literally died each morning, such was the finality of that last, choked attempt to stay alive. Yet, at night, the flame jumped awake so exuberantly and with such familiarity, he often wondered if it was in fact the same flame, not a new one at all. It certainly looked the same, a golden orb, edged in a translucent and glimmering blue corona. Perhaps, he thought, it was the same for hopes that leap full-bursting to life when Providence allows the wheel of life to turn. Perhaps what he was feeling was not the birth of a new hope but the coming to life of an old one that had never truly died, a sublime hope, per Emerson, cheering ever his faithful heart with unending love.

The Keeper went out on the parapet as he did each morning to see what he could see and, especially now, to clear his mind and ponder anew the nature of hope and love. It was there he spotted the *Maudie Jane* at tortured rest atop the line of sand hills just south of the Crossan House. At that astonishing sight, he forgot all else save to wonder in awful fear if perhaps he had not discovered a son, but had, in terrible fact, lost one.

# 47

The two U-boats edged near, then stopped. Small waves smacked the hulls, and the wind sighed through the wounds of torn steel. Krebs studied Vogel's boat, trying to determine what had battered it. Bullet holes in the tower fairing were a clear indication of fighting a surface vessel, and a big scrape on its bow indicated a collision. "What happened to you?" he hailed across the gulf between the two boats.

Vogel's executive officer, *Leutnant* Sizner, returned the call. "We fought the American patrol boat last night," he said.

"Who won?"

"We did."

"You sank it?"

"It's aground, thrown up on the beach."

Krebs surprised himself when he felt relieved to hear the patrol boat had survived. "Where's Vogel?"

"Asleep. He was exhausted after the battle." Sizner was taken aside by one of his men for a moment, there were a few words exchanged, then he returned. "*Kapitän* Krebs, I am coming across to assume command of the *U-560*."

"Come ahead," Krebs said.

Max whispered, "Sir, you can not allow this."

"I have no choice."

"There is another way."

"There is no other way." When Max started to say more, Krebs hushed him. "Don't say it and don't think it, either. One hanging is enough between us."

Sizner was paddled across in a raft, then clambered up on the tower. "You are relieved, sir," he said to Krebs upon arrival.

Krebs nodded. "What happened in your battle with the Americans?"

Sizner, a lumpish sort of a man with a dense black beard, looked troubled. "We pretended we were you, actually," he said after a moment of hesitation, as if he had to decide whether to lie or not. "We sent out a long signal so that the Americans could get a fix on where we were. We waited for them beside a wreck so they couldn't detect us, then rose and attacked just before dawn."

"You didn't use a torpedo?"

Sizner looked sheepish. "*Kapitän* Vogel didn't want to waste one. Lieutenant Schlake said he would take some men across on rafts and kill the crew. It turned into a bloody affair. Schlake was killed. I saw it, though I still scarcely believe it." Sizner's hand drifted to his throat, rubbing it. "One of the Americans, a big officer, nearly chopped off Schlake's head with a tomahawk and then killed two others in what seemed an instant. Then the patrol boat ran and we chased it until we hit a sandbar. When we got off the bar, we went looking for the Americans and found them beached. We were leaking fuel so we headed into deeper water to make repairs."

"What other damage did you sustain?"

"None structurally. However, we lost six men, including the lieutenant. Our tower machine gun was also thrown overboard when we hit the sandbar."

"My congratulations on your successful attack, *Leutnant*," Krebs said dryly. "So what are your orders?"

"*Kapitän* Vogel has decided to proceed with the operation on the island tonight," Sizner said. "It is an opportune time with the patrol boat out of action."

Krebs nodded. "I will act in the capacity as your adviser,

if that suits you. Max—you know my exec, yes?—Max will remain in his position as will the rest of my officers and subofficers."

Sizner stiffened. "I have been given no orders as to the disposition of your officers and men, sir, and I agree they will be left in place. However, I'm afraid you must go across to *Kapitän* Vogel's boat and there remain for the duration of our operations."

Max said, "That is ridiculous. Trust me, *Leutnant*, you will want *Kapitän* Krebs's advice."

"Nonsense, Max," Krebs said lightly. "The *Leutnant* knows his business. Show him around the boat, what's left of it, and let the fellows know he's in command. I'll get a few things and then go see *Kapitän* Vogel."

"He will not see you," Sizner replied evenly. "You are to be put under arrest and secured in the aft torpedo room."

"I see," Krebs said. "Well, I'll try not to get in their way back there."

"I am grateful for your compliance, *Kapitän*," Sizner said. "I will note it when I testify at your court-martial."

"And when I swing, you will even shed a tear for me, is that it, *Leutnant*?"

Sizner shrugged. "No, sir. I will be glad to see it. For treating with the enemy, you deserve to hang."

"Well, you're an honest sort, I will give you that."

Sizner squared his cap in preparation to meet the crew. "And you, *Kapitän* Krebs, are a traitor, even though I have no doubt that you are still the best U-boat commander in the fleet. I will give you that."

# 48

Preacher died that morning, to the relief of the Maudie Janes. It seemed to them that Preacher was a man who'd gone from telling the good news of heaven to take a turn in hell. They guessed there was a deep reason for that and they didn't like to be around anyone that close to Providence, for good or evil.

Their unease, however, did not keep each of them from doing his best for the man while he lay silently and indifferently dying on a sand hill gradually soaked with his gore. Each boy had made a solemn journey across the sand to where Preacher lay staring up at what had started as a crystal blue sky but was, as the day wore on, tending toward clouds. Preacher had his full length exposed, having kicked off the blanket each time it was put over him. His eyes were wide and staring and he held with one hand his bandaged guts and with the other a Bible that Dosie had brought to him, for pity's sake, when no one else had thought of it. Each boy first covered with Preacher the weather, according to Killakeet custom, and then they told him what a good shipmate he was, and how they'd enjoyed his sermons, and they sure hoped he'd be back aboard the *Maudie Jane* real soon. Except for the weather, everything they said was a lie.

But Preacher didn't know the boys were telling him lies. He clutched Dosie's Bible and heard their words, more or less, but they didn't much register. His mind was elsewhere.

It wasn't death he saw coming so much as sleep, and that was his revelation, that death *was* sleep, and it might not be dreamless. He found the revelation somewhat useless because he had no great enthusiasm to live on after death, even as a dream. What he wanted was to get near God, to have just one moment—it need not last more than the blink of a gnat—so he could figure out who God was. Preacher didn't much think he was going to get that moment, so he lay there disappointed at the prospect of death.

Then Lieutenant Thurlow came and knelt and took Preacher's hand and told him he thought the clouds would likely scud away and that Preacher was as good an auxiliary coastguardsman as there ever was. Preacher had squeezed his eyes shut and allowed a choked laugh, though it hurt like hell to do it. Preacher had watched Josh Thurlow swing his little ax—*swish, swip,* and *swop*—and three men were dead without a lingering moment to contemplate their fate and their future after death, nor make amends, nor cry for help. All they had been given was a quick death, but perhaps that was a blessing.

Josh rose to be replaced by a hangdog Dosie Crossan. Preacher gave her a thank-you for the Bible, or at least he hoped his lips moved enough that she recognized what he was saying.

Dosie left and Preacher saw a seagull come passing by against the clouds, and then Keeper Jack came. By then, Preacher was considering all the words in the Bible, how they simply lay there, and depending on how you read them, they might say anything you wanted them to say. They could be read right to left, or up and down like the Chinese did, or perhaps in three dimensions, through the book rather than on each page. As Keeper Jack knelt and prayed above him, Preacher wondered if it was dying that made him philosophical or the morphine. He regretted he would never know for certain.

Preacher wanted to tell Keeper Jack how much he would miss seeing him at the services. The Keeper was a quiet sleeper, not one of those cracking snorers who often interrupted his sermons amidst the titters of the ladies. Keeper Jack had come with Purdy, the old pelican. Purdy looked down on Preacher with a concerned expression, then winked at him. Preacher didn't know that pelicans could wink, and then he realized it wasn't Purdy winking at all. It was someone else. Stars swam in Preacher's head.

Oh, if heaven was going to be this sweet, Preacher thought, where he might consider all things in such a detached, philosophical manner, he might come to love it, even if it lasted a time too short to measure or too long the same. And then Preacher died while Keeper Jack was back to speculating on the weather, and Purdy had waddled off. Some said the man died in bitterness and loss, while others weren't certain, matching Preacher's opinion.

After Preacher had passed, Keeper Jack took Josh aside and told him his thoughts about the boy, that maybe it was possible he was Jacob. "Daddy, that's crazy" was Josh's retort.

"But what if he is? At least, consider the possibility."

"What I have to consider," Josh said, "is that all these years you've lied to me, telling me you thought there was no hope for Jacob."

"That's not the way it is at all," Keeper Jack replied, a bit testy. He hadn't had much sleep, after all. "I've always believed that eventually the sea would give us an answer."

"And you think this German is it? Daddy, there's nothing to prove it at all except for crazy little Willow."

"She sees things the rest of us don't," the Keeper insisted.

"Believe what you want, but that German is not Jacob."

"We'll soon know," Keeper Jack said. "First chance he gets, Doc is going to look into his files to see if he took Jacob's fingerprints when he was a baby."

"Doc agreed to that?"

"Of course. Why wouldn't he?"

Josh left his father before he got shouting mad at the old man and went down to his boat. "What do you think, Pump?" he asked Willow's father, who was inspecting the gash in the boat's bow.

"Fixable," Pump said. "A little planking cut just so, caulking and such." Then he said, "What wonderful news about Jacob being found. It's a miracle, that's what it is."

Josh resisted the urge to batter the man. "Pump, that German is not Jacob. Don't be starting rumors that he is."

"Well, he could be," Pump said. "I mean, it's possible, don't you think?"

Buckets O'Neal came over and agreed with Pump's assessment on the boat. "High tide will float her, Josh," Buckets said. "You want us to have a go at fixing this hulk?"

Josh did. Though he had no depth charges, he still had the three-inch gun and the machine gun. With at least two U-boats operating off Killakeet, the *Maudie Jane* needed to be out there. Since Stobs's radios were dead, Josh had sent word for Chief Glendale to call Captain Potts about what had happened, but he didn't expect any help from that quarter. None had been forthcoming before, so why now?

To Josh's irritation, Buckets also agreed with Pump's assessment of the German boy. "What a miracle little Jacob being found. Who would have believed it?"

"Shut up, Buckets," Josh growled. "That kraut is not Jacob."

"Your daddy said he could be."

"There's a considerable distance between could be and is."

Queenie drew Josh aside. "My land, Josh. The good Lord doth provide, don't He? After all these years, the boy is back. I knew you didn't lose him."

Josh slumped in despair. What, after all, did he expect—pessimism from a people who lived on a spit of sand that got swamped by hurricanes every few years? "Queenie, there is no proof whatever that that German is Jacob. Please pass that along to all the ladies and everybody else."

"But he could be," Queenie insisted.

"Jacob is dead, somewhere out there," Josh said, nodding toward the sea. "That is what I believe."

Queenie fixed Josh with a sad, motherly smile. "You should hope more, Josh."

"Well, I hope your husband and the other men can fix my boat."

Dosie wanted a minute and Josh gave it to her. She steered him over by the high-tide line of sand hills. "I've been giving this a lot of thought. It's a hard thing for me to say but I've got to say it. I love you and it doesn't even matter if you love me back."

Josh would have preferred, at that moment, that Dosie had struck him across the nose with a two-by-four. He didn't have time to think about love on a morning when his patrol boat was flung ashore, and his father had proposed that some German U-boater was actually his little lost brother and most Killakeeters seemed bound to believe it, and Preacher just dead because Josh had come up with the crazy idea that a man who'd lost his faith might as well become a machine gunner. "Well, Dosie," he said, "that's a very nice thing to say."

When he didn't add to it, she said, "That's what I thought. You don't love me."

"I didn't say that!"

"You didn't say anything worth hearing," she said, and stomped away.

Buckets came up to Josh, seeing as how he was suddenly quite alone, and tugged on his sleeve. "We're on our way back to Whalebone City for our tools and such," he said. "We have agreed to the length and width of the strakes, although I doubt we have the lumber to do the job proper, so we're likely to end up using more than a few butts or scarfs, which ain't going to be pretty. We'll tick them for rabbets so the strakes will come in pretty dear, as long as you don't mind the blocks aren't on the sheer clamp."

Josh had never been much of a boatbuilder and what Buckets had said was completely bewildering, but he nodded and answered, in his best officerly fashion, "Just as long as she don't leak much."

"That's what I told the boys you'd say," Buckets said, a finger next to his nose.

Josh looked around for Dosie but she had disappeared,

God only knew where, but likely stirring up trouble. He'd hurt her feelings, he guessed, but he didn't have time to worry about it. He spotted Herman down by the *Maudie Jane* holding a bucket of caulk. Nearly every boy on Killakeet was there, aching to help their big brothers and uncles and fathers get the patrol boat back into action. So were the little girls. In fact, now that he looked around, Josh supposed that there wasn't a soul on Killakeet that wasn't on that beach, all pitching in to help. Chief Glendale brought the jeep and Preacher was already loaded in it. He would be placed in a rude coffin of wrecked lumber and buried with all the others behind the lighthouse.

"Did you call Captain Potts about our battle?" he asked Glendale.

"I did, sir. He's up in Norfolk, meeting about something. The duty officer said he'd get back to me. I ain't heard a word."

"I'm not surprised."

"No, sir, we've been on our own since this whole shebang started. Reckon it'll stay that way for a bit longer."

Josh saw his father walking up the beach toward the lighthouse. He could also see two figures coming toward him: Willow and the German boy.

Josh was close to being overwhelmed by everything that had happened. But he couldn't be overwhelmed. He had responsibilities. On the eastern horizon was a column of smoke, likely a torpedoed tanker. The war had not stopped for all the business of Killakeet, and the U-boats were still out there doing their deadly work. But one of them, a big black one, had been knocked around, and Krebs's boat was surely damaged, too.

Josh watched the Keeper greet Willow and the German, then turn around and join them in their walk toward the *Maudie Jane*. Josh made a decision. There would be a quiet visit between him and the boy who was not his brother behind a tall sand hill where they might not be observed, and there Josh would be told all that he needed to know, through broken teeth if came to that, and he nearly wished that it might.

He smacked his big fist in the palm of his hand and waited.

Then Doc came up behind him and lifted his shirt. "Hold still, Josh," he said. Josh held still, not exactly sure what Doc was doing, then felt a sharp pain in his back. "Got it," Doc said with satisfaction.

Josh turned on Doc, who was staring with a bemused expression at an inch-long bronze sliver clamped in his pliers. Josh had forgotten he'd been hit in the back during the fight with the black U-boat. "Doc," he said, "why'd you tell Daddy you'd look for Jacob's file? Remember when I first came back? I asked you about it and you said you didn't have it."

Doc opened the pliers and let the blood-wet sliver drop in the sand. "Well, Josh, if you must know, I decided your purpose was morbid curiosity and I didn't believe it was good for you."

"Morbid curiosity? Doc, I had a long time to think while I was in Alaska. It came to me to hire a private investigator to visit orphanages to see if anybody remembered a baby like Jacob. I even told you that, if you might recall."

Doc airily waved the pliers. "I suppose I must have heard you wrong."

"I don't believe you have any files, Doc, on Jacob or any other baby. That's the truth of it, ain't it? If you do, where are they? Must be a stack of 'em tall as the lighthouse."

"They're in my outbuilding."

"That musty place? It's been flooded a half dozen times that I know of."

"They are on a high shelf."

Josh peered closely at Doc's placid face. "Why are you lying?"

Doc shrugged. "A lie isn't one until it happens."

"A favorite expression of yours. In this case, what does it mean?"

Doc wiped the bloody pliers on his pants leg, then tucked them in his pocket. "It means I have already found Jacob's file and it does indeed have his fingerprints in it. And as soon as I have yon boy's fingerprints, I shall know the answer as to who he is, or, we might suppose, at least who he isn't."

"I don't believe a word of it."

Doc raised his eyebrows. "Well, Josh, one thing I've learned over the years is that some things, even if we are certain they are not true, may well prove otherwise."

# 49

The problem with taking the German boy behind a tall sand hill and beating the truth out of him was that Josh liked him. Josh liked him because he kept saying he wasn't Jacob, and also because his face so reminded Josh of his mother. It was a contradiction but Josh was too tired to worry about it. In any case, Harro volunteered some of the information Josh was after without being asked for it. "The black submarine you fought last night was not mine," he said. "It was probably a Type Nine that is also working off Killakeet."

"Who's its captain?" Josh asked, not expecting an answer. He looked around for an appropriate sand hill to do the necessary pounding of the boy.

Harro hesitated, then shrugged. "*Kapitän* Vogel. He is the commander of all the boats along this coast. It's treason, me telling you that."

"That's all right," Josh answered, relaxing. "You would have told me, anyhow."

Dosie, unable to stand being left out, had drifted in to listen. When there was an entire second of silence, she said, "I want another word with you, Josh."

"Not now," Josh replied in as gruff a tone as he had ever used with her. As far as he was concerned, she could play her games with somebody else.

Dosie nonetheless took his arm and steered him off to the

high-tide mark. "I forgive you for not being in love with me."

"I *do* love you, you dit-dot," Josh snapped. "But you also drive me nuts."

"Well, you drive me nuts, too!" Dosie cried. Then she grinned. "Do you really love me?"

Josh tore off his cap in frustration and came near to throwing it down but decided otherwise, hats being hard to come by. He plopped it back aboard. "Yes, I do."

She turned her head in that adorable manner she had and it made Josh want to grab her and hold her and tell her how pretty she was and feel her warm body against his. Dosie saw all that in his eyes. "Why don't you come up and see me sometime?" she said, batting her eyes at him.

"You are oversexed," Josh accused. Then, he said, "I like that in a woman."

"I bet you do." Dosie walked off, her hips swaying maybe a bit more than usual.

Josh watched after her, then shook his head and went back to Willow and Harro and his father. Doc had joined them and, remarkably, had taken the boy's fingerprints on a sheet of white paper. Harro was cleaning the ink off his fingers in the sand. "I'll compare and let you know," Doc said importantly.

"It is a waste of your time," Harro said.

"I find it a most interesting exercise," Doc replied.

"This boy is a prisoner of war," Josh said. "He should be locked up."

"He's not a prisoner at all," Keeper Jack said. "He's my guest at the house."

"But the authorities will be taking him soon."

"Why do they have to even know about him?"

Josh was astonished. "Daddy, this is a German U-boat crewman, no matter who else you think he might be. Remember the *Lady Morgan* and all those bodies?"

"My boat didn't do that," Harro said.

"I will compare the prints this evening," Doc said to Keeper Jack, and went off to see about patching up Bosun

Phimble's hands. So far, Phimble had claimed to be too busy to let him pull the tiny shards of glass out of them.

Josh turned on his heel and walked toward the *Maudie Jane*. At least aboard his boat, things made some sense and he could yell and everybody would do exactly what he yelled at them to do. But then he thought of Dosie and saw she was standing in front of her house, watching him, and waiting for him, too, he supposed. She raised her hand and then he thought maybe the Maudie Janes were doing fine without his instruction and that maybe Dosie ought to have a look at the wound Doc had left in his back after pulling the sliver out. She surely had some iodine and it might do the trick, though it would burn like acid. Yes, he decided, he would let Dosie do it. It was the right thing to do, all things considered.

Once and Millie, patching the holes in *Maudie Jane*'s deck, watched Mister Thurlow walk toward the Crossan House. "Skipper's going off to throw a leg over Dosie," Once said in an envious voice.

"Who can blame him?" Millie replied. "What a woman she is!"

"Ma said she likes the skipper too much and ain't ever going to trap him," Once worried. "Said why buy the cow when you get the milk for free?"

"There's a war on," Millie said. "We might all be dead this time tomorrow."

"What's that an answer to?" Once demanded.

Millie shrugged and got back to patching. "Maybe nearly everything," he said.

# 50

Darkness, vast and black, and Vogel's raid began. Clouds had moved in steadily all day and the moon and stars were shrouded. Not even the ocean's natural luminescence provided a glimmering trail as the black U-boat, propelled by its electrics, came gliding in to Doakes Station. Quickly, nine submariners swarmed onto the dock and formed themselves into three teams. One team was to blow up the warehouses, one was to pillage the headquarters, and one, armed with a machine gun, was sent to guard the approaches to the village. No one saw them. Chief Glendale had gone home for the night.

At first, all went according to plan. The team assigned to the warehouses began to set the charges. The team assigned to the Surfmen's House kicked in the front door (had they tried the knob, they would have found it unlocked) and charged up the stairs and wrecked the empty radio room. Then they rooted through the files for secret documents. Since only one man had a rudimentary knowledge of English, this proved a fruitless search and they settled for strewing the papers about. The machine gun was set up in what its team perceived was the main road of the town, or at least the widest track of sand. There, they waited, the ugly snout of their gun pointing down Walk to the Base. Soon, the team that had pillaged the Surfmen's House joined them and sat, waiting for orders. They were nervous, and being on land felt odd, after all their weeks at sea.

Vogel came ashore and told the demolitions team to blow up the warehouses. The demolitions team rolled out the wire and took protection behind a sand hill and waited until their U-boat had backed away. Then they plunged the handle of the detonator and the warehouses went up in a mighty eruption. Then Vogel led the demolitions team to find the rest of his men. He found them watching the warehouses burn. He told the machine gun crew to fire a burst down the road. They did. "Now, round everybody up," Vogel snapped to the ranking man, a bosun named Hennsen. He and seven men went running down the sand track and began knocking politely on doors. "Kick the doors in, you fools!" Vogel yelled, just as one of the sailors was blasted away by duck shot from a shotgun poked through a window. Then someone tipped over a kerosene lantern and a fire broke out. People started running this way and that, silhouetted against the leaping flames. There was a lot of yelling, which unnerved Vogel. He wanted everybody to quietly and meekly follow orders.

Vogel tracked down Hennsen and ordered him to catch what people he could and herd them up the track. Hennsen went off, blowing his whistle. Before long, about forty men, women, and children were pushed up Walk to the Base. Dressed in their pajamas, housecoats, and hastily pulled-on whatnots, they were a bewildered bunch. A woman dressed in a pink nightgown was carrying, for no apparent reason, an old pelican.

Hennsen saluted Vogel. "We have done our best, sir," he said, which Vogel did not take to be encouraging. Vogel checked his watch. Over thirty minutes had elapsed since the operation had begun. It was time to end it and get back to the boat. He considered the situation and decided the beach was the best place to do the real work. There was plenty of room down there and he could spread the people out in a long line so they couldn't be missed even by the idiots crewing the machine gun. "Take them down to the beach," he said. "And hurry up!"

• • •

Aboard Vogel's U-boat, Krebs heard the explosions. When he asked the stern torpedomen what had happened, they shrugged. They had never paid much attention to him. He got up and walked to the hatch and they made no move to stop him. "I am going to the toilet," he said, and they didn't even bother to answer. Without Vogel aboard, nobody seemed to be in charge. Krebs kept going until he reached the galley. It was empty and the galley hatch was open. He climbed up the ladder and out on deck. Onshore, the remains of what appeared to be warehouses were smoldering, and behind them, a number of houses were burning. Then he saw a group of people being herded toward the beach. He heard one of the lookouts on the tower say, "Now, we will see the end of tonight's work."

Krebs looked around and saw nobody watching him. He eased into the cold water and started swimming.

Demands of *"Schnell, schnell!"* from the Germans sent the people to the beach. Vogel fired his pistol into the air to keep them going. Things were better now, Vogel thought. He was going to bring terror to these shores. Forty dead Americans would be impressive and Berlin would be pleased. The captured townspeople were on the beach, milling about, and his men were formed up on the line of dunes above them. Hennsen reported once more. He was a man apparently without the slightest particle of imagination. "How shall we kill them, sir?" he asked.

"Line them up and mow them down, you fool," Vogel said. When Hennsen looked blank, Vogel sighed and said, "With the machine gun."

A woman, the one carrying the pelican, came out of the crowd. "See here," she said, handing the pelican to someone else. "What are you doing?"

"And who are you?" Vogel asked, against his best judgment. He needed to shoot all these people and get away. But, he'd never spoken to an American and thought it would be interesting while he had the opportunity.

"I'm Queenie O'Neal. Why do you have us decent people standing out here on the beach?"

Vogel decided to show her the reason and shot her with his pistol but he was disappointed in the result. He had aimed at her chest but managed to only graze her arm. She grabbed it, then fell down. He wanted to shoot her again but was afraid he might miss her completely and be laughed at by the men. "For God's sake, get on with it, Hennsen!" he snapped.

When the explosions erupted on the island, followed by shooting, Max was standing beside *Leutnant* Sizner on the tower of the *U-560*. The U-boat was about a mile offshore, standing by to block any ships that might try to come to the rescue. "They're burning the town," Max said.

"And soon they will kill all the people," Sizner replied.

Max's mouth dropped open. "What do you mean?"

"This is an exercise in terror," Sizner said. "*Kapitän* Vogel means to scare the Americans out of the war."

"Is he insane?"

"No. He's brilliant." Sizner appraised Max. "Be very careful, *Leutnant*. Your neck may end up in the same noose as your captain's."

Max pondered the situation, then called through the tower hatch. "Chief, would you come up, please?"

When the Chief clambered through the hatch, Max nodded toward Sizner and said, "*Leutnant* Sizner and I have been discussing matters. It appears I was commissioned some weeks before him, which makes me the ranking officer on board."

"See here," Sizner said, "we have discussed no such thing."

"I am therefore taking over the boat," Max continued. "Take the *Leutnant* below and put him under guard. Then come back and help me. I'm going ashore."

Josh and the other men were at work on the *Maudie Jane* when they heard the explosions. "The Germans are shelling the town or they've come ashore," Josh said, and immediately started to think about what he could do about it.

Rex trotted in aboard Thunder. "The beach patrol has arrived," he reported to Josh with a salute. Dosie came running and saluted, too. She had her rifle slung over her shoulder.

"You two wait here," Josh ordered them, then went after Ready. "Get the machine gun and strap it to Thunder. Then stay with the boat and defend it."

"Ma and Pa are at the hotel," Ready said. "I ought to go help them."

"That's what I intend to do but I need to travel fast," Josh said. "Your ankle's all wrenched. Stay here, do like I tell you."

Ready reluctantly went off to tie the machine gun onto Thunder's saddle, along with ammo belts.

Josh gathered the crew and the workers around. "Rex and I will go see what's what. The rest of you stay here and get the boat ready to go to sea."

"I'm going with you," Dosie said.

"No, you need to help defend the *Maudie Jane*."

Dosie threw herself into his arms and kissed him with all her might. "I love you, Josh Thurlow!" Everybody around them grinned.

"I love you, too, Dosie Crossan!" he responded with a great, happy shout, then let her go, as it seemed he always did.

Josh and Rex and Thunder made their way up the beach, the leaping fires that marked Doakes and Whalebone City a terrible sight. At the lighthouse, they were met by Keeper Jack, Harro, and Willow. "I will go with you," Harro said. "This is surely Vogel's work. Perhaps you will need to talk to him or his men. I can translate."

That made sense to Josh so he agreed. Willow clutched at Harro. "Let go, Willow," he said, though gently.

"Why?"

"You want me to help Josh, don't you?"

Willow reluctantly let him go. "Come back," she said most plaintively.

Harro didn't reply. He fell in beside Josh.

Keeper Jack came and put his arm around her. "Josh will take care of him, Willow honey."

"He is Jacob. Oh, you must know it now," she said.

"He may be," the Keeper said, as far as he could go.

Max and two of the deck crew, carrying rifles, paddled ashore in a raft. They dodged over a line of dunes and made their way along behind them. Every few minutes, Max flashed a light toward the sea. Just offshore, the Chief directed the *U-560*, using the electrics, to keep up with the light. Max hadn't gone more than a thousand yards before he spotted Vogel and his men and the people on the beach.

Max wasn't certain of what he should do. Then a machine gun opened up and Vogel's men fell.

The people on the beach ran. Vogel yelled at his men to fire at them but they were too busy ducking bullets. The American civilians soon disappeared into the night. The wounded woman was taken with them and the pelican, too.

Vogel started sweating. Who knew what force had come across the island with a machine gun? Perhaps it was the United States Marines. This was trouble, *real* trouble.

Krebs came to what was apparently the main street of the town. Some of the houses were burning. He was surprised when he saw a little man in a derby hat pondering a shed that wasn't on fire. He was even more surprised when he saw the man pick up a burning brand, open the door to the shed, and toss it inside. The shed was soon engulfed in flames. Krebs sneaked past and disappeared into the darkness toward the chatter of the machine gun.

Vogel was scared. He had never thought about being killed or caught during his operation. If caught, he would certainly be tried by the Americans and probably hung on any number of charges, including trying to murder civilians. There would be no prisoner-of-war camp for him, nor for the men with him. He raised his head out of the sand. "Men, we must fight our way clear or every one of us will hang."

This was news to Vogel's submariners and they didn't like it. "Let's run for it," one of them said, just as a searchlight from the sea exposed them.

"It's our boat!" Hennsen cried.

A voice came out of the darkness, the voice of *Leutnant* Max of the *U-560*. "No, it isn't."

Vogel yelled back. "Come here, Max. Help us!"

"I am not here to help you, Vogel," Max said. "I'm here to stop you."


"What did those Germans say?" Josh demanded of Harro.

"It's Lieutenant Max, sir," Harro said. "Our second-in-command. That's my boat out there. But he seems to be on the beach. He told Captain Vogel he was going to stop him."

"Well, if that don't beat all," Rex said. "Krauts fighting krauts. What next?"

Josh looked over his shoulder. The people of Whalebone City had formed a bucket brigade from the sea through Doakes, throwing water on the fires. "Rex, get over there and tell those people to keep out of sight until we get things under control."

Rex went off at a lope.


Krebs was working his way through some sand hills when, to his amazement and joy, he heard Harro's voice. He crawled in closer, then went running in a crouch to throw himself beside the boy. He didn't notice for a moment the big man in khakis behind the machine gun. "*Kapitän* Krebs!" Harro exclaimed.

"Are you all right, Harro?"

Harro was having trouble getting his mouth to work. He didn't know whether to speak German or English.

Josh grabbed Krebs by the shoulder and rolled him over. "What do you know? I've been trying to kill you for nearly two months and here you are."

"Thurlow?"

"Yes."

The machine gun in the dunes erupted, and a burst of sand was tossed up in front of Josh. Cursing, he fired back, determined to chop down to beach rock the sand hills that hid the Germans. It quickly proved futile. The sand simply absorbed the bullets. When the muzzle flash stopped dancing before his eyes, Josh turned to continue his talk with Krebs. It was time to establish that the German captain was a prisoner. But Krebs was gone.

And so was the boy.

Vogel grabbed Hennsen by the shoulder. "You and the machine gunners cover the rest of us while we run to the dock. Our boat will be there."

Hennsen hesitated. He didn't like the idea of staying behind.

"You will be given an Iron Cross and a promotion," Vogel said. "And if you don't follow orders, I will have you shot."

It wasn't much of a choice. Hennsen ordered the machine gunners to start firing. Vogel and the remaining men went sprinting across the dunes.

Josh ducked when the machine gun bullets stitched the sand in front of him. Then he saw the machine gunners lift their gun and make a run for it. This time, there was no sand hill to save them. He cut the Germans down with a short burst.

Hennsen took steady aim at the men of the *U-560* clambering into the raft. They were traitors. He was truly going to earn his Iron Cross. He squeezed the trigger, nearly getting off the shot before he felt a pressure alongside his ear. A mosquito, perhaps, was his thought. He would have slapped at it except he couldn't move his arms, nor did he much care after a moment. The pressure had been caused by a bullet entering his skull, snapped off by Rex Stewart as he came walking back from town. Hennsen fell face-down into the sand. Rex came and stood over him, then twirled his rifle around and blew on the barrel. "That was for Joe Johnston," he said.

# 51

D eep water, that was their salvation. The *U-560* pounded for the Stream and some room to maneuver, lookouts posted fore and aft on the ravaged tower. Harro spelled Pretch on the radio just as a signal from BdU came pouring in. Max decoded the message and carried it to Krebs.

> KREBS. YOU ARE STILL RELIEVED. PROCEED IMME-
> DIATELY TO BASE. VOGEL. PROCEED IMMEDIATELY
> TO BASE. ALL OTHER BOATS AMERICAN STATION
> CONGRATULATIONS ON YOUR CONTINUED SUCCESS.
> STRIKE HARD. WOUND THE ENEMY. DO NOT LET UP.
> BDU

"No doubt Vogel has already contacted Doenitz with his side of the affair," Max said.

Krebs shrugged. "All he needs to do is to tell the truth and our goose is cooked. I think it's past time I talked to the boys. Set up the internal communications and I will be right down."

Max went below while Krebs took one last look around. The sea was completely empty. He felt the hairs on the back of his neck prickle. To another U-boat captain, the lack of targets might simply be a disappointment. To Krebs, all that emptiness meant something had changed and the enemy might be hatching a surprise. "You boys," he said to the lookouts, "cock your ears toward the hatch and you'll hear what I have to say. But no matter what, sing out if you see anything—and I mean *anything*." The lookouts responded affirmatively and Krebs clambered down the ladder and took the microphone from Max.

"Men of the *U-560*," he said. "I do not need to remind you of all that we have gone through together in the last weeks. During it all, I have been proud to be your captain. You have performed with distinction and courage and have never failed in your duty to your country nor to me.

"I, however, have failed you. *Kapitän* Vogel intends to bring me up on charges of treason. Likely, I will be found guilty. But at the moment, that is not my concern. My concern is that we will all return in disgrace. I cannot deny that I have put every one of you in peril. I also cannot change it. Now, as we head back across the Atlantic, I am going to ask you to vote amongst yourselves, section by section, as to whether I will remain your captain until we reach base. I will abide by your decision, whatever it is. I hope you will forgive me because I will never forgive myself for what I have done to you. Out."

Krebs hung the microphone in its holder and waited. Before long, the Chief came up the ladder into the tower control room. "Sir," he said, "the men say they have no need for a vote. They will stand with you."

Krebs was honestly surprised and touched. He went below, walked through the *U-560*, patted the arm or the shoulder of each man, and thanked them while looking into their eyes for any sign of resentment. He saw none, except for crazy Hans, but even Hans was not resentful for the noose Krebs had fashioned for his neck. He was resentful as always for the abuse of his engines. "They will not fail us, sir," he said of the roaring diesels.

"I wish our philosophy was half as good as your engines," Krebs replied. "Then we might deserve to lead the human race."

"Here's a philosophy for you, Captain," Hans replied tartly. "To hell with the human race."

Krebs made his way forward, reflecting on Hans's words. All in all, he supposed, it wasn't a bad philosophy to have if you were a motorman. But Krebs was still a captain of a U-boat, which meant he required another philosophy, the simplest of them all: *Survive*.

The inhabitants of Whalebone City wished Preacher wasn't one of the bodies going into the sand. They feared for his soul, considering that he was a preacher who had lost his faith. Dosie, seeing them all so stricken, told them it wasn't so. "Preacher was holding his Bible when he died," she said. "That meant he had regained his faith. Isn't that so?"

Nobody answered Dosie because nobody was certain of the answer. Preacher went down in his wrecked-lumber coffin and the sand was shoveled over him. A driftwood cross went up along with a hastily painted sign hung by a scrap of twine. It said, simply, *PREACHER*.

The German sailors left behind were buried, too. Doc collected their name tags to give to the authorities should any ever arrive. His infirmary had burned and he had temporarily moved into the Hammerhead. The hotel had been scorched but was still open for business. Queenie's wound had been but a scratch, although Buckets was giving her round-the-clock nursing. Purdy was back at his station on the hotel pizer, although no gulls had returned.

Doc found Keeper Jack saying a few words over the fresh German graves. "How are you, Keeper?" he asked.

"Tolerable," Keeper Jack answered.

"And the boy?"

"Ran away. Back aboard his U-boat." Keeper Jack shrugged. "Willow was wrong. He was just a German boy."

Doc raised his eyebrows, then allowed them to settle into a frown. "A German boy. Is that what you think? Well, Keeper, I compared his fingerprints with Jacob's before my records were burned."

Keeper Jack's eyes widened. "What did you discover, Doc?"

Doc's frown remained in place. "Why, that he is Jacob. Willow was absolutely correct. He is your boy."

• • •

"I'm picking up propeller sounds!" Harro cried, his hands clamped to the earpieces of the hydrophone. "A U-boat coming at us and fast! I make it near due north, two miles away."

"It's Vogel," Krebs said to Max, scanning the sea with the Zeiss glasses. He had stopped the *U-560*'s flight momentarily to give Harro a chance to listen without the distortion of the diesels. It was what he'd expected. Vogel did not intend to let Krebs and his crew return across the Atlantic to give their side of the story. "Look north," he said to the lookouts. "If you see a periscope, call out!" Then down the open hatch: "Harro, if you hear a torpedo launched, give the alarm!"

Harro responded with an affirmative and then called, "Another set of propellers coming our way, sir." He listened for a moment. "Also from the north. Sounds like something big. Not a freighter or tanker, I don't think. Something different."

The lookouts all aimed their binoculars farther out but not Krebs. He kept his focus closer in and saw a single streak of white foam, just for an instant, on a patch of otherwise clean ocean. A periscope. Vogel was lining up. Then his attention was taken by a lookout's cry. "Destroyer, sir! Coming hard at us!"

Krebs looked in the direction of the lookout's point. It was indeed a destroyer, sharp at the bow, narrow at the beam, a big crow's nest with what looked like mattress springs mounted on her mast. She was studded with guns, torpedoes, and depth charges. It was the old World War I–era destroyer observed in February. He put it at about six miles away but coming hard. It would be on them in a matter of minutes. "Chief, how deep is it here?"

The Chief called up, "Forty feet, sir, maybe less."

"That destroyer will pound us to oblivion at this depth," Krebs said, thinking out loud.

Max didn't bother to lower his voice for the lookouts. "Let's scuttle, sir. The Americans will pick us up."

Krebs did not reply. He was letting the situation run through his mind, sorting out all the variables, possibilities,

and probabilities. Vogel had been lining up to attack, but that
had surely been interrupted by the appearance of the American destroyer. "What do you hear, Harro?" he called, to
confirm his hunch on what Vogel would do.

"Destroyer propellers getting louder. I don't hear the
U-boat anymore."

"Vogel's dropped to the seabed," Krebs said, "to let the
destroyer take care of us." He called through the hatch.
"Chief, left full rudder, take a course due north. Go to the
electrics full throttle and prepare to dive!"

The Chief echoed the command and then gave the alarm.
The lookouts descended to the stutter of the diesel exhaust
winding down, leaving Krebs and Max alone on the tower.
Max had been studying the destroyer. "She's an old girl."

"Let us hope she still has her teeth," Krebs responded,
which Max thought a most curious thing for him to say since
she was hauling her bulk as fast as she could for their murder.

It was near a full moon or the tide wouldn't have reached
her quite so bursting, but luck held and the *Maudie Jane*
floated and she didn't leak. Her diesels were fired up and she
backed away from shore, alive once more, anxious for the
sea. Phimble took the wheel on the stoop bridge and jammed
the throttles hard against their stops. Stobs switched on his
radios and was gratified to see their needles twitch and their
dials come aglow. "All I needed was to get some power,"
he said to Josh as he came inside. "God bless American
engineering. What's the word, Skipper?"

"Call Morehead City and hand me the mike," Josh said.
Stobs did both and Josh quickly went through what had happened. As always, he didn't expect any help. He was just
providing information.

"Be advised," the answer came back, "the wind is turning." The last four words were said cryptically.

"What does that mean?" Josh demanded.

The Morehead City radioman sounded disappointed. "It's
in your codebook, sir."

"I don't have a codebook, you dit-dot!"

There was a long pause. "Well, you'll see soon enough. I'll pass along your information to Captain Potts. Out."

Josh shook his head. "I would like to know just once what the hell is going on in this war."

"Maybe we're too far out in front of it, sir," Stobs suggested. "Everybody else is still trying to catch up."

"You might be on to something," Josh grumbled, then went outside to make certain the boys were assigned to their proper stations. That was when he noticed the boy in a slicker atop the wheelhouse manning the machine gun. Josh couldn't quite tell who it was but he had his suspicions. He clambered up and pulled back the hood of the slicker, only a little surprised by who it turned out to be. "Dosie."

"Corporal Crossan of the United States Beach Patrol reporting for duty, sir," she said smartly. "I heard you needed a gunner."

"Get below and stay in the galley. Either go on your own or I'll carry you down there."

"I have a right to be here, Skipper."

"You have no rights except the ones I say. I'm the captain of this lash-up. Now, get below."

Dosie clamped her hands on the machine gun. "Make me," she growled.

"Skipper!" It was Once, on the bow. "There's a destroyer coming in from the northeast." He paused to look a fraction longer. "And it's bearing down on that there U-boat."

Herman agreed to help Willow haul the kerosene, step by step, up the spiraling staircase. Willow had seen the lamp lit often enough over the years when her daddy had visited Keeper Jack. She guessed she and Herman could do it if they had to, and they had to. It wasn't that difficult. Into the watch room, open the can, pour it into the tank. Crank up the weights. Up the steps into the lantern room, pull back the curtain. Light the spirit lamp, warm the kerosene flow, light the mantle. Release the mechanism and get out of the way. Herman and Willow made a good team.

Willow was gratified when it all worked and the great lens began to turn. She and Herman stepped out on the parapet while behind them, for the first time in all its existence, the Killakeet light flashed across the sea in the middle of the day. It was overcast but there was no haze from burning oil. They could see for nearly forever, and what Willow saw frightened her.

There was her Jacob, surely on that submarine that was slipping under even as a big gray ship bore down on it. And there was the *Maudie Jane* batting along toward them.

"See the light, Jacob," she said. "See the light and come home."

"Take us under, Chief!" Krebs yelled, sliding down the ladder, careful out of habit to land on one foot to avoid his bad knee. A petty officer slammed the hatch shut just as the ocean flushed across it and a gurgle of foam and water announced itself over the length of the boat. The deck was under but the top of the conning tower, even if the *U-560* scraped the bottom, was only going to barely get wet.

"Now, we see," Krebs said. All of his doubts about his own ability were swept away. He felt his old confidence suffuse his mind. "Easy on the turns, Chief. Slow speed, let momentum carry us along. Let's give that destroyer a nice, easy target."

"The destroyer is turning toward us, Captain," Harro called from the hydrophone set. Then he didn't need to call anymore. The swishing of the destroyer's propellers became obscenely loud.

Krebs had been silently counting the seconds. "Now!" he commanded. "Hard a-port, Chief, and full ahead for a count of five, then shut down the electrics!"

The *U-560* responded, although the port drive thumped like a drum. But then the U-boat struck something on its starboard side, a jarring glance followed by a terrible squalling sound like a giant animal dragging a terrible claw down the length of the hull. There was a sudden clap of shattering metal astern and the boat slewed even harder to port before grinding to a stop, the stern lifting, the bow pounding into the bottom sand. Men and stores were thrown forward. The bilge water ran toward the bow in a brown flood.

Max climbed to his feet. "What happened?"

"I figured we'd get close to it," Krebs said in some awe. "I didn't figure we'd hit it."

"Hit what?"

"Vogel's boat." Krebs yelled, "Get us moving again, Chief!"

"Starboard drive's busted, sir. I think we broke the propeller off. We're taking on water through the packing."

"There's irony for you," Krebs said. "We lost our good propeller. Chief, full electric power on the port shaft for a count of ten! We want Vogel to get the goods from the Americans, not us!"

Now Max understood. Krebs had led the destroyer to Vogel. The sound of the destroyer's propellers pounded overhead, followed by a series of splashes. Max counted them. *One, two, three, four—oh no—six, now eight depth charges.* "Holy Mother of God," he breathed as the noise from the engine room sounded as if every mechanical piece of equipment back there had decided to tear itself apart. The boat seemed to wallow, but then he felt a scraping noise beneath his feet. "Are we moving?" Max cried.

"We'd better be," Krebs answered just as the depth charges exploded, pounding the *U-560* like giant sledgehammers.

Once was pointing off the bow and was jumping up and down in his excitement. It wasn't the depth charges being dropped on the U-boat by the destroyer that had stirred him but what he was seeing on the horizon, one by one by one as they popped up. Ships—tankers and freighters by the dozens—but more than that. There, finally, was the big bad bluewater United States by God Atlantic Fleet, and the cutters of the Coast Guard, too, the big girls, 165-footers, a slew of 'em.

"It's a damned great convoy," Phimble admired. "About time they got one organized."

Josh went forward and admired the numbers of the vast fleet, which kept coming. Stobs stuck his head outside the wheelhouse. "What does it mean, sir?"

"It means," Josh replied, "that for the U-boats around here, the wind just turned."

# 52

The *U-560* was canted over on her starboard side, lying hard on the sand. Around her, diesel fuel spewed, a steady stream of rainbow bubbles flowing out of her to spread above in a great stain on the flat sea. Although the crew inside could not see the slick, they could hear the wash of the fuel streaming across the hull and knew it was making them an obvious target. Each man braced for it but no depth charges came raining down. Instead, the explosions were moving away. "Vogel has moved off," Krebs said. "But if anyone looks, they'll be able to see us. We've got to snake for deep water."

The Chief came sloshing through the bilge water into the control room. "The electrics are still on-line, sir, but if we can't stop these leaks, they won't be for long."

"How about the diesels?"

"They should work but we only have one propeller. And we've lost almost all our fuel."

"Good news all around," Krebs replied.

Another thunder of exploding depth charges rattled the *U-560*'s hull. "Vogel's really taking a pounding," Max said.

"I still hear U-boat propellers," Harro called.

"Tough things, these iron coffins," Krebs said. "Imagine, surviving all those explosives in this shallow water."

"The destroyer is moving farther away, sir," Harro said.

The crew was quiet, each man praying or thinking or simply waiting for Krebs to tell them what next to do.

"Now I hear many screws," Harro suddenly called. "An armada!"

"A convoy, I'll warrant," Krebs said. "The destroyer was an advance guard. That's why the sea was so empty. They were holding them back for the convoy." He gave the situation some thought. "The destroyer's sonar won't work well in this shallow water. Vogel might get away."

"Too many propellers now to tell anything," Harro announced.

Krebs threw his leg over the periscope tractor seat. "Give us a little buoyancy and straighten us out, Chief. Let's see what we can see."

The Chief directed the proper turning of the valves and the U-boat rolled into an upright position. The whir of the periscope's motor was surprisingly smooth and had a calming effect on all who heard it. Krebs took a quick sweep, saw the convoy he expected off in the distance heading determinedly south, then the *Maudie Jane,* and unexpectedly, the pulsing lighthouse. He called out each of his sightings as he swiveled.

In the radio/hydrophone closet, Harro smiled at the announcement of the light. Pretch glanced at him. "What's so funny?"

"My girl's calling me home," he said.

"Your girl? How long were you on the island? Two days, if that!"

"We U-boaters work fast." Harro grinned and Pretch clutched his shoulder and laughed with him.

Jimmy had given up on the sonar machine. The water was too shallow. He was getting echoes from every direction. But the hydrophones were still working, though nearly overwhelmed with all the noise from the convoy. Through all the clutter, he thought he heard the whisper of something familiar. "Skipper," he called, "I think there's a U-boat still moving out there. I put it northeast of us, about twenty degrees off our port bow, maybe a mile away."

"Ready," Josh said from the stoop bridge, "is the three-inch gun loaded?"

"Loaded, Skipper."

He recalled Dosie was still on the fifty caliber on the bow. "Once, take over for Dosie, won't you?"

"I tried already, Skipper. She said she was going to slap my face if I tried again."

"Josh!" Phimble called out, so startled by what he had seen that he called his captain by his first name. "U-boat. Just there. It's the black one!"

Through the periscope, Krebs saw Vogel's boat rise, men tumbling out of the tower to man the deck gun. "What's he up to?" he asked and then told Max what he had observed.

"He's going to sink the patrol boat," Max said.

"Why not use his torpedoes?" Then Krebs saw the reason. "His bow is a mess. He took a hit there." Krebs looked farther out. "The convoy is still running, ignoring this little battle. Odd. I guess they're following their orders exactly. Protect the tankers and freighters, never mind anything else. Wait!" Krebs pressed against the periscope eyepiece. "There's why. The convoy is being attacked. A tanker just took a hit."

The crew of the *U-560* cheered. "Give them hell, boys!" the Chief yelled. Despite all that had happened, this was still a German U-boat. Destruction of the enemy was its aim and that of its brethren.

"*Kaleu,*" Max said, suddenly caught up in the moment, "can we get out there and attack that convoy, too?" He saw a sudden hope, that perhaps if the *U-560* joined the battle, the charge of treason might be swept away.

Krebs didn't reply to Max's idea. He pulled down the periscope. "Let's surface and see if we can maneuver. We're half out of the water, anyway." He looked around the tower control room at the lookouts. "Go ahead, crack open the hatch."

A petty officer sprang for the lever and threw it over. A flush of blue-green water dropped around the edges like a circular waterfall, then subsided. Krebs went up first, throwing himself against the shredded fairing, and saw with some relief that the *U-560* had become a sideshow. Miles away, the convoy and its escorts were still charging south. Destroyers, their alarms whooping, were dropping depth charges. Closer in, the American patrol boat, the *Maudie Jane,* was rushing headlong toward Vogel's boat, her machine gun chattering and Vogel answering with a salvo of artillery fire.

Josh had to admire how Dosie immediately let fly with the machine gun even though its powerful recoil made the barrel pitch up, its tracers screaming skyward. Once helped her and together they got control of the gun and sent a stitch of bullets at the deck-gun crew. But the Germans bravely stood and started firing back. Phimble put the *Maudie Jane* through a series of sharp turns, speeding past geysers of water where the German rounds had struck. Then he aimed the patrol boat's bow straight at the U-boat.

Ready fired the three-inch gun and struck the black U-boat's mangled bow. A puff of smoke billowed and decking flew into the air. Then the Germans returned the favor, their round striking the *Maudie Jane.* Her stern exploded, the empty depth-charge racks hurled overboard, a hornet's nest of steel scouring the deck. Bobby fell, groaning and clutching his legs, and the *Maudie Jane* went dead in the water and started settling, her bow lifting. Vogel's boat moved ahead, then its stern torpedo-tube door swiveled open.

The Keeper had joined Willow on the parapet. Together, they watched the battle from the height, the light flashing behind them. The townspeople gathered around the base of the lighthouse. One by one, they began to sing the old hymn:

> *For all of us who are on the stormy deep,*
> *For all of us who 'neath the ocean sleep,*

*Thy mercy now we pray on high,*
*Great God of wave and wind and sky.*

Krebs watched as Vogel's U-boat continued its turn until its stern torpedo tube was pointing not at the American patrol boat but at the *U-560*. "So, I'm more of an enemy than the Americans, eh, Vogel?" Krebs whispered.

When nothing immediately happened, Krebs supposed that Vogel was having some trouble readying his eel. Not surprising considering all the depth charges his boat had endured. "Ready the bow tubes," Krebs ordered. U-boat against U-boat. The first one to launch a torpedo would win.

"They're jammed, sir," the Chief called.

"The stern tube, then."

"We've lost power there," came the reply. "The boys are working on it."

"Then full ahead!" Krebs demanded. "Use the rudder to counter the starboard propeller. Sound the collision alarm and bring up the machine gun!"

The *U-560* began to push through the water slowly, then increased its speed. The Chief clambered up to the tower. "The bow-tube packing has given away. The pumps can't keep up. I'm afraid we've had it." Just as he spoke, the diesels failed, sending out a last puff of black, oily smoke.

Krebs, at long last, had nothing left to do except what he'd always believed unacceptable. "Abandon the boat, Chief," he said calmly. "Get the men going and hurry. I don't think Vogel is going to give us much more time." He pointed toward Vogel's boat. Her deck-gun crew was frantically turning the 105 millimeter toward them.

The lookouts and the machine gun crew went first over the side, then the others came racing up from below. Krebs manned the machine gun, cracking out rounds toward Vogel's crew to keep their heads down.

Max made certain each boy had on his life jacket as he went past to take the leap into the sea. Finally, it was just Krebs and Max on the bridge. "Well, Max," Krebs said, "at least we didn't scuttle her. Over the side with you."

"What about you, *Kaleu?*"

"I'll keep their heads down over there until our boys get away."

"Don't stay too long."

"I'll be right behind you."

Max went down to the deck, then slipped over and allowed the current to grip him, then carry him off.

All was quiet aboard Vogel's boat. It appeared the deck-gun crew had given up. Krebs looked toward Killakeet. The lighthouse was blinking its message of a safe harbor even in the light of the day. It made him think of the lighthouse at Nebelsee and the last time he'd seen Miriam. He remembered her cross and his hand went to it just as *Leutnant* Sizner came lunging from the hatch, sticking Krebs in the stomach to the hilt with a knife taken from the galley. Then Vogel's torpedo arrived. Krebs never felt any pain. One moment he was thinking of Miriam and how much he loved her, and then he was gone.

The *Maudie Jane*'s bow was still afloat, though barely. Josh had Dosie beside him. He and Phimble checked each of the crew to make sure they had their life preservers on. Marvin was also outfitted in his own preserver. Jimmy was taking care of Bobby, whose legs were torn up and bleeding from shrapnel. "All right. Into the water, boys," Josh said. He held Dosie back. "Stay with me."

She gave him a brave grin, and hand in hand, they went overboard.

It wasn't long before the current shoved the Maudie Janes and the crew of the *U-560* together. They started to link arms, Germans and Americans, just trying to survive.

Vogel ordered his U-boat toward the men in the water. He brought up a detail of men with rifles. "Finish them," he ordered. But then a lookout started to babble and Vogel heard the whooping shriek of a cutter making a run on them. "Dive and quickly!" he ordered, and disappeared below, ahead of his men.

· · ·

The cutter ignored the rapidly submerging black U-boat and slid alongside the drifting Americans and Germans. Josh recognized the crewman on the cutter's bow. "Well, here I am, Skipper," Again said. "I finally managed to hitch a ride home on the old *Diana*."

"Again!" Once called up from the water. "There you are, Brother! I was beginning to think you'd joined the navy."

"Naw. I had my fill of them dit-dots. But why are you swimming?"

"Well, it seemed the thing," Once replied.

The cutter boys threw over mats and some of them even dived into the water to help the Maudie Janes and the Germans up the side. Josh waited until everyone else was out of the water, including Marvin, then climbed up on deck where a crewman immediately wrapped him in a blanket. A familiar face also loomed. "Sorry it took the *Diana* so long to come, but we've been a bit busy," Captain Allison said.

A mug of hot coffee was shoved into Josh's hand. "Never saw better timing, Jim," he replied. "Some of my men are wounded . . ."

"They're with our doctor now."

"Good. Why didn't you attack that U-boat?"

"Depth charges and men in the water, we've learned, are not compatible," Allison replied.

Josh nodded gratefully.

Dosie found Harro among a soaked, dispirited knot of U-boat men gathered on the cutter's bow. "Take off that life vest," she ordered. "And put this one on."

"Why?"

"Because yours is German and this one is American."

"But I am German."

"Shut up and do what I tell you."

"No! I will stay with my crewmates!"

Once and Again came over. "Problems, Dosie?"

"Yes. Grab hold of this stupid son of a bitch, strip off his life vest, and make him put this one on. Then keep him with you. If he opens his trap, knock the ever-loving hell out of him."

The brothers looked at each other. What Dosie wanted them to do didn't make sense but it sure sounded like fun. "All right, boy," Once said to the German. "You heard the little lady."

Harro shook his head. "I am German," he said weakly, which was the last thing he said before Once grabbed his arms and Again wrapped a hand around his mouth.

# PART FOUR

## NOT DEATH, BUT LOVE

# 53

Killakeet had never seen anything like it. It seemed as if the entire Marine Corps had landed on its beaches and spread across it from end to end. At the military dock on Doakes, the *Diana* pushed out her gangway and sent the German prisoners down it to be taken into custody by Naval Intelligence agents. A seaplane, of all things, landed just offshore and taxied in, the officers on board looking goggle-eyed at the still smoking evidence of a German invasion.

Captain Potts was one of the officers aboard the seaplane. He sought out Josh. "This way," he said, waving him over beside the charred remains of one of the warehouses. "The first thing I have to tell you is that everything that's happened here is to be kept secret, do you understand?" He didn't wait for an answer. "The second thing is that you're being put in for a promotion. From what I've heard, you ought to get the Navy Cross, but considering we can't let any of this get out, we'll bump you up a grade, instead. Congratulations. You're a full lieutenant."

"Thank you, sir," Josh said. "I think."

Captain Potts shook his head. "Bad business, Josh. If the newspapers find out the Germans did this, a lot of crap will come down on all our heads."

"It'll get out, sir," Josh replied. "It always does."

"Maybe, but by the time it does, the war will have ground

on. You saw our convoy system out there. Finally in place. I've been up in Norfolk to help organize them. We'll have these U-boats on the run in no time and then we'll be heading across the Atlantic to take the war to them. That's the headlines the people will pay attention to, not some rumor that a few Germans landed on a scrap of sand."

Josh got angry. "Killakeet is American soil, sir."

"I know that, Josh. Don't get your hackles up. We'll do what we can here to take care of things. Doakes will be built back, better than ever, you can count on that. I don't doubt President Roosevelt himself is going to pay a bit of attention to Killakeet now. Wouldn't be surprised if they built a road here or something."

Josh didn't want to hear any more about what the politicians and the admirals were going to do. He saw his father waiting for him by the Surfmen's House and excused himself. Captain Potts charged off to talk to every Killakeeter he could find and swear them to secrecy for the good of the country.

"He's your brother" was the first thing Keeper Jack said. "Doc compared the fingerprints. A perfect match! Isn't it wonderful?"

Josh opened his mouth to reply, then had another thought. "Wonderful," he said.

The Keeper's smile broadened. "I knew it all along. You see, Josh? You may have lost your brother, but in the end you brought him back home."

"Tell you what, Daddy," Josh said heavily. "Let's you and me go see Doc. Where's he holed up?"

"Why, I suppose at the Hammerhead. He's staying there, now that his place was burned."

Doc was indeed at the Hammerhead, sitting in a rocker, his black bag at his feet. He was looking pleased with himself, even more so than usual. Josh sat down on the edge of the pizer while Keeper Jack stood down in the sand. Purdy, who'd been asleep in the corner, woke up and waddled over to sit beside Josh.

"Well, I wouldn't have believed it, Doc," Josh said, stroking Purdy's head. "But I guess I was wrong. Thank you for saving Jacob's file for all these years."

"It was lucky I compared those fingerprints before the Germans burned down my place," Doc replied loftily. "But you know, Josh, I have a tendency to look forward and think about all the possibilities and probabilities. I didn't know my place was going to get burned down, of course, but I thought I'd better find that file and do the comparing right away. Never know what might happen."

"You're a smart man, Doc. Real smart."

Keeper Jack said, "How do you think we ought to break it to Jacob?"

"Why don't you let me do that, Daddy?" Josh said. "I lost him. I guess I should find him, you know, in a way."

Keeper Jack beamed. "I'm so happy, Josh."

"Yes, sir. Who's minding the light, by the way?"

"I guess I better go do that. Been burning all day, kerosene's probably running pretty low."

Josh waited until his father disappeared into the gathering shadows of evening and then gave Doc a long withering look. "So why this lie, Doc?"

Doc rocked placidly. "This lie? Whatever do you mean?"

"You didn't compare any fingerprints because you never had any files. Your study was all a big hoax from the beginning. I broke into your shed, Doc, just as soon as I heard you told that cock-and-bull story about the fingerprints to Daddy. There was nothing in there except trash, mildew, and silverfish."

"I wondered who left those footprints in the dust. The files were under the floorboards. You didn't look there, did you?"

Josh couldn't help but smile. "Down on the beach yesterday, you told me they were on a high shelf. But nevermind. Odd, ain't it, that those old Germans went after your place? Why, you'd think they would burn down the hotel first. What happened, Doc? Did your shed catch your infirmary on fire by mistake? I guess Mr. Shakespeare was right about mice and men and how things oft go awry."

Doc kept rocking back and forth, drumming his fingers

on the armrest of the rocker. Then he stopped and leaned forward. "You're wrong. It was Robert Burns who wrote that."

"I'll take your word for it, Doc. But I ain't wrong about you. You're the biggest liar that ever existed."

"Maybe I am and maybe I'm not," Doc replied with a shrug. "But there ain't no maybe that Keeper Jack needs a son."

"He's got a son."

Doc curled up his lip. "You? You're probably not even going to survive this war. I'm talking about a son who'll take the Keeper's place, maybe provide him with some grandkids, give him some joy in his old age. That's not you by any stretch."

Josh knew Doc had mentally skinned him and nailed his pelt to the wall. He hung his head and let a wave of guilt and shame wash over him. When it subsided, he raised his head and said, in a weary voice, "Doc, tell me something I've wondered about for a long time. When I was in college, down at the library and tired of studying, I figured to look you up in the list of physicians in North Carolina, just for the fun of it. But you weren't on that list. Nor in Virginia, either, nor anywhere else I could find. I looked all over. Who are you, anyway?"

Doc shrugged and went back to rocking. "I might lack a few credentials that would get me listed in any of those books. You see, I was a medic with the navy in Norfolk. Got myself into trouble, one thing or another, gambling debts, mostly. So I ran out here where nobody would think to look for me. Next thing I knew, I was bandaging up folks, giving them pills, and just hung out my shingle. Folsom ain't my name, of course, not that it matters. Nobody ever questioned my credentials, not even the pharmacy in Morehead City. I just took care of the people all these years as best I could. Never heard any complaints, either."

"My mother died with you tending her."

"Queenie was with me. She'll tell you I did all there was to do."

Josh nodded agreement. "I don't have to. I talked to her a long time ago. That's why you're still alive."

Doc raised his eyebrows, then tipped his hat. "Why, thank you, Josh. I heard you're pretty handy with a hatchet. But now the German boy. What's it to be?"

"Daddy can have his second son. I won't stand in his way."

"Well, aren't we the noble one?" Doc replied, sarcastically.

"At least, I didn't start this lie."

"Who says it's a lie?" Doc snapped. "Willow says he's Jacob. He looks like Jacob should look. And you have no proof that he *isn't* Jacob. Think about that, Lieutenant Josh Thurlow of the Coast Guard, who don't know Billy Shakespeare from Bobby Burns."

All of a sudden, more than anything in the world, Josh didn't want to talk to Doc anymore. The man was just too sharp for him. Josh stood, brushed the sand off his pants, and said, "Well, we're in it together, Doc, whatever you might call it."

"So we are," Doc said. "Just you and me and that there pelican. Ain't that right, Purdy?"

Purdy cocked his head at Doc, then stamped his webbed feet and waddled back to his corner for a nap.

Josh went looking for Dosie and found her on the beach with Willow and the German. The Jackson twins were trailing behind. Josh said to the boy, "You're my brother and your name is Jacob."

"My name is Harro Stollenberg," he replied defiantly.

"No, it isn't." Josh balled his big fists. "Your name is Jacob Thurlow and if you ever say a word to the contrary, I'll find you and hit you so hard, your head will ring for all eternity."

"I should join my fellows in prison. It is the only honorable thing to do."

"Listen," Josh said. "Here's the honorable thing to do. From this day forward, you are my brother and Keeper Jack's son. People along this coast have lost a lot because of your damned U-boats, yet they've opened their arms to you. You're a Killakeeter now because of their goodness. Do you understand?"

"No," Harro replied. Then he asked, "Am I really your brother?"

"Yes, you are. Your fingerprints proved it."

"You are telling me the truth?"

"Ask the doctor. He'll tell you."

Willow laughed and said, "Jacob, you are so silly. Won't you ever believe who you really are?"

Harro offered his hand to Josh. "Take it and tell me I'm your brother. Then perhaps I will believe you."

Josh took his hand and drew him into a clumsy embrace. "You're my brother and I'm proud of it. Your father is at the lighthouse. I imagine there's a lot of work to be done there. There always is. You'd best get on and start learning the ropes."

Willow took the boy's hand and pulled him toward the lighthouse. Still, he hesitated, looking toward Doakes, where the crew of the *U-560* were being interrogated. The Jackson twins moved in. "Get going," Once threatened.

"Jacob, please," Willow cried.

"Stop being such a hardhead," Again advised the German boy. "You've been handed a miracle. You'll take it and run with it if you've got an ounce of brains."

Harro looked from twin to twin, then at Willow. Something seemed to melt inside him. Willow sensed it and laughed. Soon, they were running toward the lighthouse.

Dosie and Josh watched them go. "Is he really Jacob?" she asked.

Josh told Dosie the truth, as far as he knew it. "But you know what, Dosie?" he said at last. "The thing is, I don't guess I'll ever know if he's Jacob or not and that's probably a good thing."

"What do you mean?" Dosie demanded. "Surely, you must want to know."

Josh shook his head. "Even if he was Jacob, he still wouldn't be the person he could have been. No matter what happens to him now, he'll forever be a boy from Germany." Josh tried to smile but it came out sad. "I think it's better not to know. Let it remain a possibility, at least one good thing that came out of all this bloodletting, which was for nothing."

"All wars are for something, aren't they, Josh?"

"No. Most are against things. This one is about the same."

They walked along, being quiet for a while until Dosie asked, "Are you certain you can live with things this way?"

"Yes. I think at heart that German's a good boy. I told him I was proud to have him as my brother. I think I will be."

She made him stop so she could look him in the eyes and be certain he was telling the truth. When she was satisfied that he was, she said, "You are something else, Lieutenant Thurlow. I'm right proud to know you, that's for sartain. So what would you like to do now?"

He took her in his arms. "What I've got in mind, Corporal Crossan, we will have to do together."

"Now, ain't you fresh?" She laughed.

"I can be," he said and before too long, they were hurrying down the beach toward the light, which seemed to be brighter than ever before.

# 54

Every morning, Dosie walked out on her porch, as she carefully remembered to call it instead of a pizer, lest people these days give her odd looks, and studied the vast Atlantic, whether it was placid or stormy or somewhere in between, then went down into the sand to walk the beach to see what she could see. There had been a time when she had preferred to ride her horse, either Genie or Genie II, and then Genie III, but now that she was over eighty years old, she no longer kept a horse, burying the last Genie's Magic with the others in the sand behind the stable three years before.

Genie III had not only been Dosie's last horse. She had been the last horse allowed on the island, "grandmothered in" as the federal and state officials had called it, thinking themselves gracious for allowing the old woman to keep a horse at all, considering the terrible damage they did to the ecosystem of a barrier island. That's why ecologists had removed the last of the wild horses in 1972, to stop the damage caused when they dug their water holes. The federal ecologist who made the initial study had written that "exclusion" would mean not only an end to the destruction the wild horses caused, but would also be a kindness to them, considering how hard they had to struggle just to live on an isolated island. Dosie began a one-woman crusade against the removal. She wrote letters to her congressman, who ignored them. She held candlelight vigils at the corral when the herd was put in it. She laid herself down on the ferry ramp to keep the horses from being herded aboard. It all made for good local television news, but in the end, it was all for nothing. The horses were removed. When Genie III was put down, Dosie supposed the woman ecologist who had written the initial report was finally happy, God damn her soul.

Worries over the ecosystem had not kept the island from turning into something of a playground for people who didn't live there. In the mid-1970s, off-islanders had bought up the remains of Whalebone City, torn down most of the old houses, and built three-story monstrosities, each large enough to house ten Killakeet families in the old days. They were unoccupied for the most part, except during the summer months. After the old town was filled with massive houses, and the views of the sea well blocked, a new town started marching down the beach. It stopped momentarily at the Crossan House, inconveniently occupied by Dosie, who wasn't selling at any price, then jumped to the other side and kept going nearly all the way to Miracle Point. There it stopped, the federal government having made the point into a national wildlife refuge. For now, at least, the point was off-limits to condos, high-rises, and ugly houses, but Dosie sincerely doubted that would last for long. She wasn't even sure she wanted it to last. A move was underfoot to remove all the wildlife on the wildlife refuge and reintroduce only those animals that might have predated white settlers. That, Dosie supposed, would only leave the snapping turtles and maybe the seagulls.

Dosie, in truth, was a bit tired. She had fought the good fight for the island, had done what she could to keep the old ways, to protect the sand, as she had come to think of it, but over the years she had become realist enough to know that eventually everything changed. She had also learned that if you tolerated it long enough, you could get used to anything. There was still much of Killakeet that remained as it always had been, especially the beach.

It was July so the air was mild, the breeze gentle, the skies blue except for a line of low, puffy clouds on the ocean horizon, looking for all the world like a heavenly armada of sailboats. Mornings were when the light was best, when it would show Dosie's practiced eyes all the treasures tossed up on the beach by the sea.

She rolled up her loose khaki pants and kicked off her house slippers and went barefoot onto the sand, savoring the feel of Killakeet between her toes. She knew she was spry for an old lady and was proud of it. She hoped she would never know the day when she couldn't walk on the beach. When the day came for her to die, she hoped it would be during one of her morning excursions and it would be quick. She prayed for that every night after she had finished praying for the ecologist who'd gotten rid of the wild horses to live forever in hell.

She passed under the taut lines of several obese fishermen who had baited their hooks, tossed them out beyond the surf, then flopped into lawn chairs. One of them was already drinking a beer and Dosie admired him for that, at least. She spoke to each of the men in turn but they ignored her. She knew she was not much liked, being viewed as an impediment to progress. Because she had put in the paperwork to place her house on the National Historic Registry, there was a possibility that it might be against the law to ever tear the Crossan House down. It amused her to think she would continue to frustrate the people who were after her property, even after she was dead.

The roar of the waves was loud enough that it smothered another nuisance to Dosie, the traffic along the asphalted road that went down the inland edge of the beachfront property. During the summers, there was the constant traffic of day-trippers, come across on huge ferries from Morehead City to visit the Lighthouse Park, then trundling south for a look-see at the Miracle Point Refuge. Girls, dressed in shorts and halters, walked back and forth, trying to attract the eyes of boys in sport utility vehicles. Dosie liked to hear the girls laugh, but didn't much care for the revving of the engines by the boys who confused horsepower with sexual prowess.

These days, hardly anyone knew or cared what had happened off the coast sixty-plus years ago, when once the

U-boats had come and poorly armed little boats had gone up against them. Legends abounded that the Germans had even landed on Killakeet and other Outer Banks islands, but there was nothing to substantiate it beyond anecdotes, surely much embellished by the old grayheads still around. Historians laughed up their sleeve at the whole idea that an invasion had occurred. They wrote up the technical details of the German U-boat attacks, listed the hundreds of tankers, freighters, destroyers, trawlers, and patrol boats sunk, and the few U-boats as well, and left it at that. World War II history was too grand to pay much attention to a battle along sandy islands populated by poor fishermen and lighthouse keepers. Anyway, Americans simply could not believe such a huge battle had occurred along these shores. It was hard to find a high school or even college history book that even mentioned it.

Dosie looked north to the lighthouse. It had been moved back a hundred yards from its original location after the ocean had encroached on its base. That had been something to see, the entire lighthouse jacked up, put on giant rollers, and carted inland. When Dosie had seen it, she tried to imagine what the celebrators at the fiftieth anniversary of the light might have thought had they seen their lighthouse lifted into the air and brought drifting back, like some gigantic magic trick. Of course, there had been little magic about that night when the U-boats had come. Perhaps it was just as well nobody cared. Who wanted to recall the terrible waste of lives it had caused?

But it had also led to life. Harro was no longer the keeper but he'd taken the job in 1952 and kept it until the lighthouse had ceased operation in 1980. By then, he and Willow had a family of three boys and two girls. Willow had died in 1982, leaving Harro alone. He had never remarried but he was a grandfather, and a loving, doting one at that. There was no sweeter man in the world than Jacob Thurlow, whom Dosie still couldn't help but think of as Harro Stollenberg. These days, he was a guide to the visitors of the lighthouse, which had become a tourist attraction.

Dosie turned away from the lighthouse and kept walking.

She spotted a sport-fishing boat coasting by, filled with tourists on their way out to the Stream to angle for wahoo or tuna. No commercial fishing went on these days. The Killakeet workboat existed only in museums. Then she saw another boat that contained sport scuba divers. They would dive the remains of the German U-boat that was out there or perhaps one of the many tankers and freighters with huge torpedo wounds in their sides. At least, they could guess a little of what had happened in 1942.

She thought then of Josh, of course, though not much ever stopped her from thinking of him, anyway. Josh Thurlow lived in her heart and never left it. Even though their time together might have been considered short by some folks, their love had been as vibrant and bright as sunrise. Dosie was content with Josh, and her memory of him, though she wished that he might have resolved the sadness that came back to him, ever so often, about Jacob. She wished he could have known what had really happened to his brother, one way or the other, even though he always said he didn't want to know.

The sun was perfectly angled for her to see things on the beach, even given that her eyes were failing her these days. She was always looking for beach glass. She had taken to making jewelry with it over the years, though she'd slowed since her fingers had become too arthritic to comfortably bend the silver wire.

A flash of gold caught her eye and she hurried to the spot. There was something protruding from the wet sand. She knelt and dug around it, then felt a bit faint as she lifted it into the sun. She sat down, the sea flushing up around her legs. After a while, she found her voice. "Well, hello, Captain Krebs," she said. "Where have you been all this time? Were you afraid I would shoot at you again?"

Dosie could see Krebs still, standing there on his cold steel tower, with a bemused smile and a tangled reddish brown beard, looking for all the world like some ancient Viking warrior. She clutched the object for a long time while the sea tumbled across her legs. Finally, she rose and hurried back up the beach. She accidentally ran into the line of one of the fishermen, who said something rude to her. She untangled herself and kept going up the steps to the pizer, thank you, and into her house. She went immediately to the art studio she'd constructed off the parlor, where the morning sun had warmed her while she had made her jewelry over the years. On the shelves were the cigar boxes she'd accepted from Harro and Willow after Keeper Jack had died. When they had decided to convert the old art room into a place for the children to play, they had offered the old boxes to Dosie. She had gladly taken them. Shortly afterward, she'd started making jewelry. For years, Dosie's work had been popular in souvenir shops all along the Atlantic coast.

Dosie carefully laid her find on the worktable and studied it. It was a gold cross with empty tines on each of its tips. The tines in the center, however, had held and were clasping a small piece of smooth red glass. She opened a drawer in the desk beside the table and retrieved a large manila envelope that contained a secret she'd kept for over sixty years. A month after the *U-560* had been sunk, Rex had found a shredded gray leather jacket on the beach and showed it to her. She had looked a little closer and found a letter within its folds. Not only had the writing within been terribly blurred by the sea, it had been in German. She recognized, however, the name on the envelope: *Kapitänleutnant Otto Krebs.*

Although she had first thought to hand over the letter to Naval Intelligence, she'd decided it was most likely of a private, personal nature. She also hadn't much cared for the high-handed ways of the intelligence officers during their stay on the island. A few months later, she'd decided to have the letter translated. Not trusting Doc to do it since he'd proved himself less than trustworthy, she'd gone into Morehead City and found a high school German teacher. It had been torturous work but he had finally worked his way through it. As she suspected, it had indeed been a very personal letter.

Dosie left the old, water-blurred letter in the envelope and withdrew the translation to study it anew.

*Dear Otto,*
*Miriam is gone and there is nothing I can say that will bring*
*her back. I imagine you are finding it as hard as I am to let*
*her go. She was a beautiful woman and we miss her greatly*
*here. The children ask about her all the time. What can I say*
*to them except she is in God's arms? Otto, it is so sad. Yet,*
*you know me well. I believe God has a plan and tragedy is*
*part of that plan. Something good must result. That is why I*
*don't want you to give up the idea of having a family. I want*
*all of my children to live full lives despite what might befall*
*them.*

The priest had written a full page on his concept of family
and how a man could not be complete without one. The
children of the orphanage, he wrote, were his family and he
was so worried that something horrible might befall them. It
broke Dosie's heart every time she read it. Father Josef had
not survived the war and neither had his orphanage. Fighting
back a tear, she skipped ahead to the part of the letter she
needed now to recall.

*You ask about Miriam's cross. I know she would be glad that*
*you are wearing it every day. The teardrops of amber on each*
*tip represent Christ's wounds. Be mindful, Otto, that we all*
*suffer loss and sorrow but we can find ourselves reborn and*
*renewed by it.*
   *In the center of the cross is a piece of red glass representing*
*the sacred heart of Christ. This I found in the clothes of one*
*of the orphans I took from the orphanage in Kiel. I am not*
*certain of its origin but I was struck by its beauty and kept*
*it. This is a boy who was a particular favorite of hers. It is a*
*boy whom you know well, Harro Stollenberg. It is fitting that*
*you have both the cross and Harro to keep safe.*
   *Otto, I pray for you every day, but not just for God to*
*keep you safe. I pray that you will keep Miriam in your heart*
*and remember not death, but love.*

*Yours in hope of peace,*
*Fr. Josef*

Dosie folded the translation and put it back in the manila envelope with the original letter.

*This I found in the clothes of one of the orphans.*

When she had read that passage for the first time, Dosie recalled that Josh had once told her Jacob was forever putting things in his pockets. On the morning he was lost, Josh had retrieved Jacob from his mother's art room. He had been playing with some beach glass. Rose of Sharon glass.

Dosie ran her finger across the glass in the cross, then looked at a box on her shelf, a box from Trudelle Thurlow's art room. It was marked in faded letters *Alexander Hamilton.* Inside it was the glass from the Rose of Sharon wine bottles. "You always believed the sea would give us the answer, Josh," she whispered. "Well, let's just see if it has."

Rising, she took the box from the shelf, put it on the table, and sat down again. She took one of the pieces and placed it beside the cross, then swung over the magnifying glass with the circular fluorescent light. The gold behind the red glass on the cross made it difficult to be certain of its true color. Her hands aching, she used tiny pliers to carefully bend back the tines that held it.

The sun flowed like a warm river through the window-panes. She held the two pieces, one from the cross and one from the box, so that the light would pass through them. Her eyes, still sharp for color, went from one to the other. She allowed a long sigh, then put them down. Carefully, and in some pain from squeezing the pliers just so, she placed the glass back on the cross. Then she sat there for a long time, trying to decide what to do.

After a few minutes, she decided. She rose and went into the kitchen to the telephone on the wall. She lifted the receiver and, her fingers still aching, punched in Harro's number. He wouldn't be home, she didn't think, but she believed one of his children might be there for a visit and she was right.

In fact, it was little Josh. *Little, ha!* Josh was big as his namesake, and a father twice over. "Josh," she said. "I have something to tell you. Are you listening?"

"Yes, Aunt Theodosia." Harro's children liked to call her that.

"Tell your father something for me, will you?"

"Yes, ma'am."

"Tell him I found Miriam's cross."

"Miriam's cross?"

"Shut up and listen. Tell him I found Miriam's cross and something else, too. Tell him, Josh—are you listening?"

"Yes, ma'am. I'm listening."

"Tell him . . ." She stopped and thought for a bit on how to put it into words.

"Aunt Theodosia, are you there?"

"Yes, I'm here, you dit-dot! Give an old woman time to think, won't you?"

"Yes, ma'am."

"Tell him I found Miriam's cross and . . ." She shook her head. It was not right. She needed to tell Harro to his face. He had always wondered about the truth and now she could tell it to him. She summoned her courage. "Tell your father to come and see me."

Without waiting for an answer, Dosie hung up the phone and went to the stove. She would fix some yaupon tea. That always seemed to calm her, not the tea, just the fixing of it. After it was ready, and properly loaded with honey, she carried the steaming mug and went outside and sat in one of the rockers and thought about the time she and Josh had sat there together and then had nearly torn the door off its hinges in their haste to get upstairs to the bedroom.

The recollection made her smile.

She sipped her yaupon tea and rocked a bit longer and then she put the mug down and leaned forward and put her elbows on the banister and cupped her chin in her hands. She looked across the sea and listened to the wind and the rolling thunder of the waves and the hissing of the sand, the symphony of Killakeet, and remembered nothing of death, but everything of love.

# HISTORICAL NOTE AND ACKNOWLEDGMENTS

When an author applies his imagination to history, a reader might well wonder where truth ends and fiction begins. Although Josh Thurlow, Bosun Phimble, Dosie Crossan, Rex Stewart, and the Maudie Janes are fictitious, they accurately represent the men and women who faced the U-boat onslaught along our shores in 1942. Often inexperienced, nearly unarmed, and working in pitifully small and slow boats, they fought on an ocean covered with dying ships, lakes of burning oil, and drifting bodies. Because of the necessity of compressing events, *The Keeper's Son* doesn't entirely describe the breathtaking extent of the carnage. Over four hundred Allied ships, both merchantmen and warships, were sunk by the rampaging U-boats along the American east coast from January to August, 1942, a strategic blow possibly greater than the Japanese attack on Pearl Harbor. Ultimately, the defeat of the U-boats on this side of the Atlantic required a complex convoy system and the heavy application of air power. Admiral Ernest King, who led the United States Navy in 1942, was keen to get his forces into the Pacific to slug it out with the Japanese navy. In the hope the U-boats would simply go away, he refused to release his ships and planes to plodding coastal convoy duty. Ultimately, he had no choice but to organize the convoys and see to their escort. But by then, blood and oil soaked our beaches. It was a painful learning experience for the United States and nearly wrecked our early war plans.

My interest in this battle came first in the early 1970s when a U-boat wreck was discovered off Morehead City, North Carolina. At the time, I was a scuba instructor and also a freelance writer who specialized in writing about wreck-diving. After diving on the U-boat, I became intrigued as to how and why it was there. After devouring the historical records, I started to track down Americans and Germans who had fought in the battle. My resulting book, *Torpedo Junction* (Naval Institute Press, 1989; Dell, 1992), is still the definitive account of this sprawling battle, which was far more complex than I could possibly demonstrate from the perspective of Josh Thurlow and the people of Killakeet Island.

Even though their island is fictitious, my descriptions of the characters of Killakeet are representative of the people who lived along the Outer Banks in the early 1940s. The barrier islands off North Carolina have a history of glorious beauty interspersed with death and destruction. Attacks by pirates, war, and enormous storms and hurricanes have all proved deadly over the years. During the eighteenth and nineteenth centuries, a subculture of people grew up on those sandy spits for the express purpose of salvaging wrecked vessels. When the descendents of these piratical "wreckers" were gathered by the federal government into the Lifesaving Service, they changed from colorful miscreants into heroic figures who were willing to go out in terrible seas to save lives. Surfmen, as they were called, lived in stations along the coast and waited for the call to man their pitifully fragile surfboats. One of the most famous surf stations was the Pea Island Station, which boasted an all-black unit. For the magnificent story of this brave, inspirational group of surfmen, I would recommend *Sink or Swim* (Coastal Carolina Press, 1999) by Carole Boston Weatherford, and *Storm Warriors* (Alfred A. Knopf, 2001) by Elisa Carbone. For more information on the Outer Banks in general, I recommend *Graveyard of the Atlantic* (The University of North Carolina Press,

1952) by David Stick. For accounts of what it was like to grow up in an Outer Banks lighthouse family, *Lighthouse Families* (Crane Hill Publishers, 1997) and *Hatteras Keepers* (Outer Banks Lighthouse Society, 2001) by Cheryl Shelton-Roberts and Bruce Roberts are marvelous books. For a look at the natural surroundings and ecology of the Outer Banks, *Hatteras Journal* (John F. Blair, Publishers, 1998) by Jan DeBlieu is a touching work, as is *Ocracoke Odyssey* (Down Home Press, 1999) by Pat Garber. For a discussion of the delightful dialect of Outer Bankers, I recommend *Hoi Toide in the Outer Banks* (The University of North Carolina Press, 1997) by Walt Wolfram and Natalie Schilling-Estes.

The Coast Guard Beach Patrol did indeed exist, although perhaps it was a bit more organized than how I have presented it. Many times, however, locals joined and provided their own horses and uniforms to supplement the regulars, so Dosie's experiences were not entirely unusual. Many 4-F cowboys were also recruited for the Beach Patrol, so Rex's story has a historical basis as well. For more information, *Prints in the Sand* (Pictorial Histories Publishing Company, 1989) by Eleanor C. Bishop is an excellent resource.

As for Captain Krebs, Lieutenant Max, and the men of the *U-560*, the deeds of the U-boat brethren are told in many excellent novels and books. I modeled Captain Krebs a bit after Captain Peter Cremer, who accomplished some deadly work in his *U-333* off the Outer Banks during 1942. His book, *U-boat Commander* (Naval Institute Press, 1984), is a great source for anyone wishing to understand the mindset of German U-boat captains during World War II.

I was also assisted by a number of past and present residents of the Outer Banks, who graciously provided me with old letters, diaries, logs, photographs, or simply their memories, all necessary to enrich the lives and times of my characters. I am especially indebted to John Gaskill, the Bodie Island keeper's son, and the late Rany Jennette, son of the keeper of the Hatteras light. Their assistance included personal tours of their childhood homes and the lighthouses their fathers kept so well. I will never forget climbing up the winding, echoing stairs of the old lighthouses with them, and thence into the lantern rooms that once provided safety for all those who sailed the Graveyard of the Atlantic. Thrilling and inspirational is the only way to describe standing with those men and discussing their experiences while looking out across a vast sea swept by a constant river of salt-laden air. John and Rany also provided me with details of their World War II service aboard American warships off the Outer Banks. Rany, who served aboard a coast guard 83-footer off Hatteras, was especially able to provide fascinating descriptions of what it was like to crew on those "sea-going jeeps with square wheels."

Bruce Roberts and Cheryl Shelton-Roberts, the founders of the Outer Banks Lighthouse Society, have dedicated their lives to protecting and restoring lighthouses as well as telling the stories of their keepers. With unfailing patience, they answered all the myriad questions I posed to them while working on this novel. Along the way, they became special friends. For information on their work and their many wonderful books, please see http://www.outer-banks.com/lighthouse-society.

Wendell "Wink" Weber, Jack Read, Robert Balsdon, Bill Wells, Don Gardner, and other members of the 83-Footer Sailor's Association provided me with much information and colorful war stories about life aboard the little patrol boats, one of which, the fictional *Maudie Jane*, plays a pivotal role in this novel. For more information on the association, please see http://uscg83footers.org. The following coast guard retirees and their Web sites were also extremely helpful: Kenneth T. Laesser, http://www.laesser.org/index.htm; Fred Siegel, http://www.fredsplace.org; and Jack A. Eckert, http://www.jacksjoint.com. My thanks must also include Mrs. June Brittingham, the widow of the late Arthur Brittingham, for sharing her husband's memoirs of his coast guard experiences along the Outer Banks in 1942. They were invaluable in recreating the atmosphere of the era.

Thomas A. Tag has long been acknowledged as the leading authority on the lamps, lenses, and illumination of lighthouses and provided me many technical details for this novel. For more information on Thomas and his books on lighthouse operations, please peruse the Great Lakes Lighthouse Research Web site at http://home.att.net/~tatag/.

Special thanks are due to Mrs. Judith and General Bill Fiorentino (U.S. Army, Ret.) of Steel Prize Stables in Madison, Alabama, for attempting to teach me a little about horsemanship so that I might re-create some of the equestrian scenes in this novel. Also my thanks are extended (along with a carrot) to the real Genie's Magic for teaching me humility and who is really in charge of the barn.

The late Harold "Swede" Larson, a former coast guardsman who went on to have a distinguished career in the United States Marine Corps, was a great friend and mentor for years. His memories of life aboard the USCG Cutter *Dione*, the real counterpart to the fictional USCGC *Diana* in this novel, were extremely important not only for this book but also my military history *Torpedo Junction*, which is set in the same time and place. Because of Swede's dedicated assistance, as well as information provided by hundreds of coast guardsmen, navy sailors, merchant mariners, and German U-boat men, *Torpedo Junction* is, I am proud to say, still considered the most complete account of that bloody battle along the American coast during World War II. Thanks are also due to the late Rear Admiral James Alger, USCG, who commanded the *Dione* and is the inspiration for Lieutenant Jim Allison in this book. Jim Alger and I are both graduates of the Virginia Tech Corps of Cadets. *Ut Prosim,* Jim, and *Semper Fi,* Swede. See you on that heavenly shore.

Of course, any errors in this novel are entirely my own. I have attempted to get all the details just right but I suppose dedicated rivet-counters might find something wrong. I'll keep trying, guys.

On a personal note, I want to thank Sean Desmond, my most wonderful editor of this novel, and Tom Dunne, my publisher. Both men were willing to allow a writer chiefly known as a memoirist to stretch his art form to become a novelist. For that and more, I shall be forever grateful. As always, thanks go out to my great agents, Frank Weimann and Mickey Freiberg, who keep things humming behind the scenes.

A message of thanks is also extended to Linda, my wonderful wife, who is my first reader/editor and works so hard to keep our Web site (http://www.homerhickam.com) current, answers all the fan mail, and generally softens my life around the edges so that I can have time to pursue my work. For this novel, special thanks must go as well to Maxx, one of our four cats, who kept me company throughout by sleeping on my desk and often resting her hind quarters on the shift key of my computer keyboard. This resulted in some creative though inadvertent capitalizations that I hope the copy editor and I have caught!

Finally, my sincere appreciation goes out to the armed forces of the United States and especially the men and women of the United States Coast Guard. *Semper Paratus* is the coast guard motto and you have proved yourself always ready, indeed. Over the decades, you have kept us safe along our shores, at sea, and around the world. For that, I will be forever grateful.

*The Keeper's Son* is the first in a series. Although the battle of Torpedo Junction might be won, and Killakeet Island returned to its peaceful ways, dark days lie ahead for American naval and coast guard forces in the early years of World War II, not only in the Atlantic but in the Pacific theater as well. Josh Thurlow, Bosun Phimble, Dosie Crossan, and maybe a few Maudie Janes have adventures yet to come.

Read on for an excerpt from
Homer Hickam's next book

# The Ambassador's Son

*Coming soon in hardcover from St. Martin's Press*

Commander Josh Thurlow and his Coast Guard boys lived in a cave on the green island of Melagi, high on the slope of an ancient, dead volcano. The cave overlooked a punch-bowl valley, collapsed on one side and disgorging a lake of grass into an abandoned copra plantation by the sea. The plantation, most of its royal palms cut down to stumps, served as the camp for the 5th Marine Raiders, a battalion of warriors famous for their bloody exploits on nearby Guadalcanal. Beside the camp sat a placid little scum-covered swamp which happily provided hordes of mosquitoes and the odd crocodile to keep the Raiders miserable and on their toes in turn. The Raiders regularly cursed the Corps for placing them on the island which they called "Me-Soggy" since they slept in the mud, ate in the mud, did their laundry in the mud, shook from fever in the mud, hid in their dugouts from Japanese bombers in the mud, and stood in formation to the tops of their boots in the mud.

In comparison, Thurlow's Cave, as it was locally called, was a very good place to live. It was almost cool during the blazing heat of the day, and nearly dry during the nasty little storms that intermittently battered the island. The only indigenous life, besides the usual insects and arachnids, was a small squadron of polite bats and a few quiet lizards. There was little in fact about Thurlow's Cave that wasn't good except where Melagi was, which was the hot, steamy, and malarial Solomon Islands, and the year, which was the World War–ridden 1943, and the war itself, which was everywhere one looked.

Neither the cave, the Raiders, the bats, the war, nor even his Coast Guard boys were on Josh Thurlow's mind on a morning in August, actually August the tenth. This happened to be the birthday of his girlfriend, his *supposed* girlfriend, one Miss Dosie Crossan, and Josh was wondering how she might be celebrating her birthday, and with whom. A letter had recently reached him from Dosie and its contents had kept his mind churning ever since, even dragged him from his sleep. From his cot beneath a draped mosquito net, he stared into the darkness of the cave and sensed imminent sunrise and therefore could wait no longer. He rose to deal decisively with the letter. He was, after all, a man of action which meant there were times (and Josh knew this very well from hard experience) when he didn't know how to leave well enough alone.

Josh dressed in his utilities and pulled on his boots, after turning them over and shaking them in case of pedipalpi and scorpions, then wound his way through the cots holding his sleeping boys. He was a big man, broad-shouldered, with muscled arms and stout legs supporting a heavy chest, yet he was surprisingly light on his feet and slipped soundlessly from the cave to settle on a large stone the boys had dubbed Look-it Rock. Overhead, dense clouds parted to present a swath of stars so glittering and bright they were like diamonds spilt from a smuggler's bag. But Josh took no note of the stars or much else, including the rustlings of the nocturnal owls and rats and snakes hunting one another in the black bush. The world had constricted in his mind to the one thing he felt he needed to do, even if he wasn't certain what it was. The letter from Dosie was in his shirt pocket. His thought was to read it again, just in case he had missed some subtlety. Then, if he still agreed with himself that the letter reflected a certain loss of her affection, he would decide what should be done about it.

There was nothing gentle about sunrise in the Solomons.

It always had a cataclysmic feel to it. Abruptly, with the spirit of an upthrust spear in a warrior's hand, the sun tore its way out of the sea, slashed the horizon-riding clouds of cotton into blood-red shreds, and flung its hot white light viciously across a purplish, rolling sea. Before Josh's eyes, Melagi transformed itself from the gray shadow of night into its morning color of the brightest, purest jade. Steam rose like hot smoke from the surrounding bush, birds started to chitter and squawk, and the feathery leaves of a nearby sandalwood tree shook as if in the hands of a malevolent spirit.

With light enough to read, and the damp, blood-temperature breeze ruffling his sandy hair, Josh withdrew Dosie's letter. He made it through the greeting (*Dear Josh,*) but was immediately distracted when he heard the clunk of the coffee pot being set on the little wood stove in the kitchen. The stove was half an oil drum with scrap iron legs, and the kitchen was a bamboo lean-to the boys had built just outside the entrance to the cave. Josh's stomach growled in anticipation of breakfast, and Dosie's letter drooped in his hand. Millie, the cook and medic of the team, wordlessly handed Josh a mug of hot, aromatic coffee, which sent the letter back into Josh's shirt pocket. "Thank you, Millie," Josh said, and added, "It'll rain today. And it'll be hot." Being a native of Killakeet Island of the Outer Banks of North Carolina, a place of fishermen, Josh rarely greeted anyone without a comment on the weather.

Millie, also a Killakeeter, was a skinny youth, thin-faced, with intelligent gray eyes that were still hooded with recent sleep. He nodded in silent agreement on the weather report, then went back to his bamboo kitchen while Josh noticed with some pleasure that the coffee contained a splash of Mount Gay Barbados rum. It was as if Millie (who was also a cousin) knew that his commanding officer needed something a little extra on this particular morning. All his boys were pretty good at figuring out Josh's mood, although the truth was his moods were pretty simple, either good or bad or swinging toward one or the other.

Millie next arrived with a spoon and a pan piled high with

six scrambled eggs, big chunks of Spam, a quarter-pound of melted American cheese, all covered with catsup. Josh worked away at his favorite breakfast while watching with interest the landing craft, barges, and assorted small, gray-painted naval vessels churning and chugging across the water from Guadalcanal to Melagi. The stretch of blue water between the islands had recently been named Iron Bottom Bay, its sad new title attributable to the tons of American and Japanese warships resting in broken death on its deep beige sand. Many sharks lived there, attracted by the pathetic bodies that yet regularly seeped from their rusting underwater graves.

When he had finished the pan of Millie's egg concoction, Josh put it aside and was ready to get back to Dosie's letter. But then he was distracted yet again when, one by one, his Coast Guard boys came out of the cave to go down to the slit trench to do their morning business. As they passed him by, scratching their rashes, a price of living in the Solomons, they gave him their greetings: *G'mornin', Skipper, more rain today, I'm thinking,* or *Cap'n, easy breeze, ain't it?* Josh hello'ed his boys in turn, agreeing with their estimation of the weather and calling them by their names: Here was Ready O'Neal, the bosun, with his wide, cheerful, and innocent face; the identical twins and gunnery mates Once and Again Jackson, all elbows (which they used for friendly battle on the path to the trench) and long legs of gangly youth; Stobs Mallory, the chunky radioman, his big glasses perched on his stubby nose giving him the appearance of a large white owl; and Fisheye Guthrie, the greasy-haired, fox-faced mechanic.

The boys were all Killakeeters, come to the South Pacific with Josh, the oldest Ready at twenty-one, the youngest the twins at nineteen. Escorting the boys as they accomplished their morning work was Marvin, a small black-and-white terrier dog, also brought from the Outer Banks. Marvin was smart. That's about all you needed to know about him except not to mess with him when he had a fresh bone.

The last boy, if he could be called such, out of the cave

was Pogo. Pogo was neither a Killakeeter nor even an American but a Solomon Islands bushman who'd appeared out of the jungle on Guadalcanal to attach himself to Josh when he and the Coast Guard boys had been over there helping out the Raiders during their struggle with the Japanese. Pogo was naked, save a feather in his puff of frizzy hair, an ornate necklace of cowry shells and glass beads around his neck, big wooden plugs in his earlobes, and a flapping breechcloth the locals called a lap-lap. On this particular day, he had chosen a bright blue lap-lap with, for no apparent reason, a 5th Marine Raiders patch pinned at its center. "My word, belong morning, Mastah Josh," Pogo offered, a grin on his round and cherubic face. Josh could never teach Pogo, no matter how hard he tried, to call him Skipper or Captain. Pogo, like most bushmen, was prone to being a little stubborn. At least the boys had convinced him to stop chewing betel nut. As a result, his teeth had turned brilliantly white.

Megapode Dave, who the boys had adopted since their arrival on Melagi, was a bird which looked as if it might be the offspring of a turkey and a vulture, though not as attractive as either. Dave, according to Pogo, was magic and could answer prayers if he was in the mood. Magic or not, he mostly slept. Now Dave waddled out of the cave on his big splined feet and laboriously climbed Look-it Rock, difficult since he was not designed to be a rock-climbing bird, and cuddled next to Josh for a post-sleep nap.

The boys returned from their business and set to their breakfasts while Josh idly stroked Dave's back and enjoyed the view. Millie brought him more coffee well-splashed with Mount Gay, and the morning seemed unusually pleasant until he remembered Dosie's damned letter, and so he hauled the thing out again. The first paragraph of the letter was the good one where Dosie told Josh the news of Killakeet, that his father, the lighthouse keeper, was doing well, as was his brother who was now the assistant keeper. She also reported that she had placed some flowers on his mother's grave, though for what purpose, other than respect, she didn't say. He got no further because Dave, his tiny black eyes suddenly popped open and looking as serious as death, erupted with a loud *squawk* and stuck his neck out straight as a finger. Josh followed the megapode's trembling beak and saw a dot in the northern sky over a channel known famously as the Slot, a constriction of the sea between the northern Solomons that the Japanese navy used like a highway for their swift destroyers and barraging cruisers and sneaking armored barges.

The dot rapidly grew into an airplane which, by its raspy muttering, Josh recognized as a Japanese bomber known as a Betty, probably come to bomb either the Raider camp on Melagi or the airfield on Guadalcanal. "Stobs!" he bellowed over his shoulder, and his fat-cheeked, flaxen-haired radioman came running, though he nearly tripped over his untied boots. "Call Henderson Field, tell them they got a Betty coming their way. Call the Raiders, too, and tell them to get in their dugouts."

Stobs went off to comply and Josh took another look at the Betty, satisfied himself that it hadn't made its move as yet, had another sip of the mixed coffee and rum which he called Barbados Sunrise, then went back to Dosie's letter, determined to get through it even if the entire Imperial Japanese Navy appeared steaming down the Slot.

The next paragraph was the critical one. In it, Dosie had written she wanted to be *useful*, that it was only by being *useful* that she could know who she was. She had therefore decided to become a nurse, as *useful* a profession as there might be, and was traveling over to Morehead City for her training. Furthermore, she had left the Beach Patrol, except for weekends when she still rode her quarter horse named Genie up and down the Killakeet beaches with Rex Stewart, the old Hollywood stunt man, who had a new gelding he had named Jeubal Early. And then she mentioned a certain young doctor at Morehead City who seemed to have made quite the impression.

*He's a handsome boy*, was the way she'd put it, *and so gosh-awful smart. I am lucky to be a student nurse under his hand.* Josh read the sentence a second time and thought about the young, handsome doctor's hand, surely with fine, long fingers, capable of plucking out an appendix and stroking a woman's breast with the same tenderness and care. The heat in his face rose, so much so that his cheeks turned rosy, even through his deeply tanned face.

Josh looked up just as the Betty let two bombs go over the Raider base. He watched them fall until they splashed amongst some tents, throwing up huge clods of brown mud and shreds of canvas. He saw no bodies fly through the air and supposed the Raiders had heeded Stobs's call and repaired to their coconut palm–roofed dugouts. The bomber then turned toward Guadalcanal, but it didn't get far before it was surprised by two American P-40s. The big-nosed fighters pounced, guns blazing, and filled the unfortunate Betty full of holes, whereupon it broke apart, crashing into Iron Bottom Bay with one wing left to flutter down like an autumnal leaf. The P-40s did a couple of victory barrel-rolls which made Dave's neck nearly twist into a knot to watch. Dave loved airplanes, odd for a bird who couldn't fly.

Ensign Eureka Phimble ambled out of the cave with his morning cup of coffee, idly watched the Betty's wing crash into the water, then smirked when he noticed that Josh was reading Dosie's letter again. He and Josh had been together for nearly a decade, beginning their association on the Bering Sea Patrol, and Phimble knew all the man's foibles. Women was one of them. Josh Thurlow had always been a fool for women, even on the Bering Sea where there were virtually none. Yet, the man had managed to marry an Aleut maiden, then was required to avenge her murder. It had all been a nasty, sad business. Phimble had been an ordinary seaman then and Josh an ensign, both of them assigned to the cutter *Comanche*, commanded by Captain Phineas Falcon, the legendary Arctic brawler.

Afterwards, they had served at the Coast Guard station on Killakeet and chased U-boats for a living. Since coming to the South Pacific with Josh (who was there by orders of the Secretary of the Navy himself with further orders to report back all that he observed and to make recommendations for improvements in the conduct of the war), Phimble had re-

ceived a battlefield promotion and was now an officer and
the pilot of a PBY seaplane the boys had rebuilt after the
Japanese had battered it to pieces and the navy had abandoned it as scrap. Upon first observing Phimble in action,
Colonel Montgomery Risling, commander of the 5th Raiders,
had said to Josh, "He's got potential, that is, for a Negro."
It was a comment that had stopped Josh in his tracks and
caused him to reply, most tartly, "That Negro, as you call
him, is a better man than either of us, Colonel, and make no
mistake." Risling, normally combative about everything, had
not seen fit to contradict him.

Josh took note of Phimble taking note of him. "A letter
from Dosie," he said. Then he added, though he instantly
regretted it, "She's fallen for another man."

"If that was true," Phimble replied, tamping down his
smirk, "I'd have heard about it from my Talky. I got a letter
from her the same day you got one from Dosie, as you will
recall. Nary a word except Dosie's going to be a nurse."

"She says that, too. But she's still got herself a new
fella."

"She wrote that?"

"Not in so many words."

"Dosie knows lots of words," Phimble answered, with a
smile meant to soothe. "She's the kind who'd use them, too,
if she had something to say. I think you must be wrong in
your assessment."

Before Josh could retort, a Marine Raider by the name of
Captain Lester Clooney abruptly appeared out of the bush,
his helmet askew and his shirt soaked with sweat from the
exertion of climbing the volcano and probably a low-grade
fever. While Josh and Phimble stared at him in surprise, the
Raider officer wiped his face with a scrap of an old gray
towel that was draped around his neck, set his helmet aright,
took several long breaths, then looked Josh square in the eye.
"Josh Thurlow," he said in an official, though (since he still
didn't quite have his breath) somewhat thin, voice, "Colonel
Montgomery Risling of the 5th United States Marine Corps
Raiders told me to come after you. Here, as you may notice,
I am."

Josh eyed the pistol strapped to the captain's waist and further eyed the hand that was wrapped around its grip. "You aim to use that Huk-killer on me if I don't, Lester?"

Clooney took several more breaths, then finally seemed to find his wind. "Monkey said if you didn't come, I was to," he replied, using the familiar nickname for the Colonel. "He said he's been asking you to come see him for two solid weeks. Now, he's run out of patience. He wants you in his office by oh eight hundred on this very day, and he said dead or alive, it don't make no difference."

"I don't answer to Colonel Montgomery Risling," Josh replied in a relaxed tone, "and you can tell him I said so. Anyway, I happen to know he only wants to give me a medal I don't want."

"It might have been about your medal before but now it ain't," Clooney said with the squinty eyes of a gun fighter and his hand unrelaxed on his pistol. "There's something new just come up. Anyway, you live on his island, and I guess he figures that gives him some rights to your time."

Josh conceded the point. "Are you really prepared to shoot me if I don't go?"

Clooney's squint disappeared, and he answered, after a moment of contemplation, "I don't know. This place does strange things to a man's head. I might not think so, but then go ahead and do it, anyway. Good morning, Eureka. Good morning, Dave. I'm sorry I didn't greet you until now. I was required first to accomplish my official duty."

Megapode Dave had fallen asleep, worn out from watching the air combat, and therefore didn't respond. Phimble, however, replied, "Good morning, Captain Clooney. You did an excellent job on your duty, I swan. Don't look like it'll rain again for another hour. You want some coffee?"

"Don't mind if I do," Clooney answered. "As for the rain, I guess it'll rain when it rains which will be about ten times today. In between, the sun will shine and the steam will rise and the mosquitoes will bite and the mud on Me-Soggy will get ever deeper. End of prediction."

Josh folded Dosie's letter, his mind made up on what to do about it. "All right, Lester," he said. "I have one thing to do and then you and I, we'll go see the Monkey."

Clooney took the mug of coffee brought out by Millie who had been listening from the cave. "Thank you, Millie. As for you, Josh, you go see Monkey yourself. If I'm standing by, he's liable to send me with you."

"Send me where?"

"Wherever it is, I don't want to go. Liable to get killed."

"You plan on living forever?" Josh asked, sincerely interested.

"Something wrong with that?"

Josh was an honest man, one of his many faults. "Nothing except it ain't likely, considering where you are at the moment and Jap ain't about to surrender any time soon."

Clooney gestured toward Josh with the mug. "Maybe I ain't going to live through this war, Josh, but I ain't no fool. I've heard some rumors. Monkey's after you because he's got something bad and terrible that he can't trust a stupid jarhead like me to do. Likely it involves killing with a good chance of getting killed. You're as bloody-minded as Monkey, I reckon, so you're a good man for the job. Well, killing might come easy for you and Monkey Risling and old Bull Hawsey, too, with his awful *Kill Japs* sign, but it still don't to me. Sure, most likely I'm not gonna make it through this war, but I ain't gonna go to St. Peter as a volunteer and that's all I've got to say."

"Well, I suppose that's enough, Lester," Josh tenderly allowed and went inside the cave where he sat down at the rude table the boys had built from scrap lumber, took up a thoroughly chewed pencil, and wrote on a blank sheet of paper:

*Dear Dosie:*
*I guess you've found somebody what's good enough for you at last. I never much thought I was, anyway. I hope you and your doctor will be happy. Not much else is happening around here. Eureka and all the boys are fine and I am, too. Say*

*hello to Rex and tell him I'd sure like to get old Thunder and
ride the beach with him and his new horse.*

*Good luck, fair winds, and following seas.*

Josh

*PS - Thank you for putting flowers on Mama's grave.*

Josh put the note in an envelope, sealed it, then wrote
Dosie's address on it, which was simple:

*Miss Dosie Crossan*
*Killakeet Island*
*North Carolina*

He called for Stobs. "Put this in the bag going out with
my reports." Then he strapped on his pistol and the razor-
sharp Aleut ax he'd carried since his service on the Bering
Sea, and went over to the crate used for storage of this or
that and retrieved a half-full bottle of Mount Gay rum. He
walked outside and tipped the bottle into Captain Clooney's
mug, three glugs. "Have a bit of this, Lester. It'll soften your
day."

"It's too early," Clooney protested, though he tossed it
back instantly, then whistled out a breath and put a hand on
his pistol. "Are you going or not?"

"I am," Josh replied, then handed the bottle to Phimble,
and went on down the volcano to see the Monkey where,
just as Clooney had predicted, he would be asked to accomplish a terrible thing that even a Marine Raider wouldn't do.